D0015405

ALPHA GODDESS

Also by Amalie Howard

Bloodspell
Waterfell (The Aquarathi)
The Almost Girl

Forthcoming by Amalie Howard

Oceanborn (The Aquarathi)
The Fallen Prince

ALPHA GODDESS

AMALIE HOWARD

Sky Pony Press
New York

Copyright © 2014 by Amalie Howard

All Rights Reserved. No part of this book may be reproduced in any manner without the express written consent of the publisher, except in the case of brief excerpts in critical reviews or articles. All inquiries should be addressed to Sky Pony Press, 307 West 36th Street, 11th Floor, New York, NY 10018.

Sky Pony Press books may be purchased in bulk at special discounts for sales promotion, corporate gifts, fund-raising, or educational purposes. Special editions can also be created to specifications. For details, contact the Special Sales Department, Sky Pony Press, 307 West 36th Street, 11th Floor, New York, NY 10018 or info@skyhorsepublishing.com.

Sky Pony® is a registered trademark of Skyhorse Publishing, Inc.®, a Delaware corporation.

Visit our website at www.skyponypress.com.

10 9 8 7 6 5 4 3 2 1

Library of Congress Cataloging-in-Publication Data

Howard, Amalie.
 Alpha goddess / Amalie Howard.
     pages cm
 Summary: "Sera is a Hindu goddess incarnate and must battle between her good and evil sides in order to save the world from becoming hell on earth"—Provided by publisher.
 ISBN 978-1-62636-208-6 (hardback)
 [1. Hindu goddesses—Fiction. 2. Hindu mythology—Fiction.] I. Title.
 PZ7.H83233Al 2014
 [Fic]--dc23
                                    2013035687

Printed in the United States of America

For my parents,
who encouraged me to look beyond,
to seek more, and to find my own voice.

"Blow O wind to where my loved one is.
Touch him and come touch me soon.
I'll feel his gentle touch through you and
meet his beauty in the moon.
These things are much for the one who loves.
One can live by them alone:
that he and I breathe the same air and that
the Earth we tread is one."

Translated from The Ramayana

CONTENTS

Imaginary Demons

❦

She was nothing but flame in the deep of hell's embrace.

"Welcome Serjana," whispered a throaty voice. "I have been waiting for you."

Sera lurched upright in bed, gasping, images from her nightmare still flashing like lightbulbs in her brain: a sea of moaning, bloody mouths and tongues pressing beneath her feet—razor sharp fangs slithering against her skin—a boy swathed in shadows beckoning, calling to her. A flicker of a kiss that tasted like blood.

The numbers on her bedside alarm clock glared red, two fifteen in the morning. Sera swallowed, her throat dry like gritty sandpaper, the lingering taste of something sour and tangy against her gumline. She needed water. Sitting up, her eyes focused on a smear of red on her sheets. Was that blood? A sharp graze throbbed along the inside of her heel in answer to her question. Sera touched her fingertip to the raw scrape, frowning. A glimmer of sharp teeth slithering along her foot jerked in her memory and she shoved it away, squeezing her eyes tightly shut. She must have scratched herself during the night.

Sera sighed, shrugging out of her damp pajamas and pulling on a cotton cami. The sweating was new, too. She'd had to change her clothes almost every night during the last

1

two weeks. It was starting to become tiresome, and she was sure that her mother would notice the doubling of her laundry, which would only lead to questions—ones Sera didn't want to answer. She stuffed the wet clothing under her bed.

Careful not to make any noise, she padded toward the bathroom, her bare feet curiously hot against the cold tiles as though she'd been walking on some scorched surface. Maybe this was some kind of hormonal phase, like teenage hot flashes. Whatever it was, she'd have to get through it on her own; she didn't have any girlfriends to talk to and there was no way she was going to tell her parents about getting the sweats over a couple gory nightmares.

Lately, her mother's obsession with dreams—Sera's in particular—bordered on creepy-crazy, and the last thing Sera needed was to have her mother dissecting hers to pieces. The dreams were bad enough without her mother weighing in on why her daughter was dreaming of blood and carnage and being the queen of the dead.

Sera closed the bathroom door quietly and chewed on her lip. It *was* a little strange though, she admitted silently to herself. Maybe her mother had a point. Seriously, what kind of person had dreams about heaven and hell *all* the time? At first, they'd been sporadic, but recently, they'd become consistent, *too* consistent . . .

Like they meant something.

She coughed, spitting into the sink, and frowned. Her saliva was tinged with pink against the white porcelain. On cue, a fleeting memory of the kiss in her dream winked into her brain. A shudder rolled through her. It'd been some kind of faceless monster, half-boy, half-something else. Had the blood been hers? His? The bitter coppery taste filled her mouth and this time she gagged, spitting again.

"Get a grip," Sera told herself. "It's not real."

But the monster's faceless shape still loomed on the edge of her thoughts like a dark stain; mocking her, taunting her with the fact that she'd liked it, that she'd enjoyed its kiss, that she'd begged for more. Refuting the poisonous thoughts, Sera took a deep slow breath, clearing her mind. She drank a glass of water and washed her face, the cool water refreshing against her flushed skin. But still, the taste was there like salty cotton, coating the inside of her mouth with scummy residue. She brushed her teeth with minty toothpaste and gargled with antiseptic mouthwash. Better.

"You need to get some sleep, or you'll start looking like a zombie," she told the girl in the mirror. A thin face plastered with dark stringy purple and black hair, with fierce dark eyes, stared back at her. She grimaced at her reflection, baring her teeth. In the fluorescent lighting, her skin was sallow and her eyes a lightless black. She pinched her cheeks to give them some color and sighed. "Too late, you're already a zombie. It's no wonder that monster boyfriends come looking for you," she sniped to her image.

Not only was she bony and pale, but she was also almost six feet tall. At sixteen, looking like a tall skinny gargoyle didn't win her any popularity contests at school. Sometimes she wished she looked more like her mother: petite, doe-eyed, perfect. From her mother's glossy dark hair to her sun-kissed skin, Sera would pick her exotic North Indian looks in a heartbeat if she could. She sighed again and examined her face critically. If she did look more like her mother, would things be any different? Would she have more friends? A boyfriend? A life?

The inside of her left palm ached and she stared at the curved scar on the fleshy part just under her thumb. She had an almost identically placed one on the inside of her right palm, but it was a completely different shape, nearly a reversed image of its sister scar. Her parents had told her that she'd fallen on some jagged rocks when she was a baby. The skin there felt raw and hot, and Sera rubbed it absently with the thumb of her right hand, staring back into the mirror.

An unnatural sensation zinged suddenly from her palm to her navel, and she grabbed the edges of the sink, disoriented by an odd feeling of weightlessness. For a split second, the mirrored glass seemed to shimmer, and then the face looking back at her wasn't even hers. A heart-shaped face with eyes so clear they were almost the color of light, framed by a cloud of silken red hair, stared curiously at her. The girl's eyes were rimmed in kohl, her lips stained the color of a rose. Even her skin glowed gold as if lit from within.

Sera's lips parted and the face in the mirror followed suit, the silvery eyes widening in confused disbelief as their hands slid toward each other. Their fingers met against the cold glass, and the girl in the mirror frowned, her face an echo of Sera's own confusion. Red-etched lines swirled in an intricate design on the girl's hands and palms. Mehndi, Sera knew. She'd seen pictures of her mother wearing the same hennaed skin decorations on her wedding day—an ancient Indian tradition. The girl smiled as a waterfall of scarlet flames cascaded down her shoulders.

Sera shook her head, closing her eyes, and when she looked back, the face in the mirror was the one she'd always had—stringy purple hair, black eyes, non-descript. What the hell had just happened? Was she still dreaming?

Either you are still asleep or you are seriously losing it, Sera, she thought.

Her left palm burned, the strange scar white-hued against her flushed skin. It pulsed This time she didn't touch it. She splashed her face again and walked out of the bathroom, grabbing her iPod and sketchpad on the way to her bed. She turned the volume up full blast, her thoughts fading to nothing as her pencil scratched against the white paper.

Sleep was overrated anyway.

༺☙༻

Sera woke to the smell of pancakes and coffee, and rubbed her eyes tiredly. She'd finally fallen asleep at around five in the morning, and thankfully, that last hour of sleep had been dreamless. She showered and brushed her teeth. No metal aftertastes or strange faces in the mirror this time, and the scars on her hands were pale and ordinary, barely noticeable. She must have been half asleep when she'd gone into the bathroom earlier.

The sheet of paper with the graceful anime four-armed girl rising from a lotus flower in her sketchpad suggested otherwise, but Sera didn't want to think about what that meant. She traced the long wisps of hair and the barest hint of flames spiraling below the girl's outstretched arms. Mehndi art wound its way up each of her four arms to her neck, where it sat like a strangled bruise. The girl was reaching for something, the expression on her face beseeching. Something about it made her inexplicably uneasy, and instead of tucking the sketchpad into her backpack as she normally would have, Sera tossed it onto her desk before wandering downstairs.

Her parents' hushed voices floated up the stairs, the conversation tapering off quickly as soon as she entered the kitchen, but not before she'd caught the tail end of her father's last sentence.

" . . . sixteen. We have to tell her eventually."

"Tell me what?"

"Nothing, darling. You want some breakfast before school?" Her mother's voice was over-bright and forced, but Sera was too tired to press them about their conversation.

"No, just OJ." She plopped her bag on the stool next to her ten-year-old brother, watching him ladle giant spoonfuls of Cheerios into his mouth. They couldn't look like more polar opposites considering they were brother and sister. Nate was the image of their father, with the exception of the hair color he'd inherited from their mom. She rumpled his bright, blond curls. "Nate, you're going to turn into a Cheerio one of these days, you know."

"Like . . . oomph . . . eerios . . . oletrol . . ."

"Slow down, piglet, you're way too young to be worrying about cholesterol."

"That's not what the AAP says," Nate said, finishing his mouthful. "Saturated fats are the new teen killer. You should have a bowl."

"Seriously, who *are* you?" Sera shook her head, yawning, and rolled her eyes.

"You look like you had a rough night," her father said. His smile was also forced, and for a brief second, Sera *wanted* to know what they'd been talking about. But wanting to know something and getting it without a guaranteed lecture were two separate things. Any discussion with her parents these days covered three subjects—bad grades, bad choice of friends, and lately, bad dreams. She'd take a pass.

"Couldn't sleep," Sera replied, rubbing bleary eyes as she walked to the refrigerator and grabbed the orange juice.

"Why?" Her mother's tone was sharp, unlike her normal mellow voice. "Nightmares?"

Sera poured herself a glass of juice and sat at the counter, answering without thinking: "Like you wouldn't believe. Even scratched myself in my sleep."

Both her father and mother's gazes converged on her like laser-beams, and Sera stiffened, realizing her mistake too late.

"What kind of nightmares?" her father asked.

"Making out with a hot demon. You know, the usual dream fare of teens my age," Sera joked weakly, kicking herself that she'd said anything at all. From the expressions on her parents' faces, she could see that her joke fell flat. Way flat. They didn't look amused; they looked worried.

"Demon?" her mother repeated, staring at her with a piercing intensity. "What happened? Did it hurt you?"

"In my dream?" Sera asked, taken aback by her mother's tone. The lies came easily. "No, Mom. Nothing happened. I was just kidding," she said, avoiding her mother's acute stare and focusing on the glass of juice. "It's not like it's real or anything." She could feel them all staring at her, even Nate, who'd stopped chewing. "What's the big deal?"

Her father stood up and rumpled her hair, his face strained. "It's no big deal, Sera. But sometimes dreams have a way of telling us important things. Even the bad ones."

"I know, and I'm sorry," she said. "I didn't mean to make a joke, but in all honesty, my nightmare was probably because of watching scary movies all weekend. I'm fine, really," she added more gently. Outside, a horn blew loudly, interrupting the heavy tension that had descended in the kitchen. Sera gulped the rest of her juice and grabbed her backpack, grateful for the excuse to leave. "That's Kyle. I'm late. See you guys later." She glanced at her mother, who was still frowning. "Sorry, again."

The frown deepened. "Sera, about Kyle, I'm not entirely comfortable—"

"Mom," Sera said quickly. "Kyle's fine. He's a good driver and it beats walking or taking the bus. Look, I'm late. Gotta go, love you."

Sera raced out of the house, ignoring the anxious look that passed between her parents, desperate to get out of her mother's line of sight. Notwithstanding their completely bizarre reaction, her parents had become really overattentive the last few weeks, especially after she'd turned sixteen, as if they were expecting her to mutate into some kind of teenzilla at any moment. And their obsession with her dreams bordered on bizarre. If she even told them what she'd been dreaming of nightly for the past several months, they'd pull her straight out of school in favor of the dreaded homeschooling, which she'd endured the first thirteen years of her life. She'd rather be locked up in an entire room full of teenzillas than return to that.

Sera had only been allowed to go to the public high school in Silver Lake after her mother had found out that a close friend of hers, Eleanor Davenport, had two children at the same school. Her parents weren't strict, but they'd always been fiercely protective of her and Nate. Winning the battle to attend high school had been a major milestone in the Caelum household, with Nate constantly reminding her not to mess it up for him.

Sera tossed a glance over her shoulder. Her mother was standing at the front door, looking as though she were contemplating hauling Sera back into the house and locking her in the basement without a key. Her normally tranquil face was troubled. Sera couldn't fathom why she'd gotten so worked up over a silly dream that meant absolutely nothing.

As if in response to the tune of her thoughts, Sera thought of the demon-boy in her dream, and she fought back a shiver.

I've been waiting for you.

She shook the image from her head, frowning, and climbed into Kyle's car. Dreams were just dreams. They weren't real. Because if they were, she'd have a whole lot more to worry about than just a pair of fiery wings and a pretty face. And there were some things that just weren't possible.

Like demons.

Underneath

❧

"W"hat's up, loser?" Sera said, tossing her bag in the back-seat of Kyle's beat-up Jetta convertible. Kyle gave her a ride most days since he lived in the apartment block just beyond Sera's neighborhood. He'd gotten his license at the start of the year.

With the piercings in his nose and brow, and the black wheels in his earlobes, Kyle looked like a thug and dressed like a goth. He was every parents' nightmare, hers included. His thick, coarse, curly hair was tufted into a green mohawk—the sides of his head shaved to showcase two black dragon's wings on either side that stretched down to his darkly tanned neck. Wearing beat-up black leathers, he definitely wasn't "boy-next-door" material, but he was her friend, and Sera didn't have many of those.

"Nada," said Kyle. "You look like crap. Still not sleeping?"

"I'm fine, dreams again. Parents being a pain. You feel like ditching today?"

Kyle smirked. "Do I look like I ever want to go to school? The quicker we are out of that hellhole, the happier I'll be."

Sera laughed, the tension of the confrontation with her parents draining away. She half expected Kyle to drop out of school most days—he complained about it nonstop. But his foster mom, Carla, insisted on him graduating, saying it was the one thing she'd promised herself he would do under her watch. Carla was great and, though she gave him a lot of freedom, she was adamant about him finishing high school.

Kyle had been in and out of foster homes his whole life, some pretty terrible. His last foster parents had been evangelists who'd left on a missionary expedition to Africa when Kyle was twelve. He hadn't seen them since and didn't care one way or another. As far as negligent parents went, they'd been the bottom of the barrel, caring more for saving their congregation than nurturing a child in their own home. Kyle's real parents had died when he was five, some kind of accident he'd told her. When Kyle was placed with Carla four years ago, it was the only time in his life he'd actually been happy.

"Hey, Sera!" a voice yelled out as they drove past a large house just down the street from hers.

"Oh hi, Dev." Sera waved back, recognizing the voice's owner as a tall boy who had moved to the neighborhood that spring. She smiled as he brushed his mop of dark hair out of his face with his forearm, squinting against the glare. In the sunlight, his tanned skin glowed gold, and for a second, her memory jerked back to the girl in the mirror.

"How's it going?" she said.

"Any chance I can get a ride with you guys? My car's in the shop—"

Before he could even finish the sentence, Kyle floored the accelerator and the car lurched past the driveway. Sera waved apologetically to Dev, mouthing a silent apology before turning to Kyle.

"What is your *problem*? Slow down, it's like a fifteen-mile-per-hour zone." She shot him a surprised look. "That was really rude. He just wanted a ride."

"I don't like him. And it's my car," said Kyle. "I'm not taking him to his stupid uppity private school."

"His school is like three blocks from ours. And we're not even going to school today, remember?"

"It's my car," said Kyle stubbornly.

"Look, don't get snarky just because he goes to private school. I told you he's nice. I hung out with him over the summer."

"Whatever. He has a girl's name."

"It's unisex, and it's short for Devendra."

"Yeah, short for *girl*."

"Leave him alone, he's cool. And I like him."

Kyle made a sour face and looked over at Sera twirling a strand of purple hair in her fingers. "Well, he's weird, and what's with those blue tattoos anyway?"

Sera burst out laughing. "Are you kidding? You don't like him because he has tattoos? Isn't that the pot calling the kettle black?" she said, jerking her eyebrows pointedly to his own inked skull.

"They're girly," Kyle said defensively. "Probably got them from wherever he came from with his cab-driver accent."

Sera shot him a disgusted look. "My mother has an accent like that, too."

"That's different," Kyle shot back sourly. "And you know what I mean."

"No, I don't know what you mean. What is up with you today? Seriously, Kyle, stop being such a snob. You sound like one of Ryan Davenport's crew."

"*Me*? A snob? Come on, I'm a foster kid, remember," Kyle said waving a hand for emphasis before jabbing her in her side. "And Ryan Davenport's a tool."

Ryan Davenport, the son of her mother's friend Eleanor, was captain of the hockey team at Silver Lake High School, and his group of friends included all the more popular kids at school; a group that neither she nor Kyle wanted anything to do with.

"So what?" Sera said. "That doesn't exonerate you from being a snob if you look down on someone just because you don't know them. It makes you as bad as they are."

"*Exonerate*? Is that from your official SAT dictionary?"

"Shut up. Some of us still plan to go to college, Mr. I-couldn't-care-less-what-I-do-after-high-school. Whatever, I think the tattoo is super artistic, it's like fifteen different shades of blue, and it's across his whole chest and back."

Kyle stared at her sharply. "How would you know that?"

Sera stared back, surprised by what sounded like jealousy in his tone. "Who are you and what have you done with Kyle?" she said. "When most kids swim in a pool, they wear bathing suits. I told you, I hung out with him over the summer while you were doing community service. Since when are you the jealous type anyway?"

"I'm not. Just don't like the guy, is all."

Sera rolled her eyes, refusing to start the day with a full-out argument. "Fine. Forget it. Let's just go to Sal's. I didn't have breakfast and I'm starving."

Sal's was a seedy local diner on the outskirts of Silver Lake. It was empty except for a couple of people on their way out. The staff there didn't talk much and didn't ask questions, which was a nice relief from the general consensus in their small town that everyone should be in everyone else's business. It was also the type of establishment that most of their upper-class town residents wouldn't deign to patronize.

They sat in a booth close to the back and ordered the breakfast platter. Service was quick.

"So tell me about your dream," said Kyle, stuffing his mouth with fried potatoes. "Was it gory like last time?"

"I don't really want to talk about it," Sera replied as thoughts of walking on human brains and entrails flashed through her head. "Last night, they were so . . . real."

"Details, please," Kyle said, leaning forward expectantly. "Seriously, you're like my own personal muse."

"You're the one who's into that sort of thing, not me. I don't even believe in heaven and hell. I don't even know why I'm dreaming about flying demons or mythical gods with ten arms." Sera stared at him accusingly. "I think it's because of *you* and all those stupid movies you make me watch with flying Valkyrie-devil-angel-thingys."

"Come on, you know the devil exists. At least admit that," said Kyle.

"I'm an atheist."

"You don't believe in an afterlife? That there's somewhere we all go after we die? Or even that we could come back as something else. You know, like karma?" Kyle's voice had gone strangely quiet and he'd actually stopped shoveling food into his mouth.

She stared at him for a second before responding. "No."

In earlier dreams, she'd dreamed of heaven, too, and for a second, Sera wondered at the feeling of knowing that she'd experienced, as if she'd been there before, which was impossible. Heaven didn't exist, and neither did hell. They were both creations of a morally diseased world.

"Why?"

"Because it's impossible, that's why. The science of evolution teaches that we came from monkeys, some dumber than others—like yourself, for example, you big ape," said Sera. "Darwinian evolution is the only scientific explanation for life on Earth."

"But that still doesn't explain how life began," countered Kyle.

"Microorganisms. When did you suddenly become a theologian?"

"When did you become such a cynic?" Kyle launched back. "Look, as much as you don't want to believe it, there *are* other things out there, things that neither of us can see. Some people say that the gods walk among us."

"What, like in the *National Enquirer*?"

Kyle shot her a glare. "You know, it wouldn't hurt you to be more open-minded."

Sera shrugged. "Sure, let's hold hands and sing 'Kumbayah,' and while we're at it I need to stop by Madame Girard's for a crystal ball reading on whether my best friend is secretly some outlaw deity."

"I'm not," he sputtered, nearly choking on a piece of toast. "But just because you don't believe in them doesn't mean immortals don't exist."

Sera sighed and drank some of her lukewarm coffee. "OK, fine, I'll bite. Have *you* ever *seen* one of these alleged immortals?"

"I—"

Kyle's answer was interrupted by the sound of obnoxious laughter as a group of boys entered the diner.

"Great, your buddies just arrived," Sera said, hunching down in her seat to avoid eye contact.

"Hey, Sera," a tall, red-skinned boy drawled. "Slumming again? I'm sure Mommy and Daddy won't be too happy with you skipping school."

"What do you care, Jude?" she said evenly.

Sera always felt uneasy around Jude. His stare made her feel exposed in a seedy, dark alley kind of way—as though she were a thing rather than a person. Jude grinned and slid into the booth next to Kyle, while the other four guys sat in the booth next to them, leering over the divider. They all had the same tattoos that Kyle did, the strange black dragon wings in various places on their bodies, like they were part of some cult. Jude's tattoos extended from his neck and shoulders, all the way to the tops of his fingertips. His grin turned conciliatory.

"Come on, Sera. We haven't seen you in ages. Surely you missed me," he pouted, watching her in that unnerving way of his, drumming his long fingers on the table. His fingernails were bitten to the quick, their edges dirty. Sera ignored him, knowing he was trying to get a rise out of her. Jude threw an arm around Kyle, who shot her an apologetic look.

"Kyle, you tap that yet?" He licked his lips, and Sera reddened. She had the sudden urge to slap the suggestive smirk off his face, but laying a hand on Jude would be unwise. He seemed like the kind of boy who would explode in a second. She bit her tongue.

Jude smiled, exposing stained teeth that made Sera want to retch. They'd been filed to sharp points. For a moment, the air shimmered and Sera could swear she saw the tattooed wings along Jude's arms undulate. Her eyes flicked to the others, and their faces rippled with elongated eyes and distorted mouths full of broken, pointy teeth. The air was suddenly hot and suffocating. Why was she hallucinating again? In broad daylight?

She blinked and realized one of the boys, Damien, had asked her a question. "Wh . . . what?"

"Are. You. Going. To. Eat. That?" Damien repeated his words like he was talking to a toddler, indicating her untouched plate. She flinched at the movement of his finger near her face and felt the stares of the other boys settling on her like moths.

"Yes. I mean, no. You can have it. Look, I have to go. Kyle, I'll catch you later," Sera said, lurching out of the booth and throwing a five-dollar bill on the table.

"What's the matter, little girl? The big bad wolf scare you?" Jude said, grinning, his teeth normal: small, white, and unfiled. He leaned back and cocked an eyebrow, spreading his arms along the back of the booth. It was not an aggressive movement, but Sera felt some sort of unspoken challenge from him all the same. She couldn't get away fast enough.

She raced to the door, feeling like her chest was imploding. Sweat was dripping down her back as though she'd been sitting in a sauna and her breath was coming in shorter and shorter gasps—the beginnings of a colossal panic attack.

Breathe . . . breathe . . . breathe.

"How'll you get home?" Kyle yelled after her.

"Bus." Sera gritted the word out and flung open the door, heaving great gulps of air into her burning lungs. It felt like she'd been under boiling hot water. She crouched down on the cracked asphalt, concentrating on inhaling and exhaling until slowly her panic subsided. She rubbed damp palms on her jeans.

"Give me a sec," she heard Kyle say as he pushed open the door after her, his face worried.

"Hey, Ser, you OK?"

She cleared her throat. "I'm fine."

"What happened in there?"

"I don't know. I swear that I just saw Jude and the rest of them . . ." She trailed off, unable to articulate what she'd seen or thought she'd seen. She shook her head. "I'll be OK. I just needed to get out of there. It was so hot, I felt like I was going to pass out. And then the way Jude was looking at me . . . it just got under my skin. The guy creeps me out."

Kyle nodded. "Yeah, I mean, you looked freaked out — like you'd seen a ghost or something — and then I got this weird vibe off you."

Sera stared at him. "Off me?"

"Yeah, like a flash of . . . I don't know." Kyle shrugged, dismissing what he'd been about to say. "It was probably just adrenaline. You looked ready to barf or bolt. So, did Jude do something?"

"No, he didn't *do* anything, it's just . . . him. The heat of the kitchen must have gotten to me," Sera said. "Forget about it. I'm exhausted, barely slept last night, and I think I'm still seeing things. I'll call you later, OK? I'm just going to head to school. My mom's probably still home and she'll flip if she finds out I've skipped."

Kyle stood, pulling Sera to her feet. "Fine, I'll meet you back there. I'll be done with Jude and the boys soon." Sera looked at him sharply. She could feel Jude's stare through the scuffed windows of the diner.

"You're not . . . dealing, are you, Kyle?"

"No, I don't do that."

"Well, why are you hanging around with Jude, then? I don't get it. He's bad news."

Kyle hesitated as if trying to find the right words. "I'm just helping him out. I keep an eye out, that sort of thing."

"An eye out for what?"

"For certain people he wants me to keep an eye out for. Look, let's just drop it, OK? I owe him, you know that."

"But that doesn't mean he owns you, does it?"

"Here we go. I'll see you later, *Mom*," Kyle joked sarcastically, rolling his eyes skyward. He peered over her shoulder. "There's your bus. You know, if you want to wait, I can take you back after I'm done."

She stared at him hard, but he wouldn't meet her eyes. They'd been through this a hundred times before, and lately it seemed that every time Jude came into the picture, they ended up fighting. She couldn't win.

Sera threw her hands into the air. "No thanks. Obviously you have priorities. Do whatever you want."

Sera stalked off to the bus. She could feel Kyle watching her, but she didn't want to give him the satisfaction of looking at him. If he wanted to do something stupid like mess around with Jude and drugs, it was his funeral. She was done caring.

Her phone buzzed. She didn't bother to read Kyle's text before hitting delete and flipped him off through the window just as the bus pulled off.

~☙~

Kyle stared after the bus until it was a tiny speck in the distance, pocketing his phone. He thought about the flash of energy he'd felt from Sera in the diner just before she'd rushed out. It had been so brief that he'd barely registered it, and the delayed recognition confused him because he was never, ever wrong. His ability had never failed him.

Until now.

Because what he'd felt was impossible. Not Sera. She was human. He'd checked often enough over the years. So either he'd made a mistake or he'd been wrong every time before. Still, the sour feeling in his stomach remained like an unanswered riddle. He must have imagined the flash in the diner. It was the only explanation.

Kyle closed his eyes, recalling the ephemeral sensation . . . like the fluff of baby feathers across his skin. There was nothing like it in the world.

Daeva energy.

BROTHERHOOD

❦〜❦

"Everything OK with your girlfriend?" Jude sneered as Kyle walked back into the diner.

"She's not my girlfriend."

"Whatever you say. She'd hardly be hanging around if she knew what you were."

"Well, she's not going to know, Jude. She wouldn't understand."

"Maybe we should mess with her mind a little. That'd be fun, wouldn't it, boys?"

The others cracked up. Kyle ignored the jibe and slid into Sera's vacated seat. Most of the leftover food from the table had already been scavenged. He remained silent, watching Jude and his crew. Even though they looked like boys, they were far from human. They were Ifrit—dark shadow demons who preyed on the energy of the living and killed for fun. They thirsted for life and ruthlessly took it any way they could.

Kyle wasn't afraid of them, but if there was one thing he was most afraid of, it was death. Because Sera was wrong. Hell did exist. Only it was called by another name and was filled with horrors far worse than the Ifrit, ones that made the versions of hell in books and movies seem like child's play. Kyle had seen one of its creatures with his own eyes when

21

he was five years old—the day he'd watched his mother turn into something not quite human.

Seeing was believing, and Kyle believed.

Jude grinned. "I'm just playing with you, man. Sera's cool. Don't worry, I'm not into her so she's all yours for now." He winked, and Kyle felt a surge of anger that he quickly suppressed. "Anyway," Jude continued, "down to business. We have to check out a new source up in Connecticut, couple hours away. I need you to come along."

Kyle relaxed the minute that Jude stopped talking about Sera. He wouldn't put it past Jude to torture Sera just for sport and to prove to Kyle that he was the alpha dog. Jude was like that. It wasn't enough to see someone unhappy, he loved to twist and push the knife in further, to make them suffer.

"When?" Kyle asked.

"Saturday. We'll be gone for a few days."

"Jude," Kyle said, "will Azrath be there? I mean, it's been a few months already. Surely he's seen what I can do, how I can serve him?"

"*Lord* Azrath, Kyle," Jude snapped, "and he's a very busy person. Trust me, he knows about you. But you have to prove yourself, and you haven't done that yet. He'll find a use for you soon enough, and then you'll get to meet him."

"Yeah, man," Damien said. "It takes a certain kind of sacrifice to prove yourself worthy. Took me a couple of weeks, I think."

"But it's been eight months," Kyle said.

"Well, maybe that's because you're a half-breed."

"Don't call me that."

"Or you're gonna do what?" The whites of Damien's eyes burned red and Kyle could feel the rage radiating off his body. He swallowed thickly but stood his ground. Jude laughed, putting a hand against Damien's chest. At Jude's touch, the waves of venomous energy receded immediately as if by silent command.

"Ignore Damien," Jude said. "He's the youngest of us and has the least control, don't you, Damien?" At the reprimand, Damien scowled, but Jude ignored him and turned to face the others. "Let's not forget—we need Kyle, and he has Lord Azrath's favor, so unless that changes, he's off limits. Got it?" Jude put his arm across Kyle's shoulder and squeezed. "Feeling safe now, half-breed?"

His laugh was spiteful, and Kyle belatedly realized that Jude's performance had all been a twisted display of power. Damien smirked as Jude pushed out of the booth.

"So, Saturday, OK?" Jude said. "Tell Carla you have a school trip or something. See you later. Give Sera a big wet one for me, will you?" He tossed the last remark over his shoulder as he exited the diner. The rest of the boys obediently followed him, laughing like a pack of wild hyenas following the call of their leader.

Kyle slouched against the cool Formica of the diner table and drew in a shuddering breath. What Jude had said about him having Azrath's favor was true. He knew that Jude only tolerated him because of that, and if he ever wore out his usefulness to Azrath, talent or not, he was as good as dead. But Azrath *needed* him, more now than ever.

Gifted with an unusual birthright, Kyle could read the auras of all manner of beings—mortal, immortal, celestial, bestial. Even if the beings were shaded or hidden, he knew what they were. He could see right through them. As a kid, the innate ability to sense hundreds of energies had been overwhelming, like too many screaming voices in his head at once. After his parents died, Kyle suppressed his gift and kept mostly to himself, falling in and out of the New York Foster Care system.

But Kyle's whole life changed once he was placed with Carla in Silver Lake when he first saw Sera, stuck in a tree near her bedroom window, one evening. She had obviously been trying to sneak out, but her skirt was tangled on a branch, rendering her unable to move up or down.

"What are you doing?" he'd asked.

"What does it look like I'm doing? I'm having a tea party," she'd hissed back. "Are you going to stand there staring or help me down?"

They'd been friends ever since.

Sera had been the only person who'd ever made him feel anything. She made him want to be . . . better. It didn't take long for Kyle to develop feelings for Sera, which he hid fiercely. He knew she didn't feel the same way about him, and he didn't want to lose her friendship. Worse, if she knew the truth about what he was, she'd think he was insane. So Kyle had convinced himself that she knew the little that was *good* about him, and that was all that mattered.

He glanced at his watch. He didn't have any other place to be, and cutting class without Sera wasn't as fun. Breathing a long sigh, he turned his car toward Silver Lake High. At least she'd be there, if she ever decided to forgive him.

Sera sat in last period study hall chewing on the end of her pencil, still stewing. She *knew* Kyle wasn't telling her everything. After four years, she could tell when he was lying, and he'd never seemed to be able to keep anything important from her.

A scraping noise interrupted her thoughts, and she jumped as the object of her thoughts slid into the seat beside her.

"What are you doing here, Kyle?" she snapped. "You don't have study hall."

"I know, but I need to talk to you." Sera could feel him staring at her, fidgeting. "Look, are we cool?"

"No, we're not," she whispered through clenched teeth with a glance in the teacher's direction. "You're going to get me in trouble. Go away."

"Well, can we talk after school?"

"We have play practice after school," she said. "Unless your warden, Jude, commanded you to be somewhere else."

Sera turned to stare at him pointedly, half joking, and then froze at the uncomfortable expression on his face. It would be the last straw if he bailed on the play. They'd both been roped into it as part of their school's diversity program, and despite Kyle's antipathy for any Silver Lake extracurricular activities, he'd agreed to help out as a stagehand.

Sera's brows snapped together at the guilty look on Kyle's face. "Seriously?"

"Ser, I'm sorry, but I won't be here for rehearsal," he began. "Jude—"

"*Seriously?*" Sera repeated, the flat of her palm slamming on the desk far louder than she'd intended. "I was just kidding about him deciding what you do or don't do. What's so important that you have to miss rehearsal?"

They both jumped at the voice of the teacher. "Mr. Knox, you are not in this class. Kindly leave or report to the principal's office. Miss Caelum, obviously I don't need to remind you that this is study hall not chatting hall."

"Sorry," they both muttered.

"Ser, I'll see you after class." Kyle stood and leaned forward on the table, his head looming inches from hers. She wouldn't look at him. "OK?"

"Whatever."

Sera didn't watch him leave, and only let out the breath she'd been holding after she heard the soft click of the door. If she'd looked at him, she would have exploded right on the spot. Sera sighed, focusing her gaze on her textbook. She had to admit, she felt really hurt that Kyle wasn't going to finish the play with her. She'd enjoyed working on the set with him and was actually looking forward to the play.

This year's play for International Diversity Day was being put on in honor of Diwali, the Hindu festival of lights. It was a reenactment of the *Ramayana*, the story of Rama and Sita—a beautiful story about the power of love and forgiveness. Sera's mother had first told her the story of Rama and Sita when she was little. When her class was brainstorming ideas for this year's IB Diwali event, Sera had been the one to shyly suggest the story. The idea caught fire, and soon she found herself trying to find a way out of playing Sita; she certainly wasn't an actress. Her skill was in art, so she was happy to work on the set and costume design instead.

The last bell rang, jerking Sera out of her thoughts, and she headed to the auditorium for the final dress rehearsals. On the way there, she spotted Kyle lounging near the doors to the auditorium obviously waiting for her, and she ducked into a nearby classroom, fuming. She didn't want to talk to him or hear any more of his tired excuses, so she took the long route to the auditorium instead. She'd finish the set work on her own. She didn't need him.

Inside, the auditorium was abuzz with activity as final touches were made to the set, and actors milled around rehearsing lines and joking about breaking legs for good luck. Sera made her way to the crowd on the far side.

"Nice work, Sera," someone called out. Her heart pounded with pride as she glanced at the set she'd helped construct — the king's palace, the forest of exile, the tower where Sita was imprisoned, all of it. She'd even designed the costume for the fearsome demon king who kidnapped Sita. Another boy echoed the sentiment, and Sera flushed, mumbling her thanks. She wasn't used to so much attention.

"Hey, Mia," she said to the sophomore who was playing the role of Sita. "You need help with makeup?"

"Sure," Mia said, smiling as she tugged on the top half of the vibrant red and green sari. After deftly finishing Mia's makeup, complete with the red bindi in the middle of her forehead, Sera had an idea.

"Give me your hands," she told Mia, pulling out a jar from her bag. Her mother wouldn't even notice that she'd borrowed some of her henna powder. "I want to try something." She glanced at Mia. "It's like a temporary tattoo, an old tradition. I'm pretty sure Sita in the stories had it on her hands. It can last a couple weeks I think," Sera warned. "You cool?"

"Yeah, sounds awesome. Go for it." Mia's eyes were wide with excitement as Sera dipped a thin paintbrush into a greenish paste and started drawing intricate swirls on the backs of Mia's hands. Sera's fingers moved fluidly and she didn't stop, giving into the bizarre feeling that she'd *done* this before. Ever since seeing the girl's hands in the mirror, she'd felt compelled to reconstruct the design, and Mia was a willing guinea pig.

Vines curled in and out with a life of their own as her vision blurred, and Sera paused for a moment, wiping sweat from her eyes. She felt lightheaded and squeezed her eyes shut, white spots dancing behind her eyelids. When she looked back at her handiwork, to her horror the vines were still moving and now coiling toward her own fingers. They slid up, winding their way across her knuckles, up her wrists, and into her palms in a complex pattern.

For a second, Sera thought she was dreaming, but she could clearly hear the conversation around her like she was in some kind of waking dream. And still the vines moved, concentric circles forming in her palm and extending to the tip of each finger, though painted by an invisible brush.

"Ouch, you're hurting me!" Mia cried.

Mia's voice was faint as tiny thorns flowered around each of Sera's scars and flowed to the middle of her wrists, creating a bow of sharp points bending outward like teeth. Sera could feel the piercing tips of them digging into her skin. She held Mia's fingers in a white-knuckled death grip. They were her lifeline . . . her only tether to the real world. If she let go, she would be lost.

Sera felt as if she were flowing out of her body, called away by some unseen presence. The boy in the Ravana costume that she'd designed rushed toward her, grinning and leering, his ten-headed mouths full of red pointy fangs. She'd never felt such eviscerating fear in her life—the fear of some long-forgotten memory now awakened. The demon's arms reached out.

Sera tumbled backward into the abyss of her vision.

Ravana had stolen her away, imprisoning her in a castle that no one but he could reach. His demon breath was foul, the stench of him decaying everything around them. Her prison was in a desolate wasteland. "Come for me, Rama," she cried, but her cries went unheard. No one could hear her where she'd been hidden. Still, she cried, pleading for her love to rescue her. But then, Ravana appeared in front of her, his ferocious heads snarling, his terrible teeth gnashing. "Forget Rama, you are mine now. For all eternity."

Sera couldn't stop screaming.

DECEIVER

⟡

Someone was shaking Sera so hard that her teeth rattled. Kyle's face swam into focus. The boy in the Ravana costume backed away, shaking his head and mouthing the word, *freak*. Sera closed her eyes, her breathing shallow.

"What happened?" she heard Kyle ask in a harsh tone.

"I don't know," Mia said. "One minute she was drawing and then she completely spaced. She wouldn't let go," she said, nursing red-bruised fingers. "And then Mark came over to say thanks for the costume, and she lost it."

"I'm sorry," Sera gasped weakly, glancing down at her bare pale hands. There were no vines, no tattooed teeth biting into her skin, and the vision of Ravana was gone. "I . . ." She trailed off with no idea of what she could say that wouldn't make her sound crazy. "I'm sorry, Mia."

Sera's pulse was still racing as Mia excused herself to finish dressing, darting another anxious look in Sera's direction. Sera looked away. It'd all seemed so real. She shook her head to clear away the fuzziness and heaved a deep breath into her lungs to dissipate the terror that still lay on the edge of her subconscious. The fear she felt had been hers—no one could imagine that kind of suffocating horror.

"Are you OK? You look like you saw a ghost," Kyle said.

Sera's heart lurched. She wasn't sure what she'd actually seen, but it hadn't been a ghost or any kind of hallucination. It'd been some kind of memory. *Her* memory. But how was that even possible? She shook her head again. She'd been spending far too much time focusing on the play. That had to be the answer . . . it was the only logical explanation.

But why had it felt so *real*?

She wet her dry lips, attacking her residual anxiety with false bravado. "I'm fine."

"You want me to take you home?" Kyle asked. Sera nodded but then shook her head, remembering their earlier exchange.

"I'm fine," she repeated. "I'm just tired. Not that I need to explain anything to you."

"You don't look fine."

"Kyle, I said I'm fine. And why are you here anyway? You're done with the play, right? Don't you have to go attend to Jude and his minions?" Sera knew her tone was scathing but she didn't care. "No one else matters to you."

Hurt flashed across Kyle's face. "Sera, you know that's not true. You do."

"So stop hanging out with him."

"It's not that simple," Kyle said. "I can't."

Sera shook her head. "I just don't get it. What's so important that you'd risk everything that matters to you—Carla, our friendship, your future?"

"I told you. Jude—"

"I know what you said. You owe him. But he can't be trusted." She stared at him in silence. It seemed so obvious that Jude was simply using Kyle. Why couldn't Kyle see that?

"I need him, Sera," he said finally.

Suddenly the lights flickered in the auditorium, interrupting their heated exchange. Dress rehearsal was about to begin. Sera stared blankly at the people on stage as everyone got into position. The lights dimmed and the first act opened, with Rama and Sita, newly married, at the palace, in edenesque bliss. But the story was soon to take a dark turn, as the king's second wife conspired to send Rama into exile so her own son could be named heir to the throne. Sera sighed. Even in the play, the characters had secrets and hidden agendas.

She jumped at the thump of Ravana's entrance on stage, and an immediate dread curdled in the pit of her stomach. She couldn't understand why the story was affecting her so viscerally, but for some reason, despite her fear, she couldn't tear her eyes away. With each stomp of the demon king's foot, her body jerked, and just as the demon snatched Sita away from Rama, Sera stood, hands shaking uncontrollably. It was far too close to what she'd imagined earlier.

"I need to get out of here," she mumbled to Kyle, suddenly dizzy. "I'm going to be sick."

It didn't take Kyle long to drive them to Sera's place, most of the ride spent in silence. She didn't even speak when he followed her up to her room. She hadn't actually invited him up, but she felt that she didn't want to be alone. And she wanted to finish their conversation.

"So, what happened back there?" Kyle ventured once they had reached her room. "Another hallucination?"

"No," she said with another deep breath. "Tell me the truth, Kyle, about what's going on. It's time for you to choose: me or Jude."

Kyle's face drew tight, but Sera didn't care. He'd told her that he owed Jude, but he hadn't told her everything. She stared at him expectantly.

He sighed. "Jude's mixed up with some . . . people called Daeva. He took something very valuable from them, a rare substance called Fyre. It can cure *any* sickness, even fatal ones."

"A drug?" Sera asked, frowning.

"Some people use it as a drug, yes, but Jude needs it to help a sick . . . uncle."

"Do I look stupid to you?" Sera fumed. She was furious. Did he think she would fall for something like this? She had never heard of anything called Fyre and, if something like that really did exist, how would Jude be the only one to know about it? And as far as she was concerned, Jude didn't have a sick uncle, either.

"Look, Ser," Kyle said. "I know it sounds crazy, but it's the truth."

Sera stared at him, pinching the bridge of her nose with her thumb and forefinger. "Kyle, you can't afford to get mixed up with Jude. Whoever these Daeva are, it's nothing to do with you. It's his problem."

Kyle shook his head. "That's where you're wrong. It has everything to do with me."

They stared at each other in awkward silence, and then jumped at the sound of a door slamming followed by footsteps on the staircase.

"Sera?" her mom's voice called. "Is that you? Are you home?" Sera whirled toward Kyle, who stood half frozen, like a deer caught in the headlights of an oncoming car.

"Don't just stand there. Move," she hissed, pushing him toward her bathroom and turning on the speakers of her iPod dock. Loud music rushed out of them. The door to her bathroom clicked closed just as her bedroom door swung open. Her mother walked in.

"Hi, Mom," Sera said, her voice calm despite her racing heart. "Aren't you supposed to be at yoga?"

"Hi, darling. I was hoping you'd be home. How was school?"

"Fine," Sera said.

"My class got canceled so I was thinking that maybe we could do an early dinner, just us girls. What do you think?" Sera chewed the inside of her lip, trying to find the most tactful way to get her mother out of her room before she was caught for having a boy—and particularly Kyle, whom her parents *really* didn't like—in her bedroom.

"Mom, I don't feel that well. Can we do it tomorrow?" Sera said, staring at the floor and avoiding her mother's eyes. "I actually came home early from play rehearsal."

"We need to talk, Sera," her mother said, walking over to Sera's desk with grim purpose. Sera frowned as she picked up a sketchbook and flipped it open. "Why don't you tell me about these?"

"You went through my stuff?" Sera said, grabbing the sketchpad and hugging it protectively to her chest.

She was mortified that her mother had seen some of the last sketches she'd drawn after her dreams—impossible beings with multiple arms and faces, creatures with snarling mouths, and flying monsters. It was all there in shades of penciled gray.

Her *insanity*.

How could she have been so stupid as to leave the pad on her desk in plain sight of her parents?

"No, of course not. I was looking for some pencils for a project that Nate and I are working on and I saw your sketchpad on your desk. I wanted to see what you'd been working on all summer."

"You could have *asked* me," Sera said.

Her mother nodded toward the sketchpad that Sera was still holding in a death grip against her chest. "Some of those drawings are dated months ago."

"Mom, please," Sera said, her eyes darting to the bathroom. "It's no big deal. Can we just drop it?"

"No, Serjana, it is a big deal," said her mother in a strange tone. "You've been having these dreams for a reason, a very real reason. It has to do with who you are, and possibly things that you're going to think me crazy for saying to you. You have no idea how much I wish we didn't have to have this conversation . . . but we must." Her mother gently brushed a thick strand of purple and black hair out of Sera's face, holding it between her thumb and forefinger and staring at it thoughtfully. A sad smile curved her lips as she released it. "And if those sketches are any indication, we need to talk now rather than later."

Something in her mother's voice tugged at Sera. "What do you mean 'who I am'?" Sera said, forgetting about Kyle for a second.

"Sera, do you sometimes dream that you're somewhere else, *someone* else?" Sera's gaze clung to her mother's. A vision of the four-armed redheaded girl flitted through her thoughts.

"Sure," Sera said carefully. "I mean, who doesn't like to pretend they're someone else?" Her mother stared at her, almost sadly. She pried the sketchpad out of Sera's numb fingers, opening it to a drawing of a beautiful dark-haired woman with ten arms playing some kind of harp. "Do you dream of the people in here, in your sketches? That maybe you're one of them?"

Sera's immediate shock was overshadowed by the audible gasp from the bathroom, and they both vaulted to their feet at a crashing noise.

"Is someone here?" her mother asked with a frown, her brows snapping together.

Sera sighed inwardly as the door opened and Kyle's green mohawk emerged, his face apologetic and fearful at the same time—which was expected, given the circumstances. Sera's mother's eyes widened, reflecting shock and alarm, her body tensing beside Sera's.

"Hi, Mrs. Caelum," Kyle said. "I was just using the bathroom. Sorry about the soap dish." He placed the broken dish on the desk as he edged around the opposite side of the room toward the door. "Sera wasn't feeling well. I just brought her home after rehearsal. I'm sorry."

Kyle was still edging around the room, almost as if he was afraid to get too close to where they stood. Sera noticed beads of sweat glistening against the dark ink of the dragon's wings on the sides of his skull. His gaze was fixed nervously on her mother, who hadn't moved an inch since he'd revealed himself.

"What's with you? Why're you acting all weird?" Sera said, starting to move toward him. But her mother shifted, placing a hand on Sera's shoulder to stop her.

Kyle also froze, his stance wary, and then mumbled in Sera's direction, "No, I'm OK. Sorry again, Mrs. Caelum . . ."

"It's all right, Kyle, but in the future, Sera's not really allowed to have friends over when we're not at home." Her mother's voice was frigid.

"Yes, ma'am. I'm sorry, it won't happen again." Kyle had almost reached the door at that point before Sera recalled the absurd conversation they'd been having before her mother had shown up.

"Wait," Sera said. "What about the thing we were talking about? The play," she added after a glance at her mother's forbidding expression. "You know, about the Daeva—"

The sudden pressure of her mother's fingers digging into the flesh of her shoulder cut off the rest of her words.

"Ow!" Sera cried, wincing and twisting away from her mother's painful grip.

Her mother's body was now rigid, her hand frozen in mid-air. Kyle looked paralyzed with alarm, his mouth opening and shutting like a fish trying to breathe outside of water. His skin had turned a sickly dull color.

"*What* did you just say?" she whispered, stormy gray eyes fixed on Kyle although the question was directed at Sera.

"Nothing, just some people that Kyle . . . forget it. It's nothing," Sera said, her voice trailing off at the sudden tension in the room. Her mother wore an expression that Sera had never seen. Sera glanced at Kyle. He looked as freaked out as she felt. "Kyle, you should go," Sera said. "I'll just call you later."

But before either could move, Sera's mother stepped toward Kyle, cornering him just before the bedroom door. She grabbed his wrist. A rapid flash of blinding white light detonated in the room the instant her mother touched Kyle. Hot white spots danced before Sera's eyes as she struggled to focus on the two of them. But they seemed unaffected by the intense blaze.

Hadn't they seen it? Was she imagining things again?

Neither her mother nor Kyle were moving, but Sera could sense something eerily silent transpiring between them. A short exchange of inaudible words followed, but Sera couldn't understand what either was saying. Straining to hear the conversation, she started to move toward them.

"Stay where you are, Sera," her mother said without turning around. Her voice was quiet but firm, and Sera automatically obeyed.

"Do you understand?" her mother said to Kyle in a normal voice.

Kyle nodded and didn't even look in Sera's direction as he left the room, mumbling what sounded like a warbled apology to her mother on his way out. It was almost as if he were afraid to look at either of them. Sera shook her head, completely rattled by the turn of events.

After Kyle left, Sera waited silently for the tirade she knew would come, but instead her mother stood motionless in a kind of dazed trance, staring at the closed bedroom door. Her eyes were wide and her breathing shallow.

"Mom?"

Her mother turned toward Sera, and for a second, her pale face looked haggard before she composed it into its normal appearance. She walked toward Sera and rested a hand against her purple-streaked hair, her thumb brushing across the softness of Sera's cheek.

Her voice was knife-like, at odds with her tender caress. "You're grounded, young lady."

"What! For how long?"

She paused at the door. "Indefinitely. Dad or I will take you to school, and you'll come straight home afterward until further notice."

"But that's not fair—"

"Unless you want to reconsider going back to Silver Lake High, Sera, you'll stop this minute, because right now I am regretting ever allowing you to go to high school."

Sera felt the bottom drop out from beneath as anger flooded her body. A sharp unexpected pain shot up her back into her shoulders, almost doubling her over.

"Because of Kyle? What are you so protective of?" she argued, nearly gasping. "You can't keep doing this to me. I just want to be a normal teenager. Is that too much to ask?"

Her mother smiled sadly. "I wish more than anything for you to have a normal teenage life but there are things you don't understand—things that will make that impossible for you. And it's my duty to protect you." She sighed, not bothering to explain her cryptic words. "And while you're under my roof, you'll follow my rules."

"This is a goddamn prison," Sera muttered.

"God has nothing to do with it." Her mother paused before continuing down the hallway. "If He did, this is the last place you would be."

"This is the last place I want to be!" Sera shouted.

"Be careful what you wish for," her mother said with no inflection whatsoever. "Because you may just get it."

Sera slammed her bedroom door so hard, the entire frame rattled. "That day can't come soon enough!"

HOUSEBOUND

❧◦❧

Kyle sat in his car, his head pressed against the leather of the steering wheel, his breath coming in short pants. His head ached. What had just happened was next to impossible. Mrs. Caelum, Sera's mother, was Daeva.

An *immortal*.

And she was strong, stronger than any he'd ever felt. Her shade was near faultless. Most deities existing on the mortal plane had shades, specifically, to cloak their energy. Usually Kyle could see right through them, but he'd never met another with one quite like hers.

When he'd come out of the bathroom, Kyle had stayed far away from her for obvious reasons—he knew she didn't like him. But when Sera mentioned the word *Daeva*, her shock had cracked her composure enough that her shade had faltered. In a single blink, her energy had been as clear as day, but then in the next moment, it was gone.

Sera obviously didn't know about her mother. Kyle thought back to the energy he'd felt earlier that morning in the diner and wondered whether Daeva could leave traces of their energy on others or on their children, even if they were human. In his world, nothing was impossible.

Kyle ground his teeth together as the pain receded to a dull thud at the base of his neck. The cell phone in his pocket vibrated. Jude—the only person he didn't want to talk to right then, but he had no choice. He took a deep, slow breath before answering.

"Hey, Jude."

"You talk to Carla about Saturday?" No precursor, no hellos, no niceties.

"Not yet."

"What's wrong?" Jude was nothing if perceptive.

"Nothing much. I was just trying something. Remember you told me about that source up in Connecticut? I tried to see if I could reach it from here. That's all."

"And?"

"It could be big." Kyle knew he was stretching, but he was banking on the fact that Jude really didn't understand the inner workings of his ability.

"Maybe we should leave tonight," Jude said after a pause.

"I need to do something for Carla. She's out of town, so later tomorrow is the earliest I can go." There was a taut silence on the other end of the phone. Kyle held his breath, knowing that Jude didn't like anyone telling him what he could or couldn't do.

"OK." The word snapped through Jude's teeth, barely more than a hiss, and then the phone clicked off. Kyle breathed a sigh of relief.

He leaned back in the seat, pondering whether he should just head home. Kyle hunkered down in the seat as a pair of headlights cut through the gloom of the fading twilight and pulled into the driveway opposite him. Sera's father got out and walked inside. In one of the windows, Kyle could see him embrace Sera's mother, and the tender intimacy of it made him feel uncomfortable, especially given what he'd discovered earlier.

Did Mr. Caelum know the truth about his wife? That she wasn't human? Earlier, she'd known exactly what he was. He could still feel the imprint of her hand on his wrist. Her words had been more than clear—she would stop at nothing to protect her family from any threats, him in particular. Something foul and vengeful unfurled in his belly, and he clawed at where her fingers had touched him.

You should have shattered the bones in her hand, a terrible voice whispered in his head. Kyle swallowed past the sudden hoarseness in his throat as self-loathing consumed him.

He could never hurt Sera's mother.

But inside, the thing within writhed, delighted at the gruesome turn of his thoughts. He'd been born to hate the Daeva and bred to track them. It was in his blood. It was who he was. He was every bit as evil as Jude . . . maybe worse because he hid his true nature, pretending to be someone else for Sera's sake. Fury and self-disgust flowed throughout him as his fingers curled into fists.

Deep down, he knew he could not be trusted.

⚜

Sera watched Kyle's taillights disappear from her bedroom window. He'd been sitting in his car for a long time, and she'd just been about to call him when her father's car had pulled in the driveway. Shortly after that, Kyle had left. She stared blankly out the window at the space where his car had been.

"Great," she muttered to herself, picking up the broken soap dish where Kyle had left it. If only he hadn't been so clumsy in the bathroom, she could have gotten her mother out of there with some excuse none the wiser. She peered down at the reddening bruise her mother's fingers had left on her shoulder and rubbed it gingerly. Her mother had practically imploded after hearing the word *Daeva*. Not to mention what she'd said about Sera imagining she was someone else. None of it made any sense.

A tinny, quiet voice pulled her from her thoughts. "Come in Dollface, Dollface come in."

Sera searched for the source of the voice. A green flashing light under her desk caught her attention—one of Nate's two-way wireless radios. She picked it up and pressed the talk button.

"Dollface to command," she whispered.

"Black Hawk here. Do you request backup? Repeat, do you request backup?"

"Request immediate extraction."

"Negative, Dollface. Enemy snipers on high alert." Sera suppressed a grin at the thought of her parents as enemy snipers.

"Request . . . um . . . snacks?"

"Operation Supply-Drop approved. Black Hawk out."

Sera soon heard a light scratching at her bedroom door. A black-clad Nate slithered in, crawling commando-style on his belly and carrying a backpack. His face was smeared with red and black.

"Does Mom know you're wearing her mascara?" She bit her lip to stop from grinning. "And is that lipstick? You're going to get in so much trouble."

"You want these or not?" Nate said, brandishing a bag of chips and some other goodies. "'Cause I can take my supplies to someone who needs them."

"Don't be mean. Hand them over."

"I'm not. You know how hard it was getting down there? The parental units are on high alert."

"Bring the bounty over here, Black Hawk." She dug in the backpack and pulled out a candy bar. She bit into it and sighed.

Nate opened a Coke, pulling off his black ski hat, his blond curls springing into disarray. Sera rumpled his hair and hugged him, grateful for his company.

"Thanks, bud. So, what are they doing down there?"

"They're talking."

"About me?"

Nate smirked. "Information has its price. Ten bucks and chores for the week."

"Five bucks and chores for two days," Sera countered, sitting beside him with her back to the bed. She grabbed a pillow and hugged it to her chest. Nate consulted a notebook he pulled out from one of the myriad pockets on his spy-vest.

"Just ten bucks, no chores."

"Deal." She gave him a crumpled ten-dollar bill from her backpack and watched as he pocketed it and wrote something into the notebook. She shook her head. "What do you need money for anyway? Mom and Dad buy you everything."

"Movie supplies. And every penny counts."

"Movie supplies? What are you doing, planning to upstage George Lucas?"

A dimpled grin. "All part of the master plan."

"Seriously, what do you need the money for?"

"I'm entering an online contest: Junior Director for Best Short Horror Film."

"Don't you have to be like sixteen to enter those?" Sera asked.

"Thirteen, and I have a fake ID."

"You got a fake ID to pretend that you're *thirteen*?"

"Shhh!" Nate said, placing his ear up to the door. He turned the lights off for good measure. Silvery moonlight filtering through the windows kept the room from being in total darkness. "If Mom and Dad found out, I'd be toast."

Sera shrugged. "Your funeral. So, what are they talking about down there?"

Nate stuffed his face with a handful of chips. "You and Kyle. They think he's bad news."

"I already *know* that."

"Well, Mom was going off on something that Kyle said, sounded like she said somebody called Davy. Who's that?"

"Not a who, it's a them. Daeva," she replied without thinking.

"Yeah, that's it. Mom said something about them finding out about who Kyle was since he wasn't Carla's real kid." He pursed his lips and frowned. "She talked about your drawings and something about her being upset that she hadn't talked to you months ago when you turned sixteen. Then Dad said something about contacting somebody to try murders."

"What? That doesn't make sense."

"That's what it sounded like," he said defensively, and then his eyes brightened with excitement. "What if they're secret assassins?"

"Don't be stupid. Mom? An assassin? Think about it for half a second. She faints at the sight of blood. And Dad? He couldn't hurt a fly."

Nate frowned. "I guess so. That would have been cool though. What else? Oh yeah, they mentioned drugs, too." He glanced at Sera with a dismissive shrug and snorted under his breath. "Like you would ever do drugs . . . way too much of a control freak. Anyway, they mentioned something else called fire."

Sera started. Kyle had mentioned both Fyre and Daevas, but maybe this was something different. "As in burning fire?" she asked carefully. She was dying to know more about the Fyre that Kyle had mentioned but continued to fake being bored to keep Nate talking.

Nate shook his head. "No, that's what I thought at first, too. It was weird, like it was something big that they were talking about, all hushed and quiet, like a *secret* thing. I mean, Mom was really freaked out. So, I tried poking around on the Internet to see what I could find out, trying different spellings, the works. It took me an hour and I still didn't find anything. I mean, not even a trace of it other than some South African farm story. That's what got me."

Nate paused to open the other candy bar. He leaned forward conspiratorially. "I mean *everything* is on the Internet if you know where to look. Like someone *wants* to keep it hidden, right? So I looked harder." He paused, a gleeful smile on his face. "And I found something."

"About this Fyre or whatever it's called?" Sera asked.

"I remembered that Mom also said a name, Zeebalba, so I cross-reffed that with Fyre. I had the spelling wrong, but it was all about hell and devils. And I found this really cool site. It was password protected but I hacked it. Some group called the Ne'feri Order. Anyway, it talked about Fyre, but I don't think it's the same thing. Way too weird. Something about torture. Freaky stuff. Some of it was creepy, but full of material and great ideas for my movie, like a hundred gods and goddesses. And can you imagine seven hells?"

"Seven *what*?"

"Jeez, Ser, haven't you been listening to a word I've been saying? It talked about that word you and Mom used, too—Davys or whatever."

Sera stared at Nate in stunned shock. Between Kyle, her parents, and what Nate was now telling her, it seemed too much of a coincidence. Suddenly, Sera wasn't so convinced. Had Kyle been telling her the truth after all? Her throat felt dry, and she grabbed one of Nate's unopened cans of soda.

"Show me," Sera said thickly, opening the can and taking a big gulp.

"Not on your computer. You'd get hacked by Mom in like five seconds." Sera stared mutely at her brother like he was an alien. He shrugged. "OK, it's not exactly hacking, more like monitoring. They have parental controls on your laptop. They know every site you visit."

Sera felt her stomach flip. In the last couple weeks, she'd done a ton of searches for demons, gods, and definitions of hell. No wonder her mother had gotten so interested in her dreams if they'd been monitoring her Internet activity.

She stared at Nate with newfound admiration. "How do you know all this stuff?"

"I'm an evil genius."

"Oh, right." Sera paused. "What about your PC? Aren't there controls on yours?"

Nate shot her a withering look. Sera shook her head in wonder. Of course there were, but Nate could no doubt circumvent them. "So, let's go to your room," she said. She'd already risen when Nate put a warning hand on her leg.

"Not so fast. No computer after ten, remember? I'm not even supposed to be in here. Mom said you were grounded and you needed your space." He glanced at the door nervously. "Maybe I should go."

Sera frowned. "No wait, that reminds me, when you were downstairs this morning eating breakfast, did you hear what Mom and Dad were talking about? What were they saying they had to tell me? About being sixteen?"

"That's going to cost you," Nate said, giving her a toothy grin. He still had that teeth-too-big-for-your-face look and it reminded her that even though he sounded a lot older than he was, he was still just a kid.

"How about I not tell Mom about your fake ID?"

His green eyes widened with betrayed shock. "You wouldn't!"

"All information, including the hiding of such information, has its price," she quoted his own words back to him, biting her lip at his anxious expression.

"OK, but you can't use that threat again."

"Fine, spill."

"It's not a big deal. I wasn't really listening. They were arguing about something really quietly, but then I heard Dad tell Mom that maybe she should tell you because you were sixteen and old enough."

"I heard that too. So, what was it?"

"Not sure." Nate screwed up his face, thinking. "I think it was something about you moving somewhere. Mom looked really nervous though—scared—like she was waiting for something horrible to happen. I've never seen her cry like that either."

"She was crying?"

"Yeah, Dad kept rubbing her shoulders and telling her everything was going to be OK. Then she said something about somebody not stopping until they found what they were looking for. And then she talked about protecting you at all costs even if they had to send you away. Nothing they were saying made any sense to me. Seriously, it was like they were talking a different language. Anyway, that's when Dad said again that they needed to tell you. I didn't understand half of what they said—they were talking in code."

"Code?"

"Yeah, you know, with the looks and mumbles and sign language." He glanced at the door again. "Look, I should go. I told you everything I remember," he said, creeping toward the door. He opened it quietly and scanned the hallway, then turned back. "Oh, Sera, I forgot, mom mentioned some guy who was azure or azura but I didn't know what that meant. His name sounded like Rat. I thought it was creepy, you know, a guy called Rat? Anyway, that's it."

Sera stared at the closed door after Nate left, her head pounding. It was total information overload. She needed to separate and process everything she'd learned, but she couldn't even think about where to start. She remembered something pushed the button on the walkie-talkie.

"Hey, Nate, can you print out some of that stuff you found for me? I'll make it worth your while."

"OK. It's a flat rate per page," he whispered back.

"Deal. And what do I owe you for the snacks?"

There was a pause on the other end of the device. Then Nate's voice said, "On the house."

Sera clicked off the walkie talkie and lay on her bed thinking about what Nate had told her. So Kyle *hadn't* been lying; he just hadn't been telling her everything as she'd suspected. And why were her parents so worried about *him*? He was just Kyle her friend, wasn't he? Paranoia started to set in on top everything else, aggravating the throbbing sensation in her head.

Along with her mounting monster of a headache, her shoulders ached like she'd been swimming for hours. She stretched each arm over her chest, trying to ease the tension. It was a futile effort. She padded to the bathroom and took a couple of Tylenol to ease the dull thud along her shoulders and neck. Waiting for them to kick in, she sat at her desk and opened her laptop. She cleared her history and the temporary Internet files she'd cached on previous searches per Nate's instruction.

She stared at the search bar. Her fingers hovered over the keyboard, and then she typed in the letters A-Z-U-R-A.

She hit ENTER.

PEACE

❧❦❧

When Sera awoke, the sun was streaming through the open blinds, dipping into the farthest corners of her room. The alarm clock read ten o'clock. Sera barely remembered going to bed, but she guessed that she must have slept a solid eight hours. Her sketchpad lay open next to her and she stared at what she'd written as memories of the night flooded back: *Azura—a being demonic in nature.* Underneath it, she'd written *Rat* and provided a drawing of a half-dragon, half-rat creature with a pointed beak full of razor-sharp teeth.

She'd also drawn the four-armed girl again, only this time she'd given it her own features. Something about it seemed unfinished, almost as if it were two separate images layered on top of each other. It was disturbing. Not quite sure what she was doing, she took her eraser and carefully rubbed out the face until it was nothing but a clear oval.

Faceless was better.

Sera closed the pad and got out of bed, feeling the tender ache of her back and shoulders. She stretched her arms and did a few stiff windmill circles. She felt as if she were growing a second set of arms in the middle of her back upon each rotation. She could hear her parents moving around downstairs. For some reason, the thought of her parents sent her stomach into a tailspin. After yesterday's revelations, she didn't want to see either of them.

The flashing red of her cell phone on the bedside table caught Sera's attention. One missed call from Kyle. Her mom didn't say that she couldn't have *any* contact with Kyle—just that he had to stay away from her. After a quick check down the hallway, she quietly closed her bedroom door and slid down its smooth surface to a seated position. Her fingers skimmed lightly over the phone's keypad as she typed.

—Are you OK?

Kyle's answer came back quickly, despite insisting that he hated texting. OK.

—Where are you?

Breakfast. Meet at Sal's?

—Grounded.

Sucks. Sorry.

—Come by later?

Trip with Jude. 2 days.

Sera stared at his response and felt something cold slide around inside her. She was sure that any time Kyle spent with Jude was just putting him in harm's way. And if Kyle had been telling the truth about Daeva being out for blood, then whatever Kyle was doing for Jude meant that they'd most likely keep coming after him. Sooner or later, Kyle would run out of luck. Sera hesitated before texting him back.

—Not good idea.

No choice. Be OK. TTYL.

And just like that, the conversation ended. She knew that he was avoiding any further discussion about Jude, but the trite response still hurt. It wasn't that he didn't have a choice—Kyle didn't *want* to make the choice to stay away from Jude. There was a big difference between the two, and it infuriated her. She placed her phone on her desk, opened the door, and headed toward the bathroom.

After a long hot shower, which helped to wash away some of the aching in her back, Sera made her way downstairs. She couldn't avoid her parents forever. Normally, her dad went to the office on Saturdays. He was a defense lawyer and usually had a backlog of cases that called him in to work on the weekends. But this morning she could still hear his voice in the kitchen with her mom. And that meant only one thing.

They were waiting for her.

She took a deep breath and rounded the corner at the bottom of the stairs to the kitchen.

"Morning Ser-bear. Sleep well?" her dad asked, looking up from his newspaper.

"Morning, Dad. Like a baby. No office today?" *May as well lead with a good offense*, she thought. He half smiled over the top of his paper and offered a slight nod in the direction of her mother, who was busy at the sink. Sera poured herself a glass of orange juice, jumping at the sound of her mother's soft voice.

"Sera, sit down, please," she said. Her face was grim, her manner agitated. Sera sat, feeling her stomach twist as her mother continued, "Last night your behavior was unacceptable. You know the rules, and yet I came home yesterday to find that boy in your bedroom."

"Mom, it wasn't what—"

"Please don't interrupt, Sera. I've told you before that he is a bad influence." Her mother's voice was a careful monotone. "Yet, you constantly defy us by spending time with him. Now, not only are you breaking house rules, but your grades have not improved, and I received a call from the principal yesterday that you haven't been showing up to class."

"I can explain that," Sera said, the words rushing out. "We . . . had a flat tire . . . and by the time it was fixed, I got to school late. I only missed first period, and it was only one time." The minute the lie left her lips, Sera felt her eyes water.

"And the lying, that's new, too," her mother said, her eyes narrowing.

"I'm not lying, Mom. Dad, you believe me, don't you?" Sera looked across the table to her father. He usually stuck up for her when her mother was on her case, but the look of disappointment on his face made her recoil.

"I'm sorry, Sera. We know when you're lying," he said softly.

"I'm not lying, I swear." Pain radiated along her shoulders and she gasped.

"You are, Sera. It's something that goes against every bone in your body, and you know that," her father said gently. "You feel it, don't you?"

Since when did it hurt to lie?

"Well, I can't tell you the truth, can I?" Sera cried, her eyes stinging from her parents' interrogation and the pain burrowing deeper into her spine. "Because you don't let me. You're just going to punish me for hanging out with a friend who needed my help."

"Help with what?" her father asked.

She contemplated lying—how could she tell them what Kyle was actually facing—but felt a warning pinch ripple along her spine. "I . . . I can't tell you."

"Can't or won't? Is he in some kind of trouble?" Her mother's stare was like ice, cold and impenetrable.

"Yes. No. It's not his fault. It's this guy, Jude. He's involved with some bad stuff and he just doesn't leave Kyle alone," Sera replied, staring at the floor.

"What kind of stuff, Sera?" her mother asked.

"Some people. Some drugs." Sera felt her cheeks getting flushed, always a telltale sign she was hiding something, and she stared at the floor, letting her hair fall forward to cover her face.

Too late.

"Drugs?" her father asked.

The words spilled out of her in a wild rush. "Ever since Jude moved here, he and his friends have been all over Kyle. He told me some story about some miracle drug and these weird people called Daeva that he and Jude are mixed up with. I don't know what to think anymore," her voice trailed off.

"What exactly about the Daeva?" Her father's voice was soft, his face expressionless.

"I don't know, Dad. He says it's some kind of underground gang mixed up with Jude. I'd never even heard of it before." At her mother's look, Sera added, "I'm not lying. Really, Mom, Dad, if I could just keep him away from Jude, he'd be better off and you'll see that he's really a good person. Carla gave him a chance? Can't you?" She stared at them. "Don't you always tell Nate and me to help people? To be kind? Well, Kyle's my friend, and he needs me right now."

She sensed that she was fighting a losing battle—that her parents' minds had been made up about Kyle long before yesterday's incident. Her mother glanced pointedly at her father. On cue, he turned to Sera, resting his fingers on her arm.

"Sera, I know you're probably confused as to why we don't trust Kyle," her father began.

"Then just *tell* me!"

"We will have that conversation soon, I promise. But for now, we have to ask that you not see him," her father said.

"But that's not fair," Sera gasped.

"I'm sorry, Sera—"

"Seriously, Dad, you don't even *know* him. You and Mom just see what you want to see, right? Some guy who doesn't look the right way, doesn't fit in with our perfect Lakewood Court slice of suburbia, isn't good enough for *your* daughter. Since when did you become such snobs?"

"Sera, that's enough," her father said, but Sera couldn't stop the flow of words that rushed past her lips.

"Well, it's true, isn't it? When we moved here, everything changed. It's been really hard, or didn't either of you notice? Do you have any idea of how tough it is to start in a new school in the middle of the year? Especially when you've never been to school before? Do you know what it's like to have people stare at you like you have some kind of disease? Or because you look like someone from the *Addams Family*? Don't you get it yet? I had no friends and Kyle . . ." Sera stared at her hands and bit her lip to stop from shaking. "Kyle was the only one who talked to me. It was because of him that I was able to even get through the school year. But you didn't know that, did you?"

"What about Eleanor's children?" her mother asked.

Sera grimaced, her teeth clenched, shaking her head in disbelief. "Ryan and Beth *Davenport*? Not likely. That would be social suicide. Befriending the new girl who looks like she belongs in a circus? Hardly."

Sera's mind flashed back to the first day she'd walked into school, thrilled to be a part of something she'd never experienced. Shyly, she'd approached Ryan Davenport and his friends near the lockers—her mother had shown her photos of the Davenport kids the night before—and Ryan had eyed her up and down, making some cutting remark about the circus being in town. They'd all laughed and walked away, and it'd been all she could do not to start crying right in the middle of the hallway. Humiliated, she'd spent the morning hiding behind the cafeteria building instead.

"I had no idea. Why didn't you talk to me . . . to us about this?" her mother said. "I could have—"

"What would you have done, Mom?" Sera said. "Force them to be friends with me?"

"I could have helped. I just wish you had come to me."

"How could I? You were both so happy with the new house and neighborhood and Dad's new job. Complaining about not fitting in was stupid. And then after a while, it didn't matter anymore because I had Kyle." Sera glanced pleadingly at her mother. "He's my best friend. I promise you, nothing more than that. And he makes me happy. Don't you want me to be happy?"

"Honey," her mom said, holding the sides of Sera's face with warm hands. For the first time, Sera really looked at her mother. Her face looked weary as if she'd been through hell and back. "It's not that I don't want you to be happy, but

Kyle is not good for you. You'll make other friends if you just give yourself the chance."

"I don't want any other friends," Sera said.

"This is for your own good, Sera," her mother said, this time more firmly, her hands falling back to her sides.

"No, it's not about me. It's what *you* want! I won't do—"

Her father's chair slid back, and Sera shrank at the intensity of his stare. He'd never looked at her like that before. "Then you'll remain grounded until further notice. Straight to school and back, either your mother or I will drive you. You don't have a choice, Sera."

Tears clouded Sera's vision as she glared at her father. "I thought you of all people would understand what it was like to have everyone not believe you, someone who gets punished even though they're *innocent*. Isn't that what you do, Dad, *defend* people? Give them the benefit of the doubt? But you're just like the rest of them." Her voice broke and she ran from the room, out the glass doors, and into the backyard. She ran until she came to the stone wall at the end of their property, and then ran alongside it until she was out of breath and out of tears.

She hated her parents. Kyle wasn't the bad person in all of this. He didn't deserve to have her not be his friend just because her parents didn't like him. Sera was sure they assumed he was into drugs, but she knew that Kyle wasn't a user. They didn't understand what he'd been through. How could they? They hardly *knew* him.

Sera glanced toward the house where she could see her parents through the kitchen window, talking. Chewing on her lip, she made a quick decision and crept back to the house quietly. She edged around the side and stood beneath the kitchen window. Nate would be so proud of her snooping efforts. Her amusement faded, however, as she heard her parents' voices.

" . . . boy has dark secrets. He's dangerous. I felt it, Sam," her mother said. "Why can't she see that? She's so head-strong!"

"Sophia," her father said gently. "He's her friend, and she's sixteen, not thirty. We can't risk pushing her a further away. Sera's too important, now more than ever, you know that."

"Maybe you're right. I can talk to the Davenports and see if they can help," her mother's voice trailed off as she moved farther from the window.

Sera frowned. The Davenports? Why would talking to them help? And why would her dad say that *she* was so important? Sera peeked through the window to see if they were still in the kitchen. She almost screamed as a small body pressed against her left side, crouching down beside her.

"What are you doing?" Nate whispered.

"Nothing!" Sera said reddening. "Go away."

Nate knowingly smiled. "Spying?"

"None of your business," Sera snapped back, forgetting to whisper. They fell silent as their mother's voice came clearly through the window.

"Who's out there? Sera, is that you?" Her voice was sharp, and Sera's entire body froze. Nate put his hand on her shoulder and squeezed sympathetically.

"Leave it to the pro, next time," he whispered. He stood up with a wink and yelled out. "Hey, Mom, it's just me. I was looking for one of my LEGOs out here. Got it!"

"OK, come have some breakfast. Is your sister outside?"

"Yes, she's sitting over by the pool." Nate shot Sera a glance—she owed him, apparently.

With a sigh of relief, Sera dashed over to the loungers next to the bean-shaped pool. Her mind was racing with thoughts of what her parents were hiding on top of what Kyle and Nate had told her. Her mind was racing with thoughts of what her parents were hiding on top of what Kyle and Nate had told her, when a small golden shape jumping between the oak trees lining the edge of the yard caught her attention. She followed it with her eyes all the way to the farthest corner of their property until it disappeared over the top of the low stone wall behind the trees. She stared into space, wondering what it had been.

"Hey, Sera," a voice called just as a long blue-patterned arm swung up over the top of the wall, followed by a familiar smiling face. Dev jumped over the wall easily with a loping grace and walked toward her. He carried something small and tan in his arms, and as he drew nearer, Sera realized that it was the same animal she'd seen earlier.

"Is that a fawn?" she asked, incredulous.

"He's just a baby," Dev said, nodding.

"Isn't that thing wild? How did you catch it? You could get rabies or something, you know," she said as he stopped just short of her lounger. Dev smiled, stroking the quivering mass of golden fur.

"No rabies. Animals like me," he said.

His voice was a lilting singsong, and Sera knew the slight accent came from Southeast Asia, where he'd spent most of his childhood. He'd lived in a handful of countries, moving around because of his family.

"Army brat?" she'd asked when they first met.

He'd responded with a smile. "Something like that."

They had developed an easy friendship that past summer, walking to and from the same art program. And unlike Kyle, her parents adored Dev, whose gracious manners had immediately won them over. Despite Sera's initial interest in Dev, which had waned considerably after her parents' obvious infatuation with him, she'd kept him at arm's length out of some perverse desire to get back at her parents for their dislike of Kyle.

"Sorry about yesterday. Kyle was just being a jerk," Sera said.

"Don't worry about it. He doesn't like me much. I get it."

"Kyle doesn't really like anyone."

"Just you," Dev said.

"I guess. Sometimes I'm not even sure about that," Sera said wryly.

"What are you up to today?"

"Grounded," she said. Dev gave her an empathetic look as he stroked the fawn and sat on the lounger next to her. "Will it let me touch it?" she asked, nodding at the fawn. He smiled and Sera reached a hand out to touch the quivering bundle. Its silver-spotted fur was soft like downy fuzz. She could feel its tiny heartbeat racing a dozen miles a minute. The fawn pushed its head against her hand, like a cat begging to be stroked.

"He likes you," Dev said.

"Yeah, right."

"Animals can always tell who they can trust," he said firmly before dumping the fawn in her lap. It squealed in protest but didn't run away. Sera stroked it again and smiled while its velvet ears tickled her fingers. "See?" Dev said. "He's falling in love. Look at him, poor thing."

Something in his tone made Sera flush.

Over the summer, Dev had made no secret that he enjoyed being with her, and Sera sometimes got the feeling that he was interested in more than just friendship. But she'd always laughed it off. Boys who looked like Dev didn't go out with girls who looked like her. Thinking of him in that light made her blush even redder. With his thick dark hair and golden brown skin and eyes, Dev was definitely good-looking. Add to that his easy charm and sharp wit, and Dev pretty much had the whole package going for him. He would have fit into her school in a heartbeat if he'd gone to Silver Lake. But his family had decided to send him to a very elite private school, not far from where they lived.

Still, Dev wasn't as stuck-up as Kyle seemed to think he was. He was down to earth and fun to be around. While Kyle had been doing community service all summer, she'd been grateful to have someone else to talk to, and as much as she loved Kyle, Dev was like a breath of fresh air. He was well-read, intelligent, and could talk about anything. He also loved art, just like her.

Despite his curiously vast knowledge of various subjects, Dev was simple, sweet, and uncomplicated. And the fact that he didn't cause a major world war with her parents every time she hung out with him was a definite plus.

He poked her in the ribs and Sera jumped, realizing he'd asked her a question. The fawn leapt off her lap and bounded across the lawn. "Sorry, what?"

"Feel like a swim?"

"No, way too chilly for me. You feel free though."

Sera couldn't help but stare as he stood up and took off his bright yellow T-shirt. She smiled. He had an unhealthy obsession with the color yellow. Dev was tall and willowy, and his blue-hued tattoos rippled across his skin as he dived into the water. They were some of the most intricate tattoo art Sera'd ever seen, extending across his back and chest all the way down his arms. They didn't seem to take any particular form, but the countless shades of blue swirling and intertwining made the patterns appear different each time she saw them. She tore her eyes away as his head popped up along the side of the pool.

"Come, sit on the edge," he said. "It's very refreshing." He flicked a handful of droplets in her direction.

"I know your tricks from earlier this summer," she said smiling. "I'm close enough, thank you."

"Suit yourself." Sera watched him push off the wall and float on his back, the sun glistening off the water and his tattoos, which looked almost alive in the shimmering sunlight.

"Your tattoos are beautiful," she blurted out before she could help herself. "Why did you choose blue?"

"Because blue is the infinite."

"The infinite what?"

"The skies, the oceans, limitless life. It's all part of me as I am part of it."

"Oh," Sera said, at a loss for words. When he said it like that, it sounded like it meant far more than his actual words. She normally didn't feel tongue-tied in front of him, but for some reason she felt very small now, as if anything

she said would be insignificant, so she went for the least sig-
nificant thing she could think of, "Too bad you don't go to
Silver Lake, you would have been perfect to play Rama in
the school play. His skin's blue, too." She cringed at how trite
her words sounded.

"Oh?" Dev swam over to the side of the pool and stared
at her in a discerning way. Sera flushed, forcing a smile to
her mouth.

"We're doing a play for the diversity day at school. Diwali?
Festival of lights? Do you know it?"

Dev smiled, his whole face lighting up and making Sera
feel flustered again. "Yes. It's an eastern tradition to celebrate
the goddess of wealth and prosperity, Lakshmi," he said.

"Yes, that's it. Anyway, you look the part," Sera finished
breathlessly. "Rama, I mean." The way Dev was looking at
her made her feel warm, waves of heat radiating up and down
her arms. "Anyway, it's a nice love story." Sera flushed again,
but Dev only smiled.

"It is one of the great love stories of our time," he said.

Again, Sera got a feeling that some hidden meaning lay in
his words. She shook her head—now she was reading into
every tiny little thing. First Kyle, then her mother, and now
Dev. *He's just talking about a play for Pete's sake,* she thought,
grimacing inwardly.

"When's the performance? Maybe I can come."

"Monday."

"I'll be there." Dev pushed off the edge to swim a lap
underwater just as Sera's phone buzzed. She glanced at it
and slid it back into her pocket, her smile fading into a scowl
just as Dev's head resurfaced. "Something important?" he

asked. Sera shook her head—she was done worrying about Kyle.

"So how come you're sitting out here all alone?" Dev asked after a while.

"Grounded. I had a blowout with my parents earlier, so homebound until further notice."

"That's good," he said, then grinned. "I like having you to myself."

"Why?" Sera stared at his impish expression, smiling despite herself.

"I need to keep abreast of the competition for your affections."

Sera couldn't help blushing at his shameless flirting. Still, she was the last person anyone would ever seriously flirt with, a fact that she was reminded of daily at school.

"That's hilarious, my *affections*. You do know what they call me at school, right?" At the shake of Dev's head, she continued. "They call me a gargoyle. Doesn't exactly go hand-in-hand with winning anyone's affections, does it? But don't worry, I like it, fits me perfectly—tall, gangly, and scary-looking."

"First of all, you're not scary-looking." Dev pulled his body lithely out of the pool and sat on the edge next to her chair. His golden eyes were intense. "Second, do you know in some parts of the world a gargoyle is a creature that looks after something incredibly valuable and rare, like a kind of guardian?" The way he was looking at her made her feel as if she were the most precious thing in the world. Her chest felt hot.

"They're still ugly."

"There's a reason for that too. More often than not, they're supposed to protect against evil spirits."

"Jeez, not you too!" She laughed. "Seriously, Kyle is always on about this stuff—mysterious spirits and gods and life after death. Doesn't anyone live in the real world anymore?"

Dev flicked the water off his arms and shook his head, splashing her with prism-like droplets before leaning backward and turning his face up to the sun. "What do *you* believe in?"

Sera mimicked his body language and turned her eyes heavenward as though she'd find the answer there. Her shoulders felt hot as she did and despite the warm sun, goose bumps broke out across the flesh of her arms. "I believe in . . . life."

A smile. "As do I. But for some cultures, all that other stuff *is* real. What about that play your school is doing? The *Ramayana*? Maybe once upon a time that was real, too." He turned to her, his eyes liquid.

Sera thought about Ravana and shivered. "That's just a myth, Dev," she said, distracted as his gaze strayed to her hands and he sat up, running his finger on the inside of her left palm, along her scar.

"How come I've never noticed this before?"

Sera glanced down at the marks below her thumbs. They had become a lot more pronounced in the last few days and shone like raised white scars. She hid her hands against her body self-consciously. "They've always been there. I fell when I was a kid. Sharp rocks."

"They remind me of sigillum."

"Of *what*?"

Another smile. "I meant a sigil, like a seal or rune of some kind. Here, let me see." Dev grasped her hand and drew it over to him, running his thumb over the mark on her left palm. Sera felt her cheeks redden at his gentle touch. Something electric unfolded inside of her, and her vision tunneled. This time it was different, though, full of light instead of darkness.

A flutter of firelight from the magical little clay pots lit all around them . . . the discordant aching sounds of a sitar strumming in the background. It was a glorious display, a triumph of good over evil in celebration of their love. His kiss was light upon her cheek, his touch a gossamer caress. She spun in a slow circle, the light on her beloved's face glowing from within him. She laughed because she was glowing, too.

"Beautiful," Dev murmured, breaking her trance, and raised the back of her hand to his lips. Sera wasn't sure whether he was talking about the marks or her. Either way, her entire body felt like it was melting.

"Whatever, they're just scars," she said gruffly, wrenching her hand away, embarrassed by the feelings—and thoughts—his light touch had provoked. Her palm stung, and she stuffed her hand into her hoodie pocket. "Anyway, I don't believe in any of that stuff. It's the invention of a morally-diseased world."

Dev raised and eyebrow. "Interesting theory."

"Actually, that sounded way better in my head. Good thing it's just you or I'd be really embarrassed at how pretentious that came out."

"So crushed!" Dev said, putting his hand to his heart as if she'd mortally wounded him. "I thought it matters what I think."

"Nope," she joked. "Not one bit."

With a playful grin, Dev grabbed her arm and pulled her over the edge of the chair, tossing her without much effort into the pool with a fluid motion. She swam spluttering to the surface only to be dunked once more as he threw himself into the pool right on top of her.

"You're going to pay for that, blue-boy!" she shouted, her teeth chattering as she heaved herself on top of him, laughing out loud as she dunked him. It felt good to laugh aloud.

Though she liked them both, her friendships with Kyle and Dev were on opposite ends of the spectrum, almost as if they aligned with two separate parts of herself. Since she'd met Dev, Sera felt like she didn't have to be the one always looking out for someone else, always worrying about Kyle or his friendship with Jude or whatever trouble he'd gotten himself into. For some reason, it always felt like Dev was the one looking out for *her*. Like *she* was worth protecting.

And it was a feeling she liked.

THE HUNT

❦❧

Kyle ordered lunch at Sal's while waiting for Jude. His body ached. He felt dirty, inside and out. The darkness within him was like a malignant, spreading stain—one that was growing harder to suppress. He'd felt like that ever since Sera's mother had touched his hand. Then his subsequent rage in the car had terrified him—as if something vile was clawing its way to freedom. One thing Kyle was certain of was that Jude must never ever know how strong Sera's mother was—it would only put Sera in danger.

The phone in his pocket vibrated and he checked the incoming message, hoping that it would be Sera, but it was only Jude saying that he was going to be late. Kyle's food came and he ate it hungrily, not knowing when he'd eat next. Jude and the others didn't stop to eat that often, especially when they were hunting. Human food was not a necessity for them.

His phone buzzed again. Jude was waiting outside. Kyle tossed a ten-dollar bill on the table and walked out, nodding to Big Jim, the owner, behind the coffee counter. Big Jim shot him a surly look, which Kyle returned evenly. Being known as one of Jude's boys didn't exactly win him any favors, even with the more seedy locals. But it had its perks—leaving the ten bucks had been pure generosity on Kyle's part. Jude never paid for anything, not even at Sal's.

"Where're the others?" Kyle asked, glancing at the empty backseat of Jude's car.

"Marcus and Raoul will meet us up there. Damien's going to stick around here to keep an eye on things, just in case anything blows up. So, where to, brother?" Jude tapped the steering wheel.

"I checked the map this morning, and it looks like north-western Connecticut. Where did Azrath say his source was?"

"*Lord* Azrath, Kyle. He said Danbury," said Jude.

"That sounds about right."

Kyle had tried to push out his senses the night before, but he'd felt nothing. Despite his underlying fear, his only hope was that as they got closer, somehow he'd be able to pick up a bigger trace of energy. Otherwise, there'd literally be hell to pay.

"So, what's Sera up to?" Jude asked, and the hairs on Kyle's neck rose.

Kyle tried to be casual. "Don't know, haven't talked to her since yesterday."

"She's pretty cool. Can't put my finger on it, but there's something about that girl that just sucks me in every time." Jude laughed. "Maybe it's her smart mouth and the way she thinks she can talk to me any way she likes. Sassy. I like it. You think she'd go out with me? I mean, as a favor to you?" If Jude wanted to go out with Sera, he'd find a way. He didn't need Kyle's help, or his permission, and so Kyle tried to remain neutral.

"I doubt it. She's got a mind of her own."

"So, you wouldn't mind if I asked her out?" Jude asked slyly.

"Why would I? She's not my girl." Kyle gritted his teeth as he felt a wave of anger wash over him. "Let's be realistic though—she isn't really your type. I mean, you don't have to fight for girls. Sera would make it a point to make you miserable. So why punish yourself? Sorry, but I just don't get it."

Jude shot him a surprised look, almost as if he'd never expected Kyle to actually stand up to him. A half-smile curled his lips. "I guess you're right." He stared at the road for several minutes, the only sound the low thrum of the wheels against the pavement. Then Jude remarked softly, as if to himself, "Although it would be fun to break her."

They drove fast and arrived in Danbury in just under two hours. Kyle hadn't tried to push his senses out with Jude in the car. It was as if a feeling of claustrophobia enveloped him when he used his senses in close proximity to Jude. Kyle was sure it had to do with the tattoos that connected him to Jude—making him feel like a dog on a leash. He needed to distance himself a bit to get any reading.

"I'll catch up with you later. Need to take a leak." He rushed out of the car before Jude could say anything, making his way toward Main Street. He sat in a local diner and ordered a cup of coffee. Then he relaxed and let his senses take over. He knew that what they were looking for would no doubt be in hiding, but it would also be no match against him at this close range.

Concentrating heavily, he pushed outward slowly and methodically, feeling the hundreds of mortal energies surrounding him. He brushed past them, extending his ability as far as he could. Every cell in his brain ached, and sweat soaked his shirt from the effort. Just when he felt his mind start to waver, Kyle felt the pull of what he was looking for toward the eastern end of town—a glimmer of immortal energy, shaded but still obvious to him. Kyle released and felt his body sag as a wave of relief poured over him. He dialed Jude's cell phone.

"You got it yet?"

"East. Come get me. I'm at the diner on Main Street. I think they're on the move. The trail was already faint and it took me a lot longer to find it this time. There must be a portal nearby."

"There's more than one?"

"I think so."

"You *think* so?" said Jude sarcastically.

"Dude, there were fragments, that's all I felt," Kyle snapped back. "That means multiple sources to me unless it's one that somehow got cleaved into two. Look, if you don't want to go now, no skin off my back. Your call." There was a long pause on the other end and for a short second, Kyle wondered if he'd gone too far.

"OK. See you in five." The phone clicked off, and Kyle breathed a shallow sigh of relief.

When Jude picked him up, they drove east following Kyle's senses until they were close enough to pinpoint the exact location, and then Jude called Marcus and Raoul.

"Now what?" Kyle asked.

"Now we stay put until the others get here," Jude said. "You know the drill. Your part's done unless you want to get in on how to do a Daeva." His tone was like saccharine, yet the suggestive venom underscoring it was obvious. "Or maybe it's time for you to get your *soul* dirty."

It was at that moment that Kyle realized that Jude hadn't forgotten the phone exchange; he *never* forgot. Kyle steeled himself, reaching into his darkest depths for the monster within, and released his ironclad control of it. This was what he wanted and if he needed to prove his loyalty, then he'd do what he had to do. He felt an odd sensation of bliss as if the beast were reveling in its freedom, and although a part of him cringed away from it, another part embraced it.

"Whatever you want, Jude. You're the boss," he said, his voice unwavering. "Just tell me when and where."

"Come on, then." Jude grinned, springing from the car. He looked like a kid with a bagful of Halloween candy. He nodded to Marcus and Raoul as they pulled into the lot.

The abandoned building was the remains of a giant decaying barn. Half of its roof was falling in, and its fading red paint was chipped and peeling. Kyle focused and could sense the energy clearly. He could also sense agitation and a curious readiness.

"They know we're here," he said to Jude in a low voice.

"Marcus, get the back. Raoul, side window. I'll take the top. Kyle's playing point today. He's got front-door duty," Jude said winking. "We move after he gives the signal." Marcus made a sound like a growl but did as he was told after a nasty glance at Kyle.

Kyle ignored him and walked to the front, pushing the heavy door open. It creaked noisily. In the shaded darkness, muted sunlight cut through the gloom in eerie slivers. They reminded him of golden bars like a gilded prison. He heard scuffling from the side and started moving toward it, his throat dry.

Before he could take two steps, a woman and a young boy of about fourteen stepped out from behind a pile of crates. They looked normal, clad in jeans and long-sleeved shirts. Kyle frowned. Knowing what they were, they seemed so young and so *human*. But it was just a shade, he knew. The woman spoke in a soft voice.

"He's not Ifrit."

"He's the one who brought them here," the boy told her, "the ones waiting outside." He was beautiful to look at with dark curling hair and the same clear eyes as his companion. "But you're right, he's not like them."

"What is your name, child?" the woman asked.

Child?

"Kyle," he responded without thinking.

"Why are you with them?" the boy said. "You're not like them. You are not what *they* are. Surely you must know that your humanity gives you a choice."

Someone outside the barn howled. Jude was getting impatient. Kyle felt the beast inside him flexing obediently in response, shoving against him, and for a moment, he wanted to scream with the force of it. Kyle shook his head, forcing the monster back as sour bile rose into his mouth. "You're wrong, I don't have a choice. You don't know what they're capable of, what I'm capable of."

"There's always a choice." Kyle's heart and conscience twisted into knots as the woman spoke, her voice soft, musical. "Will you let one of us go, then?"

Her companion turned to her, his expression concerned. "No," the boy said forcefully.

"Yes," she argued. "You have a job to do, Micah. Find him. You must, or we will be lost." They shared a brief wordless exchange, but her gaze fluttered back to Kyle. It was heavy, compassionate, and sad, and he felt it to his bones. His eyes watered, and he brushed at them blindly, furious at this unexpected display of emotion.

"It's not weakness, you know," the woman said, gently reading his thoughts. "It's empathy. Man has always held such a great capacity for it."

Kyle felt her words wash over him, for a moment clearing away the demon that hounded him. "Trust yourself, Kyle. All is never lost, not when there's love in your heart."

"I'm not human. You're wrong about me. I don't know how to love."

"Am I?" she said gently, and Sera's face clouded his vision.

"Yes." His gaze dropped from her eyes to the floor. "Go then," he said to the boy urgently, indicating the eastern side of the building. "They're coming, but not from that side so you'll have a chance. There's a portal near the lake. I felt it before." The boy stared at him. "Go now, before I change my mind."

"Thank you." The boy bowed. "Your kindness will not be forgotten." Then he was gone, slipping into the shadows of the side of the building.

"You're not afraid?" Kyle asked the woman, his skull aching from the pressure of Jude's impatience and the insistent tug of the beast within him. A part of him was angry that he'd let the boy go, turning his voice into little more than a growl. "They'll show you no mercy."

"No." Her smile was radiant. "You're not like them, Kyle. Hold on to that when the light is at its dimmest. They're coming now."

And then the roof caved in as Jude burst through it, landing on his feet. Marcus and Raoul circled from the back and the west, just as they'd been told.

"I thought you said there were two?" Jude snarled.

"I'm sorry. I was wrong." Kyle was unprepared for the backhand across the face, almost dislocating his jaw and hurling his body halfway across the room. And then Jude was on top of him, his face black with rage.

Kyle watched Jude's skin undulate, the demon within possessing its host, and he braced himself. Jude must never know that there'd been two. "It's not my fault. She's strong, stronger than I've seen."

As if on cue, Kyle's gaze was drawn to a bright white light exploding from the center of the room. The woman dropped all pretense of a shade and was holding a flaming sword in her hand. She was almost too beautiful to look upon, with incandescent silver flames rushing around her body in a gilded, shimmering waterfall. Gold designs crested her shoulders and brow, a red dot in the center. She stood in battle stance, her sword high.

A Yoddha. A warrior goddess.

Distracted by the windfall, Jude's face distorted into a greedy grin—Lord Azrath would be pleased. The Yoddha was far more powerful than lower level Daeva. But before Jude could flex a muscle, Raoul dissipated into a cloud of blackened embers as the warrior twisted, her golden sword tracing a blazing path across his chest. Jude howled and dove toward her.

"Marcus, ifricaius!" he snarled, releasing what looked like a long black whip in his hands. Marcus whipped out a similar weapon and they circled the woman. Marcus flung his whip and the barbed tip of it curled toward her. She danced out of the way, but not before it clipped the edge of one of the shimmering tendrils surrounding her like a shroud. She screamed and blood spurted from the severed edges.

"Careful, you idiot!" Jude shouted. "What do you think we're here for?"

Kyle blinked. For a second, it'd seemed like the fallen bits had turned to blackened char, but it must have been a trick of the shadows in the barn. He watched the woman move like a silver blur. She was strong, yet she'd chosen to stay and let the boy escape. Kyle couldn't fathom something stronger than she was, but the boy must have been. It made Kyle wonder what or who it was they'd actually been looking for.

Still, even with her considerable strength, the woman was tiring quickly from her wound. The edge of the laceration was darkening and spreading up her body. It looked like the vines of energy were dying, poisoned along the edges from the sting of Marcus's whip.

"Move!" Jude said. "We don't have much time."

They circled her again, Jude lunging toward her just as she swung the sword toward Marcus. Off-balance, she stumbled right into a second swing of Marcus's whip, and its end wrapped around her arm, the clawed barbs twisting into the flesh of her skin. At the same time, Jude flung his whip toward her. At the last second, it split into duplicate chains, weaving themselves around her legs and burrowing into her flesh like steel maggots.

The woman fell, the sword in her right hand thumping to the floor. Its shimmery flame died as Jude stood over her, leering. His booted foot kicked into her side, flipping her to her stomach.

"You can't win, you know," she gasped as Marcus wrapped a second chain around her free arm, pinning it to the other above her head.

"Shut up, or I'll make this even more painful than it's already going to be."

"Azrath doesn't know what he is doing. He will be stopped."

Jude smiled. "I'm only telling you this because you're going to die," he said matter-of-factly. "Lord Azrath will summon a rakshasa demon far more powerful than Ravinah this time to usher in the KaliYura, and when he is its ruler, I will be his right hand. You and your kind cannot stop us."

"Hell on Earth?" Her voice was weak, the black chains injecting her with dark demonic poison.

"That's the plan," Jude responded cheerfully. Her eyes were wide, but lucid.

"He has already failed once. You have no idea . . . this time . . . Azrath will . . . " Her voice grew faint with the effort it cost her to speak. "Total destruction . . . you must . . . not . . . "

Jude ignored her, turning toward Kyle. "Get over here. It's time to redeem yourself. You were right, she is strong, taking far longer than the others to shut up. Hold her down!"

"What?" Kyle said.

"Afraid?" he jeered. "Don't worry, touching her won't hurt you. Not yet, anyway." He paused. "Not while you're human."

"What happens if you touch her?"

"See what happened to Raoul? Pretty much the same, I expect." He jerked his head toward the dull sword. "Remember the glow?" Jude pulled on a pair of thick rank-smelling gloves. "That's what their energy is, deifyre."

Despite Jude's biting sarcasm, Kyle couldn't help himself. "I don't understand. Why can't she just escape by dying? Go back to where she came from?" Jude didn't answer, stuffing a dirty-looking gag into the warrior's mouth. It was Marcus who answered, staring at Kyle with a disgusted look on his face.

"Don't you know anything?" Marcus hissed. "Our ific-aius weapons bind them to the earth."

"Bring the tools," Jude said to Marcus and then glanced at Kyle. "They trap humans to the earth, too," he said in an oily voice. "So do as I told you. Hold her the hell down."

Kyle slammed his hand across the woman's back, an odd sense of pleasure consuming him. His dark nature soared. The skin above her shoulder blades felt soft and warm, like velvet fuzz. He squinted at the silver flames that danced across her skin. Their light was almost blinding, like looking directly into the sun. At first glance, they seemed like wings, but they weren't exactly. They were more like a blazing aura surrounding her entire body. Kyle realized that they weren't like anything he'd ever seen, probably because he'd never seen a Yoddha this close.

He blinked, frowning as a thought occurred to him. "What exactly *is* deifyre?"

"Watch. You'll see."

"Kyle . . . " The voice was weak and Kyle tightened his fingers across the woman's neck. He heard it again and then realized her lips hadn't moved around the gag in her mouth. He'd heard her voice in his head!

Kyle.

His palm against her skin warmed, and Kyle realized that the direct skin-to-skin contact had somehow made him able to hear her voice in his thoughts. He closed his eyes and tuned in to the connection between them. Her voice came again, more clearly.

You must . . . stop . . . them.

Why? he thought back to her.

Azrath must not be allowed to succeed. He plans to open a reverse portal from the Dark Realms to the Mortal Realm. You must find Micah . . .

Where? How?

But their connection was sliced apart as Kyle felt a horrendous spasm of pain ricochet through his body. The Yoddha's screams of anguish stunned his senses and he rocked back onto his heels, his eyes snapping open.

In horror, he watched Jude methodically stripping the surface of the goddess' skin with a black-and-red serrated blade. It was an ugly weapon, a double-edged curved sword that twisted into an inverted V at the top. Its inner blade was indented with sharp, tiny teeth, which scraped along the shimmering bands of her deifyre, a fine drizzle of shimmering powder floating into a silver chalice that Marcus held just below.

Her body lurched. "Hold her down, Kyle!" Jude snarled as a spray of blood spurted from the lower part of the rachis he'd been scraping.

Jude hissed through his teeth. "Damn it. Now we've lost most of this. Marcus, give him the chalice and put the gloves on. You hold her down."

"No, I've got it," Kyle said. "It's just that she's still alive. Maybe we should wait."

"Of course she's alive," Jude snarled. "If she dies, the deifyre dies. And we've got nothing but ash."

Tell . . . Mi . . . cah . . . beg . . . you . . .

Each word was like a welt of agony slicing deep into his subconscious. Kyle couldn't even begin to fathom how she was able to endure it. He could already see her light waning. It wouldn't be long now.

How do I find him? he thought urgently. Jude gave a grunt of approval, piercing his fog of concentration, and Kyle realized how hard he was digging his nails into her back. He pulled his fingers away, gaping at the four red crescents marring her perfect, smooth skin. Something dark inside of him swelled with pride.

"Don't worry, she's almost gone. We got most of it though. Lord Azrath will be happy," Jude said, leaning back on his haunches, flushed with exertion. "Watch this."

Jude flipped the knife to its non-serrated edge and grasped the tops of where the silver flames began at the base of her neck. In a smooth movement, as if he were scalping someone, he cut the whole thing off. It crumbled to nothing but specks of white ash into his gloves. To her credit, she didn't make a sound, even though Kyle felt her pain as acutely as if it were his own.

Kyle kept his face carefully composed, knowing Jude would find any excuse to belittle him. "What's the point of that?"

Jude shot him a look. "She's mortal now. Shred a Daeva of deifyre and they're killable." He wiped the blade clean on a white cloth and put it back into a black case with silver markings. He looked at Kyle, his stare disconcerting, his voice quiet like a snake's hiss. "So, what did she say to you?"

"What?" Kyle's stomach plummeted.

"When we came in, I heard her talking. What was she saying?" Jude's voice was nonchalant, but Kyle knew that he was carefully listening for his response. He weighed his answer carefully in his head. Jude had just given him exactly the opening he needed.

"She . . . she said I didn't belong with you."

Jude's eyes narrowed, his gaze snapping to Kyle's. "And then what?"

"Then nothing. You came through the roof." Kyle paused and eyed Jude. "So, do I?"

"Do you what?" Jude growled.

"Belong."

Jude shot him another assessing look, but Kyle kept his face blank.

"I suppose now that Raoul ate the big one, you can take his spot. Don't get excited yet, though. I'll need to clear it with Lord Azrath." Jude smiled. "And then there's the first order of business."

"What's that?"

"Prove yourself. Kill her." He nodded at the body on the ground. "She's still alive. Take care of it, and meet me out front."

Kyle knelt next to the woman. Her back was slick with blood. He barely sensed any light in her at all. He took the sword out of the box Jude had left behind and held it across his lap. It was almost two feet long and reeked of death. He hated the way the hilt rested in his hand, as if it belonged there and the odd sense of power it gave him.

"I'm so sorry," he whispered aloud. Checking around, he brushed the hair out of the Yoddha's face and felt the same connection when his skin touched hers. There was no voice this time, just emptiness. He held the weapon against the side of her chest with shaking hands and closed his eyes.

You have to do this, he told himself roughly. *She's as good as dead anyway.*

But the blood will be on your hands, an inner voice argued.

It's already on my hands.

Kyle . . .

He opened his eyes and stared into a pair of eyes like clear silver pools. He almost jerked back but a hand held his, and the sword, in place against her ribs. He saw where the barbs of the steel ifricaius whip had ripped into the flesh of her wrists and he wanted to vomit. Black tendrils of poison curled outward from the wounds, an intricate tattoo of evil.

"I can't do it," he whispered.

You . . . must.

I can't, he thought. His tears were reluctant and hot.

Kyle felt her fingers slide against his, squeezing gently. Before he could guess her intent, she gave a last, labored breath, and pushed against the heel of the blade. Its razor sharp edge slid home between ribs and muscle, and her eyes glazed over. Kyle grasped her face between his palms.

Wait, what about Micah?

Sa . . . sam . . . sar.

And then she was gone, those clear eyes fading and darkening in death, nothing but a lifeless shell left behind. For an instant, the darkness arched inside him — revoltingly joyful — until Kyle dug his nails into his palms, burying its demonic bliss with his own pain.

He pulled the sword from her chest, thick blood pooling out from the vacated wound, and felt the bile rising in his throat. He cleaned the weapon and threw it into its box, wiping his tears furiously.

They killed *gods*.

Suddenly everything became clear. He'd known about Fyre, but he never actually realized *how* Jude got it or what his group did every time Kyle waited outside one of those buildings. Now he knew and it sickened him, even while thrilling him. Bile choked him and he vomited. He'd never thought about it in detail until then. By nature of what he was, he was already damned. Being part-Azura meant that his position in the Daeva–Azura war was already decided. And dying after all he'd done meant that there was only one place for him.

Xibalba. Hell.

The thought of it made his bowels loosen. The torment of Xibalba was unimaginable. So why did he now feel so conflicted? Was it because of the Yoddha's words? She'd made it sound like he had some kind of a choice in his future. Deep down, Kyle knew that he was only deluding himself. She hadn't known who he was — the real truth of what he was. In a world ruled by gods and demons, his fate was tied to the side of the dark. There was no chance of redemption for him. He deserved Xibalba, and more.

His heart conflicted, Kyle walked outside with the weapon's case in hand. Jude grinned at him and shouted to Marcus and Damien. Jude licked his lips, his expression lurid. The monster inside him made his eyes red with glee.

"Burn it!" Jude crowed.

SERIANA

Sera sat in geography and chewed on the end of her pencil, staring absently at the empty seat beside her and then to the window across from it. Kyle had said he'd be gone only a couple days, but it was already Monday and she still hadn't heard from him. He wasn't answering any of her texts and Carla said he was still on some teenage team-building retreat. If only she knew . . .

"*Miss* Caelum?" her teacher said sharply. Sera's gaze snapped to the front of the room and she felt a dull flush crawl into her cheeks. She heard stifled laughter behind her. "Perhaps you can enlighten us on what is so interesting outside of this classroom."

"Sorry, Mr. Watts," she muttered, ducking her head into her textbook. She felt something nudge the back leg of her chair.

"Hey, gargoyle, see some of your friends outside?" a girl's voice hissed. More smothered snickers.

"Yeah," Sera tossed back. "They said to tell you thanks for last night."

A glare from Mr. Watts silenced them. Though the rest of the class passed in relative quiet, she could still feel mocking looks thrown toward her. She usually just ignored such remarks, but sometimes she couldn't help herself from sinking to their level and giving as good as she got.

A piece of balled paper hit her ear, and then another, followed by a giggle. Sera could feel the fury rippling hotly against her back and found herself struggling to breathe. She glanced at the clock above Mr. Watt's desk—only a couple minutes left. She wouldn't let her anger get the better of her so she slowly counted backward from sixty, breathing in through her nose and out through her mouth.

"Where's your *boyfriend*? Slumming for drugs?" someone whispered.

The muscles in her neck tightened. She'd never wanted to hit anyone so badly in her life. At the sound of the bell, Sera grabbed her books and lurched out of the classroom, running toward the bathroom. White spots danced in her vision.

She threw some cold water against her face and stared at her reflection in the mirror. Her skin shimmered around her eyes and she blinked dizzily, swiping the tears from them with her fists. Her back ached.

The door to the bathroom opened and Sera quickly ducked into a stall just as three girls walked in.

"Do you think Ryan's going to ask me to the winter dance?" one of them said. Sera could see her applying lipstick in the mirror through the crack in the stall door—Caroline, a snarky girl from geography class. "It's only two weeks away."

"I really can't see him going with anyone else, Caroline," another voice simpered.

"So who do you think'll ask the gargoyle?" Caroline said nastily.

"*If* she gets asked, you mean. Who would want to be seen with someone like her?"

"I don't think she's that bad looking," the third girl said quietly. "Her face isn't bad. She just looks weird because her hair and eyes are so dark against her pale skin." Sera peered through the crack but couldn't see the girl's face enough to recognize her.

"Come on," the second girl said with a snicker. "You're joking right?"

"No, seriously, she'd look OK with a softer hair color and maybe a bit of lip gloss."

"You're only saying that because you feel sorry for her and you know she's hiding in one of the stalls," Caroline said. She jerked her head toward the row of stalls. "We know you're there, gargoyle, we saw you come in here." Sera pressed herself back against the toilet holding her breath.

"Let it go, Caroline," the third girl said.

"And what are you going to do about it, Beth?" Caroline mocked just as Beth came into Sera's view. Beth Davenport, Ryan's sister. She was a senior. "She your new charity case?"

"She's hardly anyone's charity case, and you know what I can do, Caroline," Beth said quietly. Sera watched the standoff through the crack, her breath caught in her chest, as the two girls glared at each other. Sera's hardly expected Beth to come to her defense on anything.

"Why does it matter?"

"It just does."

"Is this because of your *mother*?"

"Shut up, Caroline. You don't know what you're talking about," Beth snapped.

"Whatever," Caroline huffed. "You coming, Lisa?"

A door slammed shut, clipping off the sound of their shoes and voices. Beth spoke again, this time in Sera's direction. "It's OK, Sera, you can come out. They're gone."

Sera emerged from the stall, wary at Beth's unexpected kindness. "Thanks."

"You don't need to thank me. I should have said something a long time ago, about the names and the taunts. I just didn't realize who . . . " She trailed off as if she couldn't find the right words and stared at Sera instead, shrugging.

"It's OK, they don't bother me," Sera said, still guarded. "Why did Caroline say that you were being nice because of your mother?"

Beth shot an odd look in Sera's direction before turning back to the row of mirrors. She brushed a hand through her brown curls before responding.

"Our parents are friends."

"Yeah, so? You never cared about that before," Sera said. "Neither does your brother."

"Our parents have known each other a very long time. I didn't know how important their friendship was until recently."

Sera frowned again. "So they were BFFs in high school a hundred years ago. Why are you telling me this now? What does it have to do with you and me? We're not friends. You don't even *like* me."

"I didn't know before," she said earnestly. "I only just learned—" She broke off as a group of girls trooped noisily into the bathroom. Sera made to leave and Beth grabbed her arm. "Wait, look, the whole thing is complicated, but I need to talk to you about something," Beth whispered with an urgent tone.

"About what?"

"About Kyle."

"Kyle? What? *Why*?" Sera asked heatedly, backing away from Beth. "Did my *mother* put you up to this?" she accused. She saw guilt flash across Beth's face and Sera's anger exploded. "You don't know what you're talking about. You and your stupid friends, you don't even *know* him!"

"No, Sera. *You* don't know him."

Without a backward glance, Sera stalked out of the bathroom and headed toward seventh period Study Hall. She was seething. How dare Beth lecture her about Kyle. How could her mother share any of this with the Davenports? None of them knew anything about him—or her, for that matter.

The minutes ticked by, and Sera felt her anger draining away as she stared at her notes for the play. Beth had only been trying to help. If Sera was going to be mad at anyone, it was her mother for putting Beth in that position in the first place. Sera shuffled her papers, staring blindly at the clock until the bell rang, lost in her thoughts. They had a half hour to curtain. She was lucky that her parents were even allowing her to participate in the play after the blowup over the weekend.

The auditorium was packed with people by the time Sera dropped her stuff off at her locker. Tiny little tea lights adorned the edges of the auditorium for added ambiance in honor of Diwali, and huge garlands of threaded marigolds decorated the stage. Sera busied herself with last minute details, making sure the stage backgrounds were in the correct order and that costumes were on hand for scene changes. She saw Mark in his Ravana costume, but he made sure to stay far away from her and didn't even glance in her direction. Sera knew she deserved it after the way she'd fallen apart on Friday. She didn't blame him.

She peeked through the side curtains once more and saw her parents sitting near the front. Nate was with them, and so was Dev. Her pulse quickened at the sight of him, and astonishingly, he met her eyes across the sea of people and he smiled. Sera flushed, knowing he'd made the effort to come for her. She waved and ducked behind the curtain just as the lights flickered and dimmed.

Intermission came and went, and the play was on its final scene by the time Sera was able to breathe normally. Everything had gone without a hitch, despite being a man down on the set, so she relaxed and enjoyed the last battle scene from the wings, watching as Rama enlisted the help of Hanuman, the Hindu monkey god, to defeat the demon Ravana. Armed with magical weapons, Rama was finally able to rescue his beloved Sita, and their reunion was celebrated with song and dance.

"Hey," a soft voice said, and Sera jumped. It was Dev.

"What are you doing back here?"

"This is the best part," Dev said, "so I wanted to watch it with you."

"Oh, you've seen the *Ramayana* before?" Sera asked in surprise, suppressing the blush she felt rising to her cheeks.

Dev smiled. "Yes, you could say that."

Sera's heart thumped when Dev slid his warm fingers into hers as Rama and Sita walked hand in hand through the dark forest back to their palace, with people lighting small lamps to show them the way. She was sure he could feel her pulse pounding through her fingertips and felt the urge to speak to cover her fluttering heartbeat.

"I always liked the lights as a kid," she confessed. "Mom lit them every year for the blessings of Lakshmi. She told me that's how it all started—" Sera gestured at the lights on the stage, "—people light them to guide the goddess to their homes for blessings of health and prosperity. According to many, Sita was an incarnation of Lakshmi, as Rama was of Vishnu."

"I thought you didn't believe in all that stuff," Dev said softly. Something in his voice tugged at her, and Sera stared up at him but his face was inscrutable.

"You're right, I don't, but it doesn't mean it's not a beautiful tradition."

Dev didn't answer her and, for a moment, they just stared at each other in silence, the lilting sounds of sitars strumming in the background. Time slowed as he reached down to brush a strand of hair out of her face, and Sera felt herself leaning into his touch. His hand slid down to cup the side of her face, and his golden eyes glowed amber.

"Why do I always feel like you're saying more with your eyes than with actual words?" Sera murmured against his palm, mesmerized by the music onstage, the sight of the lovers in happy reunion, and Dev's compelling stare.

"Is that a bad thing?"

"Yes. I never know what you're thinking, and I don't want to assume that you . . . " Sera trailed off, heat scorching her ears at what she'd almost said . . . *that you like me.*

But before Dev could reply they were jostled apart by the rush of students moving off and then back on the stage as the curtains closed. The hall erupted in thunderous applause, and Sera was dragged away from Dev onto the stage with the others for their final curtain call. They all received a standing ovation.

On stage, Sera couldn't stop staring at Dev or forget the velvet touch of his skin against hers. Her fingers were still tingling. He'd made his way back to his seat and was clapping along with her parents and Nate, but his eyes hadn't left hers either. She smiled at him and then at her parents. She was still grinning as she walked off stage to collect her belongings before joining her family.

Sera sighed, noticing the person waiting at her locker. She really didn't want to deal with Beth, after being on such a high from the play, but it seemed that Beth wasn't going to let her mother's orders go that easily. At the thought of her mother's interference, Sera felt anger start to simmer in her belly.

"Great job on the play," Beth said.

Sera slammed her locker shut, slinging her backpack over her shoulder and glaring pointedly at Beth. "Thanks, but you weren't waiting here just to tell me that, were you?"

Beth's face was distressed. "Look, I'm sorry about earlier. And yes, your mom did ask me to talk to you, but Sera, you have to trust us about Kyle. I have to protect you."

"You don't know a thing about him," Sera said, her voice rising. "You don't know him, or me. And I don't need a baby-sitter, Beth, I'm a big girl."

"Sera, please," Beth said, something akin to desperation coating her words. Other kids from the play were starting to whisper as they walked past them and Beth dragged her into a nearby bathroom, her fingers clutching Sera's arm. "I know a lot more than you think. He's a bad influence."

"Let go of me," Sera gritted out through clenched teeth, the anger in her stomach on full boil now. "Don't. Tell. Me. What. To. Do." She wrenched her arm out of Beth's grip. Her left palm stung, and she almost doubled over from the sudden electrifying pain shooting up her back through her shoulder blades. Something hot snaked out from the middle of her back, making her skin feel as if it were pressing against the rack of a burning stove — as if she were being branded.

"Sera," Beth said, a tremor in her voice. "What's wrong?"

She felt Beth's hand gripping her shoulder once more, and her words came from far away. She couldn't hear anything over the thundering of her pulse in her ears. Beth's anxious and terrified face swam into focus for a second. Sera wanted to ask her what she was so afraid of, but the words wouldn't come out, lodged like barbs in her throat. She choked on them as wave after wave of boiling agony radiated through her veins. Sera lips were dry, her back arching as pain lanced across her entire body.

What is happening to me?

Sera opened her eyes and, for an instant, light blinded her. It speared from her fingers, across her forearms, shimmering through her skin like a prism. Her eyes locked onto Beth crouching beside her, jabbing numbers into her cell phone. She kept darting panicky glances to the door and then horrified ones back at Sera.

Everything faded to black and then Sera rocked backward as a new blade-like sensation ripped through her. Something was slicing through her skin. It felt as if the bones of her spine were suddenly too big for her body, pushing outward, spearing into the outer casing of her skin and muscle tissue.

"It hurts!" she screamed. "What's happening?"

"Please, Sera, try to calm down. I don't know what to do!" Beth shrieked the last words to herself, gripping Sera's hand tightly.

Despite the cloud of alternating sharp and dull pain, Sera could sense Beth's fear. Her fingers were ice-cold against her own. Another thrust of agony made Sera keel forward, her back arching like a bow.

"There's something sticking into me, Beth. Against the wall," she gasped. "Cutting into my neck. Can you see it?" Sera turned her head, grimacing from the effort, and realized that something wasn't sticking into her.

Something was sticking *out* of her.

She twisted weakly, looking underneath and behind her arm. Something hot and fiery gold spun outward from her back. They looked like curling flames. Sera stared at Beth, whose eyes were round and frightened.

I'm dreaming. I have to be. I passed out, and I am dreaming.

But Beth's hand squeezing her fingers tightly was too real to be imagined. Sera pulled herself to her feet and weakly stumbled to the mirror. Strangely enough, the pain had receded, the only indication she'd been in sheer agony seconds before was the odd heaviness settling across her back . . . and a feeling that she was wearing some kind of thick cloak. She stared at her reflection.

Only it wasn't her.

It was that girl again—the one with the clear eyes and the titian hair, the one from her drawing. Sera raised her arm and the girl in the mirror followed. Phantom arms moved in the flames in the mirrored reflection. Sera blinked and watched as the girl in the mirror did the same, half expecting her to disappear as she had the last time. But she didn't.

Beth moved to stand beside her, and Sera felt the world start to tilt beneath her feet as Beth's reflection appeared in the mirror. The realization was slow, sticky, even as her knees buckled and she fell back against Beth.

She was the girl.

A familiar voice broke through the charged silence. "Open the door, Beth. It's Sophia."

"It's OK, Sera. Your mom's here," Beth said, brushing a strand of hair out of Sera's face before leaning her against the wall. She opened the door and Sophia closed it quickly behind her before rushing to Sera's side. Beth's mother also squatted beside them. Sera barely heard their fuzzy voices.

"How long has her shade been off? What happened exactly? Was anyone here?" she heard her mother interrogate Beth. What they were saying made no sense at all. Her *shade*?

"No, I tried to tell her about the boy and she lost it. I didn't know what to do. That's when I called." Beth wrung her hands. "Nothing happened until we were alone in here."

"She's getting stronger," Sophia said, her hand cool against her daughter's forehead. "Sam was right. My shade won't work for much longer. She's the only one who can do it now. We have to tell her."

"You haven't told her?" Beth's mother said.

Told me what?

Her mother's beautiful face swam into her clouded vision. "No, not yet," she murmured.

"Because of Azrath and whatever he's plotting?"

Her mother's voice held a warning. "Not here, Eleanor, but yes. Can you tell Sam to get the car?"

Sophia pulled Sera into her arms, pressing her forehead to her daughter's. Sera felt a warm sensation envelop her body as strength flowed into her. A sense of clarity chased away her haziness, and suddenly her mind no longer felt like it was full of fiery spiderwebs.

"Honey, wake up. I'll take you home, but you have to wake up." Sera felt heat against her head where her skin met her mother's. She took a deep breath into her lungs as her mother's lips pressed into her cheek. "Come on, darling. Let's go home."

By the time they'd reached the car, Sera was starting to feel more like herself, even though her mind was still reeling from what she'd just experienced—and seen. It couldn't possibly have been real.

"I have questions," Sera whispered to her mother as she was helped into the car.

"And it's time you heard the answers."

As they drove off, Sera saw a lone figure leaning on the hood of his car. Their eyes met and Sera felt the rest of her fear dissipate as if by magic. His eyes were full, once more communicating without words. But this time Sera knew exactly what he was saying.

Be still. You're going to be all right.

Sera nodded automatically, and Dev's answering smile brightened. He blew her a kiss, and Sera swore she could feel the barest shimmer of it across her cheek as they drove past.

DISCLOSURE

❧❧

S era's father enveloped Sera into a bear hug once home. "Ser-bear, you OK?"

"Hanging in there, Dad." Her father's face was lined with worry, just like her mother's. They sat in the kitchen in silence as her mother busied herself making three cups of tea. Sera sipped hers as her parents sat at the breakfast island facing her. No one spoke for several minutes.

"So, what am I?" Sera joked weakly after a while. "Some kind of ancient angel princess?"

Her father's face was expressionless, but his voice was tender. "Sort of."

"I was joking!" Sera nearly spat a mouthful of tea across the counter and instead started choking as it went down the wrong way. "What do you mean 'sort of'?"

Sera's gaze rocketed between her parents. Her mother reached across to grasp her ice-cold hand. "You're not an angel, Sera. You're far more than that." Sera remained silent, her lips clamped together. "You're a . . . deity," she said gently. "A Sanrak. A type of guardian."

"A *what*? Did you just say a deity? Like a god?" Sera's voice came out shrill.

Her mother nodded. Sera wanted to shout, "Where are the cameras? I know this is some skewed reality television show!" But it wasn't a prank. She stared at her parents' sincere faces, struggling to hold on to her tenuous grip on reality. "So, the girl in the mirror at school, the one with the clear eyes and red hair, that's who I am?"

"Yes," her father answered.

Sera looked at her mother. "Show me. Take off the . . . shade," she told her, remembering what Beth had called it. With an anxious glance in her father's direction, her mother complied.

A bright glow filled the room. Sera stared down at her hands—the luminescent shimmer beneath the skin was mesmerizing. A lock of hair curled over her shoulder and she held it between her fingers, the reddish gold strands impossibly soft.

"What exactly is a shade? Is it some kind of disguise?" Sera was proud that her voice didn't waver as she spoke.

Her father had turned away against her light but her mother continued staring at her. "It's a muted version of yourself. Your energy and your light are too blinding for human eyes. Most of us only reduce the light. In your case, I had to change other things."

"Why?"

"I didn't want to draw attention. People are naturally drawn to us. I mean look at you," her mother said sadly. "You're radiant."

"So you made me ugl . . . different."

"It was a mistake," her mother said softly. "I see that now. I only wanted to make you inconspicuous, and instead I made you more noticeable. I'm sorry for that."

"But it accomplished what we wanted it to do," her father added, squeezing her mother's shoulder. "You've been well-protected all these years."

Sera flinched at his words. If by "well protected" they meant friendless and ridiculed, then they had succeeded. She'd spent years feeling less than ordinary and invisible when the truth was she was anything but ordinary. The same odd heat she'd experienced earlier in the girls' bathroom engulfed her back and shoulders once again. Was it because her entire life had been a lie?

Were gods supposed to get this worked up? Weren't they supposed to be serene and composed and, well, godlike?

There was no way she could express or explain the firestorm of feelings inside her. And if what her parents said was true, then it was all real—the dreams, the drawings, the voices. All of it. Which meant that not only were the gods real, but the monsters were real, too.

"You OK, honey?" her mother asked, after a while. "I know it's a lot to take in."

Sera nodded. As much as she didn't *want* to know what made her so special that she had to be protected from everyone, she knew she had to. She took a deep breath, going for the least overwhelming question. "So, what's with the lotus flower flame thing?" she asked, her tone shaky. She turned to peer over her shoulder.

A tiny smile graced her mother's lips. "Deifyre."

"Deifyre?" Sera echoed, with a panicky glance at her mother.

"Yes. It's not really fire; it just looks like it. It's part of you . . . part of your aura, if that makes sense. Sam?" Her mother glanced at her father and he stepped out of the room.

Sera watched agape as her mother dropped her own shade, the sudden white light glowing from every part of her. Sera blinked as her own nonhuman eyes quickly adjusted.

"Ready?" Sophia asked, and Sera nodded, half excited, half scared out of her mind.

Spellbound, she saw a liquid white-gold shower spiral from her mother's shoulders down to the floor and flutter into something made entirely of a white fiery substance that covered her arms, torso, and back. Sera gasped.

Shimmering silks made of the same deifyre covered her mother's entire body. Gold mehndi adorned her arms and face, and a gold circlet rested upon her forehead. Every part of her was incandescent—so bright that Sera had to look away for a moment, awed.

As the light dimmed and her mother returned to normal, Sera felt herself release the breath she'd been holding.

"And I'm like that? Like you?" she exhaled.

"Similar."

Her father stepped back into the room, and Sera stared from one to the other as if what she'd just seen had been some magical illusion. If she was like that, no wonder they'd had to hide her.

"It's OK, Ser-bear," her father said. "We understand it's a lot to take in, but it's important that you know. We're just sorry that it had to happen like this, so abruptly. We waited too long. I think we were hoping that we could keep you little forever." A sad wistful smile curved his lips, and Sera fought the urge to fling herself into his arms and have him whisper soothingly into her ear that everything was going to be all right.

There was so much more she wanted to ask, but the thoughts jumbled together in her head, rendering her speechless. She'd just witnessed her mother shimmer into an immortal being and she could still hardly believe it.

"What about Beth? The Davenports?" Sera asked shakily, recalling that both Beth and Eleanor had been in the bathroom to witness her metamorphosis. "Are they like us, too?"

"No, they are Ne'feri. Mortal protectors, fighters. Beth was only recently initiated. Ryan will become Ne'feri, but only after he turns eighteen. They are guardians of the portals between this dimension and the others."

Sera opened her mouth and then shut it. Other people knew. Kids she saw in school knew about all of this: about her parents, about *her*.

"No wonder Beth got all weird at school. She said she had to protect me." Sera shook her head and stared at her father. "So, are you like mom, too?" Her parents exchanged a look.

"Perhaps we should start closer to the beginning, Sophia," her father suggested.

"Think back to everything you know about heaven and hell," Sophia told Sera. "What do you think they are?"

Sera frowned, thinking back to her days of religious education. "Some people believe they are both places you go after you die. If you live a good life, you go to heaven. If you don't, you go to hell." She glanced at her parents, remembering what her mother had said about the realms of existence and hell being plural. "But I guess you're going to tell me that isn't true, right?"

"You're on the right track. It's true and not true at the same time."

"How is that possible? It either is or it isn't."

Her mother smiled. "Things aren't always that black and white, Sera. In this world—the Mortal Realm—humans have many versions of heaven and hell, many different beliefs and teachings. All of them are, to some degree true, the truth. But what exists beyond this realm is an amalgamation of all religious teachings, not just one. Our heaven is called Illysia, and our hell, Xibalba. There are hundreds of different gods and goddesses walking among us, all incarnations of one Supreme Being, but meant for different purposes."

"So, do these gods live in Illysia?" Sera couldn't keep the disbelief from her voice despite all that she'd just seen.

"Most of them do, like the Sanrak and the Yoddha, although the Daeva, as lower level deities, are sent to the Mortal Realm as guardians to watch over people here."

"I thought you said you were Sanrak," Sera said. "How come you're here, then?"

"For you," her mother responded. Sera saw her parents link hands and the realization hit her. They lived here because of her. "This was the only realm where we could exist together as a family. Your father could not come to Illysia, but I could come here. The Trimurtas allowed it."

The strange name struck a memory chord. Nate had said something about it, about the mysterious "try murders." Obviously, he'd meant Trimurtas. Sera nodded, trying to get her mind around what her mother was telling her. "So, are the Trimurtas some kind of tribunal? Like the gods of Olympus?" she asked, trying to make some connection in her mind.

Her father smiled, looking at her with approval. "Yes, you're exactly right. The Trimurtas are the three Lords of Illysia—the Creator, the Protector, and the Destroyer. The Sanrak, like your mother, protect the Trimurtas. Beneath them are the Yoddha, the warrior gods of Illysia. Lastly, the Daeva are the ones who live here on Earth, in the Mortal Realm, to guide and protect humanity."

"Wait, why couldn't you go to Illysia?" Sera asked her father. "Aren't you Sanrak, too?"

"No," her mother said. "Your father is—was—Azura."

The sanity she'd held together by a thin thread started to unravel. Her Internet search from the other night hit her with the force of a freight train. Sera felt herself starting to sway.

Azura—a being demonic *in nature.*

"A what?" she whispered.

"As much as the Daeva are the guardians of humanity, the Azura are its enemy." Her mother's words were flat.

"Enemy," Sera repeated dumbly, her gaze twisting from her father to her mother like a pendulum. *Demonic.*

"Yes," her father said, moving to stand behind her and squeezing her shoulders with reassuring hands. "And not anymore. Seventeen years ago, Azrath, another Azura, summoned a terrible demon to wreak havoc on Earth, and the Trimurtas sent your mother here to defeat it."

Sera gasped, unable to conceal the shock on her face.

"Azrath was crazed, consumed with power," her father continued. "The demon wounded and trapped your mother, and I—" He broke off as the thought of it consumed him, his fingers gripping Sera so tightly that she winced.

"It's OK, Sam," her mother interjected, turning to Sera. "The short version is that your father saved me, sacrificing himself in the process. He defeated Azrath to free me from the rakshasa demon's hold. For his sacrifice, the Trimurtas granted him one wish—his desire to remain in this realm as a human." Sophia raised her eyes to her husband and the unmistakable love in them made Sera's heart wrench. "And I chose to be here with him, and you."

"A rakshasa?" Sera gulped. "Like Ravana from the play?"

"Yes," her mother said.

"So, are those stories all *real*?" Sera's voice rose. "Ravana? Rama and Sita?"

"Yes, my darling." Her mother brushed Sera's face gently. "Lord Vishnu is one of the Trimurtas, and the goddess Lakshmi is his wife. The *Ramayana* is about them, you know that."

Sera's head was spinning—all of her mother's stories had been true. And their whole family was part of it. "What about Nate? Is he like us?" she asked her mother.

"No." Her mother leaned forward to grasp Sera's face in her palms. "Nate came after Sam was human." She glanced at her husband. "I loved your father from the moment we met, even when he was an Azura lord. You were born of that, but Nate was not."

"So, he's human?" Sera said slowly.

107

"Half human, half Sanrak. Nate, like you, is very special. He's probably the only human who can visit Illysia in mortal form."

"But what does that make me?" Her parents exchanged a long glance. "And don't say 'very special.'"

"But you are, Sera. Born of my blood and your mother's blood, it is the reason you can enter all the realms of existence," her father said gently. "*All* of them, including Illysia and Xibalba. Even the Trimurtas cannot venture into Xibalba."

"Xibalba," Sera repeated. "What's that?"

"The hells," her father said simply. "Seven of them. Each one worse than the last."

Sera blanched. "And *why* would I want to go there?"

Her father laughed. "Not that you would, darling, but that you could, because you could take anyone with you between the realms. There are many who covet such an ability, none more so than Azrath."

"The guy you mentioned before?" Sera asked. "But why?"

An odd expression, almost of pain, slashed across her father's face. "Like me, Azrath was an Azura Lord," he said quietly. "He was known as the Azura Lord of Death, claiming the souls of those mortals destined to pass through the Portal of Xibalba. When the Trimurtas cast the demon he'd summoned back to its demon world, Azrath was banished from the Mortal Realm into exile. Ever since, he has been plotting to return. He is consumed by a lust for power, not just for Xibalba, but for *all* the realms of existence."

"You mean Illysia too?"

"Yes."

"But demons can't go there, right?"

"They can, with you," her mother said gently. "And Azrath is not a demon. He is an Azura Lord—an immortal—and one of the strongest of his kind."

"Oh." Sera's gaze spun slowly from her father to her mother, her mind whirling.

Her father hugged her, his arms reassuring and strong. "Don't worry, we will protect you. But it would probably be best for you to remain at home for a few days, at least until we can get some information from the Ne'Feri. We don't know if anyone saw what happened with you, and we don't want to expose you to unnecessary risk, especially from Azrath."

"But how do you know for sure he'll come after me?"

"Because I would if I were him," her father said rather calmly. "Azrath was my blood-brother. When the Trimurtas made me human, they cleansed me of all my Azura blood, but occasionally I have been able to sense him even though he no longer senses me. He will stop at nothing if he knows what and where you are."

"To get to Illysia," Sera finished, the realization hitting her with full force. "I thought you said he was banished from entering this realm?"

"We think that he has found another way to get beyond the wards of his exile," her mother offered softly. "Celestial wards bind him from returning here, but he must have circumvented them somehow."

A thought occurred to Sera, and she stared at her father for a long minute. "Dad? Before, when you say you were his blood-brother, were you like him, too?"

Her father's eyes turned sad. "Yes. As Azrath was known as the Azura Lord of Death, so I was known as the Azura Lord of Judgment. I sentenced. He punished. For what it's worth, I was fair to those who came before me."

"It was the reason I sought him out," her mother said. "He was the only one who could help me find Azrath and defeat the rakshasa demon."

Sera frowned, her heart heavy. "What made you do it, Dad? What made you turn against your brother?"

Sera felt the strong need to reconcile the fact that her *father* had been *Azura* with everything she knew about him. She needed to know what her father being Azura made *her*. She didn't miss the tender glance her parents exchanged or the way her father slid her mother's hand into his and squeezed her fingers.

"I did it for her," he said simply. "Azrath was killing her. I couldn't let her die."

"And the Trimurtas forgave you for your sacrifice, so now you're human." Sera studied her fingernails, trying to make sense of everything she'd just learned. "You said Daeva were guardians on Earth. They protect people from the Azura?"

"Yes," her mother responded. "The Daeva fight to protect humanity and the good in people, and the Azura to defeat and diminish it. Man's capacity for love has always been undermined by his desire to destroy. Illysia has to fight for its souls as much as Xibalba does." Her mother's face grew troubled. "Lately, with the Fyre assaults, it has become much more difficult."

"Fyre?" Sera's head snapped up. She felt the knot in her stomach tighten as Jude and Kyle popped into her head.

Something ugly unfurled inside of her, and an odd coldness settled over her shoulders. "What is Fyre, exactly?"

At this, Sophia's face paled, like a ghost. Her shoulders twitched in some kind of phantom pain, and she leaned heavily against Sam. Sera's trepidation mounted as her stomach began a slow, nauseating free fall. Her mother's voice came out in a pained rasp.

"Fyre comes from *deifyre*. From us, when we die," her mother whispered, tears soaking her cheeks. Sera shrank back from the expression on her face, her heart plummeting to the floor. So Fyre *was* real. It came from gods. Dead gods. Her blood turned to ice inside of her as everything connected at that instant, crashing together like monstrous cymbals.

Gods. Demons. Fyre. Jude. Daeva.

Kyle.

AZRATH

Kyle sat in the passenger seat of Marcus's car, staring mindlessly out the window. What had happened with the Yoddha had been earth-shattering for him. Jude had gone back into the barn after the goddess was dead and had seemed satisfied. He hadn't asked Kyle any questions, preoccupied as he'd been with getting the precious cargo to Azrath, and had taken off quickly afterward.

"Make sure it burns to the ground," he'd told Marcus with a scowl at the dilapidated building and then at Kyle. "And bring him with you to Lord Azrath after it's done."

He'd turned to Kyle, his smile little more than a sneer. "Nice work. It's about time we made it official. I'll tell Lord Azrath of your commitment and you can swear your fealty to him yourself."

In the car, Kyle was torn. What he'd wanted for so long was now about to become a reality: immortality on Earth just for the tiny fee of his soul. Before, doing whatever Jude and Azrath wanted seemed like a small price to pay given the alternative—eternity in the Dark Realms—but now, everything he'd believed was upended.

Kyle held a palm up, and it shook uncontrollably.

"That's because you're human," Marcus said with a laugh, watching him out of the corner of his eye.

"What?"

"The shaking. It's natural for humans. Ifrit don't suffer from emotion." Marcus grinned. "Just pleasure."

"Will it go away?"

Marcus's smile widened into a rictus grin. "After you've killed enough of them, sure."

Kyle felt the bile rise into his throat again and fought the wave of sickness down. There was no way he could ever do this again. Nothing made sense to him anymore. His plan had always been to pledge himself to Azrath and to escape Xibalba. And with Jude boasting about Azrath's coming apocalypse, Kyle still wanted to make sure that he was aligned with the right side, if only to protect Sera. The warrior goddess had been wrong about him. He was worse than the Azura. His *real* father had made sure of that.

Kyle's mind jerked back to the last time he'd seen his mother, lying in a pool of blood on the kitchen floor, a long wooden-handled blade slipping from her hand. She had tried to kill him and slipped, impaling herself instead. "You are cursed," she'd gurgled.

Kyle had stood petrified as she writhed, watching her transform before his eyes into something monstrous. She spoke again, as if possessed, in a different, terrible voice—a male voice. "Take heed, my son. You belong to Xibalba. In your seventeenth year, you shall return. That I promise you."

The thing that had been his mother laughed, its tone chilling.

The police had found him there in the kitchen, screaming, sitting beside his dead mother. It had taken four grown men to hold him down in order to sedate him. Kyle was placed in state foster care soon after that. From that moment on, the young Kyle lived with a reckless abandon and such careless disrespect for his own life that he'd been sentenced to a Juvenile Youth Hall four times before his twelfth birthday. The memory of what had happened that night had faded to something dull and colorless. He'd rationalized that if he was cursed and going to hell anyway, he'd do it in grand style.

Until he'd met Sera, Kyle had had no reason to change. He'd never had a friend, never felt real love. But the minute he'd met her, all Kyle wanted was Sera. He *needed* her. He'd do *anything* to avoid going to Xibalba, even if it meant sacrificing others just to remain near her.

Suddenly, Kyle's head ached, the skin of his skull pulling tight. The dragon wings were stretching painfully along his head, almost separating from the flesh that held them prisoner. Kyle glanced over at Marcus's arms and saw the tattoos along them undulating. Marcus turned to him and smiled.

"Happens when we're close to a portal," he said. "Are you afraid, half-breed?"

"Don't call me that. And no, I'm not afraid."

"You should be," Marcus sneered, pulling off the road in front of a small, dilapidated shack. Jude's car was already there.

Even before Marcus stepped out of the car, the smell of burning sulfur stung Kyle's nostrils. Everything about this place felt dark, evil. A cloud of ice descended into his bones, chasing away any life with its dead fingers. It sank deeper with every breath.

"Come along," Marcus said as if he were talking to a stray dog. He'd already begun to transform, his face rippling into a leathery, puckered mask akin to a horned lizard. Grotesque black webbed wings extended beneath his arms, his body enshrouded in hazy flames. Kyle blinked but Marcus's form remained—the Ifrit's true form.

He'd seen glimpses of Ifrit before, but the flashes had always disappeared after a couple seconds. This time, though, it wasn't a mere glimpse. Marcus's human form had metamorphosed into a terrifying hulking creature with dead eyes and a razor-sharp triangular beak, and Kyle had to keep reminding himself that it was only Marcus. One of the Ifrit's yellow eyes winked as it hunkered past him, slipping through the open doorway, a string of guttural sounds falling from its lips. Kyle still shuddered.

"Take a breath," he whispered to himself harshly. "You're going to meet Azrath, something you've always wanted. Don't punk out now!"

He followed Marcus to the doorway of the shack and bumped against something very solid—an unseen barrier. The doorway was open but he couldn't go through it. The darkness of the shack was impenetrable.

What the hell?

"Marcus?" he called out, his fingers resting against the invisible wall in front of him.

Without warning, a taloned hand ripped through the fabric of air just beneath his chin and grasped his neck, jerking him carelessly through the portal. The tattooed wings on his head stretched so tightly, it felt as though his skin was ripping away from his skull one shaved hair at a time. Hot bile soared into his chest.

Suddenly he was kneeling on a white marble floor, dry-retching to the sound of cacophonous laughter. Swallowing past the knot in his throat, Kyle stood his watery eyes focusing on a tall figure moving down a staircase toward him. Out of the corner of his eye, he registered the human forms of Marcus and Jude across the room, lounging on pillowed white sofas. They continued laughing.

Kyle stared at the floor-to-ceiling windows surrounding him. A massive bone-white marble staircase curved in front of him, flanked by carved ivory pillars. The pure white of everything was confusing, but he didn't have time to focus as something approached him.

In his confusion, he registered that the being was Azura, but there was something else, too—something that was opposite of what Azura energy should have felt like. It was similar to Daeva energy, which couldn't be the case. Kyle shook his head to clear the murkiness. The portal had made his head fuzzy.

Shadows filled his bleary vision as a person dressed in a red dress stopped in front of him. "Welcome, Kyle," a lilting voice said. "I am, as you may have guessed, Lord Azrath."

"But . . . you're a *woman*!" Kyle stuttered. A musical laugh spilled from the woman's mouth.

"I am many things," Azrath said. "Does this form suit better?"

Suddenly, she shifted into a tall slender man with platinum white hair and a clean-shaven face. He wore a tailored suit and an arrogant expression. Kyle gaped.

"Or perhaps this?" the man said, his voice deep and masculine.

Azrath shifted again, but this time his figure rose to more than eight feet tall. Blood-red dragon-like wings arced above and behind his arms. The creature was terrible and beautiful at the same time. Its face was perfect in its symmetry, artistic lines of smooth fire and ebony, with eyes like burning coals — eyes that boasted of hidden horrors and unseen agonies.

The Azura Lord of Death.

Kyle's breath caught in his throat. His hands fluttered in front of him, useless, and he felt the bile rise again in his throat.

"Or this?" The monster's voice was mellifluous, at odds with its horrific exterior yet strangely familiar, as it began yet another effortless transformation. This time, Kyle backed away on his hands, scuttling across the room as the figure of his mother strode toward him.

"No. You're dead!" Kyle whispered.

"Am I?" his mother said mockingly. "Perhaps I should finish the job I failed to do?" she said, walking toward Kyle, hand outstretched.

Kyle cringed and closed his eyes. The barest, gentlest touch made his eyes snap open. His "mother" had shifted forms to the woman he'd first seen. She knelt beside him and drew his shaking body into a soft embrace.

"It's all right," she soothingly cooed against his ear. A scent of rose curled around him, but beneath it lay something cloying and sour with a touch of death — more like dying roses on a grave. Kyle shivered involuntarily and the woman pulled him closer.

"Don't be afraid," she said to him. "Most of it isn't real." She laughed, the sound like tinkling crystal. "Sometimes the ones destined for Xibalba face the ones they've wronged the most. Other times, it's loved ones or feared ones. For you, that could be your mother."

"How do you . . . " Kyle murmured, trailing off amid her embrace. "She said I was . . . cursed."

Another laugh. "And so you are. But to me your curse has been a windfall, and you shall be rewarded for your loyalty, my darling boy." Her voice was magnetic, seductive.

Kyle looked up into her face. In her female form, Azrath was beautiful. Striking would be more fitting, with the darkest curling hair and emerald green eyes. Her skin was like rich cream. She was sultry and provocative, a courtesan with the face of an angel, the timeless dichotomy of the sinner and the saint. She smiled into his eyes and Kyle felt blissful. He shook it off roughly, steeling himself. He knew *exactly* what Azrath was and that this form was just an illusion.

"Jude has told me so much about you," she continued, drawing him up as she stood. "Now that you've proved yourself worthy, I'd like you to join me."

"Just like that? That's it?" Kyle almost breathed a sigh of relief as Jude and Marcus began cackling.

"Not so much," Jude said with a sneer. "You have to get through the initiation."

"I thought I did before in the barn?"

Marcus grinned. "That was just a taste, half-breed. Now for the ritual."

"Calm down, boys," Azrath laughed. She walked toward the sofa and sat, the slit in her dress falling open to reveal long, slender legs. Kyle hastily averted his eyes. "Come," she said to Kyle. He obeyed and sat beside her as she'd indicated. "Leave us," she commanded the others. They, too, obeyed without question.

"You must swear loyalty to me and renounce any other," Azrath told him. "After the ritual, in death, you will be bonded to me in service forever."

"The ritual?"

Her voice was like a caress. "You have to die to serve me, Kyle. You will become Azura, immortal as I am, and more powerful than you ever imagined."

"In this realm?"

"Yes, and in Xibalba when I choose to have you accompany me after we have opened the portals between the realms." She tapped the side of his head gently, her fingers tracing the wings. "These tattoos, the mark of the Ifrit, connect you to Jude as pack leader, but you won't need them anymore." She studied him like a cat toying with a mouse. The foul stench under the roses grew stronger, and Kyle almost gagged. "Before the ritual, I want to see for myself what you see—this ability of yours intrigues me. And so, you must let me into you and we will become as one."

"Let you into me? Like a possession?" Kyle asked, almost gasping for breath. Whatever she was doing, it was near impossible to resist. Her eyes were so luminous and compelling. Kyle thought he understood now why she'd chosen this form. It would be easier to get what she wanted from him— seduction was, after all, one of the tools of sin.

She laughed. "Yes, that's as accurate as anything, I suppose. I will know your every thought, and whether you are as loyal to me as you claim."

Kyle felt the air leave his body. She would see *everything* inside of him. He thought about what he knew about Sera's mother and suddenly his plan seemed full of so many holes that he couldn't breathe. The Ifrit would find and kill her immediately—he knew it. Then they'd kill him, if Azrath didn't do so first.

He felt Azrath's soft caress against his head and steeled himself from flinching. Her touch, so soft before, suddenly felt menacing. He knew Azrath would discover that he lied to Jude and, in effect, betrayed her. He was worse than dead, as far as he could tell, and there was nothing he could do about it. Azrath slipped an ugly bone-colored dagger from a red sheath lying on a table next to the sofa.

Kyle tensed. She had said that he would have to die. For a second, he wondered whether it would be painful. Azrath smiled as if reading his thoughts and leaned closer. She stroked his leg, her hands slipping along his thigh. "Don't worry, it won't hurt, if that's what you are afraid of. Now, let's begin the ritual."

Without warning, an explosion rocked the floor of the room. The white pillars shook as Jude and Marcus rushed toward them.

"The portal, Lord Azrath!" Jude screamed.

Azrath's face twisted with rage. Her ebony hair seemed alive, burning like liquid black fire and making Kyle think of the Gorgon in Greek mythology. He shrank back at her rage.

"Samsar," she gritted through clenched teeth. Something clicked in Kyle's head and he realized that it was the name the warrior goddess had called just before she'd died. *Samsar.*

"Go!" she snarled toward Marcus and Jude. "Destroy them." She turned to Kyle, her eyes now the color of ichor, yellowish-green bile. "We shall have to finish this ritual another time. Being discovered here will undermine everything." Azrath leaned in toward him. As she came closer, Kyle noticed a deep red scar running from the base of her ear into her neckline. She pressed an open-mouthed kiss against his cold lips. Her breath was hot and tasted of cinnamon spice mixed with something sour. "Stay close to the Ifrit. You will have your wish soon. Serve me, and you will be rewarded with your every desire."

And with that she was gone in a swirl of black mist. Kyle wiped his mouth with the back of his hand, resisting the urge to spit.

But he had worse things to worry about. The whites of the walls had begun to crumble in front of his eyes, and suddenly he wasn't standing in the cavernous room anymore but within the dark walls of the shack he'd encountered when they'd first arrived. Bolts of white fire speared the darkness beyond the doorway and he moved toward it on shaky feet.

Marcus and Jude flung their black whips repeatedly as they fought against a blur of gold, but they were no match for its speed. Golden fire tore through their limbs, and with howls of agony, they fled into the blackness of the night sky. Their pursuer did not chase them but rather stood still until the shine of gold dimmed to a pale white glow.

It was the boy from the barn.

"Child," the boy greeted him. "Stand behind me. I must destroy this place."

Kyle did as he'd asked and watched the boy wield a thin strand of deifyre from his fingertips that swung around the entire structure. The glow was almost blinding and Kyle felt the ground rumble beneath his feet. The shack looked the same and the smell of ichor had disappeared. He turned to the boy.

"Are you Micah?"

The boy's eyes widened at the use of his name. "Aria told you."

Kyle nodded. "How did you find me?" he asked.

"I found the portal as you said, and then tracked the Ifrit back here. It was a long shot, but I hoped you'd be here as well. I came as quickly as I could. Were you hurt? Were there others in there?"

"No, I'm OK. I don't think there are any more," Kyle said, evasive. Micah shot a piercing look in his direction but Kyle dropped his eyes to the ground. "I'm sorry about your friend, Aria."

Micah smiled grimly, his perfect face betraying an instant of suffering. "Sacrifice in these times is necessary. Even for my kind."

"Wouldn't she go back to your realm in death?"

"Not the way she died," Micah said gently. Kyle remembered that Aria had slid the dagger home herself. "The part of her spirit that remains will rest here."

Kyle frowned. "She's here then because of me. Because I couldn't do it. Because I'm a coward."

"I am sure Aria had her reasons for choosing the path she did."

"Micah," Kyle began, "there's something I need to tell you. I'm not entirely human. I don't know what I am." He stared at the floor. "Something else, something worse."

The boy's eyes were gentle. "As long as you have a drop of human blood in you, there is always hope." Micah walked over to where Marcus's car was parked. "Come, we must get you somewhere safe," he said, fumbling with the passenger door. "I destroyed the portal that brought me here. I am sure the Ifrit are still close, so we must travel by less obvious means. Do you have keys?"

"No need," Kyle said, hotwiring the car with a deft twist of a few wires. At Micah's dry look, he shrugged. "Tricks of a misspent youth. Where to?"

"Back to your town. We must speak with Samsar."

"Who is this Samsar?"

"Someone who can help."

"And *he's* in Silver Lake? I don't think I know him."

Micah shot him a measured glance. "You've known him for years. He's your friend Sera's father."

Infinity

❧ ❧

Sera lay on her bed, her iPod turned up full blast, trying to let the music drown out every thought in her head. She'd spent the entire day at home, analyzing what she'd learned into tiny, bite-sized pieces. Her whole life—everything she'd believed in—had been a lie. Especially Kyle. And that was the one that stung the most.

She'd tried to call him after her "revelation," but it went straight to voicemail. She needed to speak to him, to hear him tell her the truth in his own words—she needed to know that their entire friendship had been based on more than just another fabrication.

Kyle was one of *them*.

She almost jumped out of her skin as a head poked up from the side of her bed.

"Nate! You scared the crap out of me!" Sera shrieked.

"Sorry. I knocked and you didn't answer, so I came in," Nate said apologetically.

"What's wrong?"

"Nothing. Did you get the packet I put under your pillow?" Sera's face was blank. "You asked me to get you the information on the hell stuff, remember?"

"Oh right." Sera drew the thick envelope from under her pillows. Nate had marked "five dollars" on the outside.

An involuntary smile crossed her lips at this. She pulled the handful of papers out, scanning them. Her eyes widened at the graphic text describing Xibalba and its demons in all their horrific glory. A shiver wound its way up her spine.

"Crazy, right?" Nate whispered. "You think any of it is real?"

Sera steeled her voice. "Of course it's not real, dummy. People make this stuff up and believe in all kinds of things. Besides, I thought you said yourself that you can find anything on the Internet?" She shoved the papers back into the envelope. "I have half a mind to go make up my own vision of heaven and see what people think about that."

"They won't think anything because hell is way cooler," Nate informed her. "I think I'm definitely going to use this in my short film. Maybe *Nate's Journey to Hell* could be the title. With the right effects, it could be pretty sweet. What do you think?"

"I think it's dumb."

Sera doubted that anyone would be pleased about some kid, especially the son of a Sanrak and an ex-Azura, making a movie about Xibalba. There was a reason no one knew about it. And if Nate went poking around, it would only draw attention to them all—the one thing her parents told her they must avoid.

"Whatever, I'm the creative genius in this house," Nate said, turning to leave.

"Nate, wait," Sera said, grabbing his arm, desperate. "Maybe you should do something else, like zombies. You love zombies, remember? All that blood and gore? That's what people want."

"Been done. I need something new. This is it."

"Nate, I really think you—"

"Sera. It's just a movie. You said it yourself. It's not real." Her ten-year-old brother was speaking to her as if she were a scared child. He must have heard the underlying desperation in her voice. "What does it matter anyway? I've already submitted the outline."

"Just do something else, or I'll tell Mom," Sera hissed, frantic.

"You wouldn't!" Nate gasped. The look of broken trust on his face was almost her undoing. But she couldn't let him go through with it, not after all she'd learned. Azura killed Daeva. What would they do to a defenseless boy?

"I mean it, Nate. This stuff is bad news. It's like some kind of . . . cult. Will you please just leave it alone. OK? You have to promise me!"

"OK, I get it, it's bad," Nate said, backing away from her near manic fervor. "Look, forget the five bucks. It's on me. You look terrible, Ser. Maybe you should get some rest. I'll see you later."

Before she could respond, he slipped out of the room, the door clicking shut behind him. Sera frowned. She'd have to keep an eye on him—Nate was far too clever for his own good.

Lying back against her pillows, she tucked the ear buds in her ears and pulled Nate's packet out, spreading the pages on her bedspread. Some of the pictures were explicit, hideous. She had to keep reminding herself that it was all real.

Hell existed. These *things* existed.

Some of the information confirmed what her parents had already told her or what she'd guessed on her own. There were seven hells and seven Demon Lords. Azrath, as her father had said, was the Azura Lord for the Portal to Xibalba. Apparently he could travel freely through all of the hells and held more power than any of the other Demon Lords—with the exception of one, Ra'al.

There was no "king" of the Dark Realms, but if there were one, it would be Ra'al, the Demon Lord of the lowest, most horrific dimension of Xibalba—home to the worst of the worst of humanity. He was so strong that it was rumored he'd once portaled to the Mortal Realm himself.

According to one of the sources, centuries before, Azrath had tried to coerce the others to unite against Ra'al, but it had been a futile effort; he could not unite nor control the other Azura. They were too driven by their own greed. Ra'al, for his part, was not threatened by Azrath's antics—Ra'al held the most power as ruler of the largest hell dimension.

Strangely enough, there was no description of Azrath, the being she was most interested in. All she found what that he, more often than not, took the form of a mortal. Sera stared at the ugly descriptions of each of the seven Demon Lords.

"Ra'al is formless," she read aloud. "The worst thing about this Demon Lord is that he takes the form of what a person trusts the most and then betrays them. He reigns through hate and fear. His dimension boasts torture of the worst kind, the fear that embeds itself into tissue and bone, burrowing deep and inescapable for eternity." Her throat dry, Sera didn't even want to imagine what form the demon would take for her. Her parents? Nate?

"The sixth dimension," she read, "is home to Temlucus, the Demon Lord of Torment. This dimension is where the expression 'burning in hell' gets its reputation. Temlucus's body is all fire and to look upon him means to suffer an eternity of fiery death." There was no picture of Temlucus, just a sea of burning bodies, hands reaching out of the fire in desperate supplication, never to be answered. Sera shivered.

"The fifth dimension is ruled by Wyndigu and is marked by decomposition and decay." Sera tasted sour bile in the back of her throat and blinked away the horrific accompanying image of a faceless rotting corpse. She could feel the gaping holes of its eyes boring into her as if it were alive and suppressed a shudder. She flipped the page over quickly.

"Lamasha is the fourth Demon Lord," she read. "This dimension is overrun with disease and depravity of all kinds. Lamasha has the head of a lion with a deformed, hairy body and the taloned feet of a vulture.

"The third dimension is home to Belphegar, the Demon Lord of Lust, Excess, and Excrement." This one had an accompanying image. She stared at the likeness of Belphegar in horror. He had the body of a huge, slovenly beast with horns and a gaping mouth merged with the body of an enticingly beautiful woman. Sera retched at the grotesque rendition of a disgusting beast on one side lusting after a woman on the other side in the same body. It was a revolting combination.

Sera skipped quickly ahead to the last two Demon Lords. "Nequ'el is the Demon Lord of the second dimension. He is shown here with the head of a black dog with razor sharp teeth and the body of a man. His dimension is one of war and unending enslavement." In the illustration, Nequ'el was shown whipping his naked victims as they lugged heavy rocks in a single line up a mountain. Their thin and broken bodies were stained with blood and raw, open wounds.

"Dekaias is the Demon Lord of Vanity and Arrogance," she read. "His first dimension is marked by opulence and overindulgence, but don't be fooled: hedonism has a heavy and oftentimes hidden cost."

To Sera, the first dimension seemed to be the easiest to take in until she saw the image on the next page. In profile, Dekaias had the face of a beautiful boy with a head of twisting serpents. His tongue was forked. A pair of both feathered and dragon's wings arced from his back. The picture showed him drinking the blood of a beautiful boy with a head of blond curls, his face angled away in the image. The floor on which he stood was a sea of bloody mouths and faces and teeth, moaning in supplication. The phantom pain of a graze on her heel throbbed, and Sera gasped aloud.

It was the exact image from her dream.

Sera raced for the bathroom, her hand clapped over her mouth. She vomited into the toilet and then wiped her lips with the back of her hand. Was Dekaias the owner of the dream voice? Had he been the boy she had seen? She frowned, trying to recall if the shape she'd envisioned had been his. Gooseflesh broke out along her arms. Deep down, she knew it was him. Sera rinsed her mouth with cold water and hauled deep, cleansing breaths into her lungs, banishing the horrific images of the demon lords. One thing was for sure—Xibalba was far worse than she had ever imagined.

She walked back into her bedroom and almost screamed at the figure sitting on the edge of her bed.

"It's OK, Sera," Dev soothed. "It's just me."

"What are you doing here? Does my mom know you're in here?" she asked with a panicked look at the bedroom door.

"She told me to come up," he said, and then added quickly, "she thought you'd need some company. You don't look so great." His golden brown eyes were full of concern. "What's going on?"

If only he knew.

Her eyes watered again, threatening to go into full-on flood mode. "I'm fine," she said gruffly, her gaze slipping from his face to his bare feet. "Why are you wearing rings on your toes?"

He grinned as he wiggled his toes. "I like them."

"They're weird." Despite her glib comment, the strange rings seemed to fall in effortlessly with Dev's personal style. He had rings on his thumbs, too, and even had gold rings in his ears, which should have made him look girly, but didn't. Instead, combined with his golden coloring and inked skin, he just looked like an extraordinarily pretty pirate.

Sera frowned, noticing that Dev held some of the papers from Nate's packet in his long fingers. He raised an eyebrow.

"A . . . paper I'm working on," she said hurriedly. The familiar twinge rippled along her spine as the lie sped past her lips.

"Pretty graphic stuff," Dev commented in a mild tone. She took the papers from his hands and stuffed them out of sight beneath her duvet. "What's your paper about? Maybe I can help?"

"I doubt it," she shot back but something in his words made her reassess her immediate response. She studied his open, earnest face and gave in to the need to make some sense of her churning thoughts. "Do you think people believe in heaven and hell?"

A smile as if he'd expected her question. "People believe in a lot of different things, but at the core it's all really the same—good versus evil, gods versus demons. But what people believe in may not be the whole reality; they could just be parts of one giant truth or versions of a single truth."

Sera stared at him. "So, what is that truth?"

"Well, what I think doesn't really matter, does it? It's what you think."

"I don't know what I think," she hedged. "Did you ever have one of those days where everything you thought you knew was suddenly not the same? When everything that was so clear before suddenly turned gray and indistinct? Like you woke up in a different reality?"

Dev laughed, a huge belly laugh that made her smile and frown in confusion at the same time. "All the time," he said, wiping his eyes. "You have no idea. We live in a socially engineered world."

"So, what do you believe, then?"

"I believe in three things. I believe in life. I believe in love. And I believe in the inherent goodness of people to bring those two things together to discover meaning in life."

"What about hell?" She reached for the pile of papers she'd hidden and waved it in front of his face. "This stuff? Demons? Death, anarchy, the end of the world? If this is true, then those three things have no hope of survival."

"Yet they do survive, regardless of those things," Dev said matter-of-factly. "Because other things exist to protect that life, to guard against those very ones that would destroy it."

"Like the gods?" Her voice broke on the last word.

Dev's eyes were filled with an odd compassion, and suddenly Sera felt as if he somehow understood the topsy-turvy world she now lived in.

"Like the gods," he agreed softly.

"I don't believe in them."

"Don't you?"

His knowing eyes unnerved her. "No. Stop playing games, Dev. You offered to help, remember?"

"You're right, I did," he agreed.

Sera flounced off the edge of the bed and walked to her desk, pretending to check her email. She could feel him staring at her but focused on her screen instead. Without turning, she asked, "Have you ever heard of anything called the Trimurtas?"

"Yes. The three lords of Illysia." His calm tone made her jerk around.

"And Xibalba?"

"The Dark Realms, the hell dimensions?"

"How many?"

"Seven."

She advanced on him, eyes narrowed. "Daeva?"

"Guardians. The good guys."

"Azura?"

"The bad guys."

Sera was almost on top of Dev at that point. "How do *you* know all of this? My parents, Kyle, Beth, now you! Why does everything feel like it's all some giant *conspiracy*?" She threw her hands up and slumped on the bed next to him. Dev remained silent, his eyes sympathetic. Sera glared at him. "So you *do* believe in all of these things then? Azura? Daeva?"

"Yes." Dev stared at her with a peculiar expression. "But it's not about what I believe, but what you believe, Sera," he repeated, his tone soft. "You have to come to terms with what is right in your heart. You can't find those answers with anyone else—not me, not Kyle, not your parents."

He leaned in toward her, his golden eyes compelling, and reached a long blue arm across her shoulders to pull her to sit next to him, drawing her head against his shoulder. He smelled of spice and marigolds, an odd scent. But it suited him. Distracted by the sudden warmth in his eyes and the accompanying rush in her chest, Sera dipped her head into the crook of his arm.

Dev was very appealing, especially in the way that he was looking at her just then. It made her insides feel a little jittery. He kissed her forehead and the jittery feeling was eclipsed by something else entirely.

He was still looking at her with a serene expression, a lock of dark hair curling into his cheek. She brushed it away before she could stop herself, her fingers trailing through the softness of his hair, and then dropped them hastily, appalled at her spontaneity.

"Don't be afraid, Sera," he said.

"Of what?"

"Of me."

"I'm not—"

"Or of this."

Dev leaned down and held her chin between his thumb and forefinger. Her breath constricted in her chest. He was going to kiss her! A flush of warmth rushed up into her ears, obliterating all thought, and Sera closed her eyes as he turned her face up to his.

The kiss was the barest touch, his warm lips brushing gently against hers, but Sera felt it to the ends of her toenails. Her entire body tingled, like a live electrical wire, and then all of a sudden, it was over. She pulled back, eyes wide.

As far as first kisses went, it'd been pretty great. She felt warmth flush her cheeks at Dev's amused look—obviously it hadn't been *his* first. She turned redder as he smiled widely and kissed her on the nose.

"So?" he said.

"So what?"

"Did I measure up to all your other suitors?"

Sera laughed. "Suitors? Seriously, where are you from? The middle ages?" She pretended to fiddle with the forgotten sheaf of papers on the bed next to her. "If you must know, I don't have any suitors. Not a lot of guys lining up around the block to date this masterpiece."

"So number one, then?" Dev said with a wink. She punched him playfully in the shoulder at his arrogance and Dev grabbed her fist and pulled her toward him again. This time the kiss was not a tentative brush like the first, but something deeper, sweeter. All the darkness in her head disappeared, and every part of her was immersed in light. She felt weightless, anchored to Earth only by Dev's warm lips.

Flashes of memory burst like lightbulbs in her head.

She was running in a field, a beautiful meadow filled with every color imaginable. Dev was chasing her, laughing, his face happy and brilliant. A flash, and then they were floating hand in hand in a lake resting against the backdrop of a magnificent waterfall. Blushing lotus flowers dotted its edges. Sera could see the bright blue of a perfect sky above them. In the next instant, they were counting shooting stars lying on a warm beach with waves lapping at their toes, and then in another flash, she was dancing with Dev, his forehead pressed to hers, in a golden hall while others spun around them.

Sera blinked and jerked away.

"What's the matter?" Dev said.

"I . . . I *know* you," she whispered, a hand fluttering to her lips.

"Do you?" Dev asked softly, his eyes penetrating, perceptive.

She shook her head, feeling as if she was going to faint. Something about the kiss had felt so familiar, like she'd done it before. But she'd never kissed Dev before—they'd only just met eight months ago. He didn't look at all surprised by her whispered confession. Instead he drew his fingers along her hairline down toward her chin, his touch like velvet.

"That doesn't sound weird to you?" she asked, breaking the warm spell of silence between them. The moment faded as Dev leaned back slightly.

"Not at all. It's possible that we knew each other in another life, another time."

"Like reincarnation? *Come on*," she scoffed, confused by something in his eyes she couldn't define.

"So that's not possible? Or is that out of the realm of what you believe these days?" Dev said, his voice suddenly cool.

He stood, stretched, and walked toward her window, peering thoughtfully beyond the glass panes.

"I'm not sure what I believe anymore," Sera said, bewildered by his sudden coldness. Was he upset that she didn't believe in reincarnation? A flash of what her mother had told her about Rama and Sita entered her mind—they'd been reincarnated, but they were gods, not normal mortals. Sera shoved the thought away. She hugged herself around her middle, unconsciously echoing his cool tone. "Why don't you enlighten me?"

"Anything can be reborn into something else. Just because you may travel to heaven or hell at one point, it doesn't mean that your spirit may not return to the Mortal Realm at another time. It's all based on choice to some degree."

Sera thought of the seven Demon Lords and the horrific things she'd read about them—they would hardly let their prisoners go just like that. "So, you're saying that if you go to hell, assuming it's real, which I'm not agreeing to, you can leave of your own free will?"

"I don't think it's that simple, but yes. Easier from heaven than hell, though, would be my guess."

"How do you know?"

"I don't, but I have to believe that remorse and redemption play some role in the universe, otherwise what are we here for?"

"But what about us possibly knowing each other before in another lifetime? What does that mean?" She snorted and rolled her eyes. "That we're meant for each other?"

"Why is that so inconceivable to you? I didn't pick you for a cynic, Sera." For some reason, his words stung.

"Well, I never picked you for an incurable romantic either," she shot back. "Plus, I hardly think you'd be my type anyway in this life or any other." The lie was sour as it left her mouth.

Dev turned and Sera thought she saw a flash of something like hurt in his eyes. "And just what would be your type? The thug-with-the-mohawk type? The guy-you-can't-trust type?"

"Don't bring Kyle into this, you don't even know him!" she snapped.

"Do you, Sera?"

His cool words had the desired effect that nothing else could. Like an avalanche, all of her fear and confusion and anger from the last day roiled into an uncontrollable thing. The truth was she *didn't* know Kyle. Her fists clenched at her side, and she felt the hot sting of helpless tears behind her eyes. Sera blinked furiously. She hated crying.

Her parents were wrong about her—no goddess could feel like this!

Dev stood his ground as she advanced upon him, her jaw clenched. He stared down into her face, his golden eyes distant.

"I know it hurts you to hear it, and I am sorry for that, but I'm not saying anything you don't already know. In fact," Dev said, walking past her toward the door, with a shrug toward the window, "he's parked outside if you want to ask him yourself. I'll see you later, Sera."

HIDDEN THINGS

❦⬥❧

Kyle chewed on his lip, staring at Micah out of the corner of his eye. Micah hadn't said much on the entire ride back, not even to elaborate on his knowledge about Sera's father. Instead, after giving Kyle explicit instructions to drive directly to Sera's house, he'd closed his eyes and gone into some kind of meditative state.

The quiet was unexpectedly calming, and Kyle had spent most of the three-hour journey dwelling on what he'd say to Sera. Knowing her, she'd be so mad that he hadn't answered her texts or calls that she probably wouldn't speak to him for weeks. But he didn't have that much time.

Kyle glanced over at Micah as he pulled to a stop across from Sera's house. The boy was awake and staring at him with eerie clear eyes. He made no move to get out of the car.

"So what are you? Are you Yoddha, too?" Kyle finally asked.

"Sanrak."

"*Sanrak?*" Kyle choked. So Aria must have been *his* protector. No wonder she'd told him to go. "But your kind . . . you only come here when—"

"Yes," Micah said. "Azrath must be stopped or everything will be lost. What he is planning will only bring about the end of the world. It has been foreseen."

"Can't you and the Trimurtas stop him?"

Micah leaned toward him, his voice soft. "That is part of the reason I am here. The Trimurtas cannot. At least not right now."

"Why?" Kyle asked, unprepared for the real fear he glimpsed in Micah's eyes.

"Because one of them is missing. He came here, and now we cannot find him."

"He came *here*?" Kyle's voice was a whisper, barely concealing his terror.

"Yes, in the form of an avatara. You understand what this is?"

Kyle blinked. "It's when a god takes the form of something mortal in this realm."

Micah nodded and Kyle slumped back into his seat. Over the years, Kyle had read of old legends of the Trimurtas taking the form of human avataras to visit the Mortal Realm as a way for them to reconnect with humanity. Other stories told of the avataras visiting the Mortal Realm to divert world calamities or to prevent human tragedy. But despite their immortality, the avatara form was vulnerable because it was susceptible to the frailty of its mortal body. In short, it was a risk not taken lightly.

"What do you mean you can't find him? Surely you can feel his energy somewhere. Don't they have guards?"

"He left alone. We cannot sense him in Illysia or here." Micah threw open the passenger door. "Come, let's go. Samsar is waiting."

Kyle hesitated, closing his gaped mouth. The thought of facing Sera's mother again made him feel ill. "Micah, they really don't like me. I'm not sure it's a good idea if I go in there. Can I just wait out here?"

To Kyle's surprise, Micah nodded and walked across the street without a second look. *Micah trusts me*, he thought. It was a good feeling, one that Kyle hadn't felt in a long time. Trust was hard to come by, especially for someone like him. Given what he was and what he'd helped Jude and his friends do to Micah's kind, it was shocking that Micah hadn't dispatched him immediately.

Sitting in the car, Kyle remembered the words Sera's mother had said to him when they last met. He still felt the hot grip of her fingers on his wrist.

You are not welcome here, Azura. Return, and I will not be this merciful.

The threat, though spoken with a measure of kindness, had been real. She'd meant every word. He had to find a way to talk to Sera alone—to explain it all properly. Kyle clenched his fingers into fists, consumed by doubt. He'd participated in the killing of Daeva, even if he hadn't done the deed himself. Aria had died because of him. What was he thinking? He'd be stupid to confess anything to Sera—she would never be able to forgive him . . . even if she believed him.

What was he even *doing* here?

Just as he was turning the keys in the ignition, a face at the window made him freeze.

Sera.

She tapped on the glass, and he rolled the window down.

"What are you doing?" Sera asked. Kyle glanced back at the house. Micah was nowhere in sight.

"Nothing." He fidgeted with the steering wheel. "Look, Sera, I'm sorry about not answering your texts or calls. It's been a pretty rough time, and I . . . " He trailed off, hardly able to look at her.

Sera frowned then slipped around to the other side of the car, falling into the front seat. "Let's go to your place. We need to talk."

"Are you sure? Your parents—"

"—will understand," she finished without hesitation, despite an anxious look toward her house. "Just drive. I need to get out of here, too."

As he drove, he could feel her staring at him, but she remained quiet, which wasn't at all like her. Instead of ripping into him for being a jerk, she simply sat with her hands clasped across her lap, watching him with thoughtful eyes until he pulled into Carla's driveway.

"Carla's away for a couple days at some conference," he said, unlocking the front door. Sera followed and almost crashed into his back as he stopped short in the entry hall. The house was completely trashed and reeked of sulfur. Kyle shoved Sera behind him with one hand, placing the other to his lips. She nodded, eyes wide.

"Wait here," he mouthed to her. He crept forward and peered into the living room. Tables and chairs were flipped over. Holes were gouged into the walls and blackened spots tarred the carpets.

"Carla?" he called quietly.

There was no answer. He crept back into the hallway and inched toward the kitchen. Broken glass and china littered the floor. The refrigerator lay on its side like a casket, its doors wide open and gaping. The smell of half-spoiled food wafted in between the layers of sulfur. He gagged.

Something touched his back and he swung around, almost knocking Sera off her feet. "What?!" he hissed. "I told you to stay over there."

"Sorry!" she hissed back, eyes narrowing. "I heard a noise. Upstairs. It sounded like someone crying."

Kyle grabbed a sharp butcher's knife that was on the floor and turned back to Sera. "Maybe you should go wait in the car."

She glared at him. "I'm not leaving you. You have no idea what I've been through the last couple days, Kyle, so don't tell me what I should or shouldn't do." Any amusement Kyle may have felt quickly faded as another noise came from upstairs. It sounded like something scratching at the floorboards.

"Just stay behind me. And don't go getting any wild ideas," he warned.

Silently, Kyle expanded his energy. He couldn't detect anything out of the ordinary on the landing. He expanded his awareness to the rooms beyond it and pain jackknifed through his brain like a lance. He bounded up the stairs, with Sera close behind him, and pushed open the door to the master bedroom. Carla lay on the bed, looking almost like she was sleeping.

Kyle frowned, a sudden pressure tugging at his head again. Something wasn't right. Movement distracted him as Sera rushed toward the bed. "Wait."

Sera halted in her tracks, her face terrified. "She's hurt, Kyle. I heard her crying, remember?"

"No, wait. Something's wrong, I can feel it." Kyle pushed back against the pressure that had caused him to see spots before. It was local, clouding his thinking. It was so close that he could almost push past it . . .

Instinctively, he closed his eyes to focus, but a sudden gasp made them snap open. Sera had turned back toward the bed and stood still, her mouth wide in horror. He followed her gaze. They both stared as Carla transformed into what looked like a giant feline creature, although twice the size of any normal cat. A nekomata demon.

Nekomatas were a particularly clever brand of shape-shifter that bore little allegiance to anyone but their own kind and served whomever fed their fancies and their bellies. The nekomata yawned lazily, opening two pairs of eyes on either side of its head, and licked one of its front paws while honing in on them both.

"Sera," Kyle said. "Take a step back toward me. Slowly."

"What the hell is *that*?" she whispered back. She half-stepped back, and the demon uncurled itself from a sitting position. Sera froze. It lengthened its red hairless back into an inverted semicircle as it stretched, its two tails waving in grotesque deformity.

"Slowly. Try not to move too suddenly," Kyle warned. "It's a nekomata demon. A shape-shifter."

"A *demon*!" He glanced at her as she took another barely perceptible step backward.

"I tried to tell you."

"When did you ever try to tell me that you had demons in your house, Kyle Knox?" Her whisper was shrill, causing the nekomata to flatten its ears against its head. Kyle waved his arms, drawing its attention.

"You're here for me," he shouted to the creature. "Not her. What do you want?"

Out of the corner of his eye, Kyle saw Sera take another small step toward him. He gauged the distance in his head and knew he could knock her out of the way if need be. Closer would be better. He gestured to her urgently with a small jerk of his head.

"It talks?" she whispered, creeping back another inch.

"I don't know. I've never actually been this close to one." He turned as the nekomata jumped off the bed and circled the edge of the room toward the doorway, effectively blocking any escape. Kyle's stance widened. At least it put Sera behind him.

"What do you want?" he repeated to the demon.

"Prisssse, come," it hissed. Sera jumped, her ears ringing. The demon's voice was like the sound of nails screeching across metal. "Kahlllisssss."

"What's it saying?" Sera said in another shrill whisper. "What does it want you to do? Press what?"

"Your guess is as good as mine," Kyle said, brandishing the knife he'd kept hidden behind his back. The nekomata snarled, its body swelling to double its size. Its eyes rolled back and foam pooled at the corners of its mouth.

"Prisssse, come!" the nekomata growled, agitated now, and scratched at the wall with both of its tails. Red fire spurted from where the tails grated across the brick. "Girl, eat."

"Now would be a good time for a plan," Sera said. "I don't want to be that thing's dinner." Kyle glanced behind him. She was frozen, staring at the creature.

The nekomata continued to scratch against the wall with its tails. With a final swish and a streak of red fire, it twisted its tails in a low arc and stopped. In slow motion, the tails started moving back and forth like twin sharks. Its black lips pulled back from its jaws, exposing its deadly fangs, and it crouched low, belly to the floor.

"Kyle . . ." Sera warned. Kyle glanced at her quivering body.

"Sera, when I move, try to get near the bed," he gritted through clenched teeth. "If you see an opening for the door, you run! Do you hear me?" She nodded as if in a daze, meeting his eyes briefly. "Now!" he yelled.

Before the thing had a chance to react to his shout, Kyle dove at it, his large arms grabbing the creature around its midsection as he plunged the knife into its left flank. A terrible howling burst from the demon's mouth as they both fell to the floor, a mass of thrashing limbs and claws.

The nekomata's powerful hind legs dug into Kyle's exposed stomach as it bucked wildly to get him off. Ignoring the sharp tear of nails ripping through his skin, Kyle swung a knee up over its lower body and plunged the knife into its side. The demon screeched, greenish ichor pouring over Kyle's hand. His stomach heaved at the rotten odor.

"Sera, *go*!" he screamed. Jolted into motion, Sera scrabbled around them, skidding toward the door.

With a powerful shove, the nekomata kicked Kyle halfway across the room and twisted toward her, saliva spraying from its mouth. Sera grabbed the only thing within her reach, a small iron stool, and hurled it at the creature. The edge of the iron smashed into its head, the sound of wetly crunching bone echoing in the room. Still, the nekomata was undeterred, launching itself at her with uncontrollable hunger. She flung her arms up in a futile block.

Shrieking, Kyle threw himself at the nekomata in a football tackle and they both crashed into the wall, bits of wood and brick bursting apart. Kyle screamed as the demon buried its serrated fangs into his arm—he stabbed at its eyes with his free hand until it released him, howling. His left arm hung useless at his side, dripping blood, and he backed away.

The nekomata now stood between him and Sera, the doorway blocked by its muscled bulk. Sera stared at it silently, holding a lamp base in her hands. The demon hissed, unmoving, thick fetid blood oozing from its wounds. The air stank of blood and gore. Then Kyle saw the gouges where the demon's eyes had been. He'd blinded it.

"What now?" Sera whispered.

The creature whipped its tails against its body at the sound of her voice, its head swaying back and forth. It was blinded but its other senses were still sharp. With a snarl, it leapt toward her, claws extended, and smashed into Sera's shoulder, sending her careening into the side of an armchair. And then it was on top of her, even as Kyle flung himself after it, grasping at its hind legs and dragging it off her body.

Sera's screams split the air as the cat's claws raked through her jeans into bone and muscle like butter. Kyle climbed over the demon's body until his hands reached around the nekomata's neck. He didn't stop squeezing despite teeth shredding his leg. His mind started to dull, but he couldn't stop until he felt the neck change shape under his fingers, and his brain barely registered that he was strangling something human.

"No!" he shouted, pulling away automatically.

Confused, he leaned back, seeing another Sera crawling on her hands and knees toward him, her face horrified. The moment of indecision cost him dearly as the shape-shifter reared up toward him and rammed a broken piece of wood right into his rib cage with human hands. He gagged, vomiting blood, and heard a terrible scream.

Black spots danced before his eyes and then hands were pulling the creature off him as if it weighed nothing; a deformed hellish thing with a cat's face on a human's body was before him and then there was a flash of blinding light as a flaming golden sword stabbed through the creature's body. It screamed as it died, flipping backward onto its shrinking form, until it was nothing more than a dark patch of ash on the carpet.

Behind it, all Kyle saw was Sera standing behind the dying creature, hair in her face and a golden sword flaming from her right hand. Its flame flickered as she stood, her face trance-like. Kyle blinked and the sword was gone. All that was left was Sera, kneeling over him, her face displaying sheer terror.

"Kyle? You OK?" Sera pressed against his side and he whimpered. "I don't even know how you are still alive. You've lost so much blood." She touched the piece of wood jutting out of his chest. "If I take this thing out, you'll bleed to death."

"Take . . . it . . . out," he said, his voice barely a rasp. "Be OK."

"You sure?"

"Trust . . . me."

Sera ripped his T-shirt away from the edges of the piece of wood and grabbed it with two hands, pressing her foot against his shoulder for leverage. Then she heaved backward.

Kyle screamed, and he felt Sera press the heels of her palms against the skin of the gaping wound, applying pressure. "There's too much blood. We have to call 911. Where's my phone?"

"Be OK, wait," Kyle said, coughing. His voice was thready but getting stronger. "Keep pressure on."

"Why was that thing here?" Sera whispered, pressing until almost all her weight rested on top of Kyle's chest. "It wanted you to go somewhere with it."

"I don't know," Kyle gasped.

But he did know who'd sent the nekomata. It had to have been a pet—a spy of Azrath's. He shivered, and wondered whether Azrath would know about the demon's death. And *who* had killed it.

With several deep breaths, Kyle focused on healing himself from the inside out. After a few moments, he felt better, his Azura blood assuaging his mortal pain. He wasn't immortal, but at least his Azura blood kept him from dying.

He stared at Sera's hands against his chest and thought of the glowing weapon they'd wielded. As if sensing his stare, she pulled her hands away, wiping them on her jeans.

"We need a bandage or something," she said, using a piece of his ripped shirt to mop up some of the blood pooling on his chest. Suddenly she froze, frowning at the gash.

"Sera—"

Her frown darkened as she watched his muscle and skin knitting back together. She leaned back slowly.

"Kyle? You're—" She scooted her body back until she was a foot away, her expression accusing. "Your wound, it's not bleeding anymore." He drew himself into a sitting position, grimacing at the sore stiffness of his body. "You should be dead," she said softly, watching him. "But you're not."

"No," he said. "You saved me." He stared at her hand intently and Sera pulled it self-consciously against her body. "What was that, Ser?"

"I don't know what you mean."

"The golden sword," he said. "Where did it come from? How did you know it would kill the nekomata?"

"I didn't—" She frowned again, this time staring down at her empty palms, and then glared at him. "You first. Why are you still alive? Anyone else would be dead."

"Looks like we both have secrets," Kyle said, and coughed, tasting blood. "I don't want to keep anything from you anymore, Sera. I have something to tell you, something about me. It's why I can heal so easily, why I didn't die." He coughed again and spat a mouthful of scarlet phlegm to the side. "I'm not exactly . . . human, as you may have already guessed."

Sera's smile was unexpected. Kyle could have sworn her whole face glowed from some light burning inside of her. "Me too," she said with a shaky smile. "I guess I'm not either."

Kyle frowned. Sera *was* human, he was sure of it. His ability had never failed him before. Then he thought of the mystical weapon she'd wielded with such ease. Another fit of coughing overcame him then.

"It's a long story, my—" Sera turned as a light from the wall to the right of them caught her attention. Kyle followed her gaze. It was a glowing circle, like red embers left behind from some fire. "What's this?" She reached toward it, her fingers grazing the shimmering outline.

"Sera, no!" Kyle bolted upright, the pain doubling him. He remembered the nekomata scratching at the wall with its tail, the burst of sparks. "Don't touch that! It's a—"

But it was too late.

The portal sucked Sera through it, her body melting into thin air, her face frozen in belated surprise at the last-minute understanding of his shout. And then she was gone. The echo of his roar reverberated against the walls.

In vain, Kyle pounded against the wall until his battered fingers bled, but the portal had already closed—its shape only built for one single transfer . . . meant for *him*. The glowing circle faded and disappeared, thin lines of blackened ash the only memory of its existence, and then they, too, disappeared.

And Sera had been taken instead.

To the bowels of hell.

THE PORTAL

⧉

Kyle dug his fingers against the wings tattooed on his head, but they remained flat, unresponsive. He couldn't reach Jude no matter how hard he tried. And he could guess why—they weren't anywhere in the Mortal Realm. He felt the panic settle into his bones. If Sera was human, she would die on the other side of the portal. But if Sera wasn't just human, then she was in even more danger than he knew. The portal had been meant for him, not her. He owed it to her to do something.

Kyle pulled himself to his feet, still woozy from the blood he'd lost, and made his way downstairs. He got into his car and drove back to Sera's. As he knocked on the door, he put all thoughts of what he was about to do out of his head.

Mrs. Caelum answered, her eyes filled with mistrust. "Yes?"

"I . . . " Courage failed him.

"It's OK, Sophia," Micah said, walking past her to the door. "Kyle is a friend."

"I know who he is. I don't think it's a good idea for you to see Sera now, Kyle," Sophia said after a hard look at Micah.

Kyle felt a rush of gratitude at Micah's words and took a deep breath. "Please, listen to me. I'm here *about* Sera. She isn't here. There's been . . . an accident." He stared at Sophia's face. "Maybe you should sit down."

Once in the kitchen, Kyle explained what had happened at Carla's. Sera's parents' expressions went from shock to fear to panic in a matter of seconds. Before Sera's mother could direct her clearly mounting anger at him, he continued, "She came to me, I swear. I stayed away, like you told me. I didn't know the demon was going to be there. I know you think I'm bad news, and you're probably right, but you have to know that I would never put Sera in danger. Never."

Mr. Caelum interrupted him. "Where is the portal, Kyle?" His voice was urgent.

"I already checked, Sir. The portal is sealed."

"I know, but I can still get an idea of where it went, or at the very least try to reopen it. It's worth a shot. Some portals leave a residue, like a shadow, of their path. We can try to recreate it."

"You can do that?"

A shadowy thought niggled at Kyle's brain and he pushed his energy carefully toward Mr. Caelum. But he was human, nothing more—it was hard to believe he was the mysterious Samsar.

"I can't, but Micah can," Sam said.

Kyle shook his head. "Even if he could, I know that portal doesn't go to Illysia or anywhere in this realm. It goes to Xibalba. Which means you can't go there. You'd die." He glanced at Micah. "And he'd be too weak to even find Sera."

Sam smiled, a gentle smile that made Kyle think of Sera. "You know who I am, don't you, Son?"

"Sam," Sophia said in warning. "We can't trust him. Azrath—"

"If Azrath learns about Sera, we are lost. We have nothing to lose by trusting this boy."

"You're Sera's father. Sam Caelum." Kyle glanced at Micah, who nodded. "And Samsar."

"Yes, I am Sera's father, but what you don't know is that Azrath is my brother."

Kyle gasped. "But you're human."

"I am now, but I wasn't always. I was an Azura Lord, like Azrath, once. Up until Sera's birth." Kyle felt the blood drain out of his body, remembering how furious Azrath had been when she'd hissed Samsar's name in the white house. "Now you understand what kind of danger Sera is in, don't you?" Sam said quietly.

"But Azrath thinks she is human, too."

"As you probably realize, my brother will find out very quickly that Sera is a little more than mortal. The good thing is that she won't die there, because of my Azura blood. So we must find her before Azrath does."

Kyle was in shock. A child with both Daeva and Azura bloodlines, Sera was definitely something *more* than just another girl. "So she's Daeva, too?" Kyle asked weakly.

"Sanrak," Micah clarified.

Kyle stared at Sera's mother, his mouth going instantly dry. No wonder she'd been able to shade both herself *and* Sera so well—she was one of the most powerful goddesses, the guardians of the Trimurtas. This new revelation was staggering.

"She killed the nekomata with deifyre," Kyle said. "No Azura born has ever been able to wield deifyre."

"Kyle," Sophia said, her tone still guarded. "If Sam and Micah can recreate the portal, you're the only one who can follow her."

"You mean to Xibalba." His voice was barely a whisper, but inside Kyle knew—he'd do anything to help get her back, even if it meant going to the place that had haunted him his entire life. He nodded.

"Sophia, you stay here in case she comes back. Micah and I will go with Kyle," Sam said. Sophia whispered something to her husband that Kyle didn't catch, and they embraced. Kyle turned away, embarrassed, catching Micah's strained expression out of the corner of his eye.

The three of them drove back to Carla's place and entered the house cautiously. It was still in shambles.

"The nekomata must have been a strong one," Micah murmured as they crept upstairs. "I can still sense it even though it's dead. Only the strongest demons leave that kind of essence behind." He glanced at Kyle. "Where did it die?"

"It's in this room," Kyle said, showing him where Sera had killed the demon.

All that was left of it was a thick black burn mark that stank of decay. Micah placed his hand over it without touching the residue and closed his eyes. His forehead creased as he rocked back onto his heels.

"Very strong," he repeated. "Strange. I have met my share of nekomatas over the years and they all felt the same. This one doesn't. It was very old." He turned to Kyle. "How did it look?"

"The usual—like a giant cat. This one shifted really fast, though, once to human form. And it . . . talked."

"What did it say, Kyle?" Micah asked cautiously.

"It kept saying 'come.'" Kyle cleared his throat. "And it wanted to eat Sera."

"That's it?"

"And something about a price, but that was it."

"A price?"

Kyle shrugged. "I don't really know. It was very guttural. Before it attacked, it drew the portal with its tail. It seemed so strange to me at the time, even though it barely took its eyes off of us." He nodded toward the wall. "The portal was over there."

Micah stared again, this time in disbelief. "You saw it *draw* the portal? Are you sure it wasn't there before?"

Kyle turned his mind inward to the scene with the demon. He wasn't sure what he'd seen; the two tails scratching against the wall now seemed less than what he'd thought originally. He knew that transient demons could not portal in and out of the Mortal Realm but rather had to be summoned or sent by someone.

"Maybe you're right. It must have been there before." He glanced at the wall where Sera had disappeared, where no visible trace of it remained.

Sam raised his palm in front of the wall. "Here?" he asked Kyle, who nodded.

Micah stooped beside him. A golden light filled the room as Micah's hand glowed brightly against the wall, moving in a slow circle. Sam chanted something under his breath, his right hand on Micah's shoulder. Faint red lines appeared beneath Micah's incandescent palm.

Without warning, Sam placed both his hands directly on the red lines. He screamed as they burnt into his skin, but still he held them there, even as Micah grasped his shoulders, his blinding white aura flowing around and through them. Kyle squinted against its blaze. Then suddenly, everything went dark.

"What happened? Did Sam see anything? Does he know where the portal went? Did Sera actually go through it?" Kyle fired off in rapid succession. But Sam had collapsed against Micah, his eyes closed. They both looked drained. "Is he going to be OK?" Kyle asked Micah.

"Azura markings aren't gentle on human bodies. I absorbed as much of the pain as I could, but it wasn't enough." His face was strained.

Sam stirred and opened his eyes. His hands were criss-crossed with faint red lines and dusted in black ash. He curled them into fists, even as his face tightened in pain.

"She's there," he gritted. "In Xibalba." His eyes clouded over as they dropped from Kyle's. "Not sure where. I don't think the portal was my brother's, although I sensed him there, too."

"Azrath?" Kyle gasped. "Are you sure? I don't under-stand. I just saw him here. Why would—"

Kyle clamped his lips together, realizing what he'd con-fessed. But it was too late. Micah and Sam were both staring at him in confusion and wariness. He backed away.

"It's not what you think," he said. "I only met him today, after Micah tracked the Ifrit and showed up at the shack. But he retreated back into a portal . . . "

Sam pulled himself up to his feet and stumbled toward Kyle. His face was desperate. "Where? The portal before, was it in this realm?"

"I don't know. I went into a big white house, and Azrath appeared there as a woman."

"That doesn't surprise me. Azrath loves playing with emotions," Sam said. "What does he want with you, Kyle?"

Kyle stared at the floor, his fingers crossing over one another. Looking up at Sam's worried face, though, Kyle realized he had to trust someone, and if he couldn't trust Sera, he'd trust her father if only because he loved her as much as Kyle did.

"He wants my ability," he began after a deep breath, spitting the bitter words out of his mouth. "I can feel energies, even shaded ones. I helped them find Daeva. For Fyre. I'm not proud of what I've done, and I've done some terrible things. After I met Sera I knew even more that I didn't want to end up in Xibalba. Azrath is, was, the only way out for me to stay here, with her."

"I don't understand," Sam said. "Why would Azrath need Fyre?"

"I don't know. I find the Daeva and the Ifrit kill them. That's how I met Micah. I led them right to him and Aria. It's my fault she died." Kyle stared ahead, unseeing. "And it's my fault Sera's in danger. My mother was right," he whispered. "I am a curse to everyone around me. I should have let her kill me when she had the chance."

"It's not your fault," Sam said gently, but Kyle shied away from his kindness.

"You're wrong. You don't know what I am. My mother, she knew, and she tried to kill me. She was trying to *save* me. But she failed. And so I did everything possible to finish the job she'd started. Until I met Sera, nothing mattered to me—not death, not living, not Xibalba, nothing. I don't even *know* who

I am." Kyle crouched down to the floor, his head in his hands. "When my mother died, she —*something*—told me that I would be in Xibalba after my seventeenth birthday. When I met the Ifrit, I knew who they were, what they did. And I saw Azrath as a way out. So I took it. No matter the cost. I turn seventeen soon, so I don't have a lot of time. I was desperate."

"Kyle, does Azrath know anything about Sera?" Micah asked.

"No," Kyle said. "But I can't be sure." Sam shot Micah a worried look.

"Go," Micah told Sam. "I'll stay here with Kyle and see if we can learn anything more about the portal. Don't worry, Sophia can protect herself if need be."

Sam walked past where Kyle knelt and put a hand on his shoulder. "Don't let someone else decide who you are. *You* decide. You are free to make that choice no matter where you've come from. Blood does not define you." Sam squeezed Kyle's shoulder reassuringly and tapped his own heart. "This does, what's in here. It'll be OK. We'll get Sera back."

Kyle felt his throat tighten at Sam's compassion. It wouldn't have been easy for anyone to hear and accept what he'd just revealed; yet Sam had not shown any anger or hatred toward him. Kyle wiped the tears from his eyes with one hand, then stood after Sam left.

"Why do you trust him even though he was an Azura Lord?" Kyle asked Micah.

Micah smiled. "Now can you understand why he said those things to you? About deciding who you are? Samsar chose who he wanted to become, despite what he was—for love. So, yes, I trust him. Completely."

"But why?"

"Because his heart is pure." Micah's smile tightened. Pain slashed briefly across his face. "And because . . . Sophia loves him. Sanrak work in pairs. We were a pair. She chose to come here. To him."

Kyle shot him a speculative look. "You don't look old enough to be anyone's *pair*."

"Sanrak age differently from people, Kyle. I can shade myself to be older but I enjoy this form, the innocence of this age. I am several thousand years old, and Sophia is even older than I am. Samsar was as old as she before he turned human. And Sera is young still, in human years, just sixteen. But she will age as her mother does, with a very long life ahead of her."

Kyle frowned. "Won't Sam die eventually?"

"Yes. Sophia will shade herself to match his natural aging, and then she will return to Illysia. To me."

"And Sera?" Kyle's voice was a whisper.

Micah's brow furrowed, his face troubled. "Of all our paths, hers is the most shadowed. I do not have a good answer for you. Only Sera can decide where her path will go." He turned back to the wall. "Come over here, Azura, and make yourself useful."

Kyle walked to where Micah stood, frowning. "You called me Azura. Aren't I a Child of Man?"

"You are both, but for now, I need some Azura blood to reopen this portal." Micah pulled a silver knife from a sheath against his side and pressed the tip into Kyle's index finger. A drop of blood formed against the tip. "Retrace the markings of the portal," Micah ordered him.

Kyle placed his finger against the wall. "It's not going to work, I don't know how—"

Suddenly his hand jerked as his fingers followed a swirling circular path. His blood stood crimson against the white wall, and he watched, mesmerized, until his finger stopped moving. The markings glowed orange, and he felt the tip of his finger and then his forearm pushing into the wall, which had become the consistency of a marshmallow. A hand pulled him roughly backward.

"Enough," Micah whispered. "You've done it. The portal is open."

"But how? I've never—"

"Azura blood is also very powerful, especially within this realm. If the portal was meant for you as you've said, then it would allow you to recreate it."

"So, are we going to go after her?"

"No. You are the only one with a connection to this portal. If I lose you, I lose Sera, and I can't risk that. For now, we wait."

"But—"

Micah shot a grim look his way. "Sera's a smart girl. She'll find a way to the portal, and then we can bring her back."

"What if she doesn't come back, Micah?"

"Then we'll both go, I promise."

They sat in silence for a few minutes, the eerie sigil glowing against the wall. Kyle prayed silently that Sera would return to the portal if she had the chance. He glanced at Micah. The boy's eyes were closed, his face unlined, perfect. He seemed so young, pure. Lost in thought, Kyle jumped at the sound of Micah's voice.

"People often do that, you know. Underestimate me because of how I look."

"What? I wasn't."

"It's OK. I get it a lot."

"How old can Sanrak get?" Kyle asked. "I didn't think you actually aged."

"We don't. Years to us are meaningless. It's just time. We can choose to live forever, but most of us choose to return to Brahman, the one Supreme Being. That has always been our way."

The portal glowed red for an instant and then a black shape slithered through. Micah jumped to his feet. The snake like demon hissed and reared its head just as a golden arrow whittled through it, exploding it to black dust. The light of Micah's bow dulled and disappeared as Kyle stared at him with wide eyes. The portal's brightness faded back to its muted glow.

"That's the only problem with keeping a portal to the Dark Realms open. The demons." Micah sat back down. "Don't worry, Kyle. I'll keep you safe."

"I'm not worried about me!" Kyle's voice was shrill. "What about her? What if there are more of those things where she is? How'll she defend herself? Can she wield deifyre in Xibalba?"

"I don't know," Micah said grimly. "It has never been done before, because we are weakened by the lack of life in the Dark Realms. Our power would go toward sustaining us, not toward our weapons. But Sera is different. Who knows what she may be able to do?"

Kyle sighed. "I hope you're right, really I do. But what if you're not?"

"Pray that I am."

What Lies Beneath

❧⚘☙

Sera collapsed to the ground, gasping for breath. Entering the portal had made her bones feel liquid. She raised her head slowly and looked around, squinting in the muted darkness. Bits of sharp gravel cut into the skin of her limbs, and she could sense the jagged edges of a rock inches above her head. A thin filter of red-tinged light from a narrow tunnel illuminated some kind of low cave with barely enough space for her to move. She turned carefully, wincing as a piece of sharp rock nicked her elbow.

The ground beneath her felt damp. She didn't even want to think about where the wetness — *water? urine? worse?* — came from. A nest-like structure made of twigs and some kind of fleshy substance lay to her left next to a discarded carcass with partly rotting meat still on the bone. On cue, a rank stench filled her nostrils and she gagged.

The portal had brought her to the nekomata's lair, she realized. Which meant that she had to be in one of the hell dimensions.

I'm in Xibalba.

"Keep it together, Sera," she whispered to herself as her breathing quickened.

Her right palm stung. She rubbed her thumb against it and felt a strange tingle, which was odd, as it was her left palm that usually felt this way. She stared at her fingers, remembering that her hand had become a deadly weapon.

Deifyre.

Sera stifled the urge to make the sword reappear. Even if she could, she was pretty sure that wielding deifyre in hell would attract more attention than she wanted. Twisting backward, she felt against the wall for any sign that the portal was still there. But there was nothing except rough rock beneath her fingers. She had to find another way out.

To do that, though, she'd have to find a disguise, some kind of shade that would protect her. But she'd never done any kind of shade before. Could she even do it? She needed something that had the mark of Xibalba on it. Nearly gagging, she inched closer to the nekomata's nest but stopped short as a severed eyeball leered glassily back at her. Bile scalded the back of her tongue.

Sera scrambled backward, and then inspiration struck. Scraping her fingers against her jeans where she'd smeared what had remained of the dead nekomata, she focused on the feel of the demon just before she had killed it and rubbed her thumb against her forefingers. Focusing, Sera drew the remaining essence of the demon into herself, coating her entire aura in it. The shade felt clammy against her, ugly, as if she'd wiped the scum off the underside of a garbage bin and rubbed it into her skin. She had no idea if it was going to work, but it was better than nothing. If the nekomata were any indication of the kind of demons in Xibalba, she needed to give herself any kind of advantage, even if she had to feel like one of them for a while.

Ignoring the queasy hollowness in her belly, she crawled slowly out of the lair and emerged into another cave, which opened into a long hallway. She peered down at what looked like an underground subway tunnel lit by the same eerie blood-like light. Tentatively she walked along it, staying close to one side. Fear gripped her as two dark shapes made their way in her direction. As they got closer, she realized they were human—a man and a woman. They looked relaxed and happy, which confused her. The woman's eyes met hers briefly, and for an instant, Sera saw a flash of sickening terror before it was replaced by the blissful stare from before. She shrank back against the wall but the pair barely acknowledged her as they swept past. Sera stared at their retreating backs, belatedly noticing the mass of tiny creatures that looked like leeches covering every inch of exposed skin—feeding on them. She looked away quickly.

Nothing is normal here, she told herself. *Make no mistake, this is Xibalba. Everything that you read about is real.*

She pushed forward. A lizard-like creature snaked past her, skittering away at the sight of her. Sera expelled a shaky breath. At least the shade seemed to be working. The nekomata must have been a powerful demon. Two more demons rushed by in much the same way as the first, although this time one of them did an awkward bow. She pulled her lips back from her teeth in a snarl and they sped away.

Sera kept walking, not sure what she was looking for, until she heard the sound of voices up ahead. Sera rounded a curved entryway and instantly found herself face-to-face with a girl who could have been her twin, with long dark hair and a sallow complexion. *The twin of my human self*, Sera amended. *She'd see me as the nekomata.*

"Aziz, you have returned already?" the girl said. "Father will be pleased."

As she spoke, Sera saw that she wasn't really a girl at all. Her face was humanlike but covered in fine scales. Her black hair was more like long matted fur, curling down her neck and back. Sera pulled the shade tighter against her and retraced her steps to the door without answering.

"Aziz, wait." The girl yawned and Sera saw multiple rows of shark-like teeth along her bottom jaw before she turned her glittery yellow eyes back in her direction. "Father wants to see you as soon as he is done with Azrath."

Sera halted in her tracks. *Azrath is here?* "Where?" she hissed, the guttural sound the same as she'd heard the nekomata utter.

Her right palm stung again and Sera stared down at it, confused. The scar was now a raised, raw welt. It itched as though fire ants had just bitten her. Distracted, she rubbed it against her side. The girl's head cocked to one side, curious.

"What's the matter, Aziz? You don't look well. Did you find the boy?"

Did the demon mean Kyle? The girl was looking at her pointedly. "Yessss," Sera answered.

"Good," she said just as a boy of about fourteen wandered into the room. "Father is in the red room." The girl's smile grew into a delighted grin. "Just in time! I'm starving!" she exclaimed.

Sera almost stumbled in her haste to exit the room. The last thing she saw was the boy climbing on to the couch next to the demon-girl, whose lips had pulled back from her face in a horrible leer. The bottom half of her jaw dislocated from its top and her mouth hinged open into an impossibly wide fang-filled abyss.

Sera rushed past another empty chamber and then turned down a long hallway leading to a darkened room. Several shapes slid past her in the dark but she ignored them, focusing on the two bodies toward the far end of the chamber. The walls of the room glowed like lava and Sera understood why the girl had called it the red room. She was sure the metallic, gritty smell coming from the walls was blood. Sera eased around the side, careful not to touch the walls, and slid through a doorway, hoping that it would take her closer to the figures without her having to be inside the room with them. The last thing she wanted was to underestimate the Demon Lord of this dimension.

She crept closer to the voices, trying to make the shade as seamless as possible against her, until she was right behind where the two creatures sat.

"Azrath," the smaller of the two said in a high-pitched voice. "Where is the boy? Have you found him? If this plan of yours is to succeed, the boy is crucial. He is the key."

"I know. The Ifrit are close."

"And the portal?"

"It is almost done."

Were they talking about Kyle? Sera wondered. The girl-demon had asked her whether she'd found the boy, and the real nekomata had obviously wanted Kyle to go with it. But why did they want Kyle? She thought back to how quickly his wound had healed—how he'd admitted he wasn't human— and shivered.

Suddenly Azrath stood and walked just beyond the doorway where Sera was hidden. She couldn't help but stare.

His features were perfect—his hair a glistening gold against his snow-white skin. He looked beautiful and terrible all at once.

"I shall take my leave. I will be back just before the portal is complete," Azrath said. "Be ready to fulfill your part of the bargain."

"I will," the other voice agreed.

A small form came into view and Sera smothered a gasp. The child couldn't have been more than four years old, with perfect golden brown ringlets and a peaches-and-cream complexion. Sera knew beyond any doubt that the thing wasn't a child at all.

It was a Demon Lord.

It didn't look like any of the demons she had read about, and then she realized why as breath rushed out of her. There was one Demon Lord that had no form—it took the form of whatever one trusted the most. *Ra'al*, she thought.

She was in the seventh dimension! The lowest and worst of all Xibalba.

In that moment, Sera knew that if she didn't get out of there when Azrath did, it would be the end of her.

The child turned its face up to Azrath who bent to kiss its cheek. Sera wondered at Ra'al's choice of form with Azrath. As if he could read her thoughts, Azarth said to the child, "Perhaps next time you can take the form of something a little older."

The child grinned. "But then you wouldn't trust me, would you?"

"I already don't trust you," Azrath said smoothly, "but it may make for some more . . . entertaining discussion, don't you think?"

"Come now, Azrath. I have little time for these games. When we have played this out, you and I will have all the time in the world for entertainment. Now, go and finish the portal. One of my daughters sends word that I have pressing business to attend to."

Sera cringed back against the wall, knowing exactly what the pressing business was. The girl-demon must have told Ra'al that Aziz had returned. She had barely started inching out of her hiding place when Azrath strode into the room. He shot her a dismissive look and walked away, swinging his fingers around in an intricate design. A fiery portal appeared and he disappeared through it without a backward glance.

Sera moved to follow him but froze as a swell of cold settled about her.

"Ah, Aziz, just the demon I want to see," the child called with a tinkling laugh from the doorway. "Alis said you had returned."

Sera had never felt such dizzying fear. She suspected that it would only be seconds before Ra'al would see right through the shade. What had worked against the lesser demons would certainly be no contest to him. In his dimension, she guessed that he would have the power to unveil anything.

She glanced in desperation at the portal, which had already started to fade, and darted toward it.

"Aziz!" something terrible screamed.

She had almost reached the portal before a howl of rage crashed into her back like something solid. Lifeless fingers reached for her mind, cold and horrible, ripping her shade apart like tissue. In blind desperation, Sera reached toward the marking and turned as something sharp dug into her right leg—taloned dead fingers gripped her foot.

She wasn't going to make it! Searing pain shot up her leg as she wrenched her foot away, straining for the portal at the same time. Just as Azrath's portal sucked her through it, she glanced into the demon's face and almost cried at the face staring back at her, one that she'd never expected to see.

Dev's face.

The Demon Lord shrieked with thwarted fury as the portal closed. And then Sera was gasping for breath, convulsions rocking through her body as the portal spat her out on the other side into a wooded clearing. She stood woozily and looked around, prepared for the worst, but she was alone.

Sera collected herself, for a second wondering how Dev of all people was the person she trusted the most. She'd have thought it would have been her mother or her father. Or even Kyle. A vision of Dev's golden brown eyes filled her mind and she shoved it away. She'd dwell on it when she was in a less precarious situation. Right now she needed to figure out where she was, and whether she was safe.

She couldn't tell whether she was in Xibalba or the Mortal Realm or somewhere else entirely. The landscape was gray and empty. The sky was dark and the trees bare. Even the ground cover was little more than brown, deadened brush. It was a colorless world completely devoid of any sign of life.

Sera sighed. At least she'd escaped Ra'al. She didn't want to imagine what he would have done to her had she not been able to follow Azrath through the portal. She turned around to see where she could go and felt dust blowing at her ankles. She squinted against the dappled light and saw the air shimmer just as a bluish circle formed between the trees where the portal had just been.

Another portal.

The blue light intensified until it was electric. Sera jumped behind a bush just as two bodies emerged from the glowing blue disk.

"Seriously, I don't even know why Jude trusts him! He is not Ifrit," one of the boys sneered.

Sera recognized them immediately. Marcus and Damien. What were they doing with Azrath? And how was it that they were able to travel through the portal? What was an *Ifrit*?

"Lord Azrath trusts Kyle, and that should be good enough for you, Damien," Marcus said. "Don't go being a hothead. Jude said we just need to deliver the Fyre and head back to his place. Look, I'll take this to Lord Azrath. Stay here until I get back." Marcus walked off without another word.

Damien stared after him, his face black, and Sera groaned inwardly. Her legs were starting to cramp but there was no way she could move without drawing Damien's attention. She inched her foot to the right, grimacing with relief. She peered through the bushes and could no longer see Damien. She strained her ears but couldn't hear anything either.

Slowly, she stood. The clearing was empty, the portal glowing behind it. Two steps and she'd be through it. Sera could only hope that it would take her back home. Marcus had said that Jude wanted them to head back to his place after they delivered the Fyre to Azrath, which meant that the portal must be tethered to Silver Lake. At least she hoped it was.

Taking a deep breath, she inched forward one step before a hand wound in her hair and flung her body backward. She crashed to the dirt and pain lanced through her shoulder where she'd hit the ground. Damien leered over her.

"How did you get here? Did you follow us?" he snapped, his breath sour in her face. "Did you?" he repeated. Spit flew from his mouth.

"I didn't—"

Damien slapped her across the face. "You must have because there's no way you could get here on your own. I knew you were trouble. Don't lie to me!" Sera froze as his palm swung toward her again, instinct alone bringing her forearm up to block him. She flung her knee up into his belly and scooted out from under him, scrambling backward.

"You'll pay for that!" Damien growled. His face twisted with rage as he hunkered over, his body shifting as black leathery wings sprouted from his back and his face transformed into something hideous, pointy and scaled. Sera felt her scream lodge in her throat as he turned toward her.

"Scared, Princess?" Damien taunted. "Now that you've seen me, what am I going to do with you?"

Sera's mind whirled. They were all demons! They *worked* for Azrath. She stared at the dragon-like creature in front of her. Its tongue snaked from its mouth in a lascivious motion, and she cringed, balling her fingers into fists.

You just escaped the worst Demon Lord in Xibalba and now you're going to let some pubescent boy-demon get the best of you? she hissed to herself. *Get up and defend yourself!*

Sera stood, wiping all emotion from her face, despite her hammering heart. "I'm not afraid of you, Damien."

"You should be. I've done far worse things than I am going to do to you." He uncurled the long black metal whip at his side and flicked it toward her. Sera jumped out of the way, the barbed tip cracking perilously close to her face.

"Jude won't be happy that you didn't listen to orders," Sera said.

"Ah, so you overheard that conversation. Didn't anyone tell you that eavesdropping is rude?" Damien shrugged. "Whatever. What Jude doesn't know won't hurt him. And you're not going to be able to tell anyone our little secret, are you Sera?" He grinned, baring a row of elongated fangs. "Because you're going to disappear. Poof! And no one will ever know. But first, you and I are going to have a little fun."

"Damien, I'm warning you. Stay back. Just let me through the portal, and we can forget this ever happened."

A long slow laugh emanated from the demon. "You're warning *me*? That's funny. But it's not that simple, Princess. You've *seen* me." He advanced toward her. "And the truth is that I don't want to let you go."

Damien flung the whip toward her again and she threw herself out of the way. He growled and flung it again.

This time Sera countered instinctively with a flick of her own wrist, and a red-gold thread curled out like liquid flame, catching Damien's whip in mid-flight. For a second, Sera wondered at its odd color before hurling it to the side as his eyes widened, his weapon ripped from his fingers.

"You're *Daeva*?" he snarled. "That's impossible. No Daeva can wield deifyre here."

Sera shook her head. "I'm no Daeva," she said. "I'm something else."

Damien snarled as he flew toward her and Sera threw the flaming whip toward him, catching him across one of his wings. The stretched black skin of his wing shriveled immediately, and he screamed, falling to the ground.

In a second, he was on his feet, growling. Ifrit were certainly strong, that much she knew. He rolled to the side, grabbed the black whip with the steel barbed tips, and swung it with all his might toward Sera.

She darted to the side and tripped over a branch, the edge of the weapon catching her in her leg. Damien crowed as she went down. Sera stared at the barbs cutting into her skin, a snakelike thread of noxious black poison infecting her flesh, spreading like the lines of a spider's web. But curiously, Sera felt nothing. She wrenched the barbs out as her blood forced the poisons from the wound and raised calm eyes to Damien, who looked stunned. Confused, he stared at her, his teeth bared.

"I told you I was different," she said, spinning as she swung the flame of deifyre toward him. "Your toys can't hurt me."

The red whip curled around his neck and she yanked backward.

He screamed as it touched his skin and glowed blackly red. Damien dropped to the ground, clawing at the line around his throat. For a second, Sera wondered how easy it would be to kill him, but the thought made her sick, even though he would have killed her without a second thought. But she wasn't like them. She wasn't a demon.

Sera crouched down next to him, her words measured. "I will release you if you promise never to tell anyone about this. You do, and I will finish the job I started today. Do you understand?"

His eyes sparkled with red fury and spit coated his black lips. In one motion, Damien swung up and over, his clawed hands grabbing around her neck. "You'll die with me first!"

Sera felt the air rush out of her lungs and gasped, her hands grabbing at Damian's rigid fingers. The Ifrit's talons dug deep into her skin, and instinctively, Sera did the only thing she could. She let her shade fall. In an explosive burst, her entire body became a weapon as blinding light erupted from every part of her, shredding apart the dark creature holding her until its body exploded into nothingness. Black embers rained down on top of her like ash. The air was rank with singed flesh as the deifyre flared once more and then faded—until the clearing was silent and colorless once again.

Sera coughed, pressing her fingers gingerly to her throat. The skin felt raw and wet where Damien's nails had dug into her flesh. Tired, she crawled over to the blue portal. Without a second thought, Sera hauled herself through it, breathless as it sucked her into its vortex. Strangely, it was not as bad as the other two had been, and Sera wondered at the difference between them as it released her.

She gagged again, her bleary eyes taking in her location. It was the back of Sal's diner. Sera knew she didn't have much time before Marcus made his way back or until Jude showed up, and she was too weak to deal with either of them. She pulled her mobile out of her pocket and dialed the first number that she could think of.

"Sera!" Kyle's voice was sharp. "Are you OK? Where are you?"

"Can you come get me? I'm at Sal's."

"Be right there."

The phone clicked off and Sera stood shakily, pulling her shade together. Her hands and arms were covered in black grime and dirt. She wiped them as best as she could against her sleeves and entered the back door, trying to be as inconspicuous as possible, heading for the tiny bathroom stall in the back of the diner.

In the cracked mirror, she looked far worse than she felt. Underneath all the dirt, her neck was red raw and she had several long gashes against her cheek that were oozing blood. Her shoulder ached, and she pulled her shirt back to see a darkening purple bruise covering half her arm and upper back. She touched it and winced.

Sera washed her face, pressing a paper towel gently against the cuts, and finger-combed her hair so that most of it fell into her face. Her stare slid to the fleshy pads of her palms. She eyed the markings. Dev had called them sigils. Now they looked like actual shapes as opposed to random scars. The raised white one on her left hand was like a crescent with two swirling lines beyond it. The one on her right was neon red against her skin, the reverse to its partner, with three pronged lines going across an inverted crescent. It'd been odd that her right hand had been the one to flare up while she'd been in Xibalba. The recollection made her shiver.

Her phone buzzed as a text came through from Kyle.

—Out back.

The minute she saw Kyle, Sera completely lost it, launching herself at him. Her eyes met his, and then her lips found his. The kiss was hot and desperate. Sera crushed herself to Kyle, wanting—*needing*—to pull every cell of his body into every cell of hers, as if he were some kind of absolution from what she'd endured. She ground her fingers into his shoulders and her lips into his mouth, taking what he offered until she sagged against him. His strength was real. Regardless of his secrets, that would never change.

TRUTH

Sera sat in her living room. She'd just finished telling her parents, Kyle, and the newcomer, Micah, what had happened from the minute she'd gone through the first portal up to when she'd ended up at Sal's. Her mother's face was the most shocked, and Kyle looked like he'd eaten something rotten and was about to throw up.

"Did Azrath see you?" her father asked.

Sera shook her head. "No, only when I wore the nekomata shade, and even then he barely gave me a second glance. Ra'al did, though. I couldn't hold the shade; he was too strong. I barely got out of there with my life."

Her father's face was troubled. "Did Ra'al and Azrath say anything?"

"They kept talking about some portal being ready," Sera said and then frowned. "But Dad, didn't you say that Azrath was banished from the Mortal Realm for the last time he tried this?"

"He is," Micah responded. "He cannot open any portals to this realm, unless he has found some other way."

"I think he might have," Kyle volunteered slowly. "When I saw him via the portal, I thought it was in this realm, but I know now it must have been in his netherworld. The Ifrit can travel back and forth to him, but he cannot pass through the portal to this world because of the wards that bind him. I think he's working on something to break those wards."

"That's impossible," Sera's mother said. "The binding seals are unbreakable."

But Sera shook her head slowly as she met Kyle's eyes. "No, Mom, Kyle's right. I mean, you're right, too. The seals are unbreakable because they're celestial wards. But what if Azrath used something to bend the rules so that he could pass through the portal?" She paused. "Like Fyre."

Her mother flew up out of her seat, her hand clapped to her mouth. "You can't mean—"

"Yes, I know I'm right about this."

"That makes sense," Micah agreed. "Otherwise, why would so many Daeva have been stripped and killed? He's been planning this for years."

"So, are you saying he's been infusing himself with dei-fyre?" Her father's voice was dubious. "He is Azura. That's impossible. It would kill him."

A small voice interrupted them as Nate's blond head popped around the door. "Actually, in small doses over a very long period of time, Azrath would be able to withstand the toxins enough to control the effects."

"Nathaniel Caelum—" her mother began, and Nate started backing out of the room.

Kyle jerked to his feet. "No, wait, Sera's right. Nate, too. I thought I was imagining things or maybe I was confused, but when I saw Azrath, I sensed something else. I'd felt Daeva energy, but I thought that I couldn't possibly be right. I'd just been through the portal, and I was disoriented. But I wasn't wrong. It *was* Daeva energy, from Fyre inside of him."

"What do you mean you *sensed* energy?" Sera demanded.

"That's what I was trying to tell you before you went through the portal. Sometimes I can feel different things from people." Kyle stared at the floor, as if embarrassed.

Sera frowned, but glanced back to Nate, who stood silent in the doorway before turning to her mother. "Mom, I know you want to protect Nate, but he really knows more about this stuff than even I do. It was because of him that I knew where I was when I ended up in Xibalba. If he knows something, it can probably help us."

"You were in Xibalba?" Nate shrieked. "I knew it was real. I just knew it. Sweet!" His eyes widened. "Wow, no wonder you were so worried about my project," he stage-whispered to Sera.

"What project?" Sophia frowned and moved toward her son, but Sam held her arm.

"Sweetheart, it's OK," he soothed. "Nate's a part of this family, too, and we can only protect each other if we don't have any more secrets. Let's hear what he has to say."

Nate cleared his throat. "So, I was going to the bathroom the other day and overheard Mom talking about Fyre." He flushed at his confession. "I'd never heard about it, so I looked it up. Took me a while but there's stuff out there if you know where to look. I didn't really believe it all at first, but then Sera tried so hard to get me to drop the whole thing that it only made me want to find out more. And then I overheard you two talking to Sera about Azrath." He turned to Sera. "Remember I thought they said *rat*? So when I heard you guys talking about the deaths of all the Daeva and Fyre—"

"You were eavesdropping?" Sophia interrupted furiously, and Nate flushed.

"Sorry, Mom, I'm ten," he apologized. "It's not like I can help myself when you're all in the living room like secret agents whispering about this stuff. Anyway, so I started thinking about what I'd found about Fyre, and that it's a live godly essence. When someone mentioned just before that Rat was infusing himself with Fyre, it made sense. I mean a guy like that doesn't just give up, you know. It's like a movie. The bad guys always keep coming back until they can't anymore. I read somewhere that people used to use Fyre as a drug but it was really dangerous because the effects didn't wear off." He paused, his face animated. "That's when it clicked—*the effects don't wear off*. So someone immortal like Rat could infuse Fyre in small doses over time and it would just build and build." Nate took a breath. "That would be my guess, anyway."

Sera looked at everyone, who held expressions of dumbfounded amazement. What Nate said had an unlikely plausibility.

"One question," Kyle said. "What do you mean it doesn't wear off?"

"I read that regular people who ingested it died. You can't get off it because it's a live thing. It doesn't go away, it just . . . stays inside you. So those people crave more and, well, human bodies aren't meant to sustain that kind of energy, so they die." His voice faded.

"I can see how that would work," Micah said after several minutes of tense silence. "But I can only imagine that it would be incredibly painful even to Azrath."

"Nothing will stop my brother from getting what he wants," Sam said, his face grim. "Still, even if he were able to pass through a portal to the Mortal Realm, I don't know what he has agreed to with Ra'al. There's something missing that I can't figure out."

"Sam," Sophia said, resting her hand across his arm. "Micah wants to call for the rest of the Sanrak to come together. We have to protect Sera at any cost. If Azrath, or any of the other Demon Lords, gets his hands on her, they'll use her to breach the Mortal Realm." Sera's eyes shot to her mother, who wouldn't meet her gaze. "She needs to return to Illysia."

"No way! Why would I leave when everyone I love is here?" Sera's voice rose with each word.

"Sera, you were only meant to be here up until your sixteenth birthday," her mother said calmly. "That was the agreement that was made with the Trimurtas after your birth. You will be safer in Illysia."

"That was months ago, and I'm still here."

Her mother smiled a sad smile. "It was my mistake—my selfishness to keep you here with me. I should have taken you back the day you turned sixteen."

Sera's face was resolute. "I am not going anywhere."

"Sera," Sam began, "you must know what is at stake here. If we cannot protect you, all will be lost."

"But Mom's Sanrak, and Micah's here—"

"They still couldn't protect you from what happened today with the portal," her father said harshly. "Or from the demon that attacked you."

"That demon was there for Kyle, not for me!" she argued.

Everyone grew quiet, and Kyle flushed. "She's right," he agreed. "I think Azrath must have sent it to spy on me."

"No, Kyle," Sera snapped, her voice still heated. "I don't think it was Azrath who sent it. When I was in the seventh dimension, one of the demons asked whether I'd found the boy." She stared at him with narrowed eyes. "I think they meant you."

"Could have meant anyone," Kyle shot back defensively.

Sera stared at her parents in stony silence. She felt as if they all—even Kyle—were against her. She looked over to Kyle, who was avoiding her gaze, and it bothered her more than ever. He'd lied to her about his strange sensing ability. He'd lied about Jude. And he certainly was lying now. Her anger soared. She started pacing, hot sweat running down her back and arms. It felt like fire—hot fiery lava under her skin scalding her veins, hotter than anything she'd ever felt. Every second made the burn—and her anger—worse. White spots danced before her eyes.

She heard her father's voice as if from within dense fog.

"Sera, you have to control it!"

"Control what?" Sera gasped. The living room felt as if it were spinning into blinding white circles, the floor beneath her feet slippery. She felt suffocated by the heat.

"The part of you that is Azura," her father said gently. "That's what you are feeling right now, that fury taking over everything inside of you." He put a hand on her shoulder and Sera flinched away from his touch. He stayed with her. "Breathe, sweetheart. Don't give in to it, that's what it wants."

"You make it sound like it's alive."

"It is."

"What's wrong with her?" she heard Kyle whisper to Micah.

"The Dark Realms, I would expect," Micah said. "Going there always leaves its mark, even on the innocent. She breathed its air, saw its monstrosities. I can't imagine how she *wouldn't* be unaffected."

"But she's Sanrak."

"She's the daughter of an Azura Lord, too," Micah reminded him. "The Dark Realms always lay claim to their own."

"What should we do?"

Micah smiled grimly. "Nothing much we can do. She has to flush it out of her system."

"Why are my hands stinging so much?" Sera stared at her right palm where the mark flamed red. "First, it was that one, now this one, and now they're both burning like crazy. What's happening to me?" Her veins shone in stark contrast against the pale skin of her arms, darkening as blood pounded through them.

"It's the seals," her father said, examining the scars on each of her hands. He was careful not to touch either of them. "You were born with two, marked by both Illysia and the Dark Realms. My guess is that this one would have remained dormant but, when you went through the portal, the very fabric of the Dark Realms made it awaken."

"Xibalba claims its own," Kyle murmured, repeating Micah's words.

"Awaken? W . . . what does that mean?"

"It means that you belong to both now," Micah said slowly, "which changes everything." His face held a strange expression for a moment and then turned blank again. "I must take my leave now." He turned to Sophia. "I must seek the counsel of the Trimurtas about this."

"Micah," Sophia began, clutching his arm. Her face look pained. "Please, we have to protect her." Micah pulled away gently, taking her fingers into his hands.

"I know, and we will. I will return soon." He brushed a hand against her face, nodded to Sam, and then was gone.

Sera stood confused at what she'd just witnessed, but the pain in her palms soon obliterated everything else. She was starting to feel dizzy, as if she had vertigo. "Can I go to my room now? I need to lie down. Kyle can stay with me to make sure nothing happens." Her father nodded his consent.

"Just for a little while," he agreed. He turned to Kyle. "When is Carla back?"

"She's back from her trip in a couple days."

"Sam—" Sophia began.

"It's OK, Sophia. We all need to get some rest. Kyle can stay here tonight. I'll make up the bed in the basement." He kissed his wife's cheek. "Why don't you go up with them, get Kyle settled with a shower, and check on Nate while you're upstairs?"

Sera made her way to her room while Kyle followed her mother up the stairs. She heard the sound of the shower down the hall and lay on her bed in silence, staring at the ceiling. After a while there was a soft knock on the door, and Kyle walked in wearing a pair of her father's sweatpants and a T-shirt. His springy dark curls fell around his face.

"Lose the mohawk?" Sera said, grateful for the company and the familiarity of him, especially in a world where everything felt like it was tilting beneath her. Kyle sat on the floor and leaned back against the side of the bed.

He tucked some wet ringlets behind his ears. They covered most of his tattoo. "I figured it might make your mom a little more comfortable."

"Looks nice," Sera said, and went back to studying the lines in the ceiling.

"You OK?" he said after a while.

"Not really. How much of this stuff did you already know?"

"I tried to tell you, but I didn't know how to." Kyle turned to look at her. "Would you have believed me? You thought I was nuts when I told you about the Fyre stuff, remember?"

"You're right," she agreed. "I wouldn't have. I still feel sometimes like I'm in the middle of some unending dream, and that I'll eventually wake up, but I never do. And it just gets worse and worse." She twisted her body across the top of the bed so that her head was next to his shoulder. "Thanks for coming to get me," she whispered.

He smiled, and the sweetness of it melted her. "Any time." Her eyes dropped to his lips and she flushed. She couldn't avoid it forever.

"So about that kiss . . . "

"I was going to ask you about that," Kyle said, turning so that his face was inches from hers. "What was that about?"

Sera flushed, embarrassed by the memory. "I don't know. I was just so happy to see you, and it just happened. Are you mad?"

He laughed and stared at her as if she were crazy. "Are you kidding? I've waited to kiss you for years. Are *you* mad?"

"No, it wasn't what I expected. I mean it felt nice." She blushed and turned her face into her arm.

"Not nice like kissing-your-brother nice, right?"

Sera laughed at the look on his face. "No, definitely not like kissing my brother."

"Good, then."

Suddenly a flash of Dev's kiss filled her head and Sera banished the thought furiously. She didn't mean to compare them but once the thought got stuck in her head, she couldn't avoid it. She'd only ever kissed two guys, and by most standards at Silver Lake, she was way behind in adventures with the opposite sex.

Dev's kiss had been effortless, and the sensation that she'd done it before, even though she hadn't, still baffled her. Everything about it had felt *right*. Perfect—like a Cinderella kiss. But when she'd kissed Kyle, it, too, had felt right, just in a different way. Their kiss had been desperate and filled with friendship and longing and something else she couldn't identify. There'd been something dark in it, something fierce and primal. It had scared her, but it had thrilled her, too.

"What's wrong?" Kyle asked, as if noticing her stare.

Sera flushed and tucked her head back into the crook of her arm. "Nothing. Thinking," she muttered. "I was wondering about portals. How do they work?"

"You want to talk about portals now?"

She feigned interest. "Well, considering I just went through three of them, sure, why not?"

Kyle shot her a strange look. "There are special areas made for portals between the realms or even to other portals in the same realm. Most Azura and Daeva can't portal unless they're with a stronger deity that can. Sanrak like Micah and your mom use the ones between the realms. You have to be very powerful to travel via the portals or even to travel with someone who can take you through safely." He stared at her hard then, as if trying to work something out in his head.

"You mean, like I did."

He nodded. "You're strong, Sera. No one could have done what you did—survive in Xibalba and travel through multiple portals to get back."

"But what about the portal at Carla's? Or the one I saw Azrath make? They weren't in any portal area."

"Azrath is an Azura Lord. He has the power to open a portal anywhere he wishes in Xibalba. At Carla's—" He broke off for a moment, studying the floor. "I thought that the nekomata had created the portal, but I was wrong. Micah said that demons couldn't open portals. I know what I saw, but maybe the portal was there before."

Sera rolled onto her stomach and propped her chin in her hands, frowning. "No, I *saw* the tails draw the mark on the wall, too. And when I was in Xibalba, when I wore its shade, smaller demons there seemed afraid of me." She paused, thinking. "It spoke too, remember? Is that normal?"

"Only for very strong demons, so you may be right." Kyle fidgeted with the edge of the bedspread.

"It was strong. Ra'al trusted it. What do you think it wanted?" Kyle's face tightened more, but Sera didn't notice. "It wanted to eat me, remember? They do, you know. Eat people. I saw them doing it. You wouldn't believe some of the things I saw when I was there. Horrible, horrible things. I can't even close my eyes right now." Her fingers gripped the sheets in a death-white hold. Kyle twisted around to face her, stroking her numb fingers gently, his other arm laying across the edge of the bed between them.

"It's OK, Ser, I'm here. I'll stay here with you as long as it takes."

They sat in silence for a while, each lost in their own thoughts, with only the bedside lamp's muted glow lighting the room. At a loss for words, she followed the lamp's shadows flickering on the ceiling. They looked like black wings. She reached over and moved the hair off of Kyle's head, outlining the edge of the tattoo with her fingertip.

"Did you get these because of Jude?" she asked.

"Yes."

"Did you know what Jude was?"

Kyle looked into her eyes. He didn't want to lie anymore. "Yes."

"Why, Kyle?" she whispered. "I mean, you knew what they did, what they *do*. I don't understand what you thought they or Azrath could give you. What was so important that you'd risk your life for them?"

"I . . . you . . . "

Kyle held her face between his hands. His lips moved but no words came from them. Sera remained still as his thumbs stroked her cheeks. His eyes were pained and she could see that he was struggling to voice what was inside of him. She leaned forward and pressed a quiet kiss to his lips.

"What was that for?" he whispered, taken aback.

"Just because."

Kyle smiled and leaned his forehead against hers. They stayed like that for what seemed like forever, until a knock at the open door startled them both.

"Time for bed guys," her father said. "It's late."

Kyle stood, and placed a kiss on the top of Sera's head. "Try to get some rest, OK?" He turned off the main light and then stood at the door, looking as though he wanted to say something more.

"What's wrong?" she asked.

He shifted his weight between his feet, still hovering. "Sera, I—" His face was tormented.

"I know, Kyle. Me too," Sera said. She knew how he felt.

Kyle smiled, the corner of his mouth curling upward, and walked into the hallway, pulling the door closed behind him. "Thanks for letting me stay here, Mr. Caelum," Sera heard him say to her father, and then, "Night, Sera."

"Goodnight," she said. "Dad?"

Her father poked his head in. "Yes, Ser-bear?"

"Am I going to be OK?" Her voice broke and Sam came quickly into the room and gathered her tightly into his arms.

"Yes. You always have us with you. We'll get through this together, I promise. Get some sleep. I love you very much, don't ever forget that."

"I love you too, Dad." He moved to turn off the bedside lamp. "Can you leave it on for a little while?" she asked like a small child. Sam nodded and drew the covers up to her neck. He kissed her on the forehead.

"Night, sweetheart."

After her father left, Sera lay in bed, exhaustion driving her eyelids closed but fear wrestling them open each time they slid shut. She was weary. She felt battered and bruised. Every part of her ached: her stomach, her head, her shoulders, her palms. Sera held her hands up and stared at the sigils that lay like flags on her skin, one white and one red.

One for each side of her.

Now that she'd been to Xibalba, that other part of her had been awakened—the part that made her want to punish her parents by making out with Kyle, the part that made her feel so suddenly connected to him, the part that had made Micah run in alarm to the Trimurtas.

Sera wondered what it meant for all of them.

The red sigil flared hot and she shivered.

THE PLACE BETWEEN

❧❧

S er, just stay close, and everything will be fine. Hide in plain sight. It's part of the plan."

Sera pulled her sweatshirt hood over her head and tucked her hands under her backpack straps. She nodded dumbly to Kyle. Her mother had been summoned to an audience with the Trimurtas, no doubt to discuss what had happened to her in Xibalba and all that followed. Now that the second rune had awakened, she'd become a liability . . . unpredictable. Her eyes smarted and she squeezed them shut.

"Your dad called the Ne'feri and they're all looking out. The Daeva, too. It's only for one day. You'll be fine."

"I saw Beth just before," she said. "I feel so conspicuous. They're watching me."

Kyle held her chin with his thumb and forefinger. "Sera, that's their job. They are here to protect you."

"They're our age, Kyle. What do they know about anything?"

He stopped again to look at her. "They know a lot. You knew how to fight, with deifyre, didn't you? Micah told me that knowledge is passed down through the ranks. It's genetic or something."

"How many are there?"

Kyle shrugged. "Your dad said there's a couple kids, and I think he said the janitor too, but I wasn't sure."

"Great," Sera sighed. "Two kids and a custodian to save us from certain death in hell."

They reached the steps of the school and Kyle glanced at the paper in his hand where he'd written out their entire day. "So, Beth's in the classroom next to us. We have calc and then geography. After that, we'll navigate the cafeteria. Clear?"

Sera shot him a look. "Wait, I'm not sure what's going to happen at zero eleven hundred hours."

"This isn't a game, Sera," Kyle snapped. "Look at what happened with the portal. Your dad put your safety in my hands while your mom's gone."

"I'd be safer at home with him. You really think school is such a good idea?"

"Yes. More people. Azrath won't risk drawing so much attention this early. And I'll be with you all the time. So will a bunch of people we don't even know." He stuffed the piece of paper into his pocket. "Everything's going to be fine. We just need to stick to the plan."

"I can't believe she took Nate with her," Sera said sourly. "I'd prefer to go there than stay here."

"I thought you said you didn't want to go to Illysia under any circumstances."

"I don't. But I'd take that over school any day."

Kyle gave her shoulder a sympathetic squeeze as they walked into calculus class. "If you stop being such a baby, maybe we can get through today."

Sera glared at him, slamming her books down on a single desk at the front of the class and ignoring him pointedly. She stared blindly into her book as the teacher began to speak. Her palms itched under the extra-long cuffs of her sweat-shirt. She ignored that too.

Sera knew exactly why she hadn't been able to go with her mom and Nate. The Trimurtas were worried. They'd planned all along to keep her in Illysia, but her mother had somehow persuaded them to let her stay in the Mortal Realm as a child. The dreams had been the first sign of the appearance of her abilities, but Sera had hidden them cleverly. And Sophia hadn't wanted to lose her daughter, so she'd convinced her-self that Sera was fine. The Trimurtas had not been pleased. What had happened with the portal to the Dark Realms had been unforeseen, but it now meant that Sera could not be hidden in Illysia, not while the Trimurtas tried to understand the full extent of her power.

She vaguely heard Mr. Barnes announce that he'd be giving a pop quiz in the next class. She didn't know if she'd be around for it, though. She stared at the numbers on the board ahead of her, the squeal of chalk grating in the silence.

Sera felt an odd darkness at the edges of her vision and grew confused as Mr. Barnes and the chalkboard blurred into one dark mass. Her palms stung again and she pressed them against her thighs, agitated. A burning sensation spread across her shoulders and neck, deep into the bone. She could feel Kyle's stare on her back along with the sweat breaking out under her clothes.

She raised a shaky hand. "Mr. Barnes, may I go to the bathroom?"

He nodded in her direction and she shot like a bullet from her seat. She spared a glance at Kyle, whose frown was fierce. She ignored his obvious warning. If she didn't get out of that classroom, the same thing that had happened in the bathroom was going to happen again, in front of everyone. Every part of her ached. The last thing she heard before the door closed behind her was Kyle asking to go to the bathroom and Mr. Barnes's response about the one-at-a-time rule.

The hallway was deserted. She stared at the entry doors at the end of the hall. Everything inside of her wanted to escape. But deep down, Sera knew that what she wanted to run away from most of all was herself. And that was impossible. She fled to the girl's bathroom and turned the lock on the inside of the heavy door after checking that all the stalls were empty.

Sera stared at the spot where she'd collapsed when she was with Beth, then averted her eyes. She walked over to the sink and splashed some water on her hot face. It helped a little. She'd never be able to make it through the day. It had only been fifteen minutes since the first bell and already she was having a major panic attack. Even Beth had stared at her earlier like she was some kind of pariah, and Beth was Ne'feri—she *knew* the stakes.

Sera didn't know who to trust. Everyone had kept secrets, had hidden things, had lied.

She thought about Ra'al and about seeing Dev's face. There was only one reason she'd think about Dev when faced with the worst Demon Lord in hell—she *trusted him*. But after only a few months, how was it possible that she trusted a stranger more than her own family or even her best friend?

She frowned as a vision of Dev's golden eyes and bronze skin danced across her mind. She tasted the tartness of marigolds and flushed, confused as her heart skipped a beat.

She liked *Kyle*. She *loved* Kyle. Didn't she?

Suddenly uncomfortable with the turn of her thoughts and the fact that she didn't have a clear answer on what she felt for either Kyle or Dev, she turned the water to ice cold and splashed her face again. The coldness was numbing for a second, masking the growing warmth inside of her until it overtook everything else. She couldn't think anymore.

The heat bloomed again across her chest and back, and Sera ripped the hoodie off, then the T-shirt beneath it. Twisting to see her back in the mirror, she examined the smooth, unblemished skin. There was nothing there— nothing around her shoulder blades to indicate the presence of anything abnormal. She rotated her shoulders back, watching the bone undulate beneath the skin, and willed the aura to appear. A lacerating sensation slashed through her body, and then, like magic, it was there.

Fiery, flowing, beautiful. *Terrifying*.

The color of new blood.

Sera stared in horror as the colors of the deifyre shimmered down her arms and around her face. She looked more closely. It wasn't entirely blood red. It'd barely been a summery gold until she'd sullied it from her trip to the Dark Realms, and now it was the color of the deepening sunset with intermingling hues of scarlet, copper, and orange.

In a fretful rush, Sera backed away until she was pressed against the door of the stall behind her. Clear silver eyes stared into hers, and a fat tear rolled down the girl's face. Sera wiped it away hastily.

She was *tainted*.

The sigils on her palms tingled as if confirming what she knew. Distracted, Sera rubbed them together and winced at the sudden spark that streaked between them.

Everything slowed. She could see a single drop of water from the faucet fatten and then fall in impossible slow motion. The minute it splashed against the basin, she felt the room spin and the earth dropped out from beneath her feet.

She closed her eyes.

⚜

When Sera opened them, she was sitting in a field of yellow and orange flowers. It smelled of sunshine, grass, and summer honey.

Am I dreaming?

She glanced down at her arms and saw, with relief, that her deifyre had disappeared, and then noticed that she was dressed in a yellow and pink sari, like the ones her mother had in her closet. It was an odd choice of dress, but she loved the feel of the filmy silk against her skin. Her arms and feet were bare. A lock of hair curled into her face as she stood, and she saw that even though the fiery aura had disappeared, the scarlet and copper color of her hair had not changed. She tossed it over her shoulder with a sigh. If she *was* dreaming, she'd enjoy the peace at least for a minute.

Despite the thought that the meadow didn't look like any meadow she'd ever been in, Sera felt no fear. She felt safe — incredibly safe. Enjoying the silence and the occasional chirp of birds flying overhead, she walked aimlessly until she came to a bubbling river. She waded in and stood in the middle of its stream, letting the water curl over her bare toes, drenching the hem of her skirts. Then she walked along the river's edge for a while, noticing that the earth beneath her feet had turned from soft grass into crumbly sand.

Digging her toes in, she walked farther and saw something glistening in the distance. As she neared the glittering mass, she realized that it was the ocean. Laughing with joy, she raced to the edge of the breaking waves and jumped into them, not caring that the folds of her skirts hung in a sodden mess. She floated in the waves, feeling the sun on her face, and felt completely carefree.

Sera let the sun air-dry her as she strolled along the water's edge. She saw someone sitting on the sand farther down the beach. The blue of his arms and back undulated in the sunlight, and she smiled in recognition.

"What are you doing here?" she asked, plopping down on the sand next to him, still smiling.

His smile was white and made something go funny inside of her. "Same as you, I'd expect. Running away."

Her own smile faltered. "Is this a dream?"

"Do you want it to be?"

She scowled at him. "Do you always answer a question with a question?"

"I like people to find their own answers," Dev said, laughing, leaning back onto his elbows. "Nice sari by the way. Suits you."

Sera blushed at his sincerity, her eyes dropping to the light rippling across his lean chest. The tattoos flickered like blue-gold flame. She lowered her eyelashes and squinted carefully. To her surprise, she saw a line of gold undulate through one of the swaths of blue, and then one of the inner bands swirled into a circular shape just near his shoulder

"Your tattoos moved!" she shouted accusingly. Dev laughed again, a sound that made her laugh along with him.

"This is your world, Sera. I'm just visiting. Maybe they're moving because you want them to." Dev's hair swung into his face as he leaned forward, and he pushed it back with one hand, sand flecking through the dark strands. He cocked his head and brushed his hand along the side of her hair. "So, you felt like a change?"

She ran a hand through it self-consciously, pulling it to one side over her opposite shoulder. "It's red," she said with a sigh.

"I like it."

For an instant, her dream flashed into her head before she blinked it away. "Red's not a good color. Ask anyone. It's the color of . . . blood."

"And blood is the color of life."

She stared at him, then looked quickly away. His eyes were suddenly too penetrating, too *knowing*. "You always seem to have an answer for everything."

"Not everything," Dev said modestly.

"Can we talk about something else? Or do something else? Since this is my world, I mean?" Sera said, drawing aimlessly with her finger in the sand. Dev put his hand over hers to stop the movement. Confused, she met his eyes and flushed as the gritty sensation of his sandy fingers sliding between hers overwhelmed her senses.

"I am yours to command," Dev said with a bow of his head. "What do you have in mind?"

Dev's eyes were very golden then, like the color of warm toffee. She wanted to bask in them and leaned forward unconsciously. He met her halfway, and the kiss was just as sweet as she'd remembered. She fell into it as easily as a stone would fall through water, lost to everything but the exhilarating feeling of falling. When Dev pulled away, Sera was breathless—and mystified.

"What's wrong?" he whispered, noticing her changed expression.

She pressed a hand to her lips. "Why does that feel so familiar? It's like I've known you forever." She struggled with the words. "When I think about you, I feel safe. I mean, I know we've only known each other a few months but . . ." she faltered again. "It's like I *know* you or something." Sera stared out at the ocean, her voice a whisper. "This is a dream, right?"

"It's whatever you need it to be."

She turned to him. "In this world, then, I want you to be honest with me. Can you do that for me?" Dev nodded. "If I did live in another lifetime like you said, did we . . . were we . . . together?"

A smile spread across Dev's face that made her knees turn to water. "Yes."

"How together?" Sera pressed.

"Together, together."

Blushing furiously, she glared at him with suspicious eyes. "You're just a figment of my imagination, aren't you?

I really don't know why I keep thinking about you when I have someone perfectly normal who cares about me," she said more to herself than him. "But why would I see you, of all people? Why you?"

"When did you see me?"

"I went there, you know. Xibalba. It changed me. But I'm still me. I don't know what this is, whether it's a dream or it's real or whether I love you or Kyle, or shouldn't love anyone at all. I've known Kyle for a long time, but I feel like I've known you for even longer. You and Kyle are the exact opposite of each other. But you're the one I saw, not him." She doodled in the sand again, unsurprised when he lay his hand atop hers to stop the movement.

"Why do you keep doing that?" she snapped.

"You're drawing a portal." Her gaze dropped to the marking that matched the one on her right palm. It throbbed and she clenched her hand into a fist.

Dev drew her hands onto his lap, careful not to touch the sigils. "You have to control these. They are both powerful and will pull you to do different things."

"What do you mean?" she said, scuffing the sand with her foot, erasing the half etched marking.

"They brought you here when you touched them together. A place between the light and the dark," Dev said.

"I don't understand."

"You are bound by all three realms. That's why you come here—to escape them, to find peace. This has always been your place, yours alone. But if you unknowingly draw a portal, then others may be able to come here too."

"Why are *you* here, then?"

"You brought me here a long time ago."

"No, I didn't—" She started to speak and he placed a finger against her mouth.

"Why is that so hard for you to believe? You went to the Dark Realms. You have a Sanrak mother. You are *immortal*. Yet you can't see what is right in front of you. You *love* me, Serjana, as I love you. We always have since the beginning."

"How is that even possible? I didn't know you before—" She shook her head in denial and stood, walking to the edge of the water. The sun had begun a slow descent toward the horizon and a riot of colors blazed across the sky. The water shimmered fiery gold.

Sera knew what Dev said was entirely possible. After all, she was a *goddess*. She turned back to Dev, who was watching her with an enigmatic expression. "Are you Sanrak, too?"

He didn't answer but came to join her where she stood. "No. I am something else, like you." Sera clamped her lips together and returned her gaze to the sun and the water, sinking into each other's embrace. Light into dark. The metaphor of her life.

"Do you come here often?" she asked after a while, and then cringed at her corny choice of words.

"Whenever I want to be with you and cannot." His words were soft, and Sera felt as if he'd given her far more than just words. "I've looked for you for a long time."

"Why?"

"Because I lost you once. I cannot again."

Sera leaned into him, resting her head against his warm chest and listening to the steady drum of his heartbeat. It felt perfect. She didn't move, not even when he tucked a marigold behind her ear and kissed the top of her head.

Maybe this *was* a dream. A dream of a perfect place. Somewhere that she could escape the real world and everything that had turned inside out within it—somewhere where she was free of everyone else's secrets. Maybe, for once, she could pretend that she was happy, here with Dev. His laugh distracted her.

She scowled up at him again. "What, you can read my mind now?"

He laughed harder. "No, but I can see from your face that you are trying to convince yourself that this is not real."

"Isn't it? You said yourself before that it was a dream."

"No," Dev corrected her. "I said that it was whatever you needed it to be."

"So, it's a dream." Dev leaned in, gave her a hug, and started to walk away. Sera followed him confused. "Where are you going?"

"Back to the real world, even though it's been a wonderful afternoon. If we're gone more than five minutes, the teachers send a search party. And maybe you're just not ready."

"Wait, five minutes?"

He stopped. "Time flows differently for us here. Days here are mere minutes in the Mortal Realm. If you needed to, you could come here for weeks at a time and only be gone for an hour."

"How do I get back?"

A smile. "The same way you got here, I'd expect." His smile turned into something sad. "Give it a chance, Sera. Trust yourself. Trust in us, you always have. I won't ever fail you."

You did once.

Sera had no idea where the words had come from, but there they were, as stark as day. She blinked and Dev was gone. She touched her palms together and the same spark spun between them, and then she was staring at herself in the bathroom mirror at school.

A deafening banging on the door claimed her attention, then loud voices.

"Sera! You in there? It's Beth. We're opening the door!" A jangle of keys banged against the door. She tugged her T-shirt and her shade around her just as Beth, the janitor, and Kyle burst in.

"Hello! A little privacy please!" Sera cried. She glanced at her watch, stunned. Had she imagined it all? "I've only been in here five minutes. Can't a girl use the bathroom?"

"Are you all right?" Kyle asked, his eyes narrowing. "Who were you talking to? Beth said she heard voices."

"I'm fine." Sera let her hands fall to her side and walked past Beth and the janitor out of the bathroom. Kyle started to say something to her, but Sera just pushed past him, her face strained.

"Everything's going to change, isn't it?" Sera said as he caught up to her.

Kyle stared at her. "It already has." He reached for her hair and frowned before gently brushing the side of her face with his fingertips.

"What's the matter?"

"Nothing, it's just a bit of fluff. It's gone now."

Sera didn't notice Kyle crush the stray marigold petals in his hand or the flash of rage that darkened his face.

Confrontation

~&~

Kyle looked at his phone to check the time—thirty minutes of English to go. He glanced over at Sera, who sat staring into her textbook as if in a trance. She'd been silent for most of the day following the episode in the bathroom. Kyle knew that something had happened, but he didn't know what. After seeing the marigold petals, he'd bet his last dollar on it having to do with that neighbor of hers, but Sera was safe, and that was all that mattered. At least that was what he kept telling himself. He knew Sera would tell him when she was ready.

His phone buzzed in his pocket. A text message from Jude.

—Need to talk now. Out front.

The wings on his head stretched taut in silent warning. He stared at the phone and looked over at Sera. He couldn't risk waiting and then meeting Jude with Sera in tow, so he made a decision. He'd deal with Jude and then meet Sera back at school when they were done. He packed up his stuff and dropped a note on Sera's desk as he walked past, letting her know that he'd meet her out front after class.

"Mr. Knox, we still have thirty minutes of class," the teacher said.

"Oh, don't mind me," Kyle said over his shoulder. "Carry on."

Outside, Jude had a new convertible parked right in front of the entry doors and stood leaning against its side. "Took you long enough. I was almost going to come in and find you. You know how much I love teenage angst." He laughed but it was an empty sound. "Get in, let's take a ride."

"What's up?" Kyle said, stalling for time. He really didn't want to leave the school grounds with Sera still in the building. He knew the Ne'feri would look out for her, but he wasn't taking any chances. Jude pulled a packet of cigarettes out and lit one.

"Smoke?" Kyle shook his head. "You hear about Damien?"

"No." Kyle kept his mind closed, mindful of Jude's nearness. He knew Jude couldn't mind-read, but he wasn't taking any chances. "Why?"

"He and Marcus went to take the last of the Fyre to Azrath and something got to Damien. I mean it had to have been something powerful. The kid was strong, and now I can't even reach him." He tapped the side of his skull. "You hear of anything?"

Kyle felt something cold slide along his bones. Jude was baiting him. "I'd tell you if I did, you know that."

"So, where've you been the past couple days, Kyle?" Jude winked at him. "Slumming, I heard? You sure you didn't see anything?"

"Look, I don't know what happened to Damien. The kid was a loose cannon, you know that more than anyone." Kyle flung his backpack on the ground and leaned on the car next to Jude. "Someone or something came after me and Carla too last week. The house was a mess and it stank of demons. Not to mention the Daeva being on the warpath." He shrugged. "Just being careful. I mean, we're at the end now, right?"

Jude shot him a measured glance. Kyle held his stare squarely. He felt the wings draw tight against his skull and shoved back against it. Jude would have to do a lot more than that to intimidate him. He straightened his shoulders, tucking his hands into his pockets.

"Yeah. Everything's getting there," Jude said after a while, taking a long drag on his cigarette. "So, you staying at your girlfriend's house?"

"She's not my girlfriend."

Jude smiled. It was an ugly smile. "Yeah, I know. Saw her with some other dude the other day. Kid had blue tattoos. They looked real cozy together," Jude said slyly. His words had the desired effect.

"That's her neighbor," Kyle gritted. "They're friends."

A laugh. "Yeah, they looked like *friends* to me, especially when he had his tongue down her throat."

"You saw wrong."

"Did I?" Jude hopped over the side of the Mercedes and slid into the driver's seat. "Get in. Let's go pay blue boy a visit and see, shall we?"

Kyle felt a fury like nothing else spiral through him. He knew that Jude might be lying but he'd seen the marigold petals earlier himself. Sera was lying to him. Somehow, they'd been together. If Sera wouldn't give him the answer, maybe Dev would. He hopped over the side of the car door, tossing his backpack in the seat behind him. The Ne'feri would make sure that Sera was safe. He had a score to settle.

They drove off, heading to Knightsbrook Academy. The more Kyle thought about it, the more he fueled his anger. She'd *lied* to him. Had she been with Dev? The more worked up he became, the more he could feel Jude's pleasure, almost as if he were getting off on Kyle's own emotions. After the few short blocks to the private school, Kyle was riled to the point of no return.

"Wait here," he told Jude.

"Where're you going? Can't you see him from here? What kind of half-assed ability is that anyway?" Jude sneered.

Kyle scowled. "It detects energies, Jude. The kid is human. And so is almost every other kid in here. It doesn't work like that and you know it."

Kyle slipped into the school and walked down the hallway. He wanted to confront Dev, but he also didn't want Jude interfering and making things worse than they had to be, especially if any of it got back to Sera. A voice near the cafeteria made him whirl around.

"You are looking for me." Dev was staring at him with a curious expression, his head cocked to one side. Dressed in a button-down Oxford shirt and tie with bone-colored trousers, Dev wore the bland uniform with a careless nonchalance that was at odds with most of the students at the exclusive private school.

Dev's words were not a question, but a statement, almost as if he'd been expecting Kyle to walk through the door. This infuriated Kyle to no end. Everything about this boy infuriated him—the way he dressed, the way he talked, the way he felt that Sera belonged to him. Sera might not see the under-lying territorialism, but Kyle saw it in black and white.

He nodded toward the empty cafeteria. Dev followed him in and perched on the edge of the table. He quirked an eye-brow, making Kyle's irritation soar again.

"Did you see Sera today?"

"Not here." The answer was evasive and obvious. Kyle's anger rocketed.

"I didn't ask you that. I asked you if you saw Sera today."

"Yes. I saw Sera today."

"When?"

"Earlier this morning. We went for a walk." Dev held his stare. "Why don't you ask Sera yourself? You're good friends, aren't you?"

"Best friends." Kyle gritted his teeth. "Look, I don't know what happened over the summer with you two, but Sera is with me. OK?"

Dev studied him, a faint smile playing at the corner of his lips. "Shouldn't Sera decide who she's with? If you're here now, maybe she doesn't know that you're doing this. Let her choose."

"So there *is* something between the two of you?"

A slow smile crossed Dev's face, setting Kyle's nerves on edge. "It's more than just something, but I'm sure her best friend would only want her to be happy, even if she is with someone else."

Kyle advanced on Dev, who stood his ground. "Is that supposed to be you? You're not even her type!"

"And just what is her type? You? A boy who doesn't know who he is? What his destiny is? Where he comes from? What he's meant for?" Dev's voice had taken on a strange tone that made Kyle uncomfortable. His questions were too acute, too sharp.

He squinted at Dev. The boy was human, that much he knew from the last time he'd checked. But there was something else, something elusive under his essence. He'd felt the same thing with Sera's mother, the sensation that there was something hidden beneath. Kyle opened his gift toward Dev.

Every logical part of him said that the boy was human, but Dev felt too perfect, almost as if he were constructed out of something else. It was different from a shade, and that was what confused Kyle momentarily. There was *no* shade.

Kyle pushed harder, invoking his ability deeper than he'd ever done, searching for the boy's very essence—the source of the energy. He felt nothing. Everything around the boy felt like nothing. But there was no creature on Earth that had no energy at all, not even demons. Every *thing* had energy, whether negative or positive, bad or good.

Kyle frowned. Sera's mother had been strong enough to shade both her and Sera. Was Dev Sanrak too? The thought crippled him. He'd never be able to compete with that. He frowned again. "What are you?"

"A boy, just like you."

"Just like *me*?"

Dev's smile was mocking, perceptive. "Not exactly like you, then."

"You don't know a thing about me," Kyle snapped. "Or her."

"You're wrong on both counts. I know more about both of you than you yourselves know. And I know that you will put her in more danger than anyone, despite the fact that you claim to love her. I know that she will face death because of you. And I know that she will choose to die to save you."

Kyle felt the blood drain from his face at Dev's softly spoken words. "How could you know all those things? I would never hurt her! Who *are* you?" he said, his words like bullets.

"'The evil that is in the world almost always comes of ignorance, and good intentions may do as much harm as malevolence if they lack understanding,'" Dev quoted. "That's Albert Camus, a French writer. If you love Sera, you should send her to Illysia as Micah asked you to."

"Micah?" Kyle gasped, shaking his head, his mind reeling. "How do you know him? What do you know about Illysia?"

"I, too, have friends in *other* places." Dev glanced out the window at Jude, who sat in the car waiting. "You'd do best to reconsider some of yours, including the Ifrit. They are not to be trusted."

"Like I should trust you?" Kyle shot back, reeling from Dev's words.

Dev smiled. "If you should so choose. Sera does."

"If you hurt her—"

"Why would I hurt her? She is my heart. As I am hers."

Everything Kyle felt toward Sera drummed into view. That single moment when the blood rushed in his ears like a tsunami, his palm curling into a tight fist, and he punched Dev right in his face with all the force he could muster. He'd seen grown men fall over from his blows and not get up.

Dev's head jerked violently backward, but other than that, he didn't move from his seated position. He stared at

Kyle, his face expressionless but for a slight furrowing of his brow. A trickle of blood dampened the corner of his lip, and he touched his finger to it, staring at the blood thoughtfully.

"That really hurt," he said after a long moment. "I'd forgotten." He wiped his mouth again and moved his jaw back and forth. "I will forgive you for hitting me, because I know that you think you love her. But so do I. And I won't give her up again. I cannot."

"What do you mean, again?"

Dev didn't answer. He rose and stared out the window, studying Jude who was speaking to a pretty girl.

"There's a war coming. One she will be in the middle of. Are you prepared to protect her no matter the cost?"

Kyle thought about everything he'd learned over the last few days and where Sera belonged in it all. What Dev said was true. There was a war coming—one of epic proportions. "Yes. I would give my life for her," he finally answered.

"That's not enough. You have to be willing to take life for her. Are you?"

"Who are you?" Kyle asked, staring at the strange boy.

"Who I am is not important. It's who *you* are." He stepped past Kyle. "Now, if you'll excuse me, I need to put some ice on my face." He turned back just as he reached the cafeteria door. "You have a good heart and one that will fight for survival against your very nature. Blood is a fickle thing, but so is truth, which can be bent to suit all purposes. I'm telling you this because of her, not for any other reason, because she cares for you. You will face a choice, Kalias. One that seems to go against everything you believe. See past it even if it feels like you will be losing it all. You can't change who you are, but what you think, you become." A pause. "That one was Buddha, but it applies to you more than to anyone."

"What did you just call me?" Kyle said, taken aback.

"Kalias. Your name."

"No one knows that name," Kyle whispered, his heart jumping into his throat. "I don't get it. Why are you telling me this?"

"Because I like you. And because you love her. But you will lose nonetheless. Sita is bound to me as I am to her."

"Sita? Don't you mean Sera?" Kyle blurted out.

"Yes."

With that, Dev left, leaving Kyle in a state of complete confusion. The bell rang and he stared at the students rushing past him into the cafeteria with unseeing eyes. He couldn't even begin to process all of the information swirling through his brain.

Why would Dev call Sera *Sita*? And why would she be bound to Dev? Who *was* he? And how did Dev know his real name? Kyle had never told that to anyone, not even Sera. Kalias had died when his "mother" had.

Kyle made his way dazedly out of the building. Jude's car was gone. Kyle sighed. It was a ten-mile walk to Sera's house, and two miles to the school, but by the time he got back there, she'd likely be gone. Still, he decided to head to school first to pick up his car and then drive over to Sera's.

About a mile down the street, Jude's car slowed beside him. Kyle hesitated but got in.

"Sorry, got distracted," Jude said with a leer and licked his lips. "I love youth. It's why I choose this form."

Kyle blanched. "You didn't do anything stu—"

Jude turned icy black eyes in his direction, and the black dragon wings along his arms flexed. "Don't presume to lecture me, half-breed. You and I are not equals. Don't forget that."

"I wasn't. I'm just saying be careful, that's all. " Kyle shrugged, faking nonchalance. "Look, can you drop me back at school? I need to get my car."

Jude shot him another nasty, knowing smile. "Why don't you just *take* Sera? It's the way of the Ifrit, and you are one of our brothers now. Take what belongs to you, just as we do. As I did with that girl just now."

Kyle kept his face composed despite his immediate disgust. He needed to respond in a way that Jude would understand. "Because I want her for more than one time," Kyle said. He couldn't help adding, "And I don't want her to hate me."

"Let me guess. You want her to *love* you," Jude scoffed. "Fear is much better, for then they know their place. These kinds of weak human emotions don't belong in Lord Azrath's world. You understand that, don't you?"

Kyle nodded his head, mute. His hands shook against the side of the seat and he dug his nails into the leather.

"So, did you find her boyfriend?" Jude asked slyly.

"Yeah. I punched him in the face."

Jude threw a congratulatory thump onto his shoulder, making the car swerve dangerously into the next lane. "That's my boy. So, did he get up?"

"It'll take him a while," Kyle lied. "Next time he tries anything like that, he won't be getting up." He turned to Jude just as they was pulling up in front of the school. "You notice anything strange about him when you saw him the other day?"

"Like what?"

"Like whether he's something else, something like us, or maybe Daeva?"

Jude's face twisted into its earlier scowl, brow furrowed and eyes slits. "That's your job, isn't it?" he growled. "What did you sense?"

Kyle hesitated, walking through it once more in his head for validation. "That's just it, it's weird. I got nothing from him."

"What do you mean, nothing?" Jude snapped. "Everyone has something."

Kyle paused, trying to recall what he'd felt and whether he'd tried hard enough to get past whatever shade Dev had up. But he'd had none.

"No, nothing at all." He paused, searching for the right words. "It was almost like an invisible person wearing a mask, if that makes any sense."

Kyle was unprepared for the swift violence of Jude's reaction as the car screeched to a halt in front of the school. "Get out!"

"What?"

"I said, get out!" Jude snarled.

Kyle stepped hastily out of the car, and Jude sped off before he'd even closed the passenger door, leaving the acrid smell of burnt tires in the air. Something must have come up with Azrath for him to leave that quickly, something big. Kyle shook his head and walked over to where Sera was waiting with the Ne'Feri janitor, Uri, on the front steps.

"Who was that?" Uri said, his eyes suddenly suspicious. He stepped closer to Sera, his body poised and tense, a sharp knife materializing like magic in his hand.

"It's not what you think, Uri," he said slowly, noting Sera's sour face, no doubt because she'd seen Jude. "I'm glad you waited," he said to her.

"I didn't know if you wanted me to go home, so Uri thought we'd just stick around for a few minutes," Sera said. "So, what did Jude want?"

Her voice was calm. Too calm. She was studying her fingernails as if she didn't care about his response, but Kyle knew that she cared a lot.

"Nothing. He wanted to talk about Damien." Sera's eyes snapped to his and he saw a strange look flit across her face before it disappeared.

"Did you tell him?"

Kyle's face twisted into a grimace. "No! Of course not."

"Where did you go?"

"We just took a ride." He saw her expression and rushed to continue. "Look, I didn't want to involve you. He would have waited until after school, and I didn't want him anywhere near you or here. OK?"

He could see that she didn't believe him, and Sera wasn't the type to let things go easily. "So, where'd you go?" she repeated.

Kyle thought about lying, but he didn't know what Dev might tell her. They were friends, or more than friends if he believed anything that Dev said. He kept his jealousy in check even as it surged violently into his throat at the thought of them together.

"We went to Knightsbrook."

"*Knightsbrook?*" Sera said. "What for? Is Dev OK? What did Jude —"

Kyle could see the wheels turning in her head, her natural fear for Dev, and his stomach clenched into a solid knot. He'd thought he could handle it, but nothing had prepared him to see her feelings for Dev so clearly written on her face.

"Jude didn't do anything," Kyle said coldly. "I did."

"Kyle, what did you do?" Sera stood to face him, her expression anxious. He clenched his teeth.

"I want him to stay away from you." His voice was little more than a growl. "We can't trust anyone right now, Sera, and I don't like that he's always hanging around you. And I can't tell what he is."

She didn't miss a beat. "What do you mean, you can't tell what he is?"

Without thinking, Kyle blurted out what he'd told Jude about Dev's energy or lack of it, and he watched both Sera and Uri's expressions go from confusion to disbelief. Sera looked like she was trying to work something out in her head.

"So, how come you can't sense him?" she asked.

"If I knew, don't you think I'd tell you?" Kyle snapped back.

"Dev isn't a threat," Sera said after a while. "And don't be a jerk."

Kyle didn't bother to hide his immediate fury. "How would you know? He could be a demon! He could be Ra'al for all you know!"

Sera's face blanched, but she just shook her head. "I just know." Then her face softened as if she'd realized the source of his anger, and she stepped toward him, putting her hands on either side of his face. He shrugged away from her touch, still angry. "Kyle, please trust me."

"Don't be stupid—" Sera's eyes narrowed at his tone, but Kyle was beyond caring. His jealousy was suffocating him. He grabbed her wrist so hard that she winced. Uri stepped forward, but froze at Kyle's glare. "I don't trust him," Kyle seethed.

"But I do," Sera said. "You're hurting me, Kyle. Let go."

But the monster inside him was already provoked beyond submission. Kyle could barely control it—it wanted him to squeeze harder and inflict pain, to punish her for lying to him, for even considering being with someone else. His fingers pressed down and he watched her eyes dilate in pain. Something like fear flashed across her face. It fueled the beast pacing beneath his skin. He dragged her back against his chest so that her arm was twisted up between their bodies.

"Kyle, let go. I don't want to hurt you." Sera's voice was strangled. Her eyes darted to all the other kids in front of the school, and he knew she was considering her options. He laughed, the sound empty.

"You already have." His words were as dead as his laugh. Kyle didn't even feel like himself. He felt free of emotion. All he wanted to do was to give in to the ferocity inside of him . . . . to the lush sense of power fueling him.

Sera was his. Why shouldn't he have her? She'd kissed him, hadn't she? He could feel her body trembling against his and something inside him shuddered with the gratification of it.

"Kyle, stop this," Sera said.

He ignored her, but the cold feel of steel against his neck and Uri's sharp voice in his ear brought him swiftly back to reality. "Maybe she doesn't want to hurt you, but I will. Back off."

As if in a trance, Kyle released Sera and stepped back, watching as Uri spun her away into his car. He made no move to follow them, impaled as he was by the look of betrayal on Sera's face. He had no words to explain how close he'd come to hurting her.

But he'd wanted to.

A part of him still did.

BACK TO BEFORE

❧❧

Sera wandered along the beach again, the sand rough and warm against her toes. She let the sunlight soak into her body until its warmth chased every fear, every ache, every sadness away. She squinted, peering against the glare. She knew what she was looking for—him. He wasn't where she'd met him the last time, so she kept walking until the sand shifted into dark rich earth and then into thick grass like a soft carpet beneath her feet.

She didn't know why she'd pressed the sigils together the minute she'd gotten home. Her parents hadn't yet returned, but all she'd wanted was to go somewhere quiet and peaceful—a place where she didn't have to be *herself* for one second or to dwell on Kyle's hideous behavior. She'd been scared and shocked at the change in him—she'd hardly recognized him or the words coming out of his mouth. If it hadn't been for Uri, who knew what would have happened?

Laying on her bed, she remembered that Dev told her this world was hers, that she'd created it. It was the only encouragement she'd needed.

She walked until trees hung in a dense canopy around her. The air smelled of fresh rain. Flowers bloomed between the leaves in all possible colors—violets and yellows and blues. Lotus flowers blossomed, their fragrance enveloping her. This was her a garden of paradise. Sera smiled, and then froze as a long black snake glided across her path. She shivered and sped past the spot where it had disappeared into the brush. What was a snake doing in her paradise?

She heard the sound of water and followed it to a small brook that quickly grew into a white rushing river. Sera kept walking along its bank, twice more seeing creatures that made her shudder until the foliage cleared and she emerged from the trees. The sound of the water grew thunderous, and she realized that she stood at the edge of a waterfall. She climbed onto a rock and leaned over, watching the water cascade into a wide lagoon the same color as the sky above.

Dev was floating in the middle of the lagoon. He waved.

"How do I get there?" she shouted.

"Jump!"

"Are you *crazy*?" She estimated the distance in her head. It was about fifty feet to the water.

"You can do it!" Dev's voice floated up to her. "It's the only way down."

"I think I'll just stay here," she shouted back.

Sera sat on the edge of the rock, contemplating whether she could get hurt in her own world or not. If she broke her leg here, would it be broken in the real world? A mosquito sat on her leg and bit into her skin. She swatted it, watching a tiny smear of blood stain her skin.

She didn't know why she was so afraid of jumping. She'd jumped more than thirty feet on sky-coasters, those funny-looking bungee-type structures, with Kyle. But this was different. She had no idea what was under the mirror-like surface of the lagoon.

"What are you afraid of?" Dev shouted.

Dev was right. What was she afraid of? She'd come there to escape the fear of the real world. She stood, swaying unsteadily. The height made her dizzy, but she felt exhilarated too. She was immortal—it wasn't as if she was going to die or anything. She hoped.

"OK, I'll do it."

She stepped across the outcroppings of rock until she came to a flat ledge. A thin pool of water streamed across it, and she was careful to step firmly on the slippery surface. Sera took a deep breath, closed her eyes, then opened them. She didn't want to be afraid. She wanted to see every second of her free fall.

She hurled herself off the edge.

It felt as if she left everything heavy behind, and she was as transparent as the air that embraced her. The fall lasted for what seemed like eternity, wind rushing against her face, until her body plunged into the cool depths of the lagoon. She was surrounded by velvet. Her heart thumped in her chest, her lungs filled to bursting, and she kicked upward, breaking the surface in a shower of droplets.

Dev cheered her arrival.

"That was amazing!" she exclaimed.

"You always loved doing it," he said. "You used to say that it freed you."

She stared at him. "You're not pulling my leg, are you? I really have been here before, with you?"

"Sera, what do I have to gain by making this up? We came here a lot to escape. It's why we created this place."

"I thought you said I made up this world? And to escape what?"

Dev floated on his back and looked up at the sky. "You did dream it up. I only created it for you, made it real. And we used it to escape life. In Illysia."

"*Illysia*?" she sputtered.

"Yes, where we lived. Before."

"Before what?" He turned to look at her, treading water with his arms. His hair was slick and shiny, and tiny droplets of water glistened on his eyelashes. His eyes held hers and the silence was charged and electric. For an instant, Sera wanted to disappear beneath the water to calm her suddenly overheated body. "Before what?" she repeated, her voice shaky.

"Before you died," Dev said softly.

Sera swallowed a mouthful of water before Dev pulled her over to the grassy bank and hauled them both out of the water. She coughed, spluttering, and hugged her knees to her chest, hardly able to look at him.

"Start from the beginning," she said. "Tell me everything."

Dev shook the water from his hair and lay back against the grass, his head cradled against his palms, elbows flaring out on either side. Sera stared at him, silent, noticing the bruise on the corner of his mouth. "What happened to your lip?" she blurted.

He touched a finger to it. "Nothing. A small disagreement earlier today," he said.

Sera felt a rush of guilt. "I'm sorry about Kyle. I didn't know that he *hit* you. I don't know what's going on with him right now."

"It's OK. He needed to get it out of his system." Dev paused, letting the silence run between them for a minute. "So, are you sure you're ready for this?"

"Yes, I'm sure." Her voice was hoarse but didn't waver. She had to understand what drew her to Dev so completely, and why she trusted him—a boy she'd only known for eight months—more than everyone else in her life. She needed to know why parts of her loved him so completely.

Dev propped himself up on one elbow and stared at her for a long time, his golden eyes searching, before taking a deep breath. "You've been gone for a very long time. It's why you can't remember any of this . . . or me. Millennia," he said gently. "But in another lifetime, in Illysia, we were inseparable. You loved me, and I loved you.

"We lived in the Mortal Realm too. Your name was Sita then and mine, Rama. We always found each other, no matter the lifetime."

Sera gasped and Dev reached over to hold her cold hand in his, running his thumb along the sigil branded into her palm. She let him. His touch was comforting, the slow soothing circles hypnotic against her skin, erasing the sudden flashes of her nightmares.

"But that's not possible!" Sera said without thinking and then, more quietly, "How do you know for sure?"

"I would know her anywhere," he said thickly. "You are one and the same." His eyes grew distant as he remembered.

"Everything was different back then. Daeva and Azura both walked the Mortal Realm. Both were served and summoned equally by humanity. It was the only common ground shared by both sides. The Trimurtas allowed it because it represented balance . . . balance between the dark and the light. You loved it there for that very reason. Often, you'd disappear for months at a time, which in Illysia is but the blink of an eye. In your innocence, humanity was a tornado of color that you couldn't help but fall madly in love with. And so you did. I never faulted you for loving them, the mortals, as much as you did. You loved their ability to live so passionately, their unending capacity for emotion from fury to torment to bliss. You loved it all."

Dev stared into her eyes and brushed a copper strand of hair out of her face, holding it between his fingers thoughtfully. "You once told me you envied mortals the very brevity of their lives, and that immortality was self-indulgent."

Sera felt calm. It felt as if she were listening to Dev's story from outside of herself. It seemed surreal, but she still felt a connection to it in an odd way, as if something within her recognized and accepted what he said as truth.

"Is that why there are things here that aren't beautiful? Things like snakes and bats and mosquitoes?" she asked.

Dev laughed. "You liked the balance. You used to say that one couldn't appreciate true beauty without appreciating its opposite—two parts to create the whole." He smiled at her again.

Sera thought about the words she'd heard in her head the last time she'd been here. He'd failed her once. She had to know how it ended. "Please finish the story."

"Things started changing in the Mortal Realm. Both sides wanted to own humanity, but the Trimurtas wanted to ensure that man would always have free will to decide his own destiny. Thus the Daeva and Azura were created to guide them and to provide the balance for both Illysia and the Dark Realms. After I . . . I mean, my incarnation Rama, defeated Ravana, demons were forbidden to come to the Mortal Realm. Samsar and Azrath were appointed to guard the portal into the Dark Realms."

"My father," Sera murmured.

Dev smiled. "The man you chose to bring you back as your father, yes." He shook his head. "I don't think I ever understood you as much as I do now. I see why you chose him, and why you chose Sophia. Light and dark have always been your symbols." He stared into space as if lost in memories he no longer could give voice to.

She brushed his fingers lightly. "Dev?"

His smile was sad. "I told you before that I won't ever fail you. And I won't. But I did once." Dev sat up and grasped her shoulders, turning her to face him. "Do you recall what happened after Rama freed Sita from Ravana in the story?" Sera shook her head. "Well, he . . . I mean, I never believed that Sita had been faithful while in Ravana's captivity. I was foolish and thought she had betrayed me, and I banished her, forcing her to go through the fires of purgatory to prove her innocence. Once I realized what I had done, I forgave her, but she chose to return to the earth instead of to me." To Sera's horror, a tear fell down his smooth cheek. She brushed it away, but it was only replaced by another, and then another. She pulled him to her as he cried against her neck, his body rocking against hers. Her fingers slid through his silky hair. "I'm so sorry. How can you ever forgive me?"

"Please, Dev. It's OK. Look at me," she soothed. "I'm sure she forgave you. Sita. How could she not?"

He raised eyes that were like pools of golden light to hers. "Can't *you* remember? Remember me, us, this place? Remember this?"

And then he was kissing her, and all she could taste was honey and marigolds as the kiss splintered her into a million pieces and then brought her back together again. She pulled away, her eyes widening.

"I do know you," she whispered, her fingers trailing against his face, across his lips, his eyes, his nose. And then she was the one crying as he kissed her again, the salt of their tears mixing into the sweetness of their embrace, their reunion.

After several minutes, Sera sat back, her hand falling to grip his.

"I remember now," she said slowly, piecing together the memories his kiss had awakened that now filled her head. "I begged you to believe me. Ravana had never touched me—he'd wanted me to marry him, but I was yours. But you didn't. I felt I'd failed you, so I chose to become mortal and leave Illysia, to return to the earth."

Flashes of recollection came back to her, and suddenly she was no longer sitting on the bank of a pool. She was else-where, a waking dream. It could only be Illysia, it was so filled with light and beauty.

She saw Dev surrounded by other deities with their ethe-real beauty, only he was older than he was now. His whole body was blue, including his face, but it suited him. He was dressed in gold, his dark hair falling to his shoulders. He had never looked more unbearably handsome, and she felt love as piercingly as she'd done then.

She *had* loved him.

Trumpets blared and the sound of wind chimes filled the hall like bells. She saw herself, with dark red braided hair and dressed in a vibrant pink sari, holding his hand. They walked toward a dais with three thrones, the last of which was empty.

"My Lord," the other deities murmured as they walked past. They bowed. The Yoddha at the end stood at rigid attention, the gold deifyre of their wings matching the beautiful silks draped on their bodies. Deifyre lanced in a glowing arc from their arms to the ceiling as she walked beneath it. And lastly, nearing the dais, she saw the Sanrak, their auras the color of silvery white light, some of them so beautiful she could scarcely bear to look upon them.

But she did and gasped when she saw Micah, who also seemed much older, and then her mother, in all their divine glory. She had never looked more magnificent. A tear slid down her cheek. Sophia had been her most faithful guardian. And in the end, her spirit had selected Sophia because she had chosen to love an Azura Lord. Sera smiled softly.

Light and dark — the metaphor for her existence.

Dev's voice penetrated her thoughts. Distracted, she blinked, and the images dissipated.

"After you returned to the Mortal Realm, I searched for you forever but you never came back to Illysia," he said.

"She . . . I didn't." Sera frowned, trying to remember, separating Sita's newly fresh memories from hers. "I mean,

I stayed in the Mortal Realm even after I died. I always felt I belonged to the earth. I didn't want to return to Illysia so I chose to stay there." She smiled, realizing something else, and then laughed aloud.

"What?" he prodded.

"Now I understand why I saw your face when I saw Ra'al in Xibalba. Yours, out of everyone else in my life! Can you imagine my confusion? But you were the one I trusted the most, and the one I still trust even after so long." She stared at him. "I never forgot you, not even when it seemed that I forgot everything."

"Sera, I never stopped hoping that I'd find you one day, that I'd have the chance to redeem myself. Until now. I came right away after Micah told me he'd found Sophia."

Sera tried to piece together the remaining parts of the puzzle but they were still elusive. She didn't know why Sita had chosen to come back, only that she had. She didn't press it, diverted by something else that started to click in her mind, something she'd seen in her memories combined with something that Dev had said.

"Wait, what do you mean you came right away? You mean from Illysia?"

Sera thought about the empty throne and turned to him swiftly, gripping his arm with her right hand. Dev winced as something flared hot and red between them. He jerked backward cradling his arm. The mark on her palm glowed with an angry light, and she rubbed it against her leg.

"What's wrong?"

His voice was raw with pain. "Your sigil. It is the mark of the Dark Realms. Xibalba, as the Azura call it. I can't touch it.

My body may be mortal now but it still hurts worse than anything I've ever had to endure." He held her left hand gently. "This one, though, is mine. The symbol of the Protector and the mark of Illysia." He traced the outline with his forefinger and the sigil glowed white. He outlined the outside semi-circle, and then the two interlocking curving lines within it. "The shield, and the wing."

"What did you say?" she rasped. "The symbol of *what*?" But she'd heard him. He'd said "the Protector." She heard her mother's voice telling her about the hierarchy of Illysia and the reverent voices of the deities in her earlier vision, and started shaking her head in denial. But the truth was irrefutable. Because if in Illysia, she'd been Lakshmi, then he had to be . . .

Dev's eyes were gentle. "The Protector," he repeated. "My rune."

"But you're *mortal*!"

"It is the only way I could come to the Mortal Realm. It's not the first time, Sera." All she could see in front of her was the empty throne. "Haven't you been listening to a word I've been saying?"

"But you . . . you're . . . Trimurtas," she stuttered. "You're *Vishnu*."

"Yes. An avatara of myself in this human body."

Sera started laughing hysterically, then whirled toward him so quickly that he almost fell backward. It probably wasn't quite the response he'd been expecting. "Are you *crazy*? *Everyone* is looking for you!"

"I know. I blocked myself from them."

"*Why*? Surely you know how dangerous it is. You can be killed in mortal form!"

"No one knows who I am or that I am here, and I needed to find you. You had to trust me on your own. I couldn't very well woo you with scores of Yoddha trailing my every step, could I?"

"But you're one of the *Trimurtas*," she repeated dumbly.

He rolled his eyes. "Did you expect something different?"

"No, it's just weird. You're like a really important person. And you're here *wooing* me. It just seems . . . weird. Don't laugh, wooing was your word."

"I'm not laughing at that." Dev leaned forward to squeeze her shoulder, the laughter draining from his face. "Sera, does it not occur to you that *you* are also a really important person? I came here for you, to right a wrong I made years ago, to find my missing half. Honestly, you have become a little clueless in this incarnation of your-self," he chided with another smile.

She swatted his hand away and punched him in the shoulder. "I'll have you know that cluelessness is cool in this day and age."

"I don't think it is in any age," he said dryly. They shared a laugh, but Sera quickly sobered.

"What does this mean, Dev? I can't go back to Illysia with you. My uncle, I mean Samsar's brother, Azrath, has been planning something terrible."

"What did you just say? What about Azrath?"

"Micah went back to the other two of the Trimurtas to let them know. I think he and the rest of them have been looking for you all this time, but, of course, they were unable to see you. We don't know for sure, but it looks like Azrath has been ingesting Fyre."

"Deifyre?" Dev's face grew dark, his jaw clenched.

"Yes. We think Azrath and his minions are killing Daeva for the deifyre from their bodies. Azrath has been taking it into himself to get past the celestial wards preventing him from being able to portal to the Mortal Realm."

Sera stood and walked to the edge of the lagoon. "You need to go back to Illysia. The Trimurtas need your guidance on how to fight whatever Azrath is planning with Ra'al."

"I won't leave you, Sera. Not again." He came up behind her and buried his face in her hair. Sera pulled his hands around her waist and hugged them to her, careful not to let the sigil of Xibalba touch him.

"I'm not going anywhere, Dev. But this isn't about you and me right now. This is about the future of all the realms, of all of us. For now, Azrath doesn't know about me, but that's not to say that he won't find out. Our window is slipping closed. They need you."

Dev turned her to face him. His face was unreadable. "You're different than you used to be, but your passion is the same. And your love for humanity . . . your desire to save them hasn't changed."

"It won't."

"I know," he agreed. "I wouldn't want it to."

"So, you'll go back?"

His smile was radiant, lighting his face and eyes in an instant. Sera felt her breath catch at his grin. "They don't call me the Protector for nothing."

STRENGTH

༜

Kyle stared at the phone in his hand—Azrath wanted to see him. It couldn't have come at a worse time. He felt confused, not himself. He didn't want to be around Azrath if he couldn't even trust his own instincts, and after what had happened with Sera, he wasn't sure what to expect. Being anywhere near Azrath now would put Sera and all the others at risk. He knew too much about the Trimurtas and the rest of the Daeva.

Kyle sighed. He'd spent most of the night and morning helping Carla to clean up the worst of the damage in the house. Carla had been devastated when she'd returned from her trip to discover that they'd been burgled. Surprisingly, she hadn't blamed Kyle, even though some part of him had been expecting it. Afterward, he'd driven over to Sera's. There was only one person he could go to for help, but he was hesitant. Even though Sera's mother did not like him, he knew she was the only one who was strong enough to help him. He just hoped that Sera and Uri hadn't told her what he'd done at the school.

He got out of his car and walked up the curving driveway toward the house. There were two men—one tall and thin, the other burly—stationed out front whom he didn't recognize. They tensed the minute they saw him.

He pushed his senses out. Human, but Ne'feri.

"I'm a friend," he called out. "Kyle. I just want to see Mrs. Caelum."

They approached him and he could see the reflection of sunlight against the blades hidden in their hands. They weren't taking any chances.

"Show us your hands," the tall one said.

Kyle raised his hands, palms up toward him. The other man chanted something in a strange language, and Kyle felt something fall on him like powder—some kind of spell. He didn't have time to dwell on it, though, as the one who'd spoken dropped into a low crouch, blade in hand.

"Azura!" he snarled. The tall man whirled in a blur to step behind him in front of the flagstone path leading to the front door. Out of the corner of his eye, he saw another person approaching behind him. That last one was distinctly Daeva or higher. Already he could see the white glow of deifyre in its hands, a warrior then.

"I'm a friend of Sera Caelum's," he said, careful not to make any sudden movements. "If you just let me take my phone out—"

"Don't move!" the burly man shouted. But Kyle was already reaching into his pocket. The tall man flew toward him, and Kyle spun to avoid the attack, flinging his left foot out as he turned, causing the man to tumble to the ground.

"Listen to me, please. I am a *friend*!"

"The Azura are no friend to the Daeva," the burly man said, lunging with his knife. Kyle blocked the man's arm and countered with a swift punch to the man's face. Kyle's body felt fluid, graceful even, as his fist tore through bone like tissue paper. The man staggered back, blood pouring from a broken nose.

Kyle blinked. It was faster than he'd ever moved. Something dark uncurled inside of him as he spun to face the other man.

"A friend?" the tall man scoffed, his face angry but also fearful.

"What did you expect me to do? You attacked me!" Kyle shouted back. He dodged the deifyre arrow heading his way from the third person at the end of the driveway and tackled the tall man to the ground. He heard bone snap, and then something stung his arm. Kyle whirled as a second arrow grazed the top of his elbow. Kyle screamed—the barest touch of the deifyre on his skin was like flame scorching an open wound.

Kyle stumbled back clutching his elbow, the pain radiating up through his bones. But the arrow had barely even touched him. Something wasn't right!

He sensed someone to his left and whirled, his hand flying toward its target. He froze at the last minute, belatedly recognizing Beth. He saw an answering flash of recognition in her eyes, but it was a second too late as a heavy-looking blunt instrument swung toward his head. And then the last thing he saw was darkness.

⁓✥⁓

When Kyle opened his eyes, he was lying in the Caelum's living room. Sophia's gray eyes swam into focus.

"Kyle? It's Sophia. Can you hear me?" she asked. She waved a hand slowly in front of his face. "Are you OK? Can you see my fingers?"

He shook his head and wished he hadn't, closing his eyes tightly.

"I'm sure it looks worse than it is," a small voice said. Kyle touched his temple and winced. He turned toward the voice.

"You hit me," he told Beth, whose face was stricken.

"I'm sorry. I only saw the back of your head coming up the drive with all the tattoos and I panicked. Some demon guy named Marcus came to the house last night, so we're all a little high strung."

"Marcus?" Kyle gasped, then started coughing. He sat up and blinked, feeling woozy. "What did you hit me with? A sledgehammer?"

Beth nodded. "Sorry. You gave as good as you got. The other Ne'feri are seasoned fighters and you took them both out like they were first-timers. And with no weapons, too! That's why I panicked. You just didn't look like you—you were *so* fast."

Kyle started coughing again. Beth was right. He'd never moved that fast before. Something strange was definitely going on.

When the coughing fit ended, he asked, "How long have I been out?"

"Not very long," Sophia said, glancing at his arm. "I cleaned and bandaged your arm. Maeve's arrow just barely clipped you, so I was able to get most of it before it went too deep." She examined his head. "This wound is healing already."

"Thanks," Kyle repeated, touching his head and feeling the new skin under his fingertips. He looked up. The warrior goddess, Maeve, stood in the corner of the living room near a window. She was tall and Amazonian-looking with coffee-colored skin. She seemed fierce.

"Where's Sera? Is she OK? Why was Marcus here last night?"

"Sera's still sleeping," Beth said. "She said last night that Marcus was a friend of Jude's and that he was one of the Ifrit she'd seen at the portal."

"What did he want?"

"Marcus said he came with a message from Azrath for Sam," Sophia said flatly. "Things got heated, but he flew away before we could get any useful information out of him, like what Azrath has been planning. Maeve shot his wing, so he's hurt but still escaped." Kyle heard a strange tone in her voice. She wasn't telling him everything.

"Is Sam OK?"

"He's hanging in there. A little banged up. Mortals take longer to heal than we do."

"Where is he? Is he safe?"

Sophia nodded.

"Mrs. Caelum, I came over because I need your help. Azrath has asked to see me and I'm afraid that if I go to him, I will become the weak link in everything we are working toward. I don't know what to do, how to keep him from possessing me or getting into my head."

Sophia looked surprised. "I'm not sure what you're asking."

"Can you do anything so that I'm protected against Azrath? So that what I know remains hidden from him? I don't want to put any of you in any jeopardy, but if I don't go, he will suspect something and you'll all be in danger."

"Kyle, I'm not sure that there's anything I can do. Azrath is old and he is cunning. He'll know that you've been shaded."

"But he never knew about Sera, so it can be done, right?" Kyle felt desperate. "I have to try *something*! Maybe if Micah—"

Something clouded Sophia's face for a brief moment. Maeve, the other deity, walked over, and Kyle flinched involuntarily as she drew close. She crouched down next to him and studied him. Her eyes were sharp.

"What are you?" she said after a while, her voice like wind chimes.

Kyle stared at his hands. "I . . . don't know."

"You're not Azura," she said frowning. "At least, not all of you."

"My mother was Azura," he said in a rush. Images of the night his mother died and the thing that had spoken with his mother's voice flooded his mind.

You belong to Xibalba.

"No, there's something else." Maeve peered at the wound on his forehead, which was now only a reddened bruise. She shook her head and glanced at Sophia. "Even Azura don't heal that fast from our weapons. Show me your arm," she told him.

She peeled away the white gauze bandage carefully. Behind her, Sophia gasped.

Kyle stared down at his arm. The gash that had been there before was now closing before his eyes, stringy pieces of black gooey thread stretching across it as if it had been sewn. A fine coating of silver dust lay along its edges.

"Curious," Sophia whispered, moving to crouch beside Maeve. She touched the dust with her fingers and smelled it. "His blood is pushing the rest of the toxin from the deifyre out."

"That's impossible," Maeve said. Her face was determined. It scared him for a second until she took a silver blade from her pocket and dug it into his wound. It was nothing compared to the agony of the deifyre arrow, but he still bit his tongue to keep from shouting.

Something black fizzled and congealed against the tip of the knife.

"What is that?" he heard himself say.

Both Sophia and Maeve were staring at him. Maeve lifted the blade to her nose and smelled it as Sophia had done with the silver dust. She frowned and flung herself to her feet, flaring deifyre as a bow appeared in her hands with its arrow notched. It pointed directly to Kyle's heart.

"Maeve!" Beth shrieked. "He's a friend."

Sophia remained silent. Kyle was frozen, squinting against Maeve's light until his Azura eyes adjusted to the brightness. The second he moved, the arrow would be released. He didn't dare breathe.

"He's a demon," Maeve said flatly.

At her words, Kyle felt the world slipping away from him. They thought he was a demon? But it wasn't possible. He was Azura. He remembered the thing that spoke through his mother's mouth and felt a dark fear take hold in his gut.

"No way," Beth said, her voice trembling. "He's with us."

"That is demon blood on that knife," Maeve said. "I've killed enough of them to know."

"But Daeva can sense demons," Beth said. "How come no one sensed him? You're wrong! He's no demon. He can't be."

Sophia pulled herself to her feet, her gray eyes shaded. "Maeve's right. The blood on that blade is demon's blood. But you're right, too, Beth. I, we, didn't sense anything."

Kyle felt something jump-start inside of him, a powerful survival instinct, but he didn't move. Instead he watched the two goddesses very carefully. He didn't have a shot in hell with Maeve—she didn't trust him one bit. And Sophia barely trusted him. He read the indecision on her face easily.

Kyle knew he couldn't attack them physically. The wound on his arm was a reminder of how vulnerable he was to dei-fyre. For a second he wondered at this disturbing change. He'd been able to touch the Yoddha, Aria, in the barn, and now, like the Ifrit, he could not, which meant he had already changed and was no longer human. His eyes flitted to the wound on his elbow, now completely healed. They were right—he *was* something else.

Suddenly, Beth moved to stand behind the sofa where he sat. Neither Maeve's eyes nor her arrow wavered from him, though.

"Sophia? You can't hurt him," Beth said slowly. "Sera would never forgive you . . . us."

A flash of something that looked like doubt shadowed Sophia's face. "I'll take that risk if it means protecting her from—" She stared at Kyle. "I'm sorry, she's too important for us to take chances and you . . . I just don't know what . . ."

"Micah trusts me," Kyle whispered. He saw her almost waver and he pressed on. "And you trust him, you always have. Sam did too, he told me so. They both knew more about me than anyone, and Sam said that *I* would choose as he did, not the other way around—"

"Sophia," Maeve said warningly. "Micah wouldn't have known about this. *You* didn't. If he were here, you know what he would do." Her voice was hard. "This is a *demon*. You have to see that. Blood doesn't lie."

Sophia blinked, staring at him with new wary eyes. "What did you just do?" she hissed.

"Nothing, I didn't—"

She flared and he blinked against her light. Like Micahs, it was silvery white, unlike Maeve's gold fire. He felt his breath catch in his throat at the sight of the long spear in her hands. Behind him, Beth gripped the edge of the sofa with white hands.

"You tried to compel me," Sophia said. "A unique demon trait."

"No!" Kyle said. "I wouldn't even know how—"

But even as he said the words, he knew she was right. The low hypnotic voice had been his, and he'd felt her bend in response to it, especially when he mentioned both Micah and Sam. His mind was whirling. Maybe there was a way he could get out of this after all. He had to keep them talking.

"Mrs. Caelum," Kyle said in a normal voice. "I am not deceiving you. Micah and Sam both know that I am something else. Only I *don't* know what that is. I swear it."

As he spoke, he focused his mind on Beth's energy behind him, hoping that her newness to the Ne'feri would help him. Instead of just seeing and feeling her human energy, Kyle pushed himself into it and then swallowed as much of it as he could, holding her inside of him. It wasn't violent, although he knew without a doubt that he could be if he wanted to. It was soft, gentle, compelling . . . like a hug.

Beth, move closer. He saw her shift closer toward him. *That's it, move along the edge of the sofa. Closer. That's it.*

"I told Sam when we went to find the portal to Xibalba," he continued, speaking quietly, "the one that Sera went through." The minute he said the words, Kyle realized that it had been a mistake. Putting Xibalba and Sera in the same sentence had been a gross miscalculation on his part. Sophia hissed.

"You did that," she snarled. "You sent her there. I don't know what you are, but you're never going to get that chance again!" She swung the spear up behind her in a low arc just as Beth took a final step toward him.

With unearthly speed, Kyle spun over the back of the sofa, feeling the wind of Maeve's arrow rush past his back as he twisted up and over, and saw it bury itself into the cushion. She had another notched in the space of a heartbeat. Beth gasped as Kyle grabbed her, holding her body like a shield in front of him. Sophia's face was a frozen mask of rage.

"It's OK, Beth, I won't hurt you," Kyle said into her ear.

"You jerk!" she screamed struggling against his hold. "I was on your side."

"I'm sorry. They gave me no choice," he said, his voice low. "Be still, Beth."

"That won't work, demon," Maeve snarled even as Beth stopped struggling. "She is an easy sacrifice to get to you. Don't think I won't do it."

Beth's eyes grew wide. "Don't worry, they won't," Kyle murmured to her. She nodded, but Kyle could feel her heart racing.

He stared directly at Maeve. "I know you won't, because she's an innocent. You won't hurt her to get to me."

Kyle backed away, holding Beth against his chest until he was a few feet from the sofa. He glanced at the doorway. There would be no way he would be able to get away without taking Beth with him. By the time he looked back at the two women, Sophia had moved around the sofa to stand at his left, spear still in hand. Her wings and eyes burned like silver fire. Maeve hadn't moved.

"You won't hurt her either," Sophia said.

Kyle laughed, a sound full of despair. "Oh, you believe me now? But you wanted to kill me not ten seconds ago."

"Kyle, please," Sophia said. "Just see it from my point of view. You tried to compel me even if you didn't know what you were doing. What if there are other things you can do without knowing? You're a danger to yourself, and to my daughter. Release Beth, and we can talk about it."

"Talk about what? You just said it yourself, I'm a danger to everyone around me." His mother's words came back to haunt him.

You are cursed.

He felt hot tears sting his eyes. "My mother said that, too, you know, just before she tried to kill me. I was five! Do you know what that does to a kid? It destroys him." He'd reached the kitchen. He shoved Beth forward as he felt the tears break free. "You know what? Do your worst. I don't care. I deserve to die."

Time slowed, and in the blink of an eye, he saw Maeve's golden arrow release without hesitation just as Sophia lurched forward to grasp Beth. Kyle braced himself, his arms dropping to his side, and faced the streak of flame flying toward him. Maybe this was the best way for Sera to be protected. He locked eyes with Sophia's. Beth's face was horrified, her tears flowing as freely as his.

"Tell Sera I'm sorry—"

"No!" someone screamed. A fiery red blur whooshed past him into the path of the oncoming arrow, flinging an arm up and deflecting it into the opposite wall.

"Get out of the way. He's—" Maeve began. She had already strung another arrow.

"I don't care," the glowing creature snapped. She turned to him. "Killing him is not the answer."

But Maeve had already released the arrow. Sophia shouted a delayed warning. "Maeve, no, it's Sera." Her eyes were wide, her hands clapped to her mouth. "Sera?" she whispered. "It is *you*, isn't it?"

This time Sera grasped the arrow in midair and crushed it between her fingers. They all stared as the rush of scarlet and gold flames receded, until it was just Sera standing in their midst, her arm held out wide. "Enough!"

"Sera! Your deifyre . . . " Beth whispered. "What happened?"

"Xibalba happened," Sera said wryly. Her face turned serious, but she still wouldn't look at Kyle. He felt his heart sink. "Look, I don't really want to know what caused all of this. I don't care. We have bigger problems to worry about and right now, we need everyone who can help us. Including him."

"But Kyle—" Sophia began.

"Mom, Nate's gone."

Sera and Kyle

~∂~∂~

W hat do you mean, Nate's gone?" her mother cried. "He's in his room. I just saw him there!"

"No, he's not there. I looked."

"She's right. He's not here. I can't feel him," Kyle said, startling the others.

"What did you do?" Maeve hissed through her teeth at Kyle, her bow raised.

Sera stared coolly at Kyle, her face expressionless. She could see the remorse in his eyes but couldn't quite bring herself to forgive him. "You should go," she told him, then turned to Maeve, who still stood battle-stance ready. "I know you are here to protect my mother and me, but Kyle is not the enemy. Azrath is. Lay down your arms, *Yoddhita*."

Maeve's arms fell to her sides and she looked to Sophia in confusion.

"Sera?" Sophia whispered. "What did you say?"

"Sophia," Sera said, blinking at the shock on her mother's face. "I mean, Mom. Sorry, too many memories, it's hard to be clear." Sera walked toward her mother.

Let me in.

The words were like musical notes in her mind, soft and persuasive. Sera paused and closed her eyes as a strange feeling flooded her head. She gave in to it fully as her mouth voiced words that weren't her own.

"Sophia. I called her 'guardian,' as you were once mine." She smiled at Sophia's confusion and held a strand of hair between her fingertips. "Surely you know one other with this red coloring? Think back. You were so young then."

"No, it can't be," Sophia's gray eyes widened and her head swung back and forth. "*Sita*? It's not possible."

"Why not? I chose you," Sera said, running her hand gently along the curve of Sophia's cheek. "I chose you to return. You were my most loyal *yoddhita*, and then your love for Samsar, well, it was more than I could have hoped for."

Sera could feel the voice speaking with her lips, thought the words weren't entirely her own.

"You knew?" Sophia's voice was a dry rasp. "About Sam?"

"Of course I knew," Sera's voice said. "I had already decided to come back, but I chose you after that. I have spent the last thousand years observing humanity. Now that their darkest hour is almost upon them, I couldn't just stand by and witness their destruction."

Sophia slumped against the wall. "But that means you would have had to know this seventeen years ago." Sera felt herself nod. "I don't understand. Why didn't you say anything? Maybe we could have prevented this. Sam, Nate."

"Sophia," the goddess said gently. "Your daughter, Serjana, could not know. You know more than anyone that what is written cannot be unwritten. We can only interpret the signs. The Trimurtas are convening. The cycle of Kali is upon us—man's darkest age."

"My lady," Maeve said, her face troubled. "Micah told me that one of the Trimurtas was missing. We can't hope to do anything without the power of all three."

"We found him. He has returned."

Sophia was still staring at her with guarded eyes. "And Sera, is she . . ."

Sera blinked, trance-like, but her eyes were clear as the other part of her faded into the background of her mind. "We are the same," Sera answered hoarsely. "I'm the same. Mom, it's still me. I just have the understanding of where I came from, and who she was. She's a part of me, but I'm still me. It's OK, Mom." She gripped her mother's shoulders, her eyes fierce. "We need to find Nate."

Sera turned to Beth. "Get your mother and Uri. The Ne'feri need to be mobilized to guard the portals between the realms. Go now." Beth rushed out of the room after an uneasy glance at Kyle. He shot her another apologetic look. "Maeve, you need to let Micah and the others know. You must go to Illysia."

Sera pulled back the sleeve of her left arm. Her deifyre flared, its shades of red, gold, and orange mesmerizing. A blinding white light burst from the sigil on her palm and Sera recreated its symbol against the air.

"*Darwaaza Illysia*," she said. A white circular doorway shimmered into focus. "Go," she told Maeve. "It will take you to the Protector. Return as quickly as you can. It will remain open only for you."

Maeve bowed and slipped through it. The doorway shimmered out of sight as Sera released it. She slumped backward and flinched as Kyle lurched to catch her.

"Don't," she muttered, darting a look to her mother. Sera hadn't said anything about what had happened with him, knowing what they would all think. And as angry as she was with him for attacking her, a part of her knew that if she let him go now, he'd be lost to her forever. Kyle stepped away.

"Mom," Sera said. "You need to stay here in case Nate comes back. I need to check to see if there's anything I missed in his room. I won't go anywhere without telling you, OK?" She turned back to Kyle, addressing him without looking at him. "What are you still doing here?"

"I can help," Kyle said softly. "With Nate."

Sera stared at him, then agreed. Regardless of what was still unsaid between them, his gift could come in handy. They climbed the stairs, leaving Sophia in a daze.

"I hope she's OK," Sera said, more to herself than to Kyle, as she pushed open Nate's door.

"Well, give her a little credit. It's kind of hard finding out that your kid is the reincarnation of some goddess you served a few thousand years ago," Kyle said.

Sera shot him a look. "I guess you have a point," she said. "You heard then? About Sita? About me?"

"Yeah," Kyle said with a sidelong glance.

"And you're not freaked out at all by any of it?"

"A little, I guess, but it's not like I'm one to talk," Kyle began. "Everything seems to be happening so fast, and things have gotten so screwed up. Ser, I'm sorry about—"

"Look," Sera interrupted, cutting him off. "I don't want to talk about that. Maybe you were jealous and you let everything get to you, but right now, I need to think about Nate.

If you want to help, stay, but if not, I can't deal with you and me right now."

"I want to help," Kyle said, and bit his lip.

Inside, Nate's room was organized and neat, not a thing out of place other than the bed, which looked rumpled as if he'd just rolled out of it. Sera walked over to it and stuck her hand between the blankets and the bottom sheet.

"They're still warm," she murmured. "He hasn't been gone long. You're sure you can't sense him?"

"I'm sure." Kyle stuck his head into Nate's bathroom. "So what exactly are we looking for?"

"I'm not sure. I'm worried, but the kid is not exactly normal. He does this a lot, disappears for hours on end. What if he just slipped out to go somewhere?"

Kyle turned to check the window. "It's locked," he said, and then a thought occurred to him. "What about your dad. Would he go to him?"

Sera stared at him. "Why didn't I think of that?" She picked up the phone handset in Nate's room and dialed a number.

"Hi Eleanor, it's Sera," she said. "Is Nate there with my dad by any chance? He isn't? OK, thanks. Beth's on her way back, she'll fill you in. Bye." She replaced the handset and stared at Kyle. "No such luck."

"Your dad's at Beth's?"

"Did Mom tell you what happened last night, with Marcus?" Kyle nodded. "Well, he got pretty hurt. You remember Uri? He's a healer, so Dad went over there." Her fists tightened at her sides. "If I see Marcus, I'll kill him for what he did to my father. And if he or Jude put Nate in any danger, so help me—"

"Ser, Nate's a smart kid. We'll find him, don't worry."

Sera glanced at him, then scowled, looking away to sort through the stuff on Nate's desk. She needed his help to find Nate, but that didn't mean things were back to normal, even if he'd braved facing Sophia to apologize. She ignored the twinge of forgiveness she felt and asked brusquely, "So, what happened earlier? Looked like World War Three was about to erupt downstairs."

Kyle rummaged through the closet. "I came to find you, and one of the guys out front jumped me." He saw her look. "I'm fine. Azura blood, you know. Your mom doesn't trust me either. Kind of wish your dad was here. At least he doesn't think I'm lower than a snake's belly."

Sera shot him a look. "So, why were you giving up at the end? Did you want to die?"

There was a long silence before Kyle responded. "When Maeve shot me, I healed. But when she saw my blood, she went a little crazy, because she said it smelled like demon blood."

Sera twisted out from under the bed and stared at him. Goose bumps inexplicably prickled her flesh.

"Sera, I tried to tell you before. I don't know exactly what I am. Maybe I am a demon. And maybe that's why I almost attacked you before, why I got so jealous." He stared at the tops of his scuffed Converse sneakers, avoiding her gaze.

"Is that why your mom tried to kill you when you were little?"

"You heard that?"

"Yeah," she said. He moved to crouch beside her, and although she felt sorry for him, she moved away, keeping her distance.

"There's something else," he said. "Before my mother died, she sounded like she was possessed by something. The voice said that I belonged in Xibalba, and that I'd be there by the time I was seventeen."

"And you think she was right?" Sera said carefully.

"I don't know," Kyle said. "Maybe she was wrong. I'm seventeen today."

Sera could feel something was different. He felt different. But then again, she was different too.

Sera knew Kyle bitterly regretted what he'd done—she could see it in his eyes and hear it in every word he spoke. The truth was he was still her friend no matter how much of a misogynistic idiot he'd been, and he deserved a second chance. Her face softened.

"Birthday truce?" she offered. Kyle nodded as if he couldn't speak. She grinned. "I swear to God the last few days feel like I've been on some kind of crazy-coaster. I can't believe we didn't even go to Sal's for your birthday breakfast. It's like sacred tradition."

"Tell me about it. What I wouldn't give for some normal right now, and Sal's home fries, eggs, extra crispy birthday bacon." Kyle's eyes nearly glazed over at his words.

Sera grinned at his expression. "Tell you what, once we find Nate, breakfast on me." She peered at him with curious eyes. "Hey, when did you get your tattoos done over?"

"What?"

"They're dark red now, and the shape's different. They don't look like dragon wings anymore and they curl down the back of your neck in this intricate vine design."

"I didn't notice," Kyle said, his face conflicted. He seemed confused about the changes, but it was almost as if he didn't want to acknowledge them. He shrugged indifferently. "I don't know. Today hasn't been exactly normal, but maybe it's a good thing. I haven't felt anything from Jude in a while either."

Despite Kyle's nonchalance, Sera could see the shaded fear in his eyes. The changing tattoos obviously had some significance that he didn't want to think about . . . something that caused both her mother and Maeve to freak out. "Looks like you have something to celebrate. No more Jude. Couldn't ask for a better birthday present."

Kyle's mouth twisted wryly. "Not sure if I have that much to celebrate. I spent all morning cleaning pasted-on demon blood out of Carla's carpet, I almost got killed by two immortals, and my best friend, maybe girlfriend, will never forgive me for being a complete loser." Sera gaped at him, unable to hide her expression. "Too soon?" he asked.

"Kyle, about us, I'm—"

But Sera's voice faded as they both saw the mark exactly at the same time. It was an ashy faded symbol, barely visible against the wall just above Nate's pillow. And they both recognized it in an instant.

"Azrath," Kyle breathed.

"You know it?" Sera asked. "I saw him draw it in Xibalba." She reached forward with tentative fingers.

"Sera, no," Kyle warned. "Remember last time?"

"It's OK. Last time, I was unprepared." She leaned forward and laid her fingertips just over the symbol, not touching but hovering. The air shimmered. It *was* a portal. Sera stared at Kyle, her mind whirling. She needed to know where the portal went, but in order to do so she had to trust Kyle with her life. Sera hoped she wasn't making a monumental mistake. "Hold my arm just in case," she told Kyle, who instantly grasped her left arm.

"Don't worry, I've got you."

After a searching look, she dipped her fingers into the middle of the symbol. They sunk into the wall as if it were thick pudding. She felt the pull instantly, like a vacuum sucking her toward its exit point.

"Can you see where it goes?" Kyle said.

"Not yet, it's closing too fast. Hold me. Whatever happens, don't let go. If I squeeze once, it's OK. Twice, get me out."

Sera pushed forward again and stuck her body halfway through the portal. It felt like she was splitting into two, elongating until she emerged gasping for breath on the other side. She glanced back and saw the upper half of her body suspended in thin air, the air shimmering around her ribcage like a glowing white disk. Seeing her body severed at the chest was an ugly image and she looked away quickly, slightly nauseated.

Sera could feel the portal closing in like a noose against her skin and she knew she didn't have much time. If she didn't move quickly, she could die; even an immortal couldn't be in two realms at the same time. Sera squeezed Kyle's hand once and felt his reassuring squeeze back. She looked around. She was in a white room with a bed at one end. Something small lay motionless on it. She couldn't tell if it was Nate or not.

"Nate," she whispered. "Nate!" she called, louder. "Is that you? Can you hear me?"

A voice in her ear made her almost lurch completely through the portal. "Nate can't hear you."

Then hands grabbed her neck, holding her firmly in place. She felt Kyle's immediate concerned squeeze from the jerking movement. She squeezed back once. She had to find out why Azrath wanted her brother. Plus, if Kyle pulled her back, she'd likely be strangled.

She swiveled her eyes slowly, her heart in her throat, and saw two glowing red eyes as Jude squatted next to her. "Now this is very interesting, isn't it Marcus?" Marcus laughed, his fingers tightening around her neck.

Jude looked her up and down and twisted to look behind her missing lower half. He stood and walked toward the bed where Nate was laying.

"You leave him alone," Sera hissed. It hurt to talk with Marcus's fingers around her throat.

"Or you're going to do what, Sera?"

"What does Azrath want with Nate?" For a minute Jude looked as though he wasn't going to answer her question, but then he surprised her.

"Insurance."

"For what?"

"Simple. Your father's cooperation." Jude ran a finger through Nate's curls. Nate sighed and stirred, and Sera felt a weight lift from her shoulders. He was alive.

"Don't touch him, you filth," she said. As she said the words, the boy in the bed turned and Sera felt bile lurch in her stomach. It was some kind of demon creature with a child's face—*Nate's face*—and the rest of its wizened body covered in fur. A nekomata. It bared a row of sharp fangs in a Cheshire cat grin and the face distorted into something ugly and rodent-like.

"Where's Nate?" she gritted. "If you've hurt him—"

Jude glanced over his shoulder, his grin cold. "Why? You're going to hurt me? You think I'm afraid of a little Daeva blood?" He laughed and stroked the nekomata. "Oh, I know what you are, Sera."

"Damien made the same mistake," Sera snarled rashly.

Jude turned slowly, transforming, his face contorting before her eyes into something black and grotesque. Black scaled wings sprouted from his back, and green thorns spiked along his spine. He was bigger and uglier and more monstrous than Damien had been.

"What did you say?" Jude snarled through bared fangs.

Marcus's fingers dug into her skin like a vice. She could feel his hands twisting into talons and could smell the rancid sourness of blood on his breath. She refused to give him the satisfaction of looking at him. She reined in her anger.

"You heard me, and if you think you scare me, think again." She felt Marcus's claws almost cutting off her breath but she knew that Jude wanted to be the one to hurt her. She could see it in his hot demon eyes. She turned to look at Marcus. "Let me go, Marcus," she told him. "You will die if you keep your hands on me."

At her words, Marcus looked uneasy, but Jude's long laugh from the middle of the room erased his nervousness. Jude walked to crouch once more in front of her, his body transforming back to the boy she knew.

"You're in no position to be threatening anyone." Jude caressed her stomach with a cold finger, and Sera had to force herself from cringing at his touch. "The minute that portal closes, you are over, Daeva or not." He brushed the hair off her face, an appreciative leer distorting his features. "By the way, I like what you've done with your hair. Red suits you. I always thought you had some fire in you." His voice grew hard as he grabbed a handful of hair so hard that her eyes smarted. "Now tell me about Damien."

"I can't . . . speak," she rasped. Jude nodded for Marcus to release his hold. "Damien thought I was Daeva, too."

Sera knew she didn't have much time; the portal was a tight rubber band against her skin. But she understood the odds now and knew that revealing her power would give Azrath and his minions a tactical advantage.

"So, what are you then?" Marcus asked.

Sera looked at Jude as she responded, "Something worse."

And then she flung her fist as hard as she could into Jude's face. She heard the satisfying crunch of bone but didn't dwell on it as she squeezed Kyle's hand twice as hard as she could, and a third time for good measure.

Jude leapt to his feet, howling with rage, but he was too late as she jerked backward through the portal in half a second, crashing into Kyle.

The portal spun closed, but Sera wasn't taking any chances.

"*Darwaaza bānd*," she gasped, drawing a sealing rune on the wall and collapsing on the bed. Her body had started shaking uncontrollably.

"Are you all right?" Kyle asked. She nodded, her teeth chattering so hard they felt like they would shatter. "What happened? Did you see Nate?"

Sera told him what had happened in a few short sentences. His eyes were wide. "Did you see where they were?"

"No, it was just a white room. Probably Azrath's."

Kyle nodded his head. "Azrath is obsessed with white. What cooperation was Jude talking about?"

"When Marcus came last night, Dad said that Azrath's message was for him to stay away. Dad wouldn't agree. He told Marcus that he'd taken a vow to stand against his brother if he went against the covenant of the Trimurtas in any way. So Marcus broke two of his ribs, and now they've taken Nate to keep Dad quiet."

"That's weird. It must be something that Sam can somehow stop if Azrath's so worried about him interfering," Kyle offered.

Sera's eyes widened—Kyle was right! A crashing sound from downstairs had them both vaulting to their feet, and they almost collided on the stairs in their haste to get down them.

"Mom!" Sera yelled, rounding the corner. "You OK?"

"Yes, it's just Maeve coming back with Micah," Sophia said. "We're fine."

They encountered a white-faced Maeve, who'd stumbled into a glass end table. "Actually, we're not fine at all," she gasped. Sera stared at Micah, whose face had the same ashen expression.

"What's wrong?" Sophia said, looking from one to the other.

Maeve stared at Sera. "You said the Protector was back."

Sera frowned. "He is. I was with him last night." She could feel Kyle's eyes heavy on her back.

Micah's voice was tight. "You're mistaken, Sera. He never returned to Illysia."

AGENDAS

They drove in silence to Beth's house on the other side of town. Kyle kept shooting Sera covert glances, but she wouldn't meet his eyes. Maeve and her mother followed in the car behind. Micah had gone to Sam the minute Sera told them about Nate's kidnapping, in case Azrath tried to contact him again. Due to the the severity of her dad's injuries, they'd decided that the Davenport residence would have to suffice for a meeting place. And when Kyle had volunteered to come along, Sera had allowed him to. She wanted to keep him close—whatever was going on with him, she didn't want him anywhere near Azrath.

Before they'd left, Sera had gone next door to Dev's house, but no one had answered her knocking. So she used the backdoor key to enter the house, just to make sure it was empty. Now that she understood who Dev really was, she knew that he didn't live with anyone—it had all been a part of the facade. But the house was deserted with no sign of him at all, and a sinister feeling of foreboding spread like a cancer in the pit of her stomach.

She'd even gone to her world to look for him, but knew the second she'd arrived that Dev wasn't there. Something was terribly wrong. She could feel it.

"So . . . about the giant gorilla in the car," Kyle's voice was quiet, interrupting her thoughts. "Dev's the Protector?"

Sera glanced at him, recognizing the tightness of his mouth despite his attempt at humor. "Yes," she said carefully.

"Is that why you got so weird before? Are you with him?"

"I don't know. I'm bound to him, or Sita was to Rama, I mean," Sera said. Kyle's hands were white-knuckled against the steering wheel, his jaw clenched.

"But you're not *her*."

Sera's voice was gentle. Her hand fluttered toward him as if she wanted to touch his arm, but then it drifted to her lap. "No, I'm not. I'm me, but all her feelings for him are still real, and they're mine, too."

"And what you felt for me, was that real? You said you loved me. Or was it a lie?" Kyle said, his tone biting.

"Don't be cruel. You're still my best friend regardless of what happened the other day."

"Just not your boyfriend," Kyle said. He didn't hide the pain in his voice this time. She glanced at him, but he wouldn't look at her.

"Dev's not either," she said quietly, staring out the window, and then angling her body back to face him. "I don't know what you want me to say. I didn't ask for any of this. I never believed in any of this stuff, you of all people know that. All I'm trying to do is be fair, to do the right thing."

"So choose me."

"It's not about you or him, Kyle. Don't you get it? I think I was, like, married to him three thousand years ago." His face grew even redder and more pinched at her words. "What I feel for you won't change either, and I can't *choose* either of you because of what I feel for *both* of you. Does that make any sense?"

"No. You're either with me or you're with him."

Sera sighed. Explaining a love triangle was turning out to be more complicated than being *in* one. "Look, I don't want to hurt you."

"It's a little too late for that," Kyle muttered, turning onto Beth's street.

Sera pretended that she didn't hear him and took her jacket off underneath the seatbelt. The air in the car felt stifling. "Can you just try to understand?"

"Understand what? That you need my help to find your boyfriend?"

They stared at each other in silence. Sera felt sweat drip down her cheek. She glanced at the dashboard and cracked open her window so that some cold air rushed in. "Do you have the heat on in here? It's boiling," she snapped.

"I don't think it's the car," Kyle said. His voice sounded strained. Sera looked at him more closely and gasped. His skin was red, and she could almost see the steam rising from where the cold air brushed against his skin. She touched a cautious finger to his arm.

"Kyle, you're burning up."

"Great. I turn seventeen and all hell breaks loose." Sera's gaze snapped to him, and he laughed thinly. "I meant that figuratively, of course."

But Sera was worried about him. Too many things had clouded the obvious, and despite them skirting around what was happening, he *was* changing. First, the way he'd treated her, his blood at her house, the tattoos, and now this—his body heat could practically melt ice. Was he really some kind of demon as Maeve said? Sera chewed her lip, feeling uneasy, but didn't say anything. Kyle had given her the benefit of the doubt even when she'd gone all vile after her trip to Xibalba. She should be the last person to jump to conclusions and judge anyone.

"Are you with me, Kyle?" she asked, watching him take heaving gulps of cold air into his lungs.

"Yes," he gasped. He took several more deep breaths, and his skin lost some of the ruddiness just as they pulled up to Beth's house. Sera shot him another troubled look. "I'm fine. I think it was because I was upset. Again."

"OK," Sera said softly, stepping out of the car just before her mother and Maeve joined them. "Just get it together before we go in there."

One of the men who'd been at Sera's house earlier now stood outside the Davenport's house. He had his arm in a sling. He didn't look at Kyle, even when Kyle threw an apologetic glance in his direction.

Eleanor opened the door, her face darkening as she eyed Kyle. "You're not invited."

"He's not a vampire, Eleanor. And he's with me," Sera said flatly. She stared Eleanor full in the face. "If he's not welcome, then I'm not either."

"Sera, I really don't think it's a good idea. Beth said—"

"Eleanor," Sophia said, coming up behind them. "It's fine."

Eleanor looked confused, but she let Sera and Kyle walk past her. Beth was at the bottom of the stairs in her foyer. She wore a guarded look.

"Hey," Kyle said in a small voice. "I'm sorry about before, Beth. I never would have hurt you, I hope you know that." Beth nodded but Sera noticed that she slid away from him to stand near her brother.

"Hey, Ryan," Sera said. He stood off to the side. He wasn't quite eighteen, so not officially Ne'feri, but with what Azrath was planning, she guessed that their parents didn't think it was too early to include him in the meeting.

There were about twenty people in the room now, including her father, Micah, and a few other faces she didn't recognize. Several of them stared at Kyle with blatant hostility, and Sera bristled. She recognized Uri from school and two of the men who'd been at her house. Beth's father was also there—a tall heavily bearded man. Two dark-haired, slim men standing at the far end of the room exchanged heavy looks with Maeve. *Yoddha*, she guessed.

With the exception of those two, Sera guessed that the majority of those gathered were Ne'feri, with Micah and her mother acting as the voice of the Trimurtas.

Micah cleared his throat and spoke, not bothering with niceties. "We have convened here because Illysia is mobilizing at the will of the Trimurtas. The Ne'feri across the Mortal Realm are guarding the portals. But for a few, they have all been closed." He glanced at Sam. "Azrath has already contacted Sam and has taken Sam's son to the Dark Realms where he will remain unless Sam cooperates with him." There were several loud gasps in the room.

"Did Azrath say that?" Sera gasped, looking to her father. "That Nate's in Xi . . . *there*?" He nodded mutely.

"But the boy, he's mortal. He will not survive the Dark Realms!" Eleanor cried, and Sera felt the blood drain from her body.

Micah shook his head grimly. "No, not for long, Eleanor, which is why we don't have a lot of time. We do not know what Azrath is planning, but we do know that he has been infusing himself with deifyre, for what end we remain unsure. This boy," he pointed at Kyle, "has been the one to provide most of what we know about Azrath thus far." Kyle stared at the floor, discomfited by the sudden attention, most of it still hostile.

"He shouldn't be here," one of the Ne'feri muttered. "He's Azura."

Micah's eyes held those of the one who'd spoken. "Do not judge him because you believe him to be Azura, Gaemus. You of all people should know that being Azura does not define who you are." Gaemus's gaze darted to Sam, and he flushed.

Micah continued. "We do not know what Azrath intends to do, but he is in league with the Demon Lord Ra'al. Our guess is that he intends to open a portal, where and when we do not know. Since Sam can still detect Azrath's presence in the Mortal Realm, Azrath has taken his boy as insurance. Once Azrath opens the portal, Sam will be able to find it and him."

"How do we know for sure that he has the boy, that it's not some ruse?" one of the Ne'feri asked.

Sophia's voice rose. "Serjana, my daughter, found a portal in my son's room leading to the nether-realm. She confronted the Ifrit there and they told her that Nate was taken to coerce

Sam." Sera felt every eye in the room settle on her, and she shifted uncomfortably. Despite her newfound powers, she was still uneasy with all the attention. "There's something else you need to know," Sophia said. Her eyes flitted to Sam, her voice wavering. "Sera . . . "

Sera stood and swallowed, drawing Sita's consciousness forward. "Mom, it's all right," she said reassuringly to her mother. "I've got it." Sera faced the group, noticing that Maeve and the other two warrior gods had moved to stand behind her. She cleared her throat. "Most of you know me as Sera Caelum, but there was a time when I was also known as Sita." She heard the stifled gasps and saw the shocked looks on most of the faces in the room. Her father had half risen off the sofa, his face stricken.

"As most of you know, Sita was a deity, an incarnation of the goddess Lakshmi, and the wife of Rama, who lived many years ago but who chose to return to the Mortal Realm in death. She decided to come back in this form as it was time for her to return to the world, and to Illysia. The world as we know it, all the realms, are on the brink of complete destruction. In Illysia, they called it the *KaliYura*, a time when mankind will face its darkest hour. Such has been written."

She took a breath. "What Azrath plans to do is anyone's best guess. One thing we do know is that it will be far worse than summoning the Rakshasa demon as he did seventeen years ago, the one which my father gave his life and his immortality to subdue. I heard Azrath myself plotting with Ra'al in Xibalba—"

Several of the people in the room shot to their feet in hostile disbelief.

"But that's not possible!" someone hissed.

"You cannot survive the Dark Realms!" cried another.

"What game is this?"

The Yoddha behind her stiffened. Sera held up a hand, but the noise in the room rose to deafening proportions. Everyone seemed to be shouting at the same time.

Sera took a deep breath. She knew what she had to do. She had to show them what she was . . . *who* she was.

Deifyre blazed into the room, surrounding her with bright red light as her energy arced from her back and over her arms in a swirl of gold and copper flames. The sigils on each of her arms flared red and white, as Mehndi tendrils curled like vines along each arm, coiling up her neck and the sides of her face until they met and wound together at her forehead. A thin sword extended from each hand, one shrouded in silvery white flames, the other blood red.

Dead silence ensued.

Maybe the swords had been too much. Sera glanced at her father, then surveyed the stunned faces around her. She could feel her previous incarnations' pride and power swirling inside of her. "I am Lakshmi incarnate, goddess of Illysia and servant to the Realms. Do you question me?"

There wasn't a single sound in the room. A small smile played about Micah's lips. Even Kyle stared at her with wide eyes. Sera felt a hysterical giggle welling up at the look on his face, but quelled it immediately. She glanced over her shoulder. The three Yoddha behind her in full battle stance could have been chiseled from rock.

"This war that Azrath provokes now is but the tip of the iceberg, that I can promise you. We need to work together and gather all the help we can to stop this before it starts," Sera said quietly. "I am here to fight, but I cannot do it alone."

Micah moved to stand beside her. His face was somber as he spoke. "The Trimurtas need your help because the Protector is missing. I have hope that he is still here in this realm, but we must find him quickly. Without the protection of all three, Illysia is at risk."

"How do you know the Protector has been here?" Gaemus asked.

"I was with him," Sera said. "Last night. I told him about Azrath and he promised to return to Illysia, but he never did. Something must have happened." Sera rubbed her thumb across the sigil that Dev had told her was his, but she felt nothing. "He's not here anymore."

"He came here to find her," Micah said. "I know this because I told him who she was." He paused, his voice drained of any emotion. Sera noticed the betrayed look on her mother's face. "He was in mortal form and shaded, which is why none of us could sense him."

Out of the corner of her eye, Sera saw Kyle frown in sharp concentration at Micah's words and then his back snapped straight, as if something important occurred to him. He stared at her, his eyes bright. "I need to talk to you," he mouthed.

Sera raised an eyebrow. Couldn't he have picked a less critical time?

"Come over here," she mouthed back. He frowned but started moving along the edge of the room to her. One of the Yoddha behind her moved to block him.

"It's all right," Sera said. "Let him pass." She could feel everyone staring at them even as Micah continued speaking about their next course of action. She gestured for Kyle to go into the den just off the room they were in.

"What's going on?" she asked him once they moved, her voice loud in the quiet room. Sera noticed that Maeve had come to stand closer to the den's entrance, ever cautious.

"Did Micah say that Dev was mortal and had been shading himself?" Kyle asked in a small voice. Sera nodded. Kyle looked uncomfortable. "You know when I went over to Knightsbrook that time? Well, Dev was saying all these weird things about me not knowing who I was, so I tried to read him, you know, to sense his energy to see what he was."

"And?" Sera said.

"I didn't get anything, nothing at all. And everything has energy, right? Well, he didn't, or if he did, he was hiding it really well. I mean, he was hiding all of it."

"So, what does this have to do with Dev? Micah said he was shaded."

Kyle studied his shoes. "He wasn't shaded, Sera, because he's the Protector in avatara form. He had *no* shade."

"So, what's wrong?"

"Well, I may have mentioned that to Jude," he muttered, his face red. "At the time I couldn't understand why Jude yelled at me to get out of the car, but I think now he must have realized then what Dev was. So that means—"

"That Azrath knows . . . and so does Ra'al," Sera finished slowly.

"I'm so sorry, Sera," Kyle said, his expression fraught between jealousy toward Dev and a keen sense of yet another betrayal to Sera. He wrung his hands. "I didn't know who he was. I never would have said anything to Jude, but I was so mad that you'd been with him, and Jude just pushed all my buttons. I'm sorry. This is all my fault."

Sera squeezed his shoulder despite her sense of impending doom. "It's OK. You couldn't have known. None of us did. Thank you for telling me."

She walked to the doorway and motioned to Micah and her mother, who approached. "We have a problem. Kyle thinks that Jude may have guessed who Dev was. They were together when Kyle read Dev's energy, and Jude must have put two and two together when Kyle couldn't see anything." Kyle shot her an absurdly grateful look at her concise explanation. Sophia and Micah stared at them in mute horror.

"This is catastrophic," Micah said. "The Protector is very vulnerable in mortal form. We can only assume the worst if he has been taken."

"I can find him," Kyle said. Three pairs of eyes centered on him.

"How do you propose to do that?" Sophia asked.

"If someone did capture him, then we can assume that he won't be blocking his true form, which means I'll be able to find him. And we know that he's not going to be in Illysia, so he's either here or in Xibalba."

"But you said before you weren't able to sense anything from him. How do you know what his energy will feel like?" This time her mother's tone was dubious.

"I don't. But she does." He glanced at Sera, who was nodding in slow agreement.

"Absolutely not," Sophia said in immediate denial. "If any of the Demon Lords get their hands on her . . . "

"No, Mom, Kyle's right. I *can* help find Dev. This is the only way, and you know it. Dev comes first. If the Trimurtas are threatened in any way, then Illysia is open to attack."

"Sera—"

"No, listen. None of you can go to Xibalba. Only Kyle and I can. If Nate's there, too, we're the only ones who can help them. Mom, please, you have to trust me." Sera gripped her mother's hand tightly, but it was Micah who came to her support.

"Sophia, she's right. She and this boy are our only hope," he said. "Illysia will fall if we cannot locate the Protector, you know that."

Sophia slumped, and Micah caught her in his arms. "Micah," she whispered. "She's only a child. You've seen yourself what they do in the Dark Realms. I can't send her there. Please, I'm begging you."

"Mom, I'm almost seventeen. I'm not a child."

Micah ignored Sera's outburst, holding Sophia's face in his hands. "Sophia, your daughter is the reincarnation of a powerful goddess. *She* is a powerful goddess in her own right! If she can't help us, then no one can. Let her go. You and I both know that is what she came back for."

Sera brushed a strand of golden hair from her mother's face and stared into her gray eyes. "Mom, let me do this. Let us do this. She will protect me, you know that she will. I'm strong. There's so much of her in me, but there's so much of you, too, and Dad. She is the thread that will bind us all together. Trust in that."

Sophia hugged Sera as if her life depended on it, kissing her on both her cheeks, and hugged her again. "Go then." Her voice broke. "I love you."

"Love you too, Mom."

Sera watched as her mother rose and made her way back to her father. She looked like she'd aged fifty years just in the last ten minutes, and that was saying a lot for someone who was immortal.

With a sigh, she turned to Kyle. "Thanks for going with me."

"I owe it to Dev for getting him into this mess," Kyle said. "And to you."

"Kyle," Sera said quietly. "I need to know that I can trust you, that you're with me all the way."

"You can trust me, Ser. I'm with you."

Although Kyle's words seemed sincere, a hollow feeling in her stomach was spreading by the second. What would Xibalba do to him, considering the precarious edge he was already teetering on? Was he strong enough to suppress its pull?

Or would the darkest part of him undermine his best intentions?

THE DARK REALMS

T hey'd driven north to the secluded Rye Lake near the
Kensico reservoir, and it was freezing. The remote area
had been chosen so that no one would be in danger should
something be unleashed by the portal. Sera looked at her parents and the four warriors with them. They believed in her,
believed that she could somehow find the Protector and Nate.
Sera glanced at the forest around them. Some of the Ne'feri
were on silent guard there. Her gaze met her mother's once
more and she felt a strange sorrow at the helplessness she
saw looking back at her. Sophia would have wanted nothing
more than to take her place, but as Sanrak, she would not be
able to survive long in Xibalba, not even in the first dimension. And the last place Sera had seen Azrath had been in the
seventh. A shiver that had nothing to do with the cold ran up
her spine.

Sophia had given Sera a silver pendant on a leather
string with a marking similar to the one on her left palm,
only without a shield and with three wings layered over one
another.

"This is my symbol. If you find Nate, give it to him. It will
protect him with my strength," she'd said, her voice breaking
as she'd said Nate's name.

"I will," Sera had promised. "I'll find Dev, too. And we'll come right back, I promise." Sera smiled at her mother and took a deep breath.

"Here goes," she told Kyle. *"Darwaaza Xibalba."* She raised her right arm, removing the black glove, and drew the sigil from her palm in the air.

A hot hiss of steam erupted as the very fabric of the air tore open. The forked mark glowed red. Sera held her palm up toward it and watched as its edges flamed into a fiery burst, curling outward into a large circular shape—a shimmering red vertical body of water. She pulled her arm slowly back and stared at the glowing portal.

The doorway to hell.

With a deep breath, Sera grasped Kyle's hand with her gloved hand, her face determined despite the tremor in her voice. "This is it. Are you ready?"

Kyle checked his commando-style combat belt armed with an array of weapons—including some silver darts, several knives, a canteen, and a gun—and nodded. Sera met his gaze and said, "Where'd you get that gun?"

"Not all of us have magical flaming swords," Kyle said. "It's Carla's, and I soaked the bullets and all the rest of the ammo in holy water." He patted the canteen. "I even have a little extra for good measure."

"Holy water? Does that work?"

"Faith can destroy many things—demons are one of them," Kyle said.

Sera frowned. "Wouldn't that have to be your own faith, not someone else's?"

"We are fighting for the human race so I'd say their faith is pretty important," he pointed out. "And it can't hurt, but if it doesn't work, I have this."

Kyle pulled out a thick blade with jagged edges from a sheath on his back. It looked like black volcanic glass with a hot red spine traveling its length. Its tip angled into a reverse V at the end.

Sera felt a shudder run through her body. The weapon was clearly evil. She could feel the malevolence radiating from it. Sera eyed Kyle warily.

"Where'd you get that?"

"Jude left it in the car. It's Azrath's. They used it to . . . never mind. It's an Azura weapon, which means I can probably use it against demons." He swung once with the blade slashing a low arc from left to right. Sera frowned at the practiced ease with which Kyle wielded the weapon and the way it seemed weightless in his hands. Something about it bothered her, but she shrugged it off.

"Just keep that thing away from me," she said. "Let's go."

Sera pulled the shade that she'd crafted to conceal her goddess side closer. Without a backward glance, she pulled Kyle through the portal, feeling the familiar sucking sensation, and turning at the last minute to lock eyes with her father. She frowned. He was shouting her name and running at her, holding his ribs with one arm. He had a look of shock and betrayal on his face, his mouth open and hand outstretched toward her. He was looking at Kyle's blade, at Kyle, and then her.

And then they were gone as the darkness swallowed them.

The portal spat them out, and they crashed into each other in the cramped, lightless space. Sera lay on top of Kyle and she froze, suddenly very aware of the feel of his entire body against hers. She pushed off of him immediately, only to have her head crack into the low ceiling. She cursed and banged her head into his.

"Ouch!" Kyle muttered.

"Sorry," she whispered, edging her body nearer to one side of the small cave.

"Where are we?" He was so close she could feel his breath against her cheek.

"I think it's the same nekomata's cave from last time. Why would my portal bring me here?" she wondered aloud. Kyle shifted and his mouth grazed her cheek.

"Sorry," he murmured against it.

Sera started inching out of the cave as she'd done the last time. She heard Kyle following her. It would be a much tighter fit for him. She reached the same cave and tunnel as before and hopped into it. Kyle slid out beside her.

"It's this way," she said. "That's where I found Azrath and Ra'al."

They walked farther down the hallway, not encountering a single creature. The silence was eerie—graveyard eerie—and Sera had the distinct sensation of being watched even though they seemed completely alone.

It felt like they'd been walking for a few miles, the tunnel long and unending. Sera glanced at her watch and frowned. It had apparently stopped once they'd gone through the portal.

"Wait a minute, something feels wrong," she said. "I didn't walk this far last time." She glanced around her at the dark rock walls and the black earth beneath her feet. "Something's not right. This isn't the way."

"Sera, I've heard a lot about Xibalba," Kyle warned uneasily. "It's never the same. It changes constantly because it's a living place that thrives on fear and confusion."

"But it all looks the same. It even feels the same." Sera's eyes narrowed and she looked back the way they'd come. "I think we're being watched."

Kyle glanced around. "That wouldn't surprise me."

Something that sounded like laughter snaked through the corridor. The ground beneath their feet rumbled and the sound of something unimaginable grew, coming *toward* them.

"Run!" Sera screamed.

Kyle sprinted after her until they came, breathless, to a large open cavern holding a circular table. They stood on a ledge with a thin railing at its edge. There was no way to go but down. The rumbling behind them grew louder. They both turned and squinted into the darkness of the tunnel. It looked like the walls of the hallway were caving in.

"What the hell *is* that?" Kyle said.

"Demons, a lot of them." Sera glanced behind her. The table was about ten feet down. Kyle stared at her and nodded once.

"Jump!" he shouted. He was over the railing before she could think twice and she heard him thud onto the table below. "Sera, MOVE!"

She held her breath and kicked her legs over the railing, jumping just as wind rushed at her back. She bent her knees as her legs hit the table, absorbing most of the impact, and crouched, looking over her shoulder at the hordes of whatever demonic creatures would be descending on top of them. But there was nothing—not even a sound—just phantom wind against her face.

Her heartbeat was erratic, pounding hard in her chest as her lungs burned from the adrenaline. "What the f—"

"They're gone," Kyle said.

Sera jumped off the table and looked around the room, gesturing toward a black steel door at the far end. It seemed too convenient, too obvious. Instead, she looked around the cavern and saw an outcropping of rock that didn't look quite the same as the rest of the room. Sure enough, the rock overlapped another section of wall in the room, hiding a narrow passageway. It was all but invisible unless someone was standing right next to it or knew where it was. She glanced at Kyle and he nodded.

"This way," Kyle said, walking toward it. Following Dev's faint trail, they moved into the next room. It was one that she didn't recognize, yet it also felt strangely familiar. Faded, horrific murals adorned the white walls, pictures of demons with horns and scales and ugly red eyes tearing at each other flowed into others showing human sacrifices tied to stakes and begging for mercy. The last mural nearest an arched doorway showed a huge red demon with curled tusks and black horns sitting on a throne and staring down upon the grotesque scene as other demons cavorted and flung themselves at his cloven feet.

She caught up with Kyle, who stood hypnotized by the mural. "What's the matter?" she asked him. "Why'd you stop?"

"Can't you see it?" Kyle said, his eyes wild. "Look at it. Look at the *face*."

She complied and froze, ice crawling into her veins. "It has—"

"—my face."

Sera studied the mural. The beast was grotesque, but the features were definitely Kyle's, there was no doubt of that. She felt something uncoil in her stomach as she stared at the mural.

"It's some other trick of this place," she said slowly. "Don't look at it, Kyle. Stay focused. We need to find Dev." When he didn't budge, Sera punched him in the shoulder, trying to force him out of his trance. "Focus!" she hissed. "I need you."

Slow laughter drew their attention. "Hello, again," a cheerful girlish voice said. Sera recognized its owner as the dark-headed demon she'd seen the last time—the daughter of Ra'al. She smiled the same Cheshire cat smile, displaying several rows of needle-sharp fangs as she sauntered toward them.

"Father is not pleased with you," she told Sera, her scales reflecting light from an unknown source. "Someone killed Aziz. He was the oldest nekomata ever. Did you do it?" Sera remained silent. "He said I should watch you, but look at you, you're nothing but a silly girl."

She glanced at Kyle. "Oh, a *boy*!" Her voice turned gleeful and she clapped her hands in delight. She stepped toward him, and Sera raised her hand in warning. She'd seen what that demon did to boys. She *ate* them.

"Back off," she said warningly and moved closer to Kyle.

"Or what?" the girl taunted. "You're my guest here. It's the only reason you haven't died yet. Father will be back soon, but for now, I'm the one in charge."

"Where is Ra'al?" Sera asked. The girl's yellow eyes fastened on her, and then she smiled, flicking her head as if trying to get rid of a bothersome gnat.

"With Uncle Az. They've been spending an awful lot of time together," she added slyly.

"But Ra'al can't leave this dimension," Sera blurted.

"You'd be surprised." Her voice sounded peevish, as if she'd been left out of something exciting that she wasn't too happy about. "I'm done with you. I want him. He looks *yummy!*" she nodded at Kyle, who remained mute. He was staring at her with a strange mixture of disgust and fascination. The demon girl was voluptuous—and deadly. Sera punched him again.

"Good thing I don't want you," Kyle choked out, moving until he was beside Sera. The demon's face twisted into a grotesque snarl.

"Fine, have it your way, then." She waved her hand and scores of demons poured from every corner of the room like a dark wave.

"Kyle!" Sera screamed. "Watch out." She tried to conjure her deifyre, but nothing happened. She tried again, but didn't feel anything sparking inside her.

Kyle pulled the gun from his belt and shot into the oncoming black horde. Twelve of them fell before he snapped out the cartridge. Sera wondered where he'd learned to shoot, until a flying demon with a red beak and red talons leapt at her. She kicked it in the stomach and turned to find another of the same beast attacking from the left. Kyle shot at it wildly and tossed the empty gun to the ground.

"The holy water kills them, but they're still coming," he gasped. "I don't have many of these left." He pulled the remaining darts from his belt and hurled them into the throng of demons. "What's wrong?" he asked noticing her face.

"It doesn't work." At his expression, she said, "Me, the deifyre."

"Does Sita know why?" he said, plunging a short knife into a demon's eye. The thing sputtered and died. "In her memories, I mean?"

"No, there's nothing," Sera said. She kicked another demon in the head and swung back toward Kyle. "Probably has to do with being the offspring of a Sanrak and an Azura Lord."

"So, that's good, right?" Kyle said. "If anything, you should be more powerful than she ever was." Six more demons dropped as he darted the last of the holy-water spikes into the throng.

Sera tried again, frustrated. "It's still not working."

Kyle kicked a creature that looked like half-monkey, half-fish and crushed it under his boot. "Sera, look to your Azura side. You're in Xibalba, maybe that's why. Whatever it is, figure it out. Fast."

Sera cursed as the simplicity of Kyle's answer pierced through her—she'd been trying to call upon divine energy in hell. Releasing her shade, she touched the forked rune on her right palm and summoned its reverse into her. She gasped as her back arched. It was like being in the middle of a raging forest fire, wind and flames licking through her.

Hellfyre.

The room burst into dark red light as Sera's weapons extended from her hands like liquid flame. The hellfyre was blood red, nothing like the intertwined colors of gold, orange, and pink that marked her deifyre in the Mortal Realm.

She swung the fire swords forward without thinking, the blades cleaving through the oncoming wave of demons like softened butter. She swung again and again, her eyes filled with blood and rage. A path cleared. Sera felt a sense of satisfaction as she saw the demon girl's astonished expression through the remaining horde of hissing and growling bodies.

The demon girl snarled, extending three rows of claws, and soared toward her.

Sera deflected her attack easily. The girl spun back, her body lithe like a jungle cat, her claws barely missing Sera's exposed shoulder, but wrapping themselves in Sera's hair. The girl grinned, her teeth horrific and lethal, and yanked. Sera felt her head jerk back just as she jumped again. Her entire scalp shrieked from the pain of handfuls of hair being ripped out.

The demon's tail snaked out, caught Sera in the legs, and she went down, the air knocked out of her. She gasped, her weapons fading as she struggled for breath. The demon girl was on top of her in seconds, claws and teeth inches from her throat.

"Who are you?" she hissed at Sera. "Tell me before you die."

"Screw you," Sera spat.

A long fetid tongue snaked out to lick Sera's face and the demon giggled. "That'll be my pleasure."

Her claws extended and Sera felt sharp pressure slashing into her skin, but suddenly, the demon went crashing into the nearest wall. Kyle had knocked the flat of the black blade into her head, just enough to stun her.

"Thanks," Sera mumbled, her hand touching her neck. She stood woozily, still gasping for breath, and stared into the now silent room. There wasn't a demon left. "Nice work," she told Kyle.

They approached the girl together, and Sera summoned back her twin fiery swords, which flared red at her command. She placed one of the blades at the demon's throat and nudged her with her boot.

"Wake up! Where's Nate? The blond boy?" The demon stirred, opening one eye and then the other. Her reptilian skin sizzled where Sera's blade seared it.

"He'sss not here," she hissed, blood pooling around her black lips. "Azsss . . . "

"Not here in Xibalba or not here in this hell dimension?" Kyle asked.

The demon flashed a bloody grin, her yellow eyes full of shiny malice. "Who knowsss? Happy huntingsss," she taunted, black blood dripping down her face.

"She's not going to tell us," Sera said. She turned away in sudden frustration, the fyre winking out, and massaged her aching head. The demon had almost ripped off her scalp. What was with girls always going for the hair in a fight? She grimaced and quickly tied the remaining bulk into a thick braid.

Kyle stared at the demon with morbid interest. It stared back, insolent.

"What are you looking at, half-breed?" She saw his look. "Oh, I know what you are, I can smell it. You think you're better than I am? Inside, we're the same."

"I'm looking at a dead demon," Kyle retorted grimly.

"I am not afraid to die. Ra'al will only bring me back. I am his favorite."

"I don't doubt that, but dying will still hurt," Kyle said. "Where's the boy? Where's the Protector?"

She gave a pained laugh. "Your weak human weapons cannot hurt me as they have the lesser demons. I am Alis, daughter of Ra'al."

Without warning, the demon swung her right arm toward Sera's unprotected back, her claws bared and poison-barbed. Kyle didn't hesitate, swinging the black blade from his bag in a swift movement, over his head and around the side.

"This one can," he cried.

The demon's eyes widened just as the blade severed her arm and ripped into her upper thigh, black blood and green ichor spraying everywhere. She screamed in agony, clutching her stump of an arm and crawled backward. Blood dribbled from her mouth.

"Mor . . . das," she gurgled, staring at the sword.

"What did you say?" Sera said, but the demon ignored her, staring at Kyle, this time with some sort of strange recognition. "Pri . . . sss," she gurgled, and choked, her body arching with a painful spasm, her arm raised toward him. Kyle stepped back, his eyes narrowed. And then the demon died, her body fizzling like a piece of over-charred meat on a spit.

"Seriously, what is this price that these demons want from you?" Sera said. "And what is that *smell*?" The odor of something putrid rose in the air.

"Dead demons," Kyle said dryly. "Let's get out of here."

HELL AND
MORE HELL

᚛᚜

They were in another cavern that seemed roofless, as if it just disappeared into darkness, and the air was warm and clingy. Kyle felt the sweat pooling on his forehead and swiped it away with his sleeve. They'd already shed most of their outer layers, and even in shorts, it was boiling as they inched forward.

"Where is all this heat coming from?" Kyle said.

"Ah, I hate to be the one to tell you but um, hell is hot," Sera said. "I think those pockets of heat are from those tunnels over there." They both looked to the three black holes carved in the side of the room.

Kyle glanced around. "There's no exit in here, did you notice?"

"Hang on a sec—" She broke off near one of the steam-filled tunnels and knelt to the floor. Kyle rushed to her side as she dug something from the ground with her fingernails.

"What is it?"

"A gold ring," Sera said, clutching the item in her hand. "It's Dev's, I know it." She stared around the cavern, as if reconsidering Kyle's earlier words. "You're right, there are no exits. So it's one of these, then," she said, indicating the three caves.

"You've got to be kidding."

She stared at him. "I wish I was." She extended a glove-less hand to him. "See if you can get a sense of where he was taken." Kyle repeated the process of trying to detect Dev's energy, frowning in concentration.

"That one," he said pointing to the middle cave. They stared at it. It was the smallest and hottest of the three. "Great," he sighed. "I'm claustrophobic, did I mention that?"

"Stop complaining. The quicker we get in there, the quicker we get out."

"*If* we get out," Kyle muttered. He stared up into the darkness. He couldn't shake the feeling that something was watching them, something way above where they couldn't see. He half expected an army of demon-bats to swoop down so placed his hand on his canteen of holy water just in case. Sera had already started to crawl into the tunnel. She'd removed her outer Henley and wrapped it around her head to protect it against any sharp edges. "Sera, wait. Maybe I should go first."

"No," he heard her say. "I have hellfyre for light."

"Hellfyre?"

"Well, it's definitely not deifyre," Sera said. "Stay close."

Kyle removed his own shirt as Sera had done and twisted the sheath of his sword so that it hung under his left arm at his side. He crawled in behind her on his hands and knees, following her muted red light. The sensation of the walls pressing in around his back made him gulp.

"You think there are any demons in here?" Kyle asked. Just as he said it, he felt something wet slide along his leg and he hoped fervently that it was only condensation from the heat.

"It's widening up a bit," Sera said, and Kyle saw her peering at the side of the wall. Her mouth tightened on a swift, indrawn breath.

"What's the matter?"

"Nothing," she said quickly. "Just follow me and move fast. Don't stop." After a few more feet, Kyle noticed that she was able to stand hunched over. She was moving fast now that she was off her hands and knees, and Kyle struggled to keep up.

"Sera, wait!" Something stung his face, and he swatted it away. He felt the same thing on his neck and twisted so hard that his forehead scraped a rocky edge. He felt a warm trickle and something fastened on to it, sucking like a leech. He grasped it and ripped it off, tugging at his belt for the grill lighter he'd stuck into it at the last minute. He pressed the trigger and blinked as yellow flame lit the darkness.

He was holding a thin snakelike creature. It wriggled in his hand, struggling to get back to the blood on his forehead. He crushed it, then felt another and another attach to his skin. He ripped them off and held the flame to the wall of the cave. It was covered in hundreds of the leeches, each of them straining toward him, hungry.

His gasp blew out his light and he scrabbled toward Sera, bile in his throat, clawing at the ones that had fastened to his exposed skin. A sudden scream had him almost running as the cave widened.

"Kyle, watch out!"

He skidded to a halt just in time, his heart thudding at the sight of Sera hanging off the edge of a short ledge that had dropped off suddenly, her fingers barely holding on as her body dangled in open space. The bottom had crumbled where she'd been standing, and he shifted to the side of it, flinging himself to the ground just as her fingertips lost their hold.

"Gotcha!" He gripped her wrists above the gloves and she gripped him back. Kyle dug the toe of his boot behind a rock, his arms almost out of their sockets at the weight pulling them over the edge. A scream behind him made him jerk around, only to see something black soaring above them like some kind of huge demon-raptor. All he could see was teeth. It circled lower.

"We don't have much time. Listen carefully, Sera, pull yourself up, and grab hold," he told her, gritting his teeth as he shimmied his body back against the jagged stone ground. He groaned with effort as he pulled her up and over the ledge.

The minute she rolled to safety, Kyle was on his feet, the black blade in his hand pointed toward the gigantic creature descending to them, all razor fangs and fury. He swung and it dove beneath them, the wind off its wings blasting them up against the side of the wall. "Sera! Hellfyre. Now!"

She stood, still shaky, her fiery swords flaming from both hands just as the huge raptor attacked. Kyle hacked at one moss-green wing and Sera at its exposed underbelly. Yellow bile spurted from the creature's mouth and bubbled into the ground at her feet. "Acid! Don't let it get on you, Kyle," she shouted. "It spits like a camel."

"Great. Dragon-camels in hell," Kyle muttered, dodging the stream that came his way as he sliced a new gash on its wing. The demon's scream was horrible, echoing off the walls of the cavern. "Sera, you can make anything from hellfire, right? Like other weapons?" She stared at him in confusion. "Arro—" he shouted.

He'd barely gotten the word out when the creature's tail hit him square in the head, sending him careening into the solid rock wall. He slid against it and crumpled to the ground near the edge where Sera had gone over, and as he looked over the lip, his stomach sank. The abyss was moving. It was a sea of black writhing bodies—a sea of *rising* writhing bodies!

"Sera, we have to get out of here," he shouted over his shoulder. "Something big and ugly is coming up the bottom of the abyss."

Kyle glanced back at the cave they'd come through and it was full to the brim with the leech-like demons, the scent of fresh human blood drawing them out. He shuddered, his blood curdling at the thought of those things sucking the life out of him.

He twisted and saw Sera approaching the raptor demon that had landed on the ledge between them, gripping the wall vertically with its clawed hind legs. Kyle blinked, not believing what he actually saw, but when he looked again she was still flameless and moving closer to the demon, palm outstretched, until he couldn't see her behind the thing's neck. A soundless scream parted his lips. What was she *doing*?

"Sera!" he finally yelled.

Either she didn't hear him or she chose not to. He pulled himself to his feet, grimacing as stars blinded his vision and pain throbbed in his skull. He inched toward them just as Sera came back into his line of sight. She moved directly under the demon's neck between its body and the rock wall, her right palm sliding against its hide. Even where he stood, Kyle could see the rune glowing through her skin, her power consummate.

"Sera?" She nodded for him to approach.

"Slowly," she said softly, her palm still on the demon's side.

As Kyle got closer, he realized just how big the raptor demon was. Its wingspan was near forty feet long, those wings now folded back against its body. It was the color of green muck and was striped with black markings. Six spikes protruded from its head, with two on the underside of it. It had a long sharp beak with rows of black teeth and a black soulless eye that saw right through him. It snapped its beak when he was within a few feet of Sera, and he jumped.

"It's OK," she soothed it, rubbing her palm in circles. "He's . . . my servant."

Kyle raised an eyebrow and quelled a disbelieving snort. If Sera's new pet could get them out of the rising tide of dead things coming toward them, he'd be its number one fan. Sera looked at him, a half-smile curving her lips.

"He doesn't trust you."

Kyle kept his voice low and nonthreatening. "Now that's just hilarious. A demon with trust issues." He stepped closer. "What else does it say?"

"He says that you are a boy playing with weapons you don't understand. He says the sword's name is Mordas." Her voice grew quiet. "And he says that you will betray me."

"And you believe that? The words of a demon in hell?" His rising tone earned him another snap from the demon, one so close to his head that he jumped back.

"The girl demon called the sword by the same name, remember?"

"I'm not talking about that, I'm talking about it saying I will betray you!" Kyle said heatedly. "Sera, can't you see it's trying to come between us? We've proven already that we're strong together, so now they want us apart. You have to see that."

She smiled again, but didn't reply to him. Her behavior confused him. "Come, Izei will take us to the top." She climbed on the bend of its hind leg and hoisted herself onto its shoulders.

"Sera—"

"We don't have a choice, Kyle. We can't go back, and at some point I need to trust who I am, and that even here, there are beasts and demons who will be loyal to me." She patted the raptor demon's neck. "As Izei is."

"How can you be sure?"

"Because he's marked with my rune," Sera said. The demon turned its face and Kyle saw the same sigil Sera had on her palm etched into its first horned spike. Its other eye was blood red, and he felt another tremor pass through him.

"What if it's a trick?" he said, still reluctant to get on behind her.

"Then we die," Sera snapped, exasperated. "Either we die here with that thing coming up from the abyss, or we die this way. Get on!"

"OK, already," Kyle said as he climbed on behind her. "You don't have to be bossy just because you're the queen of hell or something." The touch of the demon's hide was not cold and scaly, as he'd expected. It was almost hot to the touch and felt like lizard skin. He held Sera around the waist. He looked down as the demon circled slowly up the cavern until the ledge where they'd stood disappeared from view, and still they kept climbing. There was no sign of anything above them except more darkness.

Kyle stared at the walls, which were covered in small grotto-like caves. He squinted, disbelieving. "Are those *people* crawling up the walls?"

Sera followed his stare and shook her head. "Not all of them. Izei says they're damned to this pit. When they try to escape, he casts them back."

Kyle felt a shudder surge through him. "Where's it taking us?"

"To the top of this abyss, where Ra'al and Azrath are . . . where Dev is."

Kyle felt the hairs on the back of his neck rise and he leaned forward, pressing into Sera's back. "What if it's a trap?" he whispered into her ear.

"I trust Izei," she said, and Kyle wanted to kick her for being so obtuse. He gnashed his teeth in frustration but remained silent until he felt the beat of the demon's wings start to slow.

After what seemed like eons, the demon rose into a black cavern with shiny lights mimicking a starry night sky and alighted. They dismounted, and Sera thanked the beast and then released it. Kyle's eyes narrowed as the demon-raptor dove off the edge, its blood-red eye lancing into him, and he could have sworn a smile distorted its mouth as it sped past, hurtling down into the pit below. Kyle rounded on Sera. "Seriously, what is *wrong* with you?" he hissed.

She returned his gaze calmly. "What would you have had me do, Kyle? Say that I didn't trust a beast *while* riding it thousands of feet above an endless abyss?"

He stared at her, mute. "I guess you have a point."

"Of course I didn't trust it, but we didn't have much of a choice back there. I recognized the rune that I saw by chance and compelled it to obey me. Izei is an overlord demon of this particular pit. He's very strong and very smart. He knew exactly who we were and that we'd fought Alis. Information spreads faster than wildfire here."

"So, does that mean that Ra'al knows we are here?"

"You can bet on it."

"What's the plan?"

Sera shook her head, momentary panic darting through her eyes. "I don't really have one. Find Dev and Nate, portal out. I'm not sure we can do much more than that."

"But if he knows we're coming, won't Dev be heavily guarded, especially if they know he's Trimurtas?" Kyle guessed that the demons were toying with them, especially if they already knew who they were and why they had come. It seemed more certain that they were being drawn into some kind of elaborate trap.

Sera sighed, shaking her head. "You're probably right, but I don't see that we have any choice. The minute we stepped foot here, the reigning Demon Lord knew it."

"But they don't know that you're Sita, so we have *some* advantage, right?"

Her lips twisted in a wry grimace. "Even if they don't, which I'm not sure about, they know who *you* are and about that gift of yours. We have to assume that whatever Azrath knows, Ra'al knows."

Kyle stared at her. "We're going to die, aren't we?"

She couldn't help but laugh at his deadpan expression. "Come on, a little optimism, please. For all we know, Dev could be in a room by himself with no demon guards, just waiting for us to spring him."

"Or, we could die."

She chucked him in the shoulder and walked toward the center of the huge cavern. For such a large open place, it smelled musty and dark, like a hot attic. Kyle followed her to the back of the room, staring at the fake stars.

"Can you see the patterns?" he whispered. Sera turned and shook her head. "They're like pictures, like constellations, only demonic ones. Just like the last room. Can't you see them?"

Sera narrowed her eyes. "I don't see anything. They just look like white dots to me." She moved back to where she'd been standing. "There's a door here. I think we should check to see if Dev's beyond it."

Kyle felt woozy, his blood thudding in his ears as the stars above started to blur and the floor felt as if it was spinning. He wanted to lie down and let it all embrace him, to close his eyes just for a minute and savor the feeling of power in this room.

"Kyle? Kyle!" Sera slapped his face and he felt his eyes move thickly to hers. "What's wrong?"

He gazed into the constructed space above them. "Maybe my mother was right. I do belong here. I haven't felt like I belonged anywhere ever, and now suddenly. . . " He trailed off.

"Suddenly what, Kyle?" Sera grabbed his shoulders and shook him roughly.

He stared at her as if he was seeing her for the first time, her features blooming into sharp focus. "I belong."

"No." She shook him again. "Look at me." His felt his eyes roll in the back of his head, something sucking him back down into that place where he felt good, comfortable. It filled every part of him with power—the darkness he'd been suffocating for months sucked it in like a starving creature. He inhaled deeply, clenching his fingers into fists.

Sera stared at him with an uneasy expression on her face. "Kyle. It's this place doing that. It's all a trick, a mind game. You don't belong here."

"And you do?" His words were softly spoken and he knew they shot her to the core. "Sita? Rama's *goddess*?"

"Yes, I mean, no. Not me, *Sera*, and not you." She stared at him. "Kyle, please. Snap out of it! I need you."

"You only need me to find Dev, the love of your life. And then I'll have nothing, so what's the point? I've just been deluding myself that you ever felt anything for me."

"No," she said, "that's Xibalba talking. You know that *I* need you. I need my friend, my *best* friend. I need you. I—"

"Why? You don't love me," he heard himself say. "You love someone else, someone you've loved for eternity. How can I compete with that? We . . . I never had a chance."

"I do love you, Kyle," she said. "I always have. You have to believe that. I don't know what's going to happen right now, but what I feel about you isn't going to change. You are the only person I'd want by my side in Xibalba, the only one I trust to be here with me. Please believe that." Her voice grew desperate. "Kyle, please, we don't have a lot of time, and you said it yourself—they are going to try to break us apart here because we're so strong together. Trust *me*, not this place!"

Slow clapping interrupted them. They spun around. A tall thin man was walking toward them. He had long white hair and a strong aristocratic face. Kyle felt Sera tense, but he let his arms hang limply by his side, staring in silent curiosity at the stranger.

"Stay back," Sera warned.

"Welcome," the man said in a sonorous voice. He looked straight at Sera. "We didn't have a chance to meet the last time. You left quite suddenly as I recall. I am Ra'al." She frowned in disbelief and a thin smile curved the corner of his mouth. "You saw what you most wanted to see the last time we met. This form is of my own choosing. I hardly think you would want to see the very person you were here to save, now would you? What's his name again?" He tapped a long finger against his head. "Ah, yes. Lord Devendra."

"What's he talking about? Why would you see Dev?" Kyle said, and then it hit him. She'd seen Dev the last time she'd been in Xibalba when she'd seen Ra'al. Because Dev had been the one she trusted the most.

"Kyle," Sera began, her eyes glued to his. "It's not what you think. I—"

He'd never felt such hot pain knifing through him. Jealousy wound into simmering violent rage. "I'm the only one you trust?" he sneered, mocking her earlier words. "Doesn't seem that way to me."

"You know I can't control what she feels!"

"But you can control what *you* feel," Kyle snapped back venomously. "Say it, then. Tell me you don't feel anything for him. Say it!"

"Kyle," she whispered, pleading. "Time and place. Snap out of it. There's a demon *lord* not ten feet from us. Pull it together. This is no time to be jealous."

Kyle glared at her in stony silence until the thin man clapped again, the sound hollow and empty in the room.

"Wonderful," he said to Sera, then looked at Kyle. His voice shifted into something dark and guttural, one that plucked Kyle's memory. "Welcome. I'm glad to see that you have already met Prince Kalias. You've been such a good friend to return him home, haven't you?"

"Kalias?" Sera said *"Prince?"*

Kyle felt himself falling into a black bottomless abyss. Then suddenly he was back in time. Five years old and crying, standing with a knife in his hand. Terrified.

He stared at the demon, backing away, his body shaking. It couldn't be, but the voice was the same. The same voice he'd heard from his mother's mouth twelve years ago.

"No," he whispered.

Ra'al's smile was icy, sly, and terrible. "Welcome home, my son."

THE SINS OF THE FATHER

❧~❧

"Your *son*?" Sera said in disbelief. She turned her gaze toward Kyle. "So, that's what the demons were saying, the nekomata and then the demon girl. They were calling you *prince*, not price."

"I don't know what he's talking about."

"Don't you, son?" Ra'al said. "I told you that you would return here and that all would be revealed in your seventeenth year." Kyle shook his head but Ra'al continued. "I told you when you were a boy, remember?" Ra'al pointed to Kyle's back. "Why do you think those markings on your head and body changed today of all days? It is your inheritance. You are bound to me." He laughed, his lips pulling back in a sneer. "You've always known who you were, and now you've fulfilled your greatest purpose. You've brought me the perfect sacrifice."

Sacrifice?

Fear slid along Sera's spine. Kyle's tattoos *had* changed. Maeve and her mother had said he had demon blood. Had this all been some elaborate trick to get them both here? Even Izei had said that Kyle would betray her.

She edged closer to him. "Kyle, it's not true what he says, is it?" He didn't answer, his mouth opening and closing without speaking.

"That blade you wield," Ra'al continued, "Mordas, can only be claimed by a descendant of mine."

"Then you're laying because I saw others use it," Kyle said hoarsely. "The Ifrit used it to get Fyre from the Daeva."

"I gave leave to Azrath to use it for that purpose," Ra'al said. "Mordas serves me and none other. Had they tried to use it for anything but what I intended it to do, they would have failed."

"And what purpose are you talking about?" Sera shot out. Ra'al turned cold black eyes in her direction. His laugh was chilling.

"You already know, Serjana," he said, spitting out her name. "The end of the world." He laughed again. "It's no secret. Azrath will now be able to open a portal to the Mortal Realm."

Sera blanched but hid her agitation with arrogance. "I'll never let you do that. The balance must be maintained. As above, so below. You know that, Ra'al."

"And so it shall remain. Only in the new world, Azrath will rule Illysia and I shall have the rest."

"Azrath is an Azura Lord. He cannot live in Illysia, no matter what desecration he has done to his immortal form with Fyre. The wards of the Trimurtas forbid it."

He sent her a cunning look. "Not if the Trimurtas are no more."

Ra'al strode to the door at the back of the room, beckoning for them to follow him. Sera hesitated, but Kyle moved forward without hesitation. He seemed to be in some kind of trance.

"Kyle, wait. What are you doing?" she whispered. He didn't answer but rather slipped into the next chamber. Sera took a deep breath and entered behind him, almost choking.

They were inside a massive cave. Fires burned all around a huge pit of molten lava, and all manner of demons crowded the edges of it, crowing and laughing maniacally as human bodies fell into the lava. It was an image of hell from books and movies, and Sera's stomach heaved from the sheer horror of it. Then she looked up.

Dev was tied upside down to a beam suspended in the middle of the cave above the swirling pit. Sera felt tears sting her eyes and her fingers curled into fists at her side.

"Is he alive?" Sera rasped.

"More or less," Ra'al said with a sly leer.

Ra'al moved to stand on an outcropping of what looked like red marble, his bearing imposing, and began to transform into the image they'd seen on the wall in one of the earlier chambers. Black horns extended from his head and his body elongated into the heavily muscled form of a terrifying beast. His face was split by a snarl, each of his teeth fanged to sharp points, his lips black as death. The true form of the Demon Lord.

"Kalias, Son, come and take your place," he growled. He turned back to the pit, globs of lava bubbling beneath him.

Sera grabbed his arm. "Kyle, no!"

Kyle turned cold dark eyes upon her. It was a look that Sera had never seen before, one that emitted sorrow, despair, and utter hopelessness. He didn't look anything like the Kyle she knew. She hardly recognized him.

"He's right, you know," Kyle said softly. "About who I am. My deep, dark secret. I'm a monster." He glanced at the demons all around them. "I'm just like them. Maeve knew it. Your mother knew it, too. You should have let them kill me when they had the chance."

Sera shook her head fervently, her mind reeling. "No. You're nothing like them, like *him*. You don't belong here no matter what this place is telling you. This isn't you."

Kyle held her shoulders, then her face, his fingers winding in her hair. "But it is, Sera. I've known all along what I was. I was never totally honest with you even though I wanted to tell you everything. I was afraid that you would run screaming. And now look at us. We're both in hell, in Xibalba, and it's not as bad as I'd imagined it to be."

"Kyle, what you see is not real," Sera said desperately. "Demons laughing and dancing? Is that what you think this place is? It's *not*. This is a show that Ra'al has put on to make you feel otherwise. People come here to suffer for eternity." Sera gestured at the pit, her voice strangled. "Look at them! They're jumping to their deaths over and over and over. This is a place of depravity and pain and hate. Those things don't define you—they never have."

"But Ra'al said it himself. I'm bound to him. It's who I am—"

"No!" She grasped his shoulders and shook him. "I've seen who you are, Kyle Knox, and it's not this. Some stupid birthmark doesn't make you his son! Your family is in here." She tapped his heart and then hers. "I'm your family."

Kyle shook his head, stepping away from her touch, his hands dropping to his sides. "You don't know anything about me. You don't know that I went to Azrath so that I could become immortal on Earth to be with you. They . . . I . . . killed Dae . . . people to make that happen. What kind of *good* person does that? What kind of good person *kills* anyone for his own selfish greed? A demon, that's what."

"Everyone makes mistakes—"

"There's no going back from what I've done, Sera."

"Micah doesn't think so, and he was there. You tried to save yourself from here, what's so terrible about that? At least you're trying now to right that wrong."

"Micah never knew about this. He thought I was a half-breed. But I'm the son of a Demon Lord of Xibalba who possessed my mother—that changes everything. Anything human in me will die." Kyle choked out the last word.

"No, it won't," Sera shot back. "Don't give up, Kyle. You only have to give in to what Ra'al wants of your own free will. He cannot force you. You don't have to do this."

Kyle stared at her and then at Dev, who still hung motionless in the middle of the cave. "What do you care, anyway? You found Dev, so now you can go live your happily ever after."

She stood in front of him now, her tears turning into steam from the heat of the pit. "Don't you get it yet, you idiot? I don't have any happy ever after without you in it!"

Kyle raised conflicted eyes to hers. "What are you saying?" he whispered.

"I'm not saying anything I haven't said before. You just heard what you wanted to hear," she said almost screaming the last words.

"And him?" He jerked his head toward Dev's body.

"I can't change what Rama and Sita shared, Kyle. All I can tell you is what *I* feel about *you*," she snapped. A startled look flashed across Kyle's face and Sera felt a small bit of hope for the first time since they'd entered the cave room. "Are you with me, Kyle?" she asked.

She could see him fighting—see the darkness within him trying to convince him that she was deceiving him. He closed his eyes and when he opened them, Sera felt faint with relief.

Kyle swallowed. "So, what's the plan?"

Sera bit her lip, glancing at Ra'al out of the corner of her eye. "I don't have one."

"How about get Dev and portal the heck out of here?"

"And him?" She nodded to Ra'al, who was addressing his minions. "He won't let you go so easily." She glanced at Dev. "And how do you propose getting to him?"

Kyle frowned. "You have a point. Well, we know Ra'al wants me. You can attack me and we can offer a trade, me for Dev. We'll pull the old bait and switch."

"But what happens after that?" Sera stared at him, agitated. "After we get Dev? What happens to you?"

"I'll figure something out." He saw her hesitation. "Don't worry, by the time you open that portal, I'll be right behind you two."

"*Prince Kalias!*"

The chanting of Kyle's name grew louder. He and Sera walked toward where Ra'al stood, and Kyle turned to her just before joining his father on the marble outcropping. He held her hand tightly. She could see every emotion he had ever felt for her glowing in his eyes.

"Trust me," he mouthed.

Sera bit her lip, unable to say anything. She squeezed his hand. She knew that if she opened her mouth, she would start crying, and that was the last thing she needed to do just then. She waited a few steps until Kyle had reached the front of the dais before she summoned the hellfyre, drawing the eyes and ire of all the demons in the cave, including Ra'al.

"I cannot let you do this," Sera said to the Demon Lord.

The hellfyre flared brighter, swirling around her like liquid flame. Sera flexed her shoulder blades and felt the hellfire burn hotter. She held both swords in her hands like a warrior of Illysia about to march into battle. The chanting of the demons fell silent.

Ra'al nodded at two demons standing behind Sera, and she swung her weapons backward without even looking, disposing of both attackers instantly. She spun to deflect a second attack from the left, and then twisted in a fluid sequence of moves so that she stood just behind Kyle, her sword across his chest. He played his part well, freezing, his eyes widening.

"Try that again," she snarled to Ra'al, "and your *prince* dies."

A hideous laugh echoes throughout the cave. "You won't hurt him. He's your best friend, is he not? Maybe more?" Ra'al's tone was slyly mocking, almost daring her to do it, but Sera knew that it was a test. Ra'al would never sacrifice Kyle, at least not to her. His monstrous pride would never allow it.

"Try me," Sera said coolly. She lowered her blade so that the tip of it drew a fiery line along Kyle's arm. He flinched and then screamed as the fiery pain sunk deep into his muscles. "Next time, it will be his throat."

She stared at Ra'al in silence, her face an indecipherable mask, jaw clenched, and waited. "What do you want?" Ra'al's manner was indifferent. But Sera knew he was seething, she could see in the taut tendons of his face. He wanted to rip her apart.

She nodded to where Dev was hanging. "I want him."

"Ah, the Trimurtas. I wish I could, but he's not mine to give."

Sera knew he was playing games. If she was going to negotiate Dev's release and save both Kyle and herself in the process, she needed to play some games of her own.

She laughed and saw a furrow shadow his face. "That's funny. I never picked you for being Azrath's petty slave." The furrow deepened. She was getting to him. "So, is that how it works? He calls the shots and you obey like a good little demon?" She glanced around, a smile on her face. "I get it. You do all the heavy lifting down here, and he gets all the glory. I thought it would be way harder to get the best of a demon lord, especially one as powerful as you."

Ra'al slammed his fist into a chunk of marble hard enough that several shards broke loose. "Enough!" he roared. "Azrath is a fool if he thinks he has gotten the best of Ra'al. I let him believe he has the upper hand, but I am the one who holds all the power. I have him," he nodded toward where Dev hung from his post, and turned to two demons who had entered the hall bearing a large mirror-like frame. Ra'al's leer was monstrous. "And I have *him*."

Nate.

Even in the mirror, Nate's little body seemed so tiny, his blond curls a tangled mess. Sera could see that he was not conscious. Was he dead? Her body went cold at the thought. She almost felt her legs buckle despite her brave stance.

"What is that? Some kind of trick?" she snapped.

"It's a special mirror."

Ra'al grinned and it was vile. Even as she fought down a wave of dread, she saw a masked face appear in the mirror next to Nate's quiet form—one of a young boy with a head full of snakes. The recognition was swift and cold.

Dekaias, the Demon Lord of the first dimension of Xibalba.

Sera remembered how she'd seen him last—drinking the blood of a child. This time he wore a sort of mask obscuring most of his face. A slender hand slid forward in the mirror to caress Nate's head and Sera could feel the demon's desire from where she stood. Her stomach heaved and she gagged involuntarily.

"Don't you touch him!" she shrieked, eyes smarting impotently. Dekaias turned to stare at her, his eyes contemptuous, and bowed.

Ra'al licked his black lips, enjoying her horror. "Don't worry, he's safe . . . for now." The mirror winked into a gray ocean of nothing.

"Why should I trust you?" Her voice was dispassionate. "He could already be dead for all I know."

Ra'al laughed again. "You can believe what you wish. The mirror is real and the boy is not dead, just sleeping. His body would not have survived the journey here."

Sera felt her rage rise to boiling point, her right hand shaking into sharp flame. "If you've hurt him, I will—"

"You dare to threaten me?" Ra'al growled in fury.

AMALIE HOWARD

Sera felt a hot consciousness that wasn't her own invade her, and she gave in to her inner rage. Grasping Kyle by his neckline, she faced Ra'al's rage head-on, her words shaking with feeling. She could feel Kyle's shock.

"Of course I dare," her mouth mocked. "You rule here because I allow it. You think because you and Azrath have some scheme to change the balance of things that I will stand by and let you destroy everything I have built? I am Serjana, goddess of all the realms, and you forget your place, *demon*."

Sera raised her right hand to Kyle's chest. Ra'al bowed mockingly, his eyes burning. "As my lady wishes," he said. "The boy is in safe health. As for the Trimurtas, I fear that I must provoke Lady Serjana's wrath. He belongs to Azrath."

"Cease your games, Ra'al. I grow tired of them. Give me the boy and the Trimurtas in exchange for your son's life."

Ra'al chuckled. "I believe the saying is 'an eye for an eye' is it not? And it appears that you only have one eye to bargain with."

"Take Dev," Kyle whispered through his teeth.

"I can't leave Nate there," Sera whispered back, her lips barely moving. "Or you."

"I'll find Nate."

Her fingers dug into his collarbone. "How?"

"Do you trust me, Sera?"

"Yes," she whispered, despite the ugly niggling thought that she was putting her trust and her brother's safety into a boy whose demon side had gotten the better of him one too many times before. Sera stared at him, hesitating. "You promise you'll get him?"

"Yes. Get Dev out. It's what you came here to do."

Sera thought about Nate. He'd looked so peaceful, so vulnerable. She'd told him she would always protect him, and now when it mattered most, she had to leave him. But her hands were tied—she didn't have a choice. She nodded to Ra'al.

"Agreed. I'll take the Trimurtas."

"So dutiful, Lady Serjana. It's almost too easy to read you." He waved his arm. "Go, claim your prize."

"Remember your promise," she said softly to Kyle as hellfyre stormed around her body like a tornado, its fiery arms lifting her off the ground.

She sped swiftly toward Dev and hovered in front of him. She almost cried aloud. Long lines of dried blood caked his face, and there were deep cuts along his neck and shoulders as if sharp talons had hooked into his body and then dragged him. There was a raw chunk of flesh gouged out of his side. The wound was covered in writhing maggots. Sera gagged and looked away.

"Dev, it's Sera. Can you hear me?" He didn't answer. He was barely alive.

She glanced back at where Kyle stood, his face unreadable. She didn't dare look at Ra'al, but could feel the malevolence of his stare.

Sera loosened Dev's restraints one at a time and held him close, the weight of him heavier than she'd expected. His unique scent curled faintly around her, the smell of spice and marigold, and Sera almost wept.

Out of the corner of her eye, she saw Kyle shift and pull the black sword out. Ra'al said something to him, and she could see his revolted expression. She whirled and spun toward him, her pace far slower, watching as he dispatched the two demons standing next to him with a howl of fury. Three more advanced his way. Ra'al snarled, his face a mask of rage, and leapt off the rock.

"What's the matter?" she gasped, almost crashing into Kyle. Dev slumped against her side like a dead weight.

"Change of plans." Kyle swung the sword in a low arc, his body twisting fluidly as a demon with the head of a jackal spun toward them. Blood spurted from the wounds of the two demons at his feet.

"What are you doing? Are you crazy? It's us against thousands." Even as she spoke, shrieks of wrath echoed within the cavern in a thunderous deafening wave.

"You were dead no matter what, there was no way he was going to let either of you go. And we die together, right?" he shouted, gripping Dev's left arm and throwing it over his shoulder. "Move!" They scrambled back through the doorway they had come through into the room full of stars.

"What do you mean?" Sera said. "Where are we going?"

Kyle held Mordas in front of them, its blade taking on a scarlet sheen from the blood it had consumed. They edged toward a back corner of the room. "It was all a game, all of it. You're a prize, nothing more, Sera," Kyle said. "Just like me. We're getting Nate and we're getting the hell out of here. No pun intended."

"What did he say to you?"

"Later. Grab him." He leaned Dev down against Sera and jumped in front of them both, swinging Mordas with all the strength he could muster.

The demons shied back, waiting, and then the room quieted as Ra'al took center stage. He eyed his son with slitted obsidian eyes, holding a gigantic spear in one muscled forearm. He bared his teeth and roared, the sound horrific. Kyle stood his ground, hefting the sword in both hands. Ra'al noticed and laughed.

"You think you can wield my own blade against me?" he taunted, twirling the spear like a baton. "Mordas only knows one master."

"That master is me," Kyle gritted back.

"The blade only obeys a Demon Lord, Kalias." Ra'al's words were like barbs. For a second Kyle faltered, his grip going slack, but then he tightened it again.

"Is that not what I am? The son of a Demon Lord?" he shot back. He thrust the blade in a high arc, crashing into Ra'al's spear as he brought it down, and then back again on the underside. The weapons crashed again, and Sera could see the ripple of force up Kyle's arm. She'd never seen him so strong—every part of him was feeding on the dark energy surrounding them. He glanced back at her. "Portal. Now!"

Ducking to avoid the spear, which was moving at lightning speed toward his head, Kyle crouched and spun the sword toward Ra'al's chest on the diagonal, throwing his body across the floor to where Sera and Dev stood. Ra'al stared in delayed shock at the black line of blood, his lips curling in a snarl as he leaped toward Kyle.

Sera gripped Dev against her left side and drew the runes on the wall with her right palm just as Kyle crashed into them from behind, sending the three of them hurtling through the portal. The last thing she saw was Ra'al's face and the tip of his spear following behind them. Her mouth opened in a scream as she was sucked through. The portal spun shut behind them, snapping the head of the weapon mid-strike.

Looking into Ra'al's soulless black eyes was like looking into the face of death.

DEKAIAS

※

"Where are we?" Kyle gasped, standing woozily, Mordas at the ready. They were in a sumptuous room, with velvet couches and long elegant drapes across wide windows. Elaborate gold-framed paintings adorned the fabric-covered walls. It was like the inside of a chalet from the fourteenth century. He looked around and said, "We're in the first."

"Kyle. You're hurt," Sera blurted.

Kyle glanced down at the severed head of Ra'al's spear gouging into his shoulder and dug it out with Mordas's point. It stung like a hive of bees, and he gnashed his teeth. The spearhead clattered to the floor and transformed into a mound of black writhing maggots.

"What the hell *is* that?" Sera cried, as Kyle crushed them under his boot.

"Demon magic, I expect," he said, grimacing and rubbing his shoulder. Despite his accelerated healing, the wound burned and seeing the maggots only made him feel like some of them were now burrowing deep into his flesh. He rubbed his shoulder harder as if to banish the phantom sensation. Sera shot him a look, but he forced a smile to his lips. "I'm fine, don't worry about me. Practically healed already."

She stared at him, frowning. "We have to go. Ra'al can travel the hell dimensions, too. He must have known that we would come here for Nate." She checked Dev, who was still unconscious.

Kyle squatted next to her, peering at Dev's wan face. "We have a little time. Ra'al has to go through all six to get here."

Sera look startled. "What do you mean?"

"The seventh is the lowest dimension of Xibalba. Ra'al must portal through each of the other six to get here. That's probably the reason Nate's being held here. Any portal to Azrath's nether-realm could only be from the first dimension. It's the law of the Dark Realms."

"But *I* can portal in and out," Sera said.

"Those laws don't apply to you because you made them, or a past incarnation of you did, for the Trimurtas. You did it to preserve balance within Xibalba."

"How do you know all of this?"

"I . . . I don't know." Kyle felt confused. He had no idea how he knew that she had made those laws, but it was simply there in his head. Just as he'd known that they were in the first dimension. He cleared his throat and wiped Mordas's blade on a nearby drape, then tucked it into the scabbard on his back. "Let's go. Dekaias will no doubt know we are here." He glanced at Dev and hoisted him up between them. "How's he doing?"

"Not sure." They both stared at the unconscious boy between them. His clothes were ripped and discolored by blood, the gaping wounds beneath festering. His lips moved soundlessly. His brown hair was matted, his skin sallow. "I did this," Sera whispered. "I did this to him."

"Sera—"

"No, he came to the Mortal Realm for me and took this vulnerable form, for *me*."

"That was his choice, Sera. He's done this before. He knew the risks."

"And now he'll die, and Nate—" Her voice choked, her knees buckling.

"Sera, focus! Don't fall apart now!" Kyle said fiercely, staring hard into her eyes. "We are going to find Nate and get us all out of here. It'll be hard enough with him unconscious." Dev stirred, startling them both.

"Dev?" Sera said softly. He groaned, then opened his eyes, squinting against the muted purple light. "Dev, it's OK, we've got you."

"Where am I?" he murmured and reached a hand up to Sera's face. She grasped it and clasped it to her cheek, kissing his fingers.

"You're safe for now, but we're still in Xibalba." She pressed her forehead to Dev's, hugging him tightly. "I'm so glad you're alive."

Kyle looked away, unable to contain the wild rush of jealousy surging through him. He forced it back, knowing the thing inside of him would be only too happy to feed on any negativity, and he was vulnerable enough already.

"We need to move," he growled, surprised at the rough edge of his voice. He moved to the door, ignoring the troubled look Sera sent him, and peered outside. He focused his energy and expanded it into the house. Strangely, he couldn't sense a thing. "No one's in this house." Kyle walked back to where Sera knelt next to Dev. "Can you walk?" he asked Dev gruffly.

Dev pulled himself to his feet, his knees buckling at the last moment and tumbling into Kyle. Kyle grabbed Dev's arms and stared into the deep golden brown eyes that lanced right through him. In that millisecond, it was as if Dev saw everything hidden inside of him.

"Thanks," Dev gasped, straightening himself, and the moment was gone.

"Here, let me help," Sera said as she moved to support his shoulder.

"You shouldn't be here, Sera. Ra'al wants you, not me." He coughed and blood flecked his lips. "You need to leave now."

"I can't, Dev. Nate's here. I won't leave him. And *you're* here so that Azrath can challenge the power of the Trimurtas." Dev stared at her with a strained expression. "Don't talk, just conserve your strength," she told him.

The trio made their way down a wide curving marble staircase, the opulence of the lower floors matching those of the room they'd arrived in. Gold fixtures adorned everything, from the stair railings to the chandelier. It was overwhelming in an oppressive way—one that took beauty to an ugly extreme.

Kyle opened the door and dappled sunlight flooded in. It wasn't warm, just an illusion of sunlight. The long cobbled street was deserted, dark buildings flanking its sides.

"Let's go," he said, nodding to Sera and Dev. He sent his energy forward and just as quickly pulled it back as a lone figure trotted up the street to meet them. "Stay behind me," he warned and pulled Mordas out of its sheath.

A young girl about ten years old approached. Her skin was like cream, and long yellow ringlets framed a heart-shaped face with eyes the color of the sky. She wore a muslin summer dress with a wreath woven through her curls.

"My Lord Dekaias bids me to welcome you," she said in a musical voice.

"That's far enough," Kyle told her.

She smiled and Kyle could see a black gaping hole where her teeth should have been. "Whatever Prince Kalias wishes," she said bowing.

Kyle could feel Dev's stare and cringed. "Where's the boy?"

The girl let out a merry laugh. "The boy is well. Shall we?" She turned and Sera's gasp was audible. The girl's scalp had been peeled away from her skull, exposing bits of bone and flesh beneath it. Teeth marks crusted with black rings ran the length of her white neck, disappearing into the back of her dress. Kyle slid back to squeeze Sera's arm. Her face was pale, and Dev's was rigid.

"She's so . . . young," Sera whispered.

"It's a demon, Sera. What you see is not a little girl," Kyle said in a dead voice.

As if the creature had heard them, she turned and skipped back in their direction, stopping short when Kyle raised Mordas in warning.

"Vanity," she said, "has its price at any age, and beauty, after all, is only skin deep." She giggled, and Kyle caught a sour unwashed smell on her breath.

"Where are we going?" he demanded.

The demon danced forward, her grin wide and macabre. "The banquet has already started. Hurry or you'll miss it."

"Nate!" Sera gasped. Her eyes were wide, panicked. Kyle wrapped her fingers in his. "Kyle, Dekaias is evil. I've seen what he does . . . " She trailed off in horrified silence, staring at the marks on the girl's flesh.

"It doesn't hurt," the demon sang, grinning. "It's like a kiss. A demon kiss." She giggled again, a child's laugh made more sickening by its gruesome source.

"Move away," Kyle warned the demon again. He waited until she was far ahead of them then he turned to Sera and Dev. "We'll get Nate. I promised, remember? Don't worry."

"It's a trap," Dev said softly.

"I don't care. I'm not leaving Nate." Sera glared at her companions. "Or either of you. We find Nate and then I portal us out of here. Deal?"

"Kyle, you must help her to see reason," Dev urged. "They want her. We are nothing to them. They need her because of what she can do, for her ability to move between the Realms. Surely you can see that. This ploy of Dekaias's is working, because we are walking straight into it." A fit of coughing overtook him. He spat a mouthful of bright red blood to the ground.

Inside, Kyle knew Dev was right, but he couldn't say no to the pleading expression on Sera's face. "We'll fight them if we have to," he said through clenched teeth.

Dev shook his head. "This isn't about you and me, Kyle," he said.

"No, you're right. It's about her."

They followed the demon to the end of the road and up a grassy knoll covered with wildflowers. The scene appeared idyllic, but Kyle knew that it was an elaborate farce. He could smell something ugly beneath the mask of beauty, something that reeked and whispered of death and decay.

Sera scrambled ahead of them, following the demon, who had already disappeared over the top of the hill.

"Sera, no. Wait." Kyle sprinted up the hill, Dev limping behind them, and almost crashed into her.

What lay before them was something out of a fairytale. All manner of creatures danced on the impossibly green grass around a circular stone structure. An endless ocean stretched behind them, its white curling waves crashing against the rocks beyond the clearing.

"Do you see Nate?" Sera gasped, breathless.

Kyle looked and saw Nate's blond head laying on a stone tablet in the middle of the circle with Dekaias sitting on a velvet chaise to his left. He was attended to by what looked like golden cherubs. "Yes, he's just over there."

Sera started down the hill, but Dev stalled her descent, a hand on her arm. "Sera, wait. You can't just waltz down there. There are hundreds of demons. Don't be seduced by what seems like a harmless garden. Don't forget for one second where we are. We are in the Dark Realms."

Her body shook beneath his fingers and her eyes were like chips of ice. "Every second we wait," she hissed, "that monster gets one inch closer to my brother." She removed Dev's fingers from her arm. "You know what I am capable of, don't you, Devendra?" Dev's eyes widened at her words.

"Sera, Dev's right—" Kyle began, hand outstretched. She glared at him and let his hand fall. He'd never seen such a look on her face, not even when she'd been her angriest. It was a cold rage, almost inhuman. But he recognized it, too, deep inside himself. His body twitched again, the heat inside like a rising tide. He took a deep breath, shoving it back.

Kyle pulled out twin silver blades from his boot and handed them to Dev. "It's not much, I know, but it's all I've got. These probably won't kill them, but it'll keep them away for a while if any get too close." Dev nodded in thanks.

Flanking Sera, they walked down the hill, demons clearing a path around them, and then closing in behind as they got nearer to the stones. A line of demons blocked their entry to where Nate lay, motionless, on a stone altar. Dekaias had disappeared.

"Dekaias," Sera shouted, her tone venomous. "I will give you one chance to release my brother."

A lazy echoing laugh surrounded them. "Why so rude, my lady? Surely I am deserving of some small measure of courtesy for keeping this delicious morsel whole."

"If you've touched him in any way, I will revisit it upon you a hundred times! Show yourself, Dekaias!"

"I'm not stupid, Sera. Can I call you Sera? So much more friendly than *Lady Serjana*. I know of your power, and of course that of the young prince who so cleverly outsmarted our father." Another laugh pierced the heavy silence and Kyle trembled slightly. "He was not pleased but quite proud at the same time." The voice continued, its tone arrogant and cunning. "How are you, my brother? Strange that it's taken this long for us to meet. I do relish the moment when we are finally face to face."

"I'd do as the lady says, *brother*!" Kyle shouted back. "And maybe you'll get your wish soon enough."

Dekaias's amused chuckle filled the air. "Spoken like a true son of Ra'al. Alas, it now falls to me to restore the balance of power, now, does it not, Serjana?"

"I will not ask again, Dekaias. Release the boy," Sera gritted.

"That I cannot do until my father arrives," the Demon Lord returned unperturbed. "It won't be too long now."

The other demons crowded even closer. Most of them had been beautiful at one time, but now stood with bare remnants of their perfect faces and pieces of their bodies dismembered or left rotting.

A creature with gossamer wings and black thorns sticking out of her head lurched toward Sera, and Kyle reacted automatically, swinging Mordas across the front of the demon.

It screeched horribly as ichor poured from its severed head as it collapsed. Ten others leapt forward to eat what was left, ripping its carcass to bloody shreds. Their mouths were ringed with blood and venom, and suddenly they were all rolling forward in a giant unstoppable wave toward them.

"Protect Sera no matter the cost!" Dev screamed, hacking at the approaching demons.

Kyle watched and then turned away as Sera flared into fiery response, the hellfyre surrounding her in a blaze as her weapons spun with immortal speed. She wasn't Sera anymore; she was fury and flame embodied.

They cut through the first and second waves of demons easily. Mordas took its sacrifices hungrily and, strangely enough, with each kill Kyle felt himself growing stronger. The heat was a volcano within him now.

A boyish scream rose above the sounds of the battle. "He's so sweet. I don't know how much longer I can hold myself back," Dekaias taunted. Sera's face tightened and she turned toward the stone circle.

"Sera, no," Dev cautioned. "He's doing this on purpose. We need to stick together!"

But Sera seemed to have lost whatever hold she had on her sanity. Her hellfyre blazed brighter, expanding from her body in an incandescent circle, annihilating any demon it touched as she spun closer to the stones.

"Kyle. Don't let her get near him. Something's wrong. I can feel it," Dev screamed as he sprinted toward Sera. Kyle dove at the same time, his body crashing into Sera's.

The pain was unimaginable. He heard someone screaming as if from afar and realized that it was his own voice as her flames sliced into him, welts of charred skin bubbling up on his arms and back. He fell to the ground, his face frozen in a scream that wouldn't end. It was his voice that made Sera stop at the very second Dev slammed into her from the other side, away from Kyle.

The flames engulfed them both.

"Sera! Listen to me," Dev said, grasping her shoulders.

She wrenched away, staring past the stones in front of her where Nate lay just beyond her reach. "Try to stop me again, and I will hurt you, Dev," she said. "I need to save Nate before—"

"Your weapons cannot hurt me, Serjana," Dev said quietly. "Even in mortal form. You cannot hurt those you love." Kyle heard the words and felt like she'd slashed him again, this time from the inside and right to his heart.

She'd been able to hurt *him*.

"Just let me go, Dev. I know what I'm doing," Sera said.

"No, you don't know anything, Sera. Don't you get it yet? They want you in there. Those stones are guarded by ancient demon magic. That's why Dekaias won't come out here. It's all a trap."

"I'm Sita . . . *Lakshmi*—"

Dev's thumb slid across her face, soothing her. "Yes, but you're Serjana now. There are things they could have done that you can't yet, just like there are things you can do that they never could. There's too much at risk to let you go in there alone. Do you understand what I'm trying to tell you?" She nodded in silence. "We'll get Nate another way."

Just as he said the last words, the sound of soft sobbing reached them. "Sera, please help me," Nate's voice cried. "I'm . . . bleeding. You're my sister. Don't leave me. Please. You promised!"

And before Dev or Kyle stop her, Sera snaked out of Dev's grasp toward the sound of her brother's voice, sliding through one of the gaps in the stones, and disappeared.

"I'm sor—" Her words were cut off as the air shimmered around where she'd entered.

In the next second, everything around them vanished—the dead demons, the live demons, everything. Everything, that is, except for the two of them and the barren wasteland where they now sat.

"What the hell?" Kyle gasped. "Where'd she go?"

"Exactly where I told her not to," Dev said grimly. "She's a lot more headstrong than I remember."

"Headstrong puts it mildly," Kyle muttered. "She jumps first and thinks later." They shared a strange, if awkward moment, before Kyle fell back onto his elbows, breathing hard. "What do we do now?"

"Not entirely sure." Dev stooped beside him and eyed the blackened scars along Kyle's arms. They were healing, but slowly. Dev stared at him. "You know if you were mortal, you would have died, right? Just like if you were full demon, you probably would have died."

"It burned like nothing I've ever felt." Kyle refrained from voicing what had torn his heart into tiny unrecognizable pieces. She'd been able to hurt him even though she shouldn't be able to hurt those she loved.

Dev stared at him again, his eyes like twin gold lasers. "You know *why* she was able to hurt you, right?" Kyle shook his head and stared at the rocky ground. Sera's choice, even if she hadn't known it, was clear.

"It's the sword," he said, indicating the black blade at Kyle's side. "Every time you use that thing, every time it kills, it transfers that into you. You change a little more each time, and in the state that she was in, she couldn't protect you. The hellfyre only understood the presence of the sword and its master."

"Why are you telling me this, Dev? You could have let me believe that she didn't love me. Things would have been much easier for you."

Dev smiled. "Because it's not the truth. And why would I hurt you when it's clear that she *does* love you? What she feels for you doesn't change what exists between me and Sera. That existed far before your time and will endure long after it. Even if she loves another, I bear that person no ill will because I love her. And love is infinite, is it not?"

"Now you definitely sound like one of the Trimurtas," Kyle said wryly. "You're probably the only person who'd allow someone you love to love someone else just for the sake of love."

Dev shook his head, a sad look darkening his face. "I didn't always. I punished her for a crime she never committed. And I lost her. It was a hard lesson, one that I do not wish to repeat." He held an arm out. "Come on." Dev pulled him to his feet.

"I have an idea," Kyle said, weighing his thoughts. "Micah told me once about recreating portals. I did it once with a portal that was meant for me, and I know that this one isn't really a portal but maybe because I'm Ra'al's son, I could recreate where she went through." He faltered. "I mean, I can at least try."

"Are you sure? We have no idea what those demon wards will do to you. You're still part Azura."

"I'm sure." Kyle glanced at Mordas's hilt still resting in his left hand. "And I'm a lot more demon than I was when I first got here. At least my becoming more like them may be good for something, if only it means saving her. That's an easy choice in any realm."

Kyle ignored Dev's look as he took one of the silver daggers and cut into his index finger, moving to the exact spot where Sera had disappeared. He held his hand up and felt the wards take hold of his demon blood offering. The portal reappeared, guiding his fingers until it was complete. The runes glowed like red embers suspended in midair.

Kyle stumbled backward, breathing hard from the effort. Everything inside of him felt hot and powerful. His shoulder ached and he rubbed it without thinking. Black stars exploded in his vision and ribbons of pain snaked into his head, his heart, everywhere. He clutched his shoulder, feeling something evil invading his system like a poison. He thought about the maggots—it *was* poison. Ra'al's poison.

"What's wrong?" Dev asked.

"Ra'al's spear, shoulder," Kyle said. "Burns like the devil." He didn't mention the maggots. "I'll be OK, give me a sec." Kyle forced deep breaths into his lungs. He glanced at Dev and was shocked by the evil rage howling inside of him—Ra'al's rage. Kyle knew he didn't have much time. He could feel it infecting him, changing him, forcing him to bend to his *legacy*.

"Ready?" he growled to Dev.

"Yes." The single word was spoken without hesitation as Dev held out his hand. Their eyes met, and Kyle felt a violent splitting feeling take hold of him once more—the visceral surge of his demon nature. He'd never wanted to kill someone more, to squash the very life out of him until he was nothing but dust. He dragged his eyes away.

With Dev out of the picture, everything would be so easy. His father's plan was faultless. He saw that now.

Take your place, Ra'al's poison hissed in his head. *He is mortal. Weak. Don't be foolish, boy. Everything you want is in your grasp. Take it. Assume your crown.*

Kyle grabbed hold of Dev's arm, his eyes rolling back in his head. His fingers were not gentle, instead digging into Dev's mortal flesh like putty. Savage hunger spiraled inside him like a tornado, eclipsing the boy he'd been. His eyes burned red, the monster writhing, celebrating his awakening.

The birth of a king.

He stepped forward and plunged through the portal.

THE PRIZE

❧❦

The smell of decay was pungent and burned through Sera's senses like wildfire. Her eyes smarted, and she retched. She couldn't see a thing and called the hellfyre to her fingertips. Its glow was muted—red flame in a red room. There was a spear of light toward the far end of the room, and she walked toward it. The surface beneath her feet felt wet and spongy. Something sharp slid against her ankle, and snatches of a dream she once had filled her mind.

No, she told herself. *Don't look down.*

Something licked the base of her calf and her eyes automatically looked at her leg. She saw that she was walking on what looked like people's faces. She could see mutilated eyeballs glaring at her and tongues snaking out to lick her ankles. Sera shut her eyes tight, the fear suffocating.

It's not real, it's not real, it's not real.

This was Xibalba. It would take everything she was afraid of and turn it against her. She thought about Nate laying in the arms of that lecherous monster and steeled herself. Sera strode on, ignoring the bites and wet caresses against her skin. She didn't want to think that her mother had been right all along—that what she'd dreamed were actually premonitions.

Sudden movement stole her attention, and she squinted into the red haze. She knew it was Dekaias even before he spoke, his boy-like figure shrouded in darkness.

"Welcome, Serjana," he said throatily. "I have been waiting for you."

Sera's breath escaped her as he moved into the light. The mask he'd worn earlier was now gone. His features came into focus, and Sera felt her bottom jaw fall.

He was the spitting image of Kyle.

Dekaias gave her a satisfied smirk. "I see you didn't know there was a family resemblance."

"You're twins?" Sera said dumbly.

"Separated at birth, as the mortals say, only just not as neatly. It was quite a bit more . . . bloody." He grinned again. "You think Kalias knows?" he asked gleefully, clapping his hands. "I cannot wait to see his face. You should have seen yours! Priceless." He waved his hand indicating the room in which they stood. "Do you like my welcoming room? I built it in your honor." The floor undulated with a collective sigh, and his smiled widened. "They like you. They say you taste like spun sugar."

"Everything about you disgusts me," Sera snapped as several tongues snaked along her feet. She fought the urge to vomit. "Where's my brother?"

Dekaias shook his finger, stepping close enough that she could see the green writhing snakes on his head—like Medusa's—exactly as she'd read from Nate's research. "Now, now. Let's not forget our manners. You know the rules here. After all, you made sure that we were in place to keep them enforced." He laughed. "Of course, I mean your old self, not *you*, darling Serjana. A trifling thing, really." He turned. "Come along. Father is waiting."

Sera felt her arms clench at her side. She wouldn't do anything to endanger Nate, and Dekaias knew it. She followed him, grinding her heel into every sickening face she could. They entered another room, this one plain but for a gigantic oval mirror with an ornate frame at one end. A single person occupied the table near the mirror.

"You know Lord Azrath, of course," Dekaias said with a sly smile.

Sera stared at her uncle, her distaste visible. His face was so like her father's that she hesitated momentarily until she realized that, like Ra'al, he could shift forms. He held a goblet in one pale white hand. "You look beautiful, Sera. That was quite a secret your mother and father managed to keep from me, but no matter. Everything is in place now. Still, I admit it would have been far easier—and far less painful—with you in the mix earlier."

"I never would have helped you," she spat.

"You mean just as you won't now?" he said smoothly. "Not even to save your dear brother."

"If you've hurt Nate—"

"Now, now. You know what they say about anger, don't you? It's the path to the Dark Realms." He shrugged an elegant shoulder. "No matter, everything is prepared. We just need to make sure that one little detail is taken care of, the tiny matter of the Trimurtas Lord you stole from me." Azrath's eyes glittered. "Let's make a trade, shall we? My young nephew for Lord Devendra? What do you say?"

"I don't know where he is," she said. Dekaias moved from behind her to sit indolently at the table. His face, so much like Kyle's, was also ugly with spite. A sour smell followed in his wake, but Sera ignored him, keeping her eyes focused on Azrath.

"Of course you don't." Azrath laughed. He drained the contents of his glass and stared thoughtfully for a second at the empty vessel. "Your mother really had me fooled thinking you were mortal." He advanced toward her. "Dev's with your other little friend, I bet. You probably were very surprised to learn about that one, weren't you? The son of Ra'al? A prince of Xibalba."

"Where's my brother?" Sera repeated.

"How does it feel to love the son of the worst Demon Lord in Xibalba? Maybe a little root of fear or of doubt has taken seed and you're not quite sure you can trust him with your or your brother's life." He stared at her slyly. "And then, of course, there's the matter of your *other* paramour. How do you think the son of Ra'al will handle that one now that you're out of the picture?"

Sera's lips pursed in a thin white line as Dekaias chimed in loudly from where he was sitting. "Maybe a sudden kick near a bottomless crevice? Or how about that sword of his? A mortal body wouldn't stand a chance against Mordas. I put my money on Kalias. It's what I'd do."

"Kyle would never do anything to hurt anyone. He's nothing like you," Sera hissed, but she wasn't so sure. She trusted the Kyle she once knew, but she didn't trust what this place seemed to do to him.

Dekaias sauntered toward them. Sera had to blink as Kyle's face swam in her vision. She knew that Kyle was nothing like his father, or his brother, but it still rattled her. "What about the Yoddha? Did he tell you about her?" Dekaias taunted. Sera felt her heart drop to her toes at his saccharine words. She took a step back. "Did he tell you about holding her down while they *razed* her deifyre from her body? With that same sword he now carries?" Sera took another step back. Dekaias's words were like bullets tearing into her already fragile trust. "Did you know that he enjoyed the sounds of her screaming as her deifyre died? Or that when he slid Mordas home between her ribs, he relished how it felt to *kill* her?"

"No, you're lying," she whispered. "You're wrong."

"Am I?" His face was convincing, but Sera believed it had to be a ruse. It *had* to be.

Images of Kyle wielding the black sword as if it was a second arm flashed through her head: Kyle wrenching her arm up behind her back; Kyle's voice saying that he'd killed . . .

The recollection struck Sera with the force of a crashing blow. He'd been about to say Daeva when he said people instead. Sera felt herself crumble inside. How could she have been so blind? So *trusting*.

"You see?" Dekaias whispered gently.

"I'll kill you!" Sera screamed, her fingers reaching toward him. Dekaias's face had suddenly become too much to bear. She wasn't sure whether she wanted to kill Kyle or Dekaias at that moment. Flames engulfed her as the hellfyre came in a hot rush, beating around her with furious power. Her twin swords sprung from her fingertips. She'd never felt such all-consuming hate in her entire life.

A look of alarm crossed Dekaias's face before Azrath stepped between them. She turned scorching eyes at him. He wagged his index finger.

"Remember your brother, Sera. Let's not act hastily. Remember, Nate, your *brother*," he said more forcefully. "Dekaias is not to blame for Kalias's deceit. Don't forget, my dear child, that it is in a demon's nature to lie."

"I'm not your *dear* anything, Azrath," Sera snapped. "You are nothing to me. I tire of this game. Where is my brother? Tell me, or all of you be damned."

"We already are, Sera," Azrath said quietly, almost sadly. Sera was momentarily stunned at this glimmer of true emotion she'd seen from her uncle. He moved forward, close enough to run a hand against the outer strands of hair that had escaped her braid. "Don't you see what this is about, my darling?" His voice dropped to a whisper. "Damned," he continued. "Do you have any idea what that is like? To live in exile? To deal with demons, lower than filth? To never see the Light Realms . . . Illysia?"

"But you're Azura," Sera said. "You couldn't go there anyway."

"That doesn't mean I don't dream of what Illysia is like, of the perfection of it?" His voice shook. "I was fine knowing that I had no hope of ever seeing Illysia until I was banished from the Mortal Realms and everything ceased to matter. Do you have any idea what it has been like with *them*?" His eyes jerked over his shoulder in Dekaias's direction. "I am *not* a demon." Spit flew from the corner of his mouth. "But with Fyre, I could. Not just return to the Mortal Realms, but finally to Illysia."

"You'll die. The wards—"

"The wards are ineffective against Daeva."

Sera stared at him, a bit shaken by his disclosure. "You'll never succeed, you know," she said. "Whatever you're plotting, the other gods will stop you."

His laugh started low, derisive. "That's why I needed Ra'al and his minions. He is as covetous as anyone and lusts for power. The other Demon Lords fear him and will follow him with the right incentive. With his army at my fingertips, once I open the portal to the Mortal Realms, those very same gods you think will stop me will suddenly find their hands very full protecting the cherished mortal lives they hold in such high esteem."

"But why would Ra'al help you?"

"Who wouldn't want to usher in hell on Earth with a front row seat?" Azrath said. "He gets the Mortal Realms, and I—"

"—get Illysia," Sera breathed. Azrath nodded. "But the Trimurtas—"

"—are broken." He peered into her eyes searchingly. "Come now, *Lakshmi*. Surely you remember somewhere deep within you how the power of the Trimurtas works? It's the power of three, a triangle within a circle. If the triangle breaks, the circle breaks."

He tapped her gently on the forehead, and Sera felt herself shiver. She knew he was right. Without Dev, Illysia would fall. If the Light Realms fell, the Mortal Realms would follow. The gods would not be able to protect the Mortal Realms *and* Illysia if both were defenseless.

"You and I both know that Illysia has never been breached," she said.

Azrath grinned a thin smile. "It is possible. As Azura, the minute I set foot in Illysia, all the wards will fall, and Azura will no longer be forbidden. There will be nothing to stop us from returning to the rightful realm of our birth."

"I will never allow it."

"You won't have a choice. You will open the portal when the time comes." His face grew cold. "We are *gods*, too."

"You chose to become Azura! To seek material comforts in your lust for power. You went against everything Illysia stands for," Sera said. "If you do this, Azrath, you condemn us all."

Azrath's eyes were like shards of ice. "As I've been condemned?"

"This isn't the way to seek forgiveness!"

His laugh was bleak. "I'm afraid it's far too late for that. The minute I took that mortal avatara of the Protector, it put everything in motion. It was the beginning of the end. There's no going back now. You know as well as I do that they will never forgive an attack on the Trimurtas."

"I would die before having any part in this."

His voice was so quiet she barely heard him. "You will have no choice. Before you had nothing to lose, and now you do. They were always your Achilles heel, the mortals, only this time your choices are intertwined with whether the ones you love live or die."

Sera felt a chill seep into her bones. Could she sacrifice Nate? Her parents? Everyone she knew? Dekaias made a loud sound, clearly aggravated by their tête-à-tête. He stomped toward them, and Sera blinked at the malice on his face.

"Father is here," he announced.

Sera turned to see a doll-like teenager standing in a jewel-colored green dress. Her golden ringlets bounced with each step she took. "Hello again, Serjana," the girl said, and Sera realized that it was Ra'al. She read Sera's expression easily. "Azrath likes to think of me as a child. It appeals to his protective instincts." She burst into tinkling laughter, and Sera fought the urge to clap her hands over her ears.

Two other Demon Lords followed Ra'al into the room. The first was a beast and a voluptuous woman wrapped in one body, a tangle of arms and legs and barely-covered body parts. A single blue eye stared at her from the woman's face as a slovenly tongue slipped from between black lips in a leering motion. It was Belphegar, the Demon Lord of Excess and Excrement.

Sera forced her attention to the second Demon Lord and felt bile crawl up her throat. The Demon Lord of the fifth, Wyndigu. Clothed in a black robe, he looked as she imagined Death would, just without the scimitar. Strips of stringy discolored flesh hung from exposed bone, and she could just see the glow of red eyes where its sockets lay deep inside the dark hood of its robe.

Ra'al smiled. "Lord Belphegar and Lord Wyndigu are here to witness the coronation of my son, soon to be the new Demon Lord of the seventh. Then we will ascend to the Mortal Realm. To the New World." She clapped her tiny shell-pink palms together in delirious glee.

"Kyle doesn't want that," Sera blurted. Four pairs of demon eyes swiveled toward her. Azrath still seemed preoccupied with the mirror, chanting something under his breath. She saw a familiar blue tinge shimmer in the air around it.

Ra'al laughed. "Then why is he on his way here with the Trimurtas slave as we speak? My son is nothing if not obedient. Mordas ensures his duty." She glanced at Dekaias, her pink cheeks flushed, and walked to embrace him. "My other son, Dekaias, has been very patient and is longing to meet his new plaything as I have promised him."

Sera realized that Ra'al meant Dev. She couldn't imagine what Dekaias would have in store for him. But Kyle would never bring Dev to them, would he? Or had she been wrong all along? In that moment, Sera realized that she knew nothing at all about Kyle, about this stranger he'd become the minute they'd stepped foot into Xibalba. Maybe what they said was true—Xibalba did claim its own. If that were true, then she was utterly alone.

"Azrath," she urged quietly. "Please, it's not too late. Don't do this." She moved as close as she dared without provoking him. "Please."

He turned to stare at her, and it was at that second that Sera realized that Azrath's clear silver eyes were the same color as hers. Only they were dead, empty. Sera swallowed the lump in her throat, raising her hand toward his, and slid her fingers into his despite the involuntary sense of revulsion at the touch. "Please, Uncle."

Azrath gripped her fingers tightly, pulling her to him as if to embrace her. Off balance, Sera tipped forward. He jerked her wrist roughly, a sneer slashing open his face as he slammed the palm of her hand into a sigil etched into the top of the mirror's frame.

Its entire surface shimmered blue as the portal swirled open, the pain searing into Sera's hand and reverberating deep along her veins. She gasped and fell to the floor.

"What have you done?" she whispered.

"The portal between the realms has been reopened," Azrath said calmly, "thanks to you."

"Azrath, don't *do* this."

His laugh was chilling. "My first visit will be to my dear brother. And I will end that betrayal that began seventeen years ago. Then I will feed your mother to Belphegar, piece by piece."

Belphegar made smacking noises with his thick lips and rubbed the arms of the woman with whom he stood in permanent lascivious embrace.

Sera recoiled from the sting of Azrath's words, as helpless tears sprung to her eyes. She jumped to her feet, feeling her weapons extending from her hands. She needed to destroy the portal. The room fell silent. She saw the other two Demon Lords staring at her, mesmerized by the bloodlike hellfyre they'd never seen.

"What about your brother?" Azrath said coldly.

"You mean *this* brother?" said a clear voice behind them. Kyle stood there, cradling Nate in his arms. Sera stared at him warily.

"Well done, Kalias!" Ra'al said, clapping. Kyle's eyes narrowed as recognition set in. "Come now, don't be shy," Ra'al continued, jeering. "You've completed your part, brought us the boy. Come, Son."

Sera could feel Kyle's eyes impaling her. She met them, shocked by the murky darkness she saw there. His face was dead, emotionless. Hot tears of denial stung her eyes. It wasn't *Kyle*.

Out of the corner of her eye, she saw that Dekaias had cornered them. Nate lay on the floor behind them as Kyle swung his blade wildly in Dekaias's direction. Kyle was *fighting* him!

Sera searched the room desperately for Ra'al and Azrath, but they had disappeared. Belphegar stood near the portal, his face triumphant. Sera spread her wings, cleaving through the demons to get to Belphegar.

But she was too late.

His bulk slid through the portal. The demons now towered over Kyle and Nate. She screamed as one of the demons touched the blond cap of Nate's hair.

"Kyle!" she shouted, desperate. "Nate."

Kyle twisted past Dekaias and swung down to collect Nate, throwing him over his shoulder as if he weighed nothing. He began to carve a path toward her and the portal. Wyndigu snarled, and Sera knew that they had only seconds. Kyle's face was tortured—the darkness she'd seen before was ever present in his eyes. But he'd kept his promise about Nate, and that had to count for something.

Sera drew a sigil over the one at the top of the mirror, watching as the blue circle grew smaller and smaller. Sera kissed Nate's forehead, fastening her mother's rune to his neck, and turned back to Kyle, doubt exploding inside of her. She could sense that something about him was different. Darkness hovered around him. But once more, As they reached her, Sera had no choice. She had to destroy the portal before any more Demon Lords could follow the others, which meant that she needed his help to get Nate to safety. She gritted her teeth.

"Take Nate and go. Remember your promise to keep him safe. Hurry, it's closing!"

"What about you?"

"I'll come through later, after this one is destroyed for good. I have to be sure." Sera watched silently as Kyle stepped through with Nate, their bodies half disappearing, then spun around as a thought jerked into her head. She started, glancing into the mess behind them, her eyes searching. "Wait, where's Dev, Kyle?"

But she already knew.

Her eyes dipped to Mordas, catching the bright red blood staining its blade, knowing that demon blood wasn't red like mortal blood. Sera felt the world disappear from beneath her as if all the breath—her very life—was leaching out of her body. Her eyes shot to Kyle's and shrank back from the emptiness of them. He didn't even try to hide his guilt.

"What did you do?" she whispered. "Where's Dev, Kyle?"

"He's dead. He—"

She could only stare at him in horrified silence as the rest of his body—and his words—slid through the portal. Then it winked shut and all hell descended.

KALĪYURA

Hell on earth. The apocalypse. The end of the world.
The portal winked shut behind her, nothing but a whisper on the wind as Sera dragged herself through, looking at the charred forest around her with glazed eyes. All she could hear were Kyle's last words that Dev was dead.

Breathe, she told herself. *You have to breathe.*

But all she wanted to do was stop breathing, to not have to feel what this sense of loss was like, what this indescribable pain inside her chest was—the relentless ache of it.

Dev is dead.

A blast of something sour rocketed past her head, startling her, and for the first time, she fully took in her surroundings. A battle of epic proportions waged despite the eerie silence in the flattened glade. She was standing in a sort of clearing that had been completely demolished. In the distance, through the thick cloak of trees, bright white flashes darted across the night sky, and the smell of burnt flesh hung thick in the air.

"Sera!" a voice cried. Her mother was in full battle armor and so bright to look at that Sera blinked in spite of her own immortal eyes. Sophia held the largest spear Sera had ever seen. "Get down!"

Sera rolled to the ground just as a bolt from Sophia's spear shot past her head into the body of something black and large. The demon fizzled to ash as the deifyre spread through its body. Sera jumped to her feet.

"Mom! What's going on? Where's Nate? What happened?"

"They're everywhere, the demons," Sophia said. She looked as if they'd been fighting for weeks. And then it hit Sera—time in Xibalba was different from time in the Mortal Realms. What had been hours to her there had actually been days on Earth.

"How?" Sera gasped.

Sophia grabbed Sera's arm and pulled her into a thick grove of trees. Her voice was a hurried whisper. "Azrath came through a portal three days ago. We expected him but not the others. They were so fast, summoning demons quicker than we were able to get rid of them."

"Nate—"

"He's safe with your father. He and Kyle came through a half a day later. Then the portal exploded. Was that you?"

Sera nodded as relief flooded her. Nate was safe with her father, and that was the one thing that mattered. "Mom, where is Azrath?"

Sophia shook her head. "He portaled out. He broke the wards binding his exile the minute he came through that first portal. He has all his powers back now. You were right about the Fyre. The deifyre in his blood voided the sigils."

"He plans to go to Illysia."

Her mother's eyes widened. "The other Sanrak, except for Micah and me, are still there to protect the Trimurtas and also some of the younger Yoddha. Azrath will have a fight on his hands if he does try to breach the shores of Illysia."

Sera felt pain stab deep inside of her stomach at the mention of the Trimurtas. "There's something else," she said. "We lost Dev."

"What do you mean you *lost* him?"

Before Sera could respond, the trees around them were shattered by the blast of something that reeked of sulfur and rotten eggs. An immense demon plodded into view.

"Find Azrath," Sophia said to her daughter, spinning her spear. "I'll take care of this."

Sera turned and raced from the glade. She unfurled her energy as she ran and flung herself above the cover of the trees, the night air cold against her cheeks. Sparks flew beneath the dark blanket below her as gods battled demons, fighting to keep them from getting to where humanity began on the edges of the huge wood. The reservoir covered the deepest abyss, one so deep that the water ran hot near its bottom. It would be the perfect place for what Azrath was planning. Sera flew faster.

The thin crescent of moon glittered on the lake's surface. A jet of something red crossed into Sera's peripheral and she banked severely as a gigantic flying raptor demon flew at her, jaws open and screeching with impossible speed.

She held the deifyre in her hands, closing her eyes for a second as she shaped the weapon, releasing the crossbow just as the hot breath of the beast reached her face. The deifyre arrows ripped into its wings and slid into its throat, rippling outward until it was nothing but glowing ash in the air. Sera spun through it and headed down toward the lake. Three more flying demons attacked her, but she dispatched of them easily with the crossbow. As she drew closer to the water's surface, the smell of death was heavy in the air—the death of gods and demons alike. It sickened her.

Sera could see Azrath now, suspended above the lake, his own black and gray deifyre spread around him like a shield. He held something—*someone*—in his arms. A wide smile broke across his face as he saw her approach. She hovered just above him, but still couldn't see who he held.

"I see you got your deifyre back," she shouted to him.

"It's funny what a little determination can do, isn't it?" He flexed, his energy curling up and outward, almost like a fountain of water. "I did miss it." His smile turned sly. "I wonder if it'll change color in Illysia."

"What you did was a disgrace." She flew lower. "I will never let you breach Illysia."

Azrath turned then, displaying Maeve's limp body. Her eyes were glazed. At Sera's look, he shrugged. "She was strong, but no match for me after all. Still, the pets will enjoy her." He glanced down and Sera followed his gaze.

Beneath them, the surface of the lake spun into a terrible boiling whirlpool. Sera could feel the heat even from where she was a hundred feet above it. "Azrath, do not do this."

"You are really starting to sound like a broken record," he said and dropped the body right into the maw of the vortex. Sera swore she saw huge black shadows twisting underneath the clear surface of the water. Maeve tried feebly to summon her deifyre, but Azrath had stripped her raw. She fell like a rock.

Sera notched the crossbow, meeting Maeve's eyes. Her finger trembled on the trigger. Maeve nodded once and Sera released the arrow, watching as it cleaved straight though the warrior goddess. She disappeared in a shower of red and gold sparks.

"Way to ruin a good show," Azrath said dryly.

"You are despicable. You'll never get away with this. I won't let you." Sera shaped the crossbow into the two long swords she favored. "We end this now, *Uncle*!" she snarled.

Azrath nodded toward the shoreline. "Anytime, darling, but aren't you a little worried about them?" He smirked at her hesitation. "My part's done to open the doors to the Dark Realms for good. All we need is the sacrifice or, as Ra'al calls it, the coronation."

"What?"

"His son, Kalias. The sacrifice. The blood of the innocent and the blood of the demon. The way between the realms will be forever open." He laughed.

"KaliYura," Sera breathed. "That's what he meant by Kyle's coronation?"

"Hell on Earth, my dear. It is the demon's way. They consume their young." He watched her carefully. "So you decide. Fight me or save him. It's your choice."

"What makes you think I care about him?" But Sera knew the words fell flat. As much as she felt the keen slice of Kyle's betrayal, there was no way she would allow his sacrifice, especially to open Xibalba. Azrath winked as she spun around, gnashing her teeth.

Spray flew against her face and she sped toward the shoreline where Ra'al stood surrounded by thousands of demons. A smaller ring of light pressed in upon them, other gods fighting to get to the Demon Lord before he did something irreversible. But what she saw from her vantage point made the odds seem slim. There were just too many of them. Ra'al was seconds away from opening the gates of hell.

Out of the corner of her eye, Sera saw Micah and her mother flying at her from the side. "Where are the others?" she screamed. "The Yoddha?"

"Surrounding the edges of the forest. We can't risk any of the demons getting to where people are."

"And the Ne'feri?"

Micah answered, his face lined and dirty. His deifyre armor was blackened with ash, soot, and blood. "They're destroying the portals as fast as Azrath opens them. The portals don't last, but enough demons come through each time that it's harder and harder to keep them at bay."

"Ra'al is going to invoke the KaliYura," Sera said to them. "Kyle's the key. He's the sacrifice—part mortal, part Azura, part demon. Azrath said his blood will unite the realms. He will call forth Kali, the worst rakshasa of Xibalba. We cannot let that happen, do you understand?"

Eight more Yoddha joined them. Sera recognized the two from Beth's house. They sped in a V formation with Sera at its head and Micah and her mother on either side, approaching where Ra'al stood.

Kyle lay on a crude stone altar in front of Ra'al, Belphegar, and three other Demon Lords. Sera signaled for the others to wait and moved forward. Ra'al stepped closer to Kyle in warning, and Sera slowed.

She alighted on the edge of the lake. The demons snarled and spat in her direction. "I cannot let you do this, Ra'al," she said quietly. "The balance cannot be shifted between the realms."

"It's too late," he said. "Azrath has already completed the rites. This is the last of his part of the bargain." He'd reverted to the red demon he'd been in Xibalba, muscled and grotesque. Smaller demons clustered around his cloven feet, groveling in supplication and adoration. He held Mordas loosely in one hand, near enough that if she took one step forward, it would be over. Kyle stared at her, his face empty.

Sera let her deifyre fade. She saw that he was tied down, his hands and legs secured to the stone. "I don't care about you or your son. You can return to Xibalba for all I care, but I cannot let you invoke the KaliYura."

"Why? It is a time when all demons will be kings," Belphegar crowed. A raucous cheer burst from the crowd. "Do it, Ra'al," he urged. "What are you waiting for?"

Ra'al hefted the black sword. "Fulfill your destiny," he said to Kyle.

"I thought you said my destiny was in Xibalba," Kyle said weakly. "That I was to take my place at your side."

"Azrath said that you were the link, the connection between the Mortal Realm and the Dark Realms. You are the one, the sacrifice."

"And you believe him?" Kyle coughed, a drip of dark blood running down the side of his face. Sera suddenly understood what he was trying to do. She slipped closer as Ra'al's face creased.

"Azrath is only looking out for himself," she said, following Kyle's lead. "What makes you think you can trust him? Not that I care one way or another about you or your *seed*." She spat the last word. "But what if he wants you to kill the one thing you value most? Your first born?"

Sera kept staring out to the lake, but she could feel Ra'al's eyes settle on her. His indecision was clear. He *didn't* trust Azrath. Sera pressed her advantage, her voice silky, deliberately insouciant.

"Kill him, then. Spill your own progeny's blood if it pleases you."

Ra'al's hand dropped to his side. Belphegar pushed forward. "What are you waiting for Ra'al? Do it."

"No," he said.

"Then I will, you fool." Belphegar rushed forward just as Ra'al spun to face him, Mordas inches from Belphegar's throat.

"Defy me again, and I will send you back from whence you came, Belphegar. Do not forget that I was the one to bring you here." Sera could see the venom in Belphegar's eyes but he didn't respond, cowed by Ra'al's rage.

Then one of the Demon Lords she hadn't seen before approached. Everything about him was black, but it was a black underscored by a glowing ember. His face was charred, his eyes two fiery orbs. Temlucus, the Demon Lord of Torment. The last dimension before Ra'al's and the one of unending torture.

"Lord Ra'al," he said in a rich tone. "Belphegar is right. We need to open the portal. Otherwise, why are we here? Kill the boy and be done with it."

"He's my son."

"You have another. Dekaias," Belphegar's female side reminded him.

"Nothing that this boy could be. He is made in my image. Dekaias was but an afterthought." Ra'al's face hardened.

"And don't think I have forgotten Azrath's last attempt to coerce you against me. This could be another ruse to kill us all and rule all three realms himself."

"Really, you are like a bunch of children," a voice drawled. "You really think I want Xibalba? I've had enough of it to last me a thousand lifetimes. Kill the boy. Open the gates. The rites have been spoken, the sigils drawn." Azrath paused as two demons trailed behind him, hauling someone bound and limping in their wake. "All I ask for is the girl."

He stared at Sera, and all she could feel was revulsion. "I told you once, and I will tell you again. I will never help you," she spat.

Azrath called the two demons forward with a flick of his wrist. They pulled their prisoner into plain view. Sera heard her mother's soft gasp behind her.

"It's OK, Sera. I'm not hurt," her father said.

"For now," Azrath added, his words soft. He turned his attention back to Ra'al and raised his eyebrows. "Well?" he said sarcastically.

Ra'al raised Mordas high and even as the scream lodged in Sera's throat, she felt the power of the ten gods behind her descending upon them. And then she was spinning toward Kyle, her deifyre blades meeting Temlucus's own fiery weapons. Her eyes darted toward Kyle and the sword that still made its achingly long descent. Another warrior pulled Temlucus away and then she was running as fast as she could toward the altar.

Mordas was right above Kyle's chest when he ripped through his bonds, his arms coming up in an X. The blade stopped short, throwing Ra'al off balance. Kyle's voice was cold. "You miscalculated, *Father*. Mordas will never hurt its master, and I have fed it more blood than you have these last few days." He paused and sat up, his eyes glittering. "*I* am its master."

Kyle swung Mordas's inverted edge back toward Ra'al. It embedded itself into his skull with sharp precision. Black blood spurted onto the altar as Ra'al collapsed, his eyes frozen in betrayed shock. Sera jerked Kyle out of the way and severed the ties on his feet. Ra'al crumbled to ash, but before he disappeared, Sera swore she'd seen a smile on his face. It chilled her.

"That was easier than I thought," Kyle said rubbing his wrists. "Is he dead?"

"No, he has returned to the seventh hell where he belongs," she answered automatically. "Demon Lords can't be killed in the Mortal Realm."

"Sera, about—"

Kyle's words were cut off as he fell backward. Sera saw the red-handled blade protruding out of his shoulder.

Singed flesh filled the air as she spun around. Temlucus. His grin was all hate even as her mother's spear ripped through the center of him. A dozen demons attacked her then, and Sophia spun in a blur. More and more warriors appeared around them, fighting off the last of the smaller demons. Temlucus stumbled forward, blackened fingers reaching for her. It took two more thrusts from Sophia's spear to make him fall.

"Too late," he grunted with a terrible smile, his hands open in affirmation before he, too, faded to ashy embers, returning to the sixth.

Sera spun to watch in horror as blood leaked down Kyle's arm into the altar's channel and fell in slow motion into the conduit that led to the lake.

"No!" she screamed.

But it *was* too late. The drop of blood rippled into the lake as if it were a boulder dropped from a great height. The ground shook beneath their feet and a huge crack spread from the edge of the water toward the middle. Sera grabbed Kyle's collar, dragging him to the ground just as the altar fell into the seething fissure.

All of Kyle's blood would have broken open the gates to hell. A single drop would only open it for a mere second— just enough for the things raging beneath the surface to get out.

Or perhaps just one.

The lake bubbled, hotter than anything Sera had ever seen as a horrific beast reared its head. Rows and rows of distended fangs lay in its pointy snout. A crown of horns surrounded its head, green dinosaur-like vertical scales ran down its back. Two more heads came into view, smaller than the first but just as terrifying. The portal pressed against the bulk of its body as it slid further out, fighting the wards that bound it.

The beast roared and even the gods clapped their hands over their ears. It surveyed them with six pairs of burning yellow eyes, steam pouring from its nostrils. Sera felt coldness invade her body.

Kali.

The apocalypse demon. The harbinger of KaliYura.

The end of the world.

Return ⊙f
The Avatara

❧

"Force it back!" Micah screamed. The three-headed beast shrieked horribly as its bulk remained caught half in each world. The stench was sickening. The monster thrashed as if trying to heave itself completely through. Scores of smaller demons squeezed from beneath its body as it writhed madly.

"It's trapped between the realms," someone shouted. "Watch out for the smaller demons slipping through."

The warrior gods surrounded the creature, deifyre shooting through the night until Sera was almost blinded by the light. She glanced up as a sliver of light shot past her head right into the giant demon's eye. Its scream was horrendous, but it was a scream of rage, not of death. The Yoddha were trying to push the demon back into Xibalba, but it was too strong and gaining every second, hauling more of itself, inch by hideous inch, into the Mortal Realm.

More warriors appeared from all parts of the forest and the sky, battling the smaller demons that seeped from beneath the monster in the lake. Sera wanted to help them, but she had something she had to do first. She shook Kyle, a little more roughly than she'd intended. He grimaced as her fingers dug into his injured shoulder. It was healing but not fast enough. Temlucus's weapon had been extra powerful.

"Did you see where Azrath went with my father?" Sera asked urgently. Kyle sputtered again and squinted toward her back just as Sera felt her senses tingle.

"Looking for me?" a drawling voice asked.

She turned. "Release my father, Azrath."

"That I cannot," he said, but Sera didn't miss the contempt in his tone.

Her father gasped. Sera could see blood crusting along his hairline and raw scratches along his arm as if he'd been dragged across sharp rocks. "Sera," he gritted. "Don't worry about me. S . . . stop him."

"Shut up, brother," Azrath snarled, a booted foot crunching into the back of Sam's legs and causing him to fold over to the ground.

"Dad!" Sera lurched and froze. Azrath held a silver dagger to her father's throat.

"Don't forget that Samsar is human now, darling niece." He slid the dagger in a line across Sam's skin. "This is all it would take, just with a little pressure."

"What do you want?"

"Open the portal to Illysia."

"I can't do that."

A thin line of red welled at the point of the dagger. "Then Samsar dies. I must repay him for the wound he gave me seventeen years ago." Sera saw the reddened scar along Azrath's neck and understood just how much pleasure it would give him to hurt her father.

"But he's your *brother*," Sera whispered.

"Sera, don't do it. I am not worth—" Sam gasped, receiving a kick this time in the ribs. Azrath bared his teeth, his eyes feral.

"My *brother* was a powerful Demon Lord once. This," he said, holding Sam by the scruff of his neck, "is but a shell of what my brother was. So you see, any brother I knew is dead." he snarled. "This mortal means *nothing* to me."

Sam gurgled as the tip of the dagger dug into the corded muscle of his throat.

"Fine, you win. I'll open it!" Sera screamed at the blood welling at the point of the dagger.

"Sera, no," Kyle whispered from behind her. Her father could only shake his head, his eyes terrified.

"Shut up, traitor," she spat in Kyle's direction. "Why don't you go and murder someone else?"

Shutters dropped over Kyle's eyes. Wordlessly, he grabbed Mordas, which still lay on the ground beside him, and walked away.

Azrath laughed. "Your words are just as effective as your blades, Serjana. Spoken like a true Azura."

"Don't confuse me with someone like you, Azrath."

His eyes hardened. "Open the portal."

Sera closed her eyes and watched as the sigil on her right palm glowed white. Dev's rune. Her fingers closed into a fist, the light from the sigil spilling between her fingers. She glanced back at the battle still raging in the middle of the lake. Kali was gaining ground. Despite the gods' valiant efforts, she could see more and more of the demon's scaled torso, and a dozen more of its forty-taloned limbs.

They needed a miracle.

She drew a sigil for a portal, watching Azrath's covetous expression, and knew that there was no way she could ever let him set foot in Illysia. She met her father's eyes. Samsar nodded.

Sera summoned the power of the Illysia rune into her until her entire body glowed white. She could feel the sigil on her left hand burning like acid as the purity of the Light Realms filled her with iridescence. Azrath blinked for a second against it; it was the moment Sera had been waiting for. She flung everything she'd gathered toward him.

The thunderbolt drove his body crashing into the forest, but he was on his feet in seconds, his face a mask of fury. His deifyre shot out and he flew at her. Sera met him halfway, their bodies crashing into each other as they spun upward into the sky and then plummeted back to Earth in an empty part of the wood. It was now just the two of them. The impact knocked the breath out of Sera. She thrust another bolt toward Azrath, which he deflected easily. He smiled coldly.

"You won't catch me unprepared again. Once is all you get." He opened his arms wide and crossed his ankles, the picture of self-sacrifice. "Do your worst."

Sera rushed toward him swinging her blades with all her might. Azrath didn't even flinch as the blades passed harmlessly through him. Sera's jaw dropped.

He bared his teeth in a grimacing smile. "Didn't you get the memo? Weapons of light won't hurt me. That's why all the wards of my exile—the ones that took my deifyre—are gone." He laughed. "We're more alike now than you think, *Sita*."

"My name is Sera," she said. "And you are nothing like me."

He flew fast at her, knocking her off her feet. A searing pain tore at her side and she stared blankly at the red blood that seeped into her shirt. Deifyre swarmed to the spot, healing it as quickly as it had come, but a dull ache remained. Azrath still wielded demon weapons, she realized.

She deflected another attack, her own swords slamming into his. Something curled toward her head and she ducked just as Azrath swung at her again, stumbling back as something heavy caught her in the back of the head. Dizzy, she fell to her knees as a black steel whip wrapped around her legs. She stared at it until a familiar greasy face swam into her vision.

"Miss me?" Jude taunted. "I've been looking for you."

Three other Ifrit surrounded them, Marcus and two others she didn't recognize. They transformed into their demon forms, leering at her. One jerked on the chain releasing Azura poison into her leg. Sera ripped it off, tearing chunks of flesh with it, and pulled herself to her feet. She flung deifyre arrows at two of the Ifrit, killing them both instantly and swung around only to feel her face crunch into a fist. She keeled backward, blood spurting from her nose and her eyes seeing stars. An Ifricaius curled around her ankles again and her body thumped to the ground just as two other chains swung around each of her arms. Jude kneeled over her.

"Looks like you're in a little bit of a mess, aren't you, Miss High and Mighty?" he sneered. "I haven't forgotten the last time we met and our unfinished business."

"Hold her down," Azrath commanded. "All I need is her right hand to create the portal."

"Too bad we don't have Ra'al's black sword," Jude said as they pulled on the chains. "I would have enjoyed peeling the deifyre from your skin inch by inch."

"It's right here," a silky voice said. "Why don't you come and get it?"

Jude's eyes widened as he saw Kyle standing behind him, patting the blade of Mordas like a baseball bat into the palm of his hand. Sera felt an unwilling smile curl her lips at his stance. She still hated him for what he did. But she almost felt sorry for Jude and Marcus. They wouldn't know what hit them.

"I wouldn't be smiling if I were you," Azrath said, leaning over her.

Sera seized the moment, white-gold fire spilling out of her right hand and red gold fire out of her left. They met in the center over her and wrapped around Azrath's body, holding him immobile. His eyes widened.

"You like deifyre?" Sera whispered. "Then have a taste of mine!"

Threads from the deifyre flames dug into every part of Azrath's body, his eyes, his ears, his mouth. Azrath threw his head back and screamed in agony—liquid deifyre scorching along his immortal Azura veins. She closed her eyes and pushed harder until it felt like she had nothing left, and then she pushed some more until he stopped struggling.

Sera opened her eyes. He was staring right into her, his eyes bright, exultant. "I'm no longer Azura," he said. Azrath rolled his neck, testing his newly tensile strength, and stared in triumph at the pale gold deifyre surrounding him. "You stupid girl, you've only given me what I wanted . . . made me stronger!" He threw his head back and laughed. "I over-estimated you, but you're just a child after all."

"You're still evil," Sera said. "And you're wrong about two things. One, I'm no child. And two, I'm not stupid. Now that you're no longer Azura, Azura weapons can kill you."

"What Azura weapons?" he scoffed.

"The worst of all of them," Kyle said from behind him, swinging Mordas down and up, cleaving through Azrath's body.

The stunned look on Azrath's face was priceless to Sera. He, the greatest of Azura Lords, had been bested by two teenagers. The two halves of his body shriveled, blackened, then fell to the ground.

Sera and Kyle stared at each other in silence.

"Did you know that would happen?" Kyle asked quietly. "That he wouldn't be Azura anymore?"

"No." She glanced down at the ugly blade in his hand, and her face tightened. "Thanks for . . . " She trailed off, noticing that Jude and the other Ifrit were also gone.

"Anytime," he said softly. "Your dad's safe."

Sera slumped over with relief, the chains falling loose Kyle shuffled his feet and then blurted out words as if he couldn't keep them inside anymore. "Sera, I need to talk to you about Dev. It's not—"

She stood, interrupting him. "Stop. I don't want to hear any more lies. I need to get back to help with the demon. If it comes through, everything will be lost. And with Dev gone, the Trimurtas need all the help they can get."

Sera raced off before he could respond, before he could see the tears that had sprung to her eyes. She hated him so much it hurt. And she hated herself even more for wanting to forgive him.

She heard Kyle running behind her and ran even faster, as if Ra'al himself were chasing her. As she rounded the bend to the lake clearing, she summoned her deifyre and jumped without looking, crashing into something and falling unceremoniously to the ground.

A smiling face filled her vision. Dev.

"But you're *dead*!" Sera glanced back to Kyle, who'd stopped, panting, a short distance away. "You said he was dead," she accused.

"He was. That's what I was trying to explain, but you wouldn't let me. He asked me to do it."

Dev jumped off a snowy white horse. It folded huge feathered wings against its side and pawed at the ground impatiently. Dev had a huge golden crown on his brow and gold circlets around his arms. He held a massive sword in one hand. He was shirtless, his hair hanging past his shoulders, and his golden eyes were piercing. His arms and chest were the blue of the summer sky. A garland of marigolds hung around his neck.

"Hi," he said with a smile. Sera stood mute, overwhelmed. "Once we had Nate, I asked him to do it. Kyle released me from my mortal body so I could return to Illysia and make the Trimurtas whole. And by releasing me, he also freed himself from Ra'al." He touched a hand to her face. "You all right?"

"Yes," she said slowly. She turned to Kyle but no words came.

He flushed. "That's why they kept him unconscious, to keep him a prisoner so he couldn't return. He was to be tortured but kept alive by Dekaias for eternity. I only figured it out after you went through the stones."

Sera bit her lip, her remorse evident. "I'm so sorry I doubted you, Kyle. You've done more than anyone else ever could." Kyle grew redder and stared at the ground. He mumbled something about not doing well with praise and raced off in Micah's direction, who was battling a horde of snake-headed demons.

"Nice horse," Sera said, turning back to Dev.

"His name is Devhadat," Dev said, patting the horse.

"Dev, like you are." Sera ran one hand along its sleek neck, her fingers meeting his and intertwining with them. Dev held her hand tightly, his thumb running across the rune on her palm. He raised it to his lips. "So, you're back? Are you mortal?" Sera asked, breath forsaking her at his gentle touch.

A smile. "Not so much this time." He glanced down at his body. "This avatara is called Kalkarys, the destroyer of darkness. It's my incarnation against that." He nodded to where Kali fought against Sophia and the others. It was still stuck in the portal but over half of its bulk lay at the edge of the lake. "They can contain it, but they cannot destroy it."

"What are you waiting for? Go save the world, then," Sera said. Dev raised a dark eyebrow.

"The Dark Realms certainly left their mark on you," he said with another grin as he pulled himself onto the white horse. "I don't remember you being this bossy—"

"Says the *protector* of the universe!" she shot back, rousing her deifyre. The tendrils flamed out around her as they raced toward the ring of light surrounding the demon.

Sera saw her mother fighting by Micah's side. As fast as they dismembered the demon, his limbs grew back. Sophia's face was strained and exhausted. "I don't know how much longer we can hold it. It's too strong. Our weapons barely damage it. Our only hope is to drive it back."

"Hopefully not for too much longer," Sera said softly. "Dev's here."

Sophia and Micah stared up to where Dev flew on the back of his steed, his face glowing with power, as he swooped down near the main head of the demon, swinging the massive broadsword in a downward stroke to the creature's jaw. Brackish fluid rained from the wound as Dev swung again, tearing another gash in the demon's throat. The chant of "Kalkarys" grew louder and louder as the demon screamed in agony.

Sera saw Kyle hacking away at one of the other heads and she flew over to him, blades in hand. He was drenched in what looked like slobber, and the stench from the beast's mouth was crippling. She dispatched the three shadow demons crawling out from the lake.

"Why'd you do it?" she asked him. "Why'd you come back after every horrible thing I said to you?"

"You know why, Sera." He flung Mordas into the demon's eye and blinded it, dodging as a forked tongue slithered from the beast's mouth. "When he asked me to do it, I knew you wouldn't understand, and I couldn't say anything there because the demon lords would have known what it meant."

"I'm so sorry, Kyle."

Kyle rolled his eyes and shot her an exasperated look. "Time and place . . . apologize later. Help me send this thing back where it came from!"

Sera was a blur of fire as she spun, her strokes cutting into Kali's hide. The demon screamed and shot its tongue in her direction just as Kyle jumped, sword down, and severed it from its mouth. Its cry was horrible.

"It's pulling back!" she heard someone shout.

Sure enough, Kali had begun lugging its bulk back into the hole. Every collective blow they dealt made it cower more like a beaten dog. Dev flew above them, his sword a blur of gold, and dove in their direction.

"This is it!" he shouted. Sera was confused. What did he mean?

As he swung under Kali, the tip of his sword traced a golden line across the demon's throat, at the lowest point of its three heads. A huge tremor shook the ground and the lake around the demon boiled vigorously. Kali threw back its wounded neck and howled.

Just before the horse reached the ground, Dev swooped low and held his free hand out, pulling Kyle up onto the horse's back behind him. Sera flew beside them. "What are you doing?"

"Kalias summoned the demon. He is the only one who can banish it."

"You're not going to kill it?"

"No matter how much we strike it, Kali will not die here." Dev's eyes were gentle and his voice soothing. Sera could feel the premonition of dread inside her.

"But . . . why do you need Kyle?" Her voice took on a desperate edge as she looked from one to the other. "The Trimurtas can banish it, can't you?"

"I have to take it back, Sera," Kyle said. "My blood summoned it. My blood must return it. It is the way of Xibalba."

"Can't you just cut your finger and drop some blood on it or something?"

A glimmer of a smile flashed across Kyle's face. "It doesn't work quite like that. Kali is tied to me. Azrath meant to sacrifice me to give life to Kali. To banish it or kill it, I must take it back. If I stay here, it does too."

"But you belong here!"

The tear that slipped from the corner of his eye was her undoing. He made no move to wipe it away. "You're wrong, Sera. I don't. I never did. I belong there. I've always known that. I just wanted to be here with you."

"Kyle, no."

"I'll see you again. I know I will."

Sera turned to Dev. "Please don't make him do this. Please, Dev."

"I have to do this, Sera," Kyle said. He clutched Mordas tightly as the horse flew closer to the gaping mouth of the largest head. "Just remember that I love you. Always have, always will."

And then he jumped. Sera angled down to fly after him, but Dev reached over and grabbed her arm.

"Let me go," she hissed. "I won't let him do this."

"It's his choice, Sera."

"You can stop him."

"I cannot."

Dev's grip was unbreakable, his immortal strength impossible. Sera could feel herself flaring hotter and hotter until she was nothing but flame, and still he held her, drew her close. Deifyre tears bled from her eyes.

She could no longer see Kyle as Kali descended back into the abyss, and the surface of the lake glassed over once more as if nothing monstrous had ever disturbed its calm surface. Hundreds of voices cheered, but all Sera felt was a terrible ache.

Then she screamed, beating against Dev with every shred of force inside of her, crying as if her heart were breaking because she knew, without a doubt, that it was splintering inside of her chest.

They stayed on the white horse, suspended above a suddenly placid lake, the first stars winking against the black infinity of the clear night sky. A flurry of shooting stars sped past them, victorious celestial fireworks.

But Sera saw none of it. Dev held her tightly, murmuring into her hair, until her screams gentled to sobs and then nothing at all. After a while, he tipped her chin toward him, the sorrow in his own eyes almost as solid as hers. She stared down at the faces beneath them: her mother's, her father's, Micah's, the Ne'feri, and swallowed past the knot in her throat. All she could see was Kyle—the only one who wasn't there. A hole in her family.

"I can't," she choked.

"I'll tell them," Dev said. "Go, find your peace."

"I don't know where—"

He held her hands gently and pressed the two sigils on her palms together, enfolding them between his. He leaned forward and kissed her forehead. The scent of marigolds filled her nostrils, and then everything was gone.

ETERNITY

❧✦❧

S he stared out at the horizon, watching the sun dip into it like the arms of a waiting lover. Red and purple, orange and gold streaked across the twilight sky in a riot of beauty. She dug her feet into the crumbly sand, the edge of a wave frothing over the tips of her toes. The air smelled of honey and salt and was still warm on her face.

It was perfect.

And it was empty.

She had no idea how long she'd been there, only that it had taken months of solitude to come to terms with the loss of her best friend. She'd run away, needing the silence to find a shaky peace within herself. With time, she'd come to understand that Kyle had had to accept what he was, and that Dev had been right—it had been Kyle's choice to make. Not hers. Not anyone else's. It hadn't made it hurt any less, but day-by-day, it became easier.

Sera pulled her shawl tighter around her shoulders, sensing the footsteps behind her long before he was near.

"Hello," she said.

"Hello, Sera."

"How long?"

"Five days."

Was that all it had been in mortal time? Time was so different here in her world between the worlds. She felt hands on her shoulders and turned around, allowing herself to be embraced. She closed her eyes, savoring the only contact and comfort she'd had in months. The scent of marigolds and cinnamon spice curled around her.

"My family's safe?"

Dev nodded.

"And Nate?"

"Back to his old tricks," Dev said. "His film got short-listed, and he said to tell you that you were right—people love zombies." Sera grinned, hugging herself around her middle. Nate was the one she missed the most; she missed his wit, his wicked charm, his smile, his love.

"He's something special, that boy," she murmured. Dev slid his hand into hers as they walked along the shoreline. She studied him. He wore dark pants and a saffron yellow shirt. His hair was shorter but still curled into his collar. "You look different. Older."

Dev didn't answer. They continued walking in silence. "I have to return to Illysia."

"Will I still see you?"

He stopped and held her face between his palms. "You can always find me here, Sera. But I want to ask you to come back to Illysia with me."

His face was expressionless, but she could see the faint hope glimmering in his golden eyes. It would be so easy to say yes, and for a second, she hesitated. "Dev, I . . . can't. I'm just not ready."

He held a sad smile. "I thought you would say that, but still, you can't stay here forever, my love." He brushed a strand of hair out of her face. "Even if you don't return with me, you do have to go back to your world some time, even if it hurts to do so. People you love need you."

"I know. I just can't face going back to life the way it was, only without Kyle." Her voice broke on his name, the wound of his death still tender.

"Life and loss are the fabric of the realms."

"Doesn't make it hurt less."

"No," Dev agreed. "It doesn't." They walked in silence for a while. "You're sure about Illysia? Unconditional love? Perfection? Me?"

She smiled at his exaggerated wink. "I'm sure."

Dev grinned. "Well, in that case, I have a message for you. Wait, let me get this right." He stared off into space for a second, tapping the side of his head thoughtfully. "The messenger said, 'Time and place, and stop feeling sorry for yourself.'" He paused. "Oh, and that Sal's is not the same without you. Who's Sal?"

"Sal's a diner," she answered automatically. It took a minute for the words to sink in. "What did you say?" she whispered in disbelief, searching Dev's face for truth. "Kyle's *alive*?"

"After he banished Kali, he chose to become the Azura Lord of the Portal to the Dark Realms. The Trimurtas agree that this is good."

"Wait, you mean what Azrath was?" Sera asked frowning.

Dev nodded. "He said at least he got to be near you."

Sera knew her face reflected her confusion. "But how is that even possible? I thought Kyle died."

"His mortal self did."

"But if he's an Azura Lord . . . " She couldn't finish her thought.

Had Xibalba claimed him?

Dev read her easily. "Samsar was an Azura Lord and one of our strongest allies. Your father, unlike his brother, was just, and those who met him were fairly judged." Dev tipped her chin up. "The sins of the fathers do not always define the child. Judge him on his own merit." He stared out at the water and the reddening sky, his face pensive. "Sita chose you for a reason, for the balance she so valued. Evil is good's shadow, a precarious balance at best; one cannot exist without the other. She understood that more than anyone. It's why the mortals are so important. They are the tipping point, the fulcrum of our existence." He sighed. He turned to stare at her, his eyes sad, knowing. "I love you, Serjana, but I can no more ask you to choose one or the other than I can change who I am. To understand everything is to forgive everything."

"Buddha?" Sera murmured, her mind still whirling.

Dev nodded, then shrugged, echoing her earlier words. "Doesn't make it hurt less."

"I love you, you know," Sera said.

"But you love him more."

Sera shook her head. "It's not that. He *needs* me more right now." She touched his face. "You have my soul. He has my heart. Without either one of those, I'd die. I cannot choose between you any more than I can choose not to draw breath." She grinned, her smile like sunshine, lighting her eyes and every part of her. "Plus, boyfriends are overrated anyway. These days, a girl needs to have options."

But despite Dev's startled grin, deep down, Sera knew that her words would only go so far. Dev *knew* her, longer and better than anyone. He'd waited for her an eternity and his love had never faltered, not even when thrown against her love for another. He deserved so much more than she could give him right then, but most of all, he needed to know just how much she still loved him. No matter what happened, no matter the lifetimes, some things would never change. She was, and would always be, his.

Sera stood on her tiptoes, her lips dipping into the soft warmth of his. The kiss was sweet. It was a kiss of hello and a kiss of goodbye, a kiss of love and of friendship. It was a bridge between the past and the present, a promise of the future.

It was a kiss for forever.

EPILOGUE

❧✍

Sal's was not crowded. In fact, it was empty except for the lone figure sitting in the back. The windows were filmy and crusted with years of singed-on grease. The smells of coffee and bacon and buttered toast wafted through the air. The faux-leather edges of the faded red booths were peeling, and the glare of the owner behind the coffee counter was distinctly not friendly.

Sera smiled at him anyway.

She made her way to the back of the diner, each step shaking a little less than the one before, not stopping until she stood a few feet away from the boy sitting there. Sera studied him, drinking in his familiar features — the bend of his shoulders, the silver stud glinting in his eyebrow, the soft curve of his mouth — and slid quietly into the seat opposite him. She heard his sharp intake of breath, and when their eyes met over the table, Sera's own breath hitched in her throat as Kyle's clear green-flecked gaze caught and held hers.

She couldn't breathe. All the warmth in the world was in those eyes.

As her heartbeat rushed in her ears, and time and space flowed around them, Sera knew without a doubt that there was no other place she needed to be . . . there was no other place she would rather be.

She was home.

꧁꧂

Love is patient, love is kind.
It does not envy, it does not boast, it is not proud.
It is not rude, it is not self-seeking, it is not easily angered, it
keeps no record of wrongs.
Love does not delight in evil, but rejoices with the truth.
It always protects, always trusts, always hopes,
always perseveres.
Love never fails.

I Corinthians 13:4-8

꧁꧂

AUTHOR'S NOTE

FOOD FOR THOUGHT ON HINDU MYTHOLOGY

Note: Although *Alpha Goddess* is a work of fiction, a lot of my inspiration for the characters and the world-building in this novel is based on Hindu mythology. My father is a second generation Brahmin (priest class in traditional Hindu society), so Indian mythology was an integral part of my childhood. Fascinated by stories and legends of various Hindu gods who incarnated as avatars to avert human tragedy, I wanted to write an epic story that encompassed some of the Hindu mythology elements I enjoyed as a child. Here are a few interesting tidbits about some of the themes/characters appearing in this novel.

HINDU PHILOSOPHY: Hinduism is one of the world's oldest religious traditions and is also one of the most diverse. It is based on an incredibly large variety of different traditions. The core of Hinduism is the belief in Brahman, the underlying universal life force that embodies existence. Hindus recognize one single Supreme Being, and all other gods and goddesses are lower manifestations of that one Supreme Being. Hinduism is the world's third largest religion and is known as one of the most tolerant religious faiths because of the diverse nature of its teachings.

REINCARNATION: The notions of reincarnation and karma are integral to Hindu philosophy. Hindu mythology defines fourteen worlds with seven higher worlds (heavens) and seven lower ones (hells). The earth is considered the lowest of the seven higher worlds. According to Hindu scriptures, man is trapped in a karmic cycle of death and reincarnation (*samsara*) until final unification with Brahman, so the ultimate goal of living is liberation (*moksha*) from this cycle of death and rebirth, and reuniting with the one Supreme Being. Reincarnation is rooted in karma, where a person's actions in one life will determine their fate in future lives.

TRIMURTI: There are hundreds of gods and goddesses in Hinduism. However, at the top are the Trimurti, which comprisesd of Shiva, the destroyer; Vishnu, the protector; and Brahma, the creator; as well as their consorts (the Tridevi), Shakti, the goddess of power and courage; Lakshmi, the goddess of wealth and prosperity; and Saraswati, the goddess of knowledge and learning.

DEVA & ASURA: Hindu texts and scriptures reference celestial creatures called Devas, which literally means the "shining ones" and loosely translates to "heavenly beings." In the scriptures, the opposite of the Devas are the Asura, power-seeking deities who are considered to be demonic or sinful in nature. They are both important parts of Hindu culture and appear in mythological scriptures, art, and poetry.

AVATARA: Hindu scriptures talk about the manifestation of a god or goddess into mortal form to avert human tragedy or to guide humanity. This incarnation is called an avatar. One of the most famous of these stories is the epic tale of Rama and Sita.

VISHNU: Vishnu is the second god in the Hindu trinity, along with Brahma and Shiva. In the Hindu Trimurti, Vishnu is known as the preserver of moral order and the protector of life, balancing the processes of creation and destruction. Vishnu is usually portrayed with four arms holding the conch, the discus, the mace, and the lotus. He has a blue body and wears yellow clothing with a garland of flowers around his neck, along with golden earrings and a crown. The blue color symbolizes infinity. Vishnu is also known for taking the form of ten avatars to restore order in the world, the most popular of which are the incarnations of Lord Krishna and Lord Rama. According to the scriptures, Vishnu returns to Earth as Kalki, seated on a white horse, as the tenth and final avatar to end the final age of darkness and the destruction of the Kali Yuga.

SITA: Known in Hindu mythology as the wife of Rama, she is one of the more powerful incarnations of the Goddess Lakshmi. In Hindu mythology, she is considered the ideal woman and the ideal wife, embodying forbearance, wifely devotion, and chastity. Sita is most popularly associated with the *Ramayana*.

KALI YUGA: Kali Yuga in Hinduism is known as the "age of vice" and is the last of the four eras that the world goes through based on Indian scriptures. The Kali Yuga is referred to as the darkest age of man, because according to the scriptures, sin is rampant and man is uninterested in spiritual pursuits or closeness to god. The Kali Yuga is also associated with the apocalypse demon Kali.

Acknowledgments

First of all, a huge thank you to my terrific editor at Sky Pony, Julie Matysik, for seeing the promise in *Alpha Goddess* and for allowing me to share this story with the world—your vision for this book has exceeded my every expectation. To my phenomenal warrior princess agent, Liza Fleissig of the Liza Royce Agency, and her partner in crime, Ginger Harris-Dontzin, another massive thank you. Once more, you have found the perfect home for my book as well as an editor who just gets it (and me). Thank you for everything you do so tirelessly to make my writing dreams a reality.

A tremendous thank you to Julie and Marissa from JKS for all their help and publicity over the course of several books and many years—thank you so much! To Kristi Cook, I couldn't ask for a better critique partner or friend—thank you for everything, and for reading pretty much anything I throw at you. All I can say is that you rock! To the ladies of my writing retreat group who keep me inspired, thank you for being some of the most amazing women I know. To all the bloggers who spread the word about my books and humble me with their unwavering support, I only have mad love for you.

Thank you to my father, Pundit Gyanendra Gosine, for his guidance on this novel and for sharing his expertise in the

Hindu religion. To my mother, Nazroon Ramsey, who keeps me grounded, thank you for always being my first reader and for all your encouragement through every single book I have written. I know this story was near and dear to you. To my extended family, friends, and fans, thank you so much for your continued love and support. It means more than you know.

Last of all, but certainly not least, to my loves—Cameron, Connor, Noah, and Olivia—you are my heart and soul. Thank you for keeping me tethered to a beautiful reality.